PUFFIN BOOKS

THE WITCH

Little Necromancy Grumblethrush is sick and tired of the cold, damp old cave deep in the forest where she lives with her father Zachary the wizard and her witch-mother Abigail. She's fed up with learning stupid spells, concocting magic potions and charms, never seeing anyone else but the pedlar on his annual visit. The tales he tells her of the outside world set her thinking. She doesn't want to be a witch and she isn't *going* to be a witch. She's going to go to school and live in a real house with windows. The problem is how to set about it . . .

Imogen Chichester

The Witch-Child

Illustrated by Charlotte Voake

PUFFIN BOOKS

PUFFIN BOOKS

Penguin Books Ltd, 27 Wrights Lane, London w8 5TZ (Publishing and Editorial)
and Harmondsworth, Middlesex, England (Distribution and Warehouse)
Viking Penguin Inc., 40 West 23rd Street, New York, New York 10010, USA
Penguin Books Australia Ltd, Ringwood, Victoria, Australia
Penguin Books Canada Ltd, 2801 John Street, Markham, Ontario, Canada L3R 1B4
Penguin Books (NZ) Ltd, 182–190 Wairau Road, Auckland 10, New Zealand

First published by Harrap 1965
Published by Kestrel Books 1984
Published in Puffin Books 1985
Reprinted 1986, 1987, 1988

Made and printed in Great Britain by
Richard Clay Ltd, Bungay, Suffolk
Typeset in Baskerville

To Holly and Anna

Contents

chapter 1

The Naming of the Witch-Child

'What in the world is this?' inquired the wizard as he peered into a little hammock that swung from the lowest branch of a chestnut tree. 'Mrs Gumblethrush? Mrs Gumblethrush! What is this object, pray?'

A small, thin witch appeared at the mouth of the cave.

'Why, Zachary,' she said impatiently, straightening her hat; 'I keep telling you – that's our daughter! Ten days old she must be by now, poor little thing, and that's the first bit of notice she's had from her father since the day she was born. You're altogether too busy trying to turn that good pewter mug into a lump of useless gold – that's the trouble with you, Zachary Gumblethrush! You've no time for anything else at all. Look at her now!' she went on, gazing tenderly at the little black-swathed bundle. 'See how she smiles! She's very forward for her age.'

The wizard craned his long neck and looked with curiosity at his witch-child; absently he twiddled his beard round and round his long, bony forefinger.

'It's very small,' he said at last. 'Needs feeding up a bit. Make it a good strong stew, Mrs Gumblethrush. Plenty of nourishment – bats' legs, fungi and so on. I don't know that I very much want a daughter, but now that she's here we may as well make the best of it. Ah, well,' he sighed, wrapping his cloak around him, 'work's work and it won't wait, as my grandfather always said ...' And he turned away and clambered up the side of the hollow.

'Oh, look! Quick, Zachary, look!' called the witch. 'She's waving to you!' But it was too late – he had gone.

For a while she stood beside the hammock swinging it gently to and fro, and her gaze wandered slowly round the hollow in which she lived. At this time of the year it was a pleasant place, cool and shady; a little brook bubbled prettily through the middle of it, making a companionable tinkling sound, so that you never felt really alone when you were near it. On the northern slope, where Zachary had felled the trees, little, sour, wild strawberries grew in their hundreds, looking like fairy lanterns; and later there would be blackberries and after that, nuts; but then, oh, then, would come the winter.

The witch shivered and put the unwelcome thought out of her mind, for in the forest winter was a bitter season, and she had the baby to think of now.

Zachary would take care of them, though, thought the witch, for he was a good man and a good wizard too, and she knew that he loved her in spite of his formal manner. He was, she thought, absurdly old-fashioned in some ways: his refusal to call her by her given name, for instance; it was ridiculous to go on calling her Mrs Gumblethrush all the time, especially when Abigail was such a pretty name. 'Mrs Gumblethrush, be so good as to pass me my hat!' 'Mrs Gumblethrush, have you any idea where you might have put my broomstick?' 'Another mug of brew, if you please, Mrs Gumblethrush.' Ah, well, she thought, shaking her head, nothing will change him now. He's dreadfully set . . .

A little smile tweaked the corners of her mouth, and

she glanced up to the brink of the hollow where the wizard sat, engrossed in his tussle with the pewter mug. In the shade of the tree the baby slept serenely.

Whether or not it was due to the diet prescribed by her father I cannot tell, but as time went by the witch-baby grew sturdy and strong and brown as a berry, and her mother thought her the most beautiful child in the whole world. Indeed, she was not bad-looking, as witch-babies go; even Mr Gumblethrush said so.

As the months went by, it occurred to the witch and the wizard that their daughter ought to be given a name, and they had many discussions as to what they should call her, but on this subject they could not reach an agreement. Abigail thought of a dozen names that were short and pretty, as those for a little girl should be; but Zachary thought only of the future, imagining his child as a beautiful, slender, dark-haired sorceress, and the names that he chose were ill-suited to the plump and dimpled witch-baby.

One day, as he sat grinding tadpoles' tails on the great flat stone which he used for preparing all his spells, he announced that they would call the baby Goneril.

'Oh, Zachary, love,' sighed poor Abigail, 'it's a horrible name!'

Secretly she was not really sure that she wanted her daughter to be a witch at all. She had often thought that the nicest thing in the world would be to have a little shop in a village, with people coming in and out all day, buying pretty pieces of ribbon and sugar buns and barley-sugar sticks. It would be a much nicer life than being a witch, stuck in a cold old cave in the middle of a forest ...

'Couldn't we have a flower name?' she asked coax-ingly. 'Celandine, now, or Daisy? She looks *just* like a little Daisy!'

'Pooh,' said Zachary scornfully, emptying the pow-dered tails into a large blue flask. 'Do you want people to take her for a fairy?' (He had a poor opinion of the Little People, whom he regarded as meddling amateurs.) 'No,' he went on, 'if you must have a flower name, though it's the silliest notion I ever heard of, then let it be Toadflax. I cannot say that I like it, but at least it's a sensible-sounding name – nothing fanciful about it.'

Abigail sighed deeply.

It seemed as if they would never agree. Then, one evening, when they had been arguing for nearly three days, Abigail suddenly leapt up from her seat beside the cauldron.

'Why ever didn't I think of it before?' she cried ex-citedly. 'I've often heard my grandmother tell how she used to do it for folks who couldn't decide, just the same as us! Why, I've heard her tell it a score of times! We must do the Naming Spell!'

Thankfully Zachary accepted the compromise: he had never realized before how strong-willed his wife could be – pig-headed, he called it – and at one time he had come perilously near to giving in to her, which would never have done.

He watched in silence as she moved swiftly among the trees on the edge of the dell, stooping to pick up various twigs and branches; he did not offer to help, for spell-making is a serious business requiring deep concentration on the part of the sorcerer, and the smallest distraction can sometimes prove fatal to the magic.

When at last Abigail was satisfied that she had collected enough wood she separated it into three piles in the form of a triangle, and in the centre she made a great fire. Then she began to walk in a circle round it, and as she passed each heap of wood she took a log and threw it on to the blaze, chanting, meanwhile, in that weird sing-song intonation peculiar to witches:

> 'Wood of Myrtle, Elm and Oak –
> Thick and Tortuous thy Smoke,
> Clear and quick and clean thy Flame –
> What shall be this Witch-Child's name?'

By now the heart of the fire was a brilliant shimmer of heat within the dark cavern of the unburnt logs, and the witch and the wizard watched tensely as the thick smoke rolled and twined upwards into the clear evening air.

Abigail stood very still beside her husband, her breath coming unevenly. Her whole attention, her whole being, was centred upon the writhing column of smoke. Suddenly she clutched Zachary's arm and pointed with her wand: the smoke had twisted into the shape of a letter N. A moment later another letter appeared; then another and another. Now they were coming in quick succession.

Zachary took the wand and wrote them down in the ashes, lest they should be forgotten as soon as the wind had blown them away. At last the smoke ceased to twist and turn; gradually it grew so thin that it was hardly visible, and the great fire itself was no more than a glowing crimson eye embedded in a feathery white mound of ash. Together the witch and the wizard spelled out the letters:

'NECROMANCY.'

'Necromancy . . .' said Zachary, thoughtfully.

'Necromancy . . .' repeated Abigail. 'Well, now, that's really rather pretty!'

Suddenly Zachary put his arm about her waist and whirled her round.

'Necro*man*-cy,' he sang, to the rhythm of a tango, 'is a name I rather *fan*-cy!'

'We could shorten it to *Nan*-cy,' cried Abigail, catching his enthusiasm; 'but I like it as it is!'

And round and round the smouldering embers they danced, until the great orange moon rose high above the forest, and they sank exhausted to the ground.

chapter 2

The Pedlar

A terrible fate had once nearly befallen Zachary's maternal grandmother. Because of this incident, too dreadful to relate, the wizard would never allow his wife or daughter to venture out of the forest, lest by some awful chance the same thing should happen to them; nor would he go himself, except upon the most urgent matters. So the Gumblethrushes had to do all their shopping once a year when the Pedlar passed through the forest. His coming was an event long-awaited and long-remembered by the witch-family, for whom it ranked in importance with the other great happenings of the year, such as the first fall of snow and the coming of spring. His visits were as regular, too, as the seasons themselves, so that they came to talk of Pedlar-time as one might say Christmas or Whitsun.

This year, when Necromancy was nearly six, the witch-family had one pound and twenty pence saved up, and as Pedlar-time drew near they spent long pleasant hours dreaming of what they would buy with it. They also had one dozen cold-cures to barter, half a dozen corn-cures, the same number of wart-charms and eight love-potions. (The Pedlar had not wanted so many love-potions last year: he said there was not much call for them nowadays when even the plainest girls painted their lips red and their brows black and dyed their hair like dandelions; he said the paint seemed to work better than the potions, and he'd been left with several on his hands which he had been obliged to sell off at cost price.)

So this year Zachary had bottled only a few, and had concentrated more on the medicinal side of the business. For several weeks now, he and Abigail had been busy collecting ingredients, some of which were rare. Lizards' tails, for instance, were only to be found in one particular place – a disused quarry on the southern edge of the forest, almost overgrown with willow-herb. It had taken them three days to collect enough tails, for lizards are in the habit of eating these as soon as they fall off, and you have to pounce on them quickly or you will lose them.

Any preparation that might be necessary, such as drying or grinding, was done by Zachary, and when everything was ready Abigail would measure the different substances with infinite care into the cauldron, while her husband chanted the magic words:

> 'By the slithery Slime of Snail,
> Blister, Verruca and In-growing Nail,
> Onion, Bunion, Callus and Corn,
> Rue the Day you ever were Born!'

Abigail loved bottling. It was so satisfactory to see all the flasks in their neat rows, sealed with beeswax and carefully labelled 'Influenza Elixir', 'Freckle Remover', in Zachary's scholarly hand.

The Pedlar bought them wholesale and sold them again at a handsome profit, charging fivepence on the bottle, for the wizard was most insistent that these should be returned: a spell looks a great deal more powerful in a crooked green flask full of flaws and bubbles that it does in a medicine bottle. Altogether Zachary reckoned that they would be able to buy nearly two pounds' worth of merchandise from the Pedlar; but it must be admitted that arithmetic was not the wizard's strong point, and once or twice Abigail had been sadly disappointed to find that, owing to some miscalculation, there was not quite as much money as she had been led to suppose.

The third week in August came at last, bringing with it the welcome sound of the Pedlar's boots, rustling through the deep leaves of the forest. He sang as he walked, and as soon as Necromancy heard his merry, pleasant voice she ran to meet him, heedless of the brambles that scratched and tore her bare legs.

The Pedlar laughed when he saw her, and patted her head and tickled her ribs and showed much astonishment about how tall she had grown. He asked how her witch-craft was getting on and vowed that his magic was better than hers.

'It's not!' said Necromancy indignantly.

'It is!'

'It's not!'

'It is!'

' "Tizzy snotty tizzy snotty," ' mimicked the Pedlar. 'Get along with you! I'll *prove* my magic is better than yours!' And he deftly pulled an aniseed ball as big as a pigeon's egg out of Necromancy's ear.

She stared at it in amazement for a moment. Then she laughed.

'Well, it's my ear, so it must be my magic and my aniseed ball too!' And she popped it into her mouth.

Then the Pedlar pretended to grow very angry, saying that it was his, and that he would have to turn her upside down and shake her to get it back again; and so they laughed and played until Necromancy brought him in triumph to the dell.

The Pedlar was their most prized and, indeed, their only guest, and in his honour Abigail always prepared her very best fungus hot-pot and a specially strong brew of infusion. Zachary wore his hat and his father's spectacles and Necromancy was allowed to stay up late listening to the grown-ups, until she fell asleep on the bearskin beside the fire.

The Pedlar was a wonderful talker: and when the buying and bartering were over and the year-long hunger of the witch-family for tobacco and sweets and haberdashery was at last satisfied, the Pedlar would stretch his legs on the bank of the stream and tell them the news. And if, in the telling, the brides were perhaps a little more beautiful, the revolutions bloodier, aeroplanes faster, and disasters more disastrous than is commonly the case, well, Zachary and Abigail were not ones to complain.

Then Necromancy's turn would come, and she would say: 'Tell us about the One-eyed Gangster!' or 'Tell us about the Elephant Man!' or 'Tell us about the Dragon Princess!'

Then the Pedlar would tell how, many years ago when he was journeying through China, he had come upon a pagoda made of solid gold in which was imprisoned one of the most beautiful princesses he had ever seen. She was guarded day and night by a green dragon of medium size but exceptional ferocity, with whom the Pedlar had fought a battle lasting almost seven hours.

He had eventually killed the dragon, whose blood also turned out to be green, very curious it was to see, he said, and set the Princess free, and she had thanked him warmly, and had given him a dear little dragon made of jade for a memento, which Necromancy was sometimes allowed to hold.

The Princess had gone away after that, in a rickshaw, and the Pedlar had not seen her again; but he had since heard that she married a very rich and powerful official and settled down quite happily.

This was Necromancy's favourite story and she made the Pedlar repeat it every year, correcting him whenever his memory played him false. Abigail and Zachary listened as avidly as their daughter, and on these nights it was well past the witching hour before they went to sleep.

chapter 3

In which Necromancy makes a Resolution

That Pedlar-time was to mark for Necromancy almost the last of her happy days, for shortly afterwards she had her sixth birthday, and her father decided that the time had come for her education to begin.

Witchcraft Without Tears, the book that Zachary had been compiling ever since his daughter was born, was finished at last, and so, indeed, was Necromancy's babyhood. From now on, all her wandering, timeless hours of freedom were to become three hundred leaden minutes of imprisonment every day; from the time when the rooks cawed their loud way over the trees to their feeding-grounds, until the sun reached its highest point in the sky, Necromancy had to sit in the cave at her lessons. She began with the alphabet:

'Z, Y, X – W, V
U, T, S – R, Q, P
O, N, M – L, K, J
I, H, G – F, E, D – C, B, A.'

Next came Spelling, and each day she had to recite the spell she had learned the day before and learn a new one as well. Her father would get very angry if she ever forgot to say at the beginning what the spell was for.

Obediently she would stand with her arms straight by her sides and recite: 'A Spell for Mending China, by Orlando Gumblethrush.

Shell of Beetle, Slime of Slug,
Stick the Handle on this Jug.'

The spells always seemed to be by one Gumblethrush or another, for they had been handed down to Zachary from his grandfather and his great-grandfather. *Witchcraft Without Tears* was full of long footnotes explaining the occasions on which the spells had first been used and giving the time and place; Necromancy found it very tedious.

The afternoons, however, were not nearly as bad as the mornings, for then it was Abigail's turn to teach her, and sometimes they did some brewing. Flushed from the steamy odorous heat of the cauldron, Necromancy rather enjoyed learning from her mother the preparation of draughts and poultices and potions, but these lessons were rare; more often the afternoons were spent learning

long lists of herbs and roots, their habits of growth and the virtues to be found in them. The names sometimes had a lovely sound, though, and Necromancy did not really mind having to learn them by heart.

> 'Basil and Bergamot,
> Rosemary, Sorrel,
> Tarragon, Turmeric,
> Marjoram, Laurel,
> Wych-hazel . . .'

'You must say what they're for, love,' Abigail would interrupt, 'or you'll never cure anything. It isn't any use giving sorrel for carbuncles, or turmeric for toothache! Oh, goodness gracious! I don't like to think what would happen then!' And she would throw her brewing apron over her head to stifle her laughter, for Mr Gumblethrush did not allow levity during hours of study.

So for the next two years Necromancy continued to spend her days in this fashion. She learned quickly and well, and Zachary was very pleased with his witch-child, and felt sure that his hopes for her would one day be fulfilled. But Abigail still cherished her own dream, and wished and wished that Necromancy could go to school like Mrs Pennyfeather's niece.

Mrs Pennyfeather was a customer who had come, long ago, wanting a spell to cure her broody hens. She was, in fact, the last customer to come to the dell, and Necromancy could still remember her sitting on the log and drinking a mug of infusion to revive her after her long walk. When she had recovered she had told them all about her little niece Linda, with her white socks, clean every day, and her hair in pigtails, and the prizes that she

won at school and the way she sang Polly-wolly-doodle
... Necromancy could have listened for ever, but all too
soon her father had appeared, carrying the green bottle
with the magic words written on the label:

Leggay eggeggs eggor yeggou
Weggill beggee eggay steggew.

And then Mrs Pennyfeather had paid him and thanked
them all, and had gone away, and they had never seen
her again. But Abigail remembered every word she had
spoken, and quite often, when the afternoon lessons grew
tedious, she and Necromancy would talk wistfully about
life as they imagined it outside the forest.

'The smoke won't be all over the house, either,' said
Abigail one day, when Necromancy was meant to be
learning a spell for flattening bat-ears; 'not like it is in the
cave. I have heard,' she went on solemnly, 'that in proper
houses the smoke all goes up a hole in the wall called a
chimney, and out at the top of the house. When I've been
flying, I've seen it myself. You get the heat just the same
as we do – even better, I believe, but there's no coughing
or choking at all.'

'Oh, Mother, how lovely!' cried Necromancy, her eyes
shining. 'And would we have a new bearskin, do you
think?'

'Two or three, I shouldn't wonder, child,' Abigail
answered, money being no object. 'And a blue-and-white
striped cup for each of us, and an extra one,' she added
recklessly, 'for visitors.'

'Visitors!' cried Necromancy. 'Would we really have
visitors? And would they bring their children? It would
be lovely to play with a real child ...'

'You'd have plenty of children to play with at school,

love,' answered her mother, 'and wonderful things you'll
learn about – great kings and battles and far countries
where you need no clothes at all, and can't tell winter
from summer, it's so hot. And other countries where it's
so cold you can't tell summer from winter and the nights
last for half the year. So Mrs Pennyfeather was saying.'

'And what else, Mother? What else will I learn?'

'Truly, child, I can't remember the half of it. I wonder
if there's any more about it in the letter . . .' and rummag-
ing in her deep witch-pocket she pulled out the tattered
remains of the letter Mrs Pennyfeather had sent by the
Pedlar, two years ago – the only letter that Abigail had
ever had. She scanned it thoughtfully, reading snatches
of it out loud, while Necromancy listened attentively,
giving no sign that she had heard it all a hundred times
before; in the forest a letter was a very rare and wonderful
thing.

'. . . Mr Pennyfeather's been poorly lately . . . indiges-
tion . . . too many eggs . . . hens laying like never before
. . . recipe for Nut Crunchies: Take 4 good-sized eggs . . .
kind regards to all . . . No,' she said, folding the letter
carefully and replacing it in her pocket, 'she doesn't seem
to mention anything else. But I do remember her telling
me how her niece Linda learnt songs and poems and all
sorts of things, and you'll learn them too, my little witch-
baby, when you go to school.'

'Oh, Mother, I'm *not* a baby any more – when *can* I
go to school?' But Necromancy knew that it was useless
to ask this question, for the answer was always the same:
'One day, love, one day . . .'

So the seed of discontent was sown, and, taking root
in the rich earth of Necromancy's imagination, grew
swiftly into a great many-branching flower of marvellous

shape and colour; and soon, so large did it grow that it almost filled her mind, leaving hardly any room at all for her lessons. Her father began to show impatience with her, for nowadays she seemed to be always dreaming, her head in the clouds, and one day he grew really angry.

'How,' he demanded, shaking his wand in her face, 'do you expect to grow up to be a clever witch, if you pay no attention to your work? *How* do you *imagine* that you are going to pass your M.C.E. if you never listen at all? Now ... let me see – where were we?'

Suddenly Necromancy leapt to her feet.

'I'm not *going* to take my beastly Magic Circle Exam, and I'm not going to be a witch at all! Not *ever*! I won't. I won't! I *won't*! So there!' And she burst into tears.

Abigail, white in the face and open-mouthed with astonishment, appeared suddenly at the entrance to the cave.

'Why, Necromancy, don't you speak to your father so! Whatever has come over you?'

Necromancy looked through hot tears of rage at the black-and-white blur that was her mother.

'What good is it being a witch when nobody has any use for witchcraft?' she asked furiously. 'And what good is it learning spells and spells and spells, day after day, when nobody buys them? I *hate* learning spells and I hate making charms *and* potions *and* philtres and anyway I *bet* they don't work! They're just *stupid*, that's why nobody wants them any more. Nobody's bought a spell since that lady in the blue dress, so long ago I can't remember when it was. If it wasn't for the Pedlar we'd never know there was anyone else in the whole world besides us! But I want to *see* the world! I want to go to school and I want to live in a proper house with windows, not a horrible, damp, stuffy old cave, bumping my head on the stalactites all day long. I *hate* it! And I hate toadstools and I hate bats'-leg stew and I never want to eat moss-porridge again as long as I live ... I don't *want* to be a witch ...' And she leant her head against a tree and wept bitterly, her body shaking with great convulsive sobs.

The witch and the wizard looked at each other in consternation: their daughter had never behaved like this in all her life. They wondered if she were bewitched.

'I'll make a nice soothing draught,' said Abigail in a low voice, and bending down she began to mend the fire beneath the cauldron.

Zachary was quite content to leave his wife to deal with the situation, and he was thankful that she had thought of the soothing draught, for, to tell the truth, he was at rather a loss to know what to do. As he climbed up the side of the hollow to his stone he could hear her chanting:

> 'Filthy temper, purple rage
> Drowned shall be in brew of Sage,
> Wormwood, Camomile and Balm,
> Banish storm and bring back calm!'

Necromancy drank the draught, for she was exhausted after her great outburst and did not feel like rebelling against anybody again that day.

'But I'll make a plan,' she thought to herself. 'I won't tell anyone at all, not even Mother, and one day I *will* go to school ...'

She climbed into her hammock, taking with her the kitten that the she-cat had given her for her birthday, and, burying her face in its silky black fur, soon fell fast asleep.

chapter 4

Flight

Necromancy went back to her studies, and nothing more was said about her misbehaviour. The incident was not repeated. Zachary felt satisfied that the child had returned to her senses, and after a while the matter slipped from his mind; but Abigail, on the other hand, did not forget it. She was terrified that Zachary might find out about the Brewing lesson conversation, which had undoubtedly been the cause of what she called the 'tantrum'.

She therefore said nothing more about school or houses or pretty clothes, and the afternoon lessons became nearly as dull as the morning ones. At the same time she did her best to make life in the cave pleasanter for them all: she cooked the toadstools with different kinds of herbs and tried various ways of serving them – sometimes sliced and sometimes diced; she took extra trouble to keep the fire burning brightly and the cave clean, and she carefully arranged in the pewter mug the wild flowers which Necromancy picked in the forest. They had to be removed at meal-times, of course, as the mug was needed for drinking out of, but they looked very pretty in between.

Necromancy, for her part, hugged her idea to herself, and kept her thoughts well hidden, concealing them beneath attentive looks and much apparent interest in her lessons, so that her father was once more very pleased with her. But at night-time as she lay in her hammock, close-slung beneath the smoke-blackened roof of the cave, she turned each detail over and over in her mind, and at last, when all the leaves of the forest had turned to gold, Necromancy's plan was complete.

The time came one night, as she climbed into her hammock, for her to chant:

> 'Cloven hoof and Bullock's Horn,
> Wake me up at Crack of Dawn!'

In the thick musty blackness of the cave Necromancy stirred; then suddenly she was awake, her eyes stretched wide in the darkness, her ears straining to catch and interpret every sound. The dawn had cracked! Her great adventure was about to begin.

She listened intently: her father's gently rasping snores came reassuringly from his pallet of bracken on the floor below, and her mother's breathing, with its curious little 'guck . . . guck' sound, was as even as the tick of a clock; there was no danger from either of them.

Cautiously she swung her legs over the side of the hammock and slid to the ground. The noise seemed dreadfully loud. For a long moment she stood, paralysed, not daring to move, waiting for her parents to wake up and ruin everything; then, in an agony of excitement and fear, she slipped past the old bearskin that hung over the cave mouth in winter, and out into the frost-sharp cold of an October dawn.

Nothing was left of the fire but a mound of flaky white ash, breathing only the faintest warmth, and Necromancy was shivering as she struggled into her black dress; with cold-stiffened fingers she tied the strand of ivy round her middle and wrapped herself in the cloak that Abigail had made for her out of an old one of her father's. It was patched and faded and the once-gorgeous embroidery had come unravelled, but it helped to keep her warm.

She took her broomstick from the cleft branch of the tree where it hung beside her mother's and father's, and clutching her cloak round her she scrambled swiftly up the side of the dell.

Every minute the sky was growing lighter, and the colours of her cloak could plainly be seen. She must hurry if she were to escape before her mother and father awoke. She trod as carefully as possible to avoid cracking twigs, which made a noise as loud as a pistol-cap – she felt certain that she would be heard.

At last she judged that she was far enough from the cave, and coming to a place where the branches were not too thick overhead, she stopped and mounted the broomstick.

Suddenly a loud 'miaow' just behind her made her jump so that she nearly fell off the handle. It was the kitten.

'Oh, Isaac!' she cried. 'What a fright you gave me! Come on, quickly then! We're going to school.' She patted the broomstick invitingly.

Isaac leapt gracefully on to the handle and took some time to settle himself; at last, however, he was ready.

'Now!' said Necromancy, 'hold tight! This is Father's spell. I *hope* it works:

> Hominy Zominy Pumpkin Pie,
> On my Broomstick will I Fly!'

The broomstick gave a wild lurch and shot into the air. Necromancy was flung backwards as her feet left the ground; she clung frantically to the handle, terrified lest she should lose her balance and fall down and down through the trees, to crash to her death on the hard earth below.

Branches and twigs whipped her face, pulled her hair, tore her hands and clothes as the broomstick plunged and swerved, and it seemed hours before she dared to open her eyes.

When she did so she was high above the forest; it stretched beneath her like a great billowing eiderdown,

looking deceptively soft and inviting in the silvery light of the dawn. In the east the sky was streaked with yellow, and the world looked very beautiful and mysterious.

Now that they were flying so high in the air Necromancy found to her surprise that she could balance perfectly easily on the broomstick – she did not even have to hold on very tightly. It was comforting, too, to know that Isaac was with her, and as the cold air streamed past her, snatching the breath out of her mouth, she felt fiercely, wildly excited.

Thick gold rods of sunlight thrust past the bearskin into the cave, and Abigail, slow-witted with sleep, wondered for a moment what they could be.

'Bless my hat!' she exclaimed suddenly as the explanation struck her. 'It's the sun! Wake up, Zachary, you dozy, idle wizard! Wake up! Fancy us all oversleeping like that, and fancy the child not waking! Come on, love, time to get up!' And she gave Necromancy's hammock a violent shake.

'Empty,' said Zachary. 'She'll have gone to search for truffles, no doubt. Probably intends it to be a surprise. Remarkable that we never heard her, though . . .'

'Ah, well,' said Abigail soothingly; 'don't worry. She'll be back when she's hungry, whatever happens. We can be quite sure of that.'

But when breakfast-time came Necromancy had not returned, and the witch and the wizard ate their moss-porridge alone. It was, however, not until she went to fetch her broomstick to sweep the cave that Abigail realized there was anything really amiss. Her sudden cry brought Zachary slithering down the slope.

'Look! It's gone, Zachary! Her broomstick's gone!' She

bit her lower lip and tried in vain to keep her voice from trembling. Together they stared at the forked branch of the tree: Necromancy's broomstick was undeniably missing.

'Wherever can she have gone to?' asked Abigail miserably. 'And her not able to fly properly at all ... She'll have come to grief, sure as frogs' eggs, poor little – sniff – poor little – sniff, sniff – poor little thing!' And overcome with grief, she buried her head in her old black apron and sobbed unrestrainedly.

'You'll have to go after her, Zachary,' she said at last, blowing her nose loudly on the handkerchief he lent her. 'You must cast a following spell or something, and set off in search. It's the only way, for she must have been thrown from her broomstick, and maybe she's hurt or stuck in a tree, and she'll never get home alone. Go on, now, Zachary, hurry, do!'

chapter 5

In which Zachary spends an Uncomfortable Day

The broomstick brought Zachary down in a churchyard on the outskirts of a small village. He felt certain that someone must have seen him as he came in to land, for in broad daylight he presented a rather conspicuous figure. The sooner he became invisible, the better it would be.

As he divested himself of his cloak he peered out through the blue-black branches of the yew tree in which he had found Necromancy's broomstick, and listened anxiously for the sound of approaching footsteps; but except for the bent figure of a grave-digger, intent upon his dismal work in the far corner of the churchyard, there was no one to be seen. He stowed his clothes neatly in a convenient hollow formed by the boughs of the tree and propped his broomstick up beside that of his daughter. The less he wore, the more complete would be the spell, but in view of the bitter east wind that whistled through the gravestones he prudently decided to stay in his under-clothes.

The cold was piercing; he blew on his hands and swung his arms round his thin body and stamped his feet. With chattering teeth he recited rapidly:

> 'Seven six five four three indivisible –
> Zachary Gumblethrush be invisible!'

By the time he reached the last syllable nothing remained to be seen of him but the vague outline of the long white combinations so lovingly spun and knitted for him by Abigail out of wool gleaned from the thorn-bushes on the edge of the forest. He set off at once to look for his daughter.

'Merciful Heaven!' cried the old sexton as Zachary passed within a few inches of him. 'A headless ghost! Good saints preserve us – and in my churchyard! Oh, mercy on us, mercy on us . . .' And dropping his spade he turned and fled as fast as his rheumatism would allow him into the familiar, musty, camphor-smelling safety of the church.

One side of the churchyard was bounded by farm buildings and these Zachary decided to explore. Accordingly, he climbed over a low wall and dropped down into the squelchy, odorous straw of a midden. His bare, invisible feet sank deep in the icy slush, and as he floundered across to the gate on the other side, the bottoms of his combinations got unpleasantly wet.

No sooner was he through the gate than he heard a fearful barking and snarling and two lean and hungry-looking dogs leapt out of an old barrel lying on its side in the yard. They hurled themselves towards him, growling viciously, their hackles standing up like the bristles of a toothbrush, their chains seeming about to snap at any minute. Considerably frightened, he rushed towards the nearest shed and wrenched open the door. Immediately, dozens upon dozens of terrified hens squawked into the air, filling the whole place with sawdust and feathers; they hurtled everywhere, panic-stricken and stupid, crashing into the perches, the windows, each other and Zachary. He buried his head in his arms and made for the door at the far end.

Once outside he stood for a moment, leaning against

the wall of the shed, trying to get his bearings; when he had blown the feathers out of his mouth and breathed the reeking air from his lungs he turned to the left down a cart-track and took to his heels.

The track was deeply rutted and it was hard to keep his footing as he leapt and hopped along on the high ridges of mud, his eyes on the ground, his ears intent upon the ferocious barking of the dogs. Suddenly to his horror he found himself in the middle of a herd of cows being driven out to pasture.

The cows, much alarmed by the panting, invisible creature that had suddenly catapulted into their midst, turned in great confusion and headed back towards the cow-shed, leaving the object of their terror somewhat shaken on the ground.

Presently, finding to his surprise that he was uninjured and that the dogs had evidently forgotten about him, Zachary slowly and carefully picked himself up, climbed a gate and dropped with a sigh of relief into an empty field.

On the far side a group of cottages huddled together, and as he walked along he looked with interest – and a certain fellow-feeling – at the lines of washing behind them. After a while he came to a house which did not have a washing-line or rows of cabbages and brussels sprouts like the others. It was larger than the rest and instead of a garden it had an ugly stone yard; from it came a loud and indefinite noise. Suddenly a bell clanged in the still, frosty air, and immediately the hubbub ceased.

All round the yard was a high stone wall, and on top of the wall, picking his way delicately between the evil-looking pieces of broken bottles that surmounted it, was the kitten. At the sight of Zachary's combinations he gave a loud welcoming 'miaow!' and leapt on to the wizard's shoulder.

Zachary was overjoyed to see him, for now he knew that his daughter could not be far away. He climbed up some steps into the yard and, standing on tiptoe, peered through the tall curtainless window. The sight that met his eyes made him gasp in alarm, for there, standing up in her ragged black dress, her feet bare, her thick brown hair a wild tumble round her face, stood Necromancy. On either side of her and in front and behind sat dozens and dozens of children, children of every size and shape and description, all staring with round, wondering eyes at his daughter.

In front of them all, sitting on a sort of platform, was a stern-looking woman in a grey dress. She had spectacles – round ones, Zachary noticed, not square like his – and she seemed to be questioning Necromancy. From outside the window Zachary could not hear what she was saying, so he removed Isaac from his invisible shoulder and quietly opened the door and stepped inside.

'Shut that door!' snapped the woman immediately.

Zachary shut it quickly and flattened himself against the wall.

'Please, miss, it's shut,' said a small, yellow-haired urchin occupying the desk nearest to the door.

'That will do, thank you, Henry. I don't need you to tell me whether the door is closed or open. Now, dear, where were we?' the woman went on, turning to Necromancy.

Zachary listened, horror-stricken. Whatever had made the child come to such a place? This must be the school she had talked about, but what in the world could have put such an idea into her head? She must be out of her senses. Suppose they were to discover that she was a witch? They'd hound her over half the countryside — they'd chase her till she dropped! Hadn't they done the same to his great-grandmother? And ducked the poor old lady in the mill-pond till she was more than three parts dead from drowning, and as if that were not enough, hadn't they left her in the stocks for seven days, till her feet had nearly fallen off from the chafing of the wood? It was only by a miracle that she had escaped being bur— Ugh! thought Zachary with a shudder – it was too frightful to think of. No wonder his great-grandfather had never touched roast rabbit to the end of his days ... He must get the child away at once, before they began to suspect.

But how? He could not signal to her because he was invisible, and if he made a noise everybody would hear, and that would make matters worse than ever. He racked his brains. The situation was desperate. Finally he hit upon a bold plan: crossing the room to where the black-board stood, he picked up the chalk and wrote in large letters: GO HOME IMMEDIATELY.

The blackboard was in front and slightly to the left of Miss Popkins's desk, so that from where she sat it was not possible to see what was written on it. She was, therefore, not a little surprised when, with a great clatter, the entire class rose to its feet and headed for the door.

'Children! Children! Have you gone mad? Sit down this minute. Return to your places at once! Silence! Whatever has come over you all? You will all spend ten minutes learning your six times table. Anyone who speaks during that time will stay behind after school. Is that clear?'

'But please, miss ... But please, miss ... You told us to! You wrote it on the board ...'

But there was nothing to be seen on the board, and the children trooped sadly back to their desks to spend ten dreary minutes struggling with their six times table.

Miss Popkins turned back to Necromancy. From behind the blackboard Zachary listened, his heart in his mouth.

'Now let me see,' said Miss Popkins, pulling out a large book from under her chair and opening it on her desk. She picked up her pen and began to write. 'Nancy *Jungle-brush*?' – she was rather hard of hearing – 'What a very unusual name'... How do you spell it, dear?'

'Oh, you don't have to spell it at all,' replied Necromancy gaily, 'and it's Gumblethrush, really. You never have to spell surnames.'

'Never have to spell surnames? What are you talking about, child?'

'Never,' said Necromancy, shaking her head. 'Only first names. You make a great fire and you say, "Wood of Myrt—"'

With a crash the blackboard suddenly and inexplicably fell to the floor, scattering children in all directions, while the misty shape of a pair of white combinations glided unnoticed into the darkest corner of the room.

'What is the meaning of this?' cried poor Miss Popkins. She really felt she was beginning to lose her grip. She would have to think about retiring if things were to go on like this. Her nerves wouldn't stand it. 'Go back to your desks this minute! There'll be no outing to the pantomime if I have any more nonsense from any of you!'

Zachary felt thankful for his invisibility. He had never encountered anyone as frightening as this schoolmistress woman. What ever would she do to his little Necromancy if she knew her to be a witch? Oh, he *must* get the child away somehow.

Order was at last restored, and Necromancy, in peril of her life, as Zachary thought, was once more being questioned.

'Now,' began Miss Popkins, puffing slightly, 'where were we? Ah, yes. Nancy *Gum* . . .?'

'*Bull Thrush*,' said Necromancy.

Miss Popkins wrote it down.

'Name: Nancy Gumblethrush. Address?'

'A dress?' repeated Necromancy, puzzled. 'Do I have to have another dress? I've only got this one, but my

39

mother might be able to make me another out of my grandmother's old cloak or something.'

'No, no, no, dear. *Address*. Where do you *live*?'

'Oh!' said Necromancy, more puzzled than ever. Why did they call a cave a dress? 'Oh, I live in the forest, in the cave, with my mother and father. The frogs and the toads, they live outside, but the cats live inside with us in the win—'

'Name of house: "The Cave",' said Miss Popkins thinking as she wrote it down that some people certainly did choose odd names.

'It isn't exactly a *house*, it's really a – '

'Bungalow, is it, dear? All on the ground floor? Very nice too.'

'Yes, it is all on the ground,' said Necromancy. 'Is that what you call it? A bungalow?'

'And it's in the forest, is it? That would be Stinchcomb Forest, I expect. What a way you have to walk, child . . .' She scratched away with her pen.

'Now, just one more thing – Father's profession. What does your father do, dear?'

'He's a wizard,' answered Necromancy proudly. 'He's *awfully* clever, he can do the most wonderful things, all sorts of sp—'

'Yes, yes, dear, I'm sure your father's a very clever man, but what does he do for a living? Where does he go to work?'

'Well, mostly he works at the Stone,' said Necromancy, 'but he doesn't have to go very far, it's only up at the top of the dell.'

'I see,' said Miss Popkins, writing 'Quarry-man' down in the book. 'Thank you, dear, I think I've got it all now. You may return to your desk.'

Necromancy's desk was in the second row from the front and about as far away from windows and doors as it was possible to be, Zachary noted grimly; but at least the danger seemed to be over for the moment. He felt quite weak from the strain of the last few minutes, and sat down to rest for a while on a fire bucket full of sand that stood in the corner. To his horror he realized that Necromancy was again being questioned.

'And now, dear,' Miss Popkins was saying, 'let's see how much you know. You know your alphabet, of course?'

'Oh yes, miss,' said Necromancy happily. 'Z Y X, W V, U T S, R Q P, O N M –'

A delighted chorus rose from every corner of the class-room:

'That rhymes! It rhymes! Say it again!'

Miss Popkins rapped her desk with a ruler. The children were really being quite impossible; she felt ex-hausted already. With a sigh she turned back to the new pupil.

'No, no, *no*. School, Nancy, is not a place for fooling. We come here to work, not to play about. Since it is your first day I will give you one more chance, but I warn you, any more of this sort of thing and you will find yourself in the corner. Now! Mathematics. First let me hear you count.'

Necromancy felt quite bewildered: she had no idea what had upset the mistress so much and she was begin-ning to feel very nervous as to what might happen next time she opened her mouth. Zachary, however, perched on his bucket of sand, began to see a ray of hope: if Necromancy were to be sent into the corner ...

'Come along, come along, we haven't got all day!'

'Yes, miss,' said Necromancy meekly. 'I mean – No, miss. Seven, six, five, four, three, two, one.'

'That's where you should have *begun*!' cried the exasperated Miss Popkins, clasping her head in her hands. Whatever was the matter with the child that she had to say everything backwards?

'That rhymes too!' shouted the children, all thought of their six times tables vanishing from their minds. Paper pellets and indiarubbers began to fly through the air in all directions, and in no time at all a splendid battle was raging, boys versus girls.

Zachary prudently took shelter in a cupboard, where he was able to watch through the key-hole as the pandemonium increased.

Not until much later, when Miss Popkins had once more established a state of law and order, did he discover that the door could be opened only from the outside.

chapter 6

The Homecoming

The fire outside the cave burned fiercely, licking the great black cauldron with its darting dragons'-tongues, bubbling the stew and sending wisps of savoury, herb-scented steam into the frosty air.

Every now and then Abigail paused in her stirring to glance upwards and listen, for it was growing dark, and as yet there was no sign or sound of a broomstick. The she-cat was anxious too, as Abigail could tell by the way she walked up and down, up and down, holding her tail erect with only the tip twitching, like a flag in the stern of a ship.

'Oh, lie down, will you! There's a good cat. You make me so jumpy, pacing back and forth. Go, curl up in the cave and rest your whiskers, for pity's sake. That kitten'll be safe enough.'

But the she-cat paid no attention, and Abigail was just about to drive her away with the soup-ladle when a faint swishing noise came to her ears, and looking up she beheld two black specks which rapidly increased in size until she could clearly make out the forms of a man and a child, mounted on broomsticks. A second later they had landed in the dell.

'Oh, glory be!' exclaimed Abigail joyfully, tears of relief coming into her eyes. 'You're back safe and sound and no harm's come to you! Now come and have some hot broth and tell your mother what you've been up to.

Don't ever go flying off again like that while your father and I are still asleep. Oh, my, what a fright we had! Whatever did you do it for?' And scolding and fussing she led her daughter towards the moss-bed by the cauldron and gently pushed her down.

'Leave the child alone,' said Zachary grumpily, 'and give some broth to your husband, you silly old witch. *She's* all right, the young idiot! *She's* had some dinner.'

Fortunately at this moment the soup was ready and the rest of his rantings were drowned in the scalding broth.

The fire was burning low and both Abigail's legs had gone to sleep, but she was too absorbed in Zachary's story to notice. Behind her, in the cave, Necromancy lay fast asleep.

'However long were you stuck there, then?' she asked. 'It's a marvel you weren't smothered in that airless place!'

'Doubtless I would have been,' replied Zachary gloomily, 'but for some holes drilled near the top. Five mortal hours I stood in that cupboard. I'd be there yet if I hadn't managed to slip out when the woman opened the door to fetch her shoes. It is indeed magical to think that we're home again unharmed; my blood runs cold when I remember what dangers the child nearly brought upon us with her silly, foolish tongue, prattling away.' It was plain that he would not forgive his daughter in a hurry.

There was a pause; Abigail cautiously moved her be-numbed feet, and pins and needles shot up her legs.

'Do you think the teacher guessed at all?'

Zachary considered for a moment, and then shook his head. 'I don't think she did, you know; though why she didn't I couldn't say, considering all the foolish things the child said. But I'm not taking any more chances – that I'm not! I'll fix that young woman properly in the morning!'

'Stand there!'

Zachary had awoken feeling very stiff. The long hours in the cupboard in nothing but his underclothes, the rough treatment he had received from the cows, to say nothing of the east wind, had all tickled up his lumbago, and the lumbago had had an ill effect upon his temper; he seemed to be even angrier with his daughter than he had been the night before. He glared at her balefully.

Necromancy's head was so full of the events of the day before that she had scarcely noticed her father's mood; she stretched sleepily, and rising from her seat beside the cauldron, walked wonderingly towards him.

'Now,' said Zachary severely, 'stand still.' He spread his arms wide in a dramatic gesture, and throwing back his head began to recite slowly and ponderously, in what Necromancy thought of as his 'magickest' voice:

> 'Earth and Air and Fire and Water,
> Knock some Sense into my Daughter – '

'Oh, no! Father, *no!*' cried Necromancy, suddenly realizing, as her father began to circle round her, what he was doing. This was the spell he had used many years ago for the nanny-goat when she had eaten her tether, and it had lasted for months before she managed to escape. 'Oh, *please*, Father …' she cried again. But it was no use; remorselessly he continued:

> 'Put no Foot outside this Sphere,
> Till you've dropped this Mad –

this idiotic – this – this moon-crazed, half-baked, nit-witted *lunatic* Idea! There!' He glowered triumphantly at her from beneath the tangle of his eyebrows and stumped away up the side of the dell. Necromancy, imprisoned in the invisible circle, flung herself on the ground and burst into tears.

'Zachary Gumblethrush! Look at me!'

Abigail's voice shook with anger, and in spite of himself Zachary could not help obeying. Without moving his head he turned his eyes to his wife.

'That was a spiteful, mean trick to play on the child, and I shouldn't wonder if she were to catch her death of cold! Making your own daughter sleep out at this time of year! Well, I'll teach you a lesson, you wicked old sorcerer – it'll be your mattress she lies upon, and your cloak that covers her, and if you get any ideas in your head about taking them away from the child, you'd do well to remember that your wife, too, is a *witch*!'

And with these words of warning Abigail turned haughtily upon her heel and returned to the fire, leaving Zachary with a faintly uncomfortable feeling.

She fetched the cloak and mattress and threw them to Necromancy, then, pulling her wand out of the voluminous folds of her gown, began to retread the circle of Zachary's footsteps.

'If foot be set' – she began, glancing anxiously in the direction of the spelling-stone – 'inside this ring, There let it stay till Cuckoo sing!'

'But, Mother!' cried Necromancy, lifting her head out of the leaves, 'that means you too!'

'Drat my hat, so it does,' said Abigail, irritated. 'Oh, well, there's no help for it now. I'll just have to put your food down outside, and you'll have to put the mug back again when you've done. You'll be mortal cold though, my poor little one, even with the cloak. It's not very thick and it's full of holes. I'll have to make you a nice fire.'

The magic circle in which Necromancy was confined was very small indeed, and as there was only one bush growing in it, and no trees at all or even toadstools, she had soon explored all its possibilities.

The kitten came to see her but refused to venture inside the ring for fear that he might have to stay there until April, under the somewhat comprehensive terms of Abigail's spell.

There was absolutely nothing to do. Necromancy began to grow very bored, and the more bored she grew the more angry and resentful she felt towards her father, and the more determined that he should not win the battle.

'I'm not *going* to give in, just because I'm spell-bound,' she thought furiously, as she lay on the ground watching her mother meandering in and out of the cave, engaged upon her household duties.

Soon an enticing smell of thyme and bog-myrtle began to rise from the cauldron, and Necromancy realized that she was feeling very hungry; and with this realization came the first faint whiff of a plan to get the better of her father. 'But, oh!' she thought to herself, 'it will be *dreadfully* hard to do!'

chapter 7

Victory

Zachary and Abigail sat on either side of the fire, holding their hands to the blaze. Their faces were red with anger and heat, but their backs were as cold as the north side of a mountain; they were arguing bitterly.

'It can't go on any longer!' Abigail was saying. 'You'll have to revoke the spell. Not another morsel do I cook for you, and not another hand's turn shall I do, until you give in to that child. Three days, and she's not eaten so much as a whortleberry. I tell you, Zachary Gumblethrush, if you don't give in to her she'll kill herself, lying out there in the open, as empty as a conker-shell. So thin, she's grown, and weak . . .' and she threw her apron over her head and moaned, rocking backwards and forwards piteously.

Zachary bit his nails.

To tell the truth he did not know what to do: he had never imagined that the child would hold out so long. He had, himself, helped his wife to prepare all the dishes that Necromancy liked best: he had gathered nuts for her and had spent hours searching for the rare brown toadstools that resemble so closely the fallen leaves of autumn, but these delicacies had remained untouched, and all entreaties were met with the same answer.

'I shan't eat anything at all until you promise to let me go to school, and if you won't promise I shan't eat anything ever again – I shall just die. I shan't mind a bit

49

if I die. It couldn't be worse than sitting in the cave all day long learning spells.' And with all the strength of her obstinate young spirit she had resisted the temptation of broths and brews, of stews and roasts and infusions, knowing that if she could just hold out a little longer – just a *little* longer, victory would be hers.

Appetite turned to hunger and hunger to an aching emptiness, until she had not the strength to move from the mattress, and her voice was no more than a whisper.

Almost hourly Zachary saw his child grow weaker. Oh, his daughter! His beloved witch-child! Supposing she were to die! What did it matter whether or not she followed in her father's footsteps, so long as she was alive? Who cared whether she became a famous sorceress so long as the woods echoed once more with the sweet sound of her laughter? Yes, his wife was right – the spell would have to be revoked. He knew he would have to do it, even though it might call down upon his head the ridicule of all his fellow sorcerers, so that as long as he lived he would be too ashamed to attend another Conclave of Magicians. Never again would he be able to hold up his head within their Magic Circle, or offer his homage to the Arch-Wizard.

To revoke the spell was to cut himself off for ever from the Brotherhood to which he belonged. But supposing the child were to die . . .

'I'll do it!' he cried at last, in anguish. 'I'll revoke the spell! She shall have her way.'

Necromancy lay on her father's mattress in a sort of half-dream, in which the only clear thing seemed to be the ache of hunger which had driven her at times almost to the point of surrender. But now even that came and went, and nothing seemed to make sense any more; fantasy mingled with reality so that she could not tell which was which, and it did not, therefore, seem to her in any way peculiar to see her father, his gown tied up above his knees, crawling backwards round and round her, repeating in an endless monotone:

'Fang of Weasel, Fur of Stoat
Evermore hang round my Throat;
Let this be the Antidote
To the spell that pegged the Goat!'

And when she felt herself being lifted and borne towards the cave in her father's sinewy arms, and heard her mother's voice, warm and tearful, close beside her, she neither understood, nor cared to ask, the reason.

Seven days later Necromancy stood beside her parents on the edge of the dell, proudly holding a brand-new broomstick and wearing the birch-bark shoes her father had made for her. Attentively she listened to their instructions.

'Pay attention!
Don't you mention
Any word of Witch or Wand,
Or they'll spurn you!
Beat you!
Burn you!
Duck you in the village pond!

Don't you whisper –
Don't you lisp a
Single word of Brew or Spell,

Lest disaster
Follow faster
Than the time it takes to tell!

One more warning!
Every morning,
Hide your broomstick with good care,
And beside it
When you hide it
Make a mark to show you where . . .'

At last they had no more advice to offer, and with her head fairly bursting with all the things she must and must not do, Necromancy kissed both her parents and mounted the broomstick.

It sailed up into the air, climbing steeply at first, carrying its small excited burden smoothly and easily.

Below, in the heart of the forest, the witch and the wizard waved and waved, long after their daughter was lost to sight.

chapter 8

In which Things take a Turn for the Better

So Necromancy's schooldays started again, and Miss Popkins, though at first a little startled by the reappearance of her strange pupil, was soon pleasantly surprised to find how quickly she could learn.

It was true, of course, that the child had no notion of English whatsoever, and Geography was just as bad; but she had an unusual aptitude for learning by heart and her grasp of the ways and customs of Stone-Age Man was positively remarkable. She understood much, too, about the weather, and could usefully foretell storms and frosts from such small signs as the hoot of an owl or a magpie's flight; indeed, her knowledge of natural history altogether exceeded Miss Popkins's own. There were, certainly, several puzzling things about the child, caused probably, Miss Popkins decided, by her lonely upbringing; but nothing that a little schooling wouldn't put to rights.

Necromancy quickly made friends, for she could always think of some game to play or song to sing, and she taught the other children many new ways of amusing themselves. At first they were full of curiosity and asked her where she lived, and why all her clothes were black, and why she had such funny shoes, and why she sometimes brought her cat to school with her; but she parried all these questions, and soon the children ceased to notice that there was anything strange about her. No one ever seemed to guess her secret.

As time went on she found that she could afford to be less guarded, and sometimes, when the smaller children fell and grazed their knees, she would repeat the spell which her mother had so often used when she herself was little:

'Necromancy with a Fancy
And a stick-stick-stancy,
And a ring-tailed, wry-tailed, bob-tailed Necromancy!'

It sounded much better, though, with short names such as Polly and Ellen. Necromancy did not really believe that it was a very powerful spell, but it usually seemed to work.

Sometimes one or other of the children would invite her home to tea, and these were times of inexpressible delight to the witch-child. She loved the old cottages with their thatched roofs and twinkling windows, but there were new ones too, of red brick, square and neat as dolls' houses, which were almost more wonderful in some ways, with their lights which turned on and off at a switch, and water which rushed uphill out of pipes.

'Why, it's like *magic*!' Necromancy would exclaim, her eyes round as saucers; and sometimes she would ask if she might turn the lights on and off once or twice, or run the taps. Her greatest treat was to be allowed to help with the washing-up, and she would polish each cup till it shone and hang it with the utmost care on its hook on the dresser.

'Haven't you got running water?' her friends would sometimes ask, surprised that anyone could get so excited about a tap.

'Oh, yes,' Necromancy would answer, going rather pink, 'we have. But it's not quite the same as this. And it's not in the house, like yours; it just runs through the – through the –'

'Oh, I see. You've got a tap in the garden.'

It was useless, perhaps even dangerous, to try to explain, and sometimes she found herself getting rather tied up.

After such visits as these, when the memory of the warm, bright room with its rugs and gay curtains was still fresh in her mind, and the whole of the rest of her felt as if it was full of buttered scones and iced cakes and chocolate biscuits, the cave in the forest always seemed darker and colder and damper than ever, and there were times when Necromancy could not help sighing: 'I *wish* we lived in a real house . . .'

Then her father would look up from his work and say: 'Whatever will you be wanting next? Dresses of silk, I suppose, and shoes made of leather! *Real house*, indeed . . .'

By the time school began again after Christmas the rich brown earth of the forest was covered with snow like a plum cake with icing. It looked very beautiful, glowing pink in the sunset and silver in the moonlight and making patterns of lace more delicate than cobwebs out of the twigs and branches of the beech trees.

Necromancy would have loved the snow as much as any child, but for one thing: when it covered the ground it covered also the witch-family's winter food – the roots and herbs and toadstools on which they lived. Their supply of dried toadstools, and the puff-ball rings which Abigail strung on ivy-strands across the cave, would not last for ever, and when it snowed Necromancy could see the fear of starvation in her mother's eyes, and her father would complain about business being bad and about the new-fangled, trumpery medicines and gadgets which people bought nowadays, instead of good reliable cures and spells.

'If only we had some money . . .' Necromancy thought desperately. 'Just a *little* money. Just in case the snow's going to stay a long time . . .'

One day, when the wind was bitter and flurries of snow-flakes had been falling all day, Necromancy came home very late from school. She made an awkward landing which brought her to her knees in the snow. Abigail ran to her in alarm.

'Whatever have you got there, child?' she asked, pointing to a big square box lying a few feet away.

Necromancy picked it up and examined it carefully, brushing away the snow.

'It's a wireless.'

'A what?'

'A wireless. Some people call it a radio, but Miss Popkins says it's a wireless. It's a box with voices and music inside it. You can turn it on and off with these little knobs, only you can't, because it's broken.'

'Well, why have you brought it home, if it's broken?'

'For Father to mend! It's sort of magic, you see, so I was sure Father could mend it. Miss Popkins said she'd be very pleased if he could and would pay him a pound. But she says not to make it worse, whatever happens, or she won't pay him anything.'

Zachary pulled his beard for a long time when he heard about the wireless; he felt rather doubtful.

'I've never seen anything of the sort before,' he said finally, dividing his beard into three and plaiting it. 'The Pedlar doesn't stock them, that I know. I doubt if there's a spell in existence for mending such things; I shall have to make a new one in all probability, and I don't very much fancy the idea of sitting up there all night in a snow-storm, I can tell you.'

'But a whole pound, Father!' Necromancy reminded him. He did not seem quite as pleased as she had hoped.

Finally he consented to try, and for a long time that night he sat by the fire, thumbing through the pages of the *Complete Encyclopaedia of Witchcraft and Wizardry*, but nowhere could he find any reference to a wireless or indeed a radio.

'I feared as much,' he said at last, rising wearily to his feet. 'There's nothing for it but to compose a new one ...'

The first light of dawn was filtering through the trees

by the time Zachary had made a spell sufficiently powerful to mend the wireless. He went into the cave to fetch
his wand. His eyes were heavy with sleep and his joints
were frozen stiff, but he thought it would be better to cast
the spell now and get the job finished.

He flung out his arms dramatically and the icicles that
had formed on the wide sleeves of his robe clinked in the
chill morning breeze. With his wand he described a large
circle round the radio, and taking a deep breath began,
in an awe-inspiring voice, to recite:

'Thunder, Lightning, Hail and Blizzard –
Breath of Witch and Hair of Wizard –
Spawn of Frog and Skin of Lizard –
Earth-worm's Spoor and Raven's Gizzard!'

The forest rang with the noise and as Zachary's voice
rose in a fearful crescendo Abigail and Necromancy woke
up. The echoes died away and away; a few startled birds
flapped noisily off into the forest, and then, once more,
there was silence. Zachary stumped into the cave, spat-
tering snow and blowing on his icy fingers.

'If that fails, well, then, I'm powerless to repair that
blessed wireless,' he said crossly, sitting down on his
mattress and removing his grandfather's boots.

All at once there was a loud crackling from outside the
cave, followed by a curious whining whistle; suddenly
Abigail and Necromancy sat bolt upright, clutching their
cloaks round them, as the loud clear tones of a man's
voice came to their ears.

'Good morning,' it said, in the most matter-of-fact way
imaginable. 'Here is the weather forecast for today, Tuesday, January the twenty-second ...'

*

After this success Zachary did not have as much time on his hands as of old. Miss Popkins had been delighted when her precious wireless was returned to her so soon and in such good order, and the word quickly spread round the village. Soon Necromancy found that nearly every day one child or another would bring a parcel to school containing some object to be repaired – worn shoes or a broken plate or an unpunctual clock. She was glad to be able to give these small jobs to her father, for the money soon mounted up, bringing with it a feeling of security and, for Necromancy at least, the possibility of a dream coming true.

Abigail was glad too: it was always better when Zachary had something proper to do, for as she confided to her daughter, she 'never could abide an idle man about the place – they do get in the way so.'

And Zachary himself, although he pretended to grumble at these interruptions to his Alchemy, his 'real work' as he called it, nevertheless whistled merrily as he prepared spells for every kind of household calamity, and the monotonous chanting of his voice became once more a familiar sound in the forest:

> 'Wet the weather, dry the leather,
> Strong as ling and tough as heather,
> Water-tight as duck's-back feather,
> Sole and upper stick together!'

Soon the green glass flasks that had stood empty for so many months were once again stacked in neat rows at the back of the cave, carefully labelled and stoppered. Business had not been so brisk for years.

Sometimes people wanted their furniture repaired, but as Necromancy could not manage kitchen dressers and double beds on her broomstick these had to be mended as usual by the village carpenter, an unreliable and cantankerous old man, who often took as long as six months to screw a castor on a chair.

'And it's not as if he were cheap, either,' remarked his customers. 'Now, if that Mr Gumblethrush only lived a bit closer there's no end to the things we'd be asking him to do, I declare! That man's a regular wizard!'

'That he is!' would come the reply. 'I was just saying the other day, he's a proper magician, the things he can do! It's a shame he doesn't live in the village.'

chapter 9

In which Necromancy makes a Discovery

Zachary kept his earnings in an old leather bag under a stone slab at the back of the cave, and from time to time Necromancy would go secretly to the hiding-place and feel the money-bag. Although her father did the work, it was she who supplied him with it, and she felt that she had a right to know how much he had earned; also, she had a very good reason for wanting to know.

Weighing the solid bulk of silver coins in her hands she would consider whether or not the hour had come to start looking for a house; but the months slipped by and summer had come again before the money-bag was stretched really tight, and only then did she decide that the time was ripe.

She began to question the children at school as to whether they knew of a cottage or dwelling of any sort, no matter how ivy-grown or tumbledown, that might be for sale; but no one had heard of any such place, and she grew very despondent. She walked many miles through the honeysuckle-sweet lanes surrounding the village, in the hope of coming across her dream-house, and she was so often late coming home that Abigail grew quite worried.

'It's the house-keeping class,' said Necromancy innocently, crossing her fingers behind her back. 'We have it after school.'

One day it happened that she had to go on an errand

to the house of an old man who lived about a mile along
the road to the east of the village; leaving his cottage she
decided to make her way over the fields to the forest,
rather than go back through the village. Accordingly she
climbed a gate and set off across a field of clover.

The sky was as blue as the bird's-eye that grew along
the side of the road in thick sapphire patches, and little
white butterflies fluttered along, chasing each other, almost under Necromancy's feet. As she walked towards
the distant green of the forest a cuckoo called and called
his two clear notes. She felt very happy.

She crossed two more fields and then she came to a
grassy track, winding its way between high hedges of dog-
rose and hazel, so tangled and overgrown that she had
to bend almost double to get through.

After a while the track widened: the turf became
springy and green and under the hedge on her left Necromancy could hear the gurgling of a little stream. It was
a lovely path. She wondered if anyone ever used it: it did
not appear to lead anywhere in particular, and the cart-
tracks that scored its surface were overgrown with grass.
It had certainly not been used for many years.

Then suddenly, just ahead of her, she saw the reason
for the path's existence: almost hidden by a tangle of
white roses and honeysuckle stood a small stone cottage, a
single chimney rising crookedly from its ancient, bird-
ridden thatch. The windows were broken, the door
gaped ajar, the fence had long since collapsed under the
weight of brambles that straggled everywhere; stinging-
nettles as tall as Necromancy herself filled what had once
been the garden.

For a long minute she stood and stared, hardly daring
to believe her eyes. Then she climbed over the broken

63

fence and stood on the threshold of – of *her* house! For was it not hers? Had she not that moment discovered it? Certainly it was no one else's, nor had it been for years and years and years. Necromancy doubted whether any-one else would even want to live in it, so dilapidated, so old and broken and neglected was it. Who else would be able to imagine as clearly as she could, the roof newly thatched and the door painted yellow? Already as she gazed about her the windows seemed mended, the nettles vanished, cat-mint and sweet-williams grew beneath the windows and there was soft green grass under the apple tree ...

She pushed open the front door. It tilted wildly on one hinge and she plunged through it, landing on her hands and knees in a heap of rubble. Scarcely noticing, she picked herself up and looked around: she was in a fair-sized room with stone flags on the floor and a huge fireplace containing a rusty and antiquated kitchen range. There was only one window, but it was quite large, and the room, although full of sticks and crumbled masonry, seemed light and airy. It had once been papered with a pattern of blue delphiniums which now peeled sadly off the walls, revealing large patches of yellowish-green plaster.

There was another door in the room which Necromancy, remembering the front door, opened with caution: it led into a second room, smaller and darker than the first. A rocking-chair with a broken leg lay on its side in one corner and there was a bucket without a bottom standing by the fireplace; otherwise the room was empty.

Then Necromancy noticed a door which she at first supposed to be a cupboard, but on opening it discovered to her delight that it concealed a dark and rickety stair-case. Two of the treads were missing, and as she climbed it she felt for the first time a little afraid; but in a moment she came safely to the top.

She found herself in a small room so close under the roof that she could barely stand upright. It had a single dormer window; the floor was littered with twigs and feathers and straw from the thatch above, as if a hundred birds had built their nests in it, and there were at least twelve places where one could look straight through the roof to the blue summer sky. Large black patches on the floorboards showed all too clearly what happened when it rained.

A door led from this room into another, slightly larger, above the room with the stove. It had two windows and plenty of ventilation in the roof; standing in the middle of it, reaching almost from wall to wall, was an enormous double bed.

'Oh!' cried Necromancy aloud, and dozens of small startled creatures scuttled back to their holes. 'A *real bed*!'

She climbed on to it and bounced on the rusty springs; they creaked and groaned alarmingly, and the wire mesh made painful criss-cross patterns on her knees. Presently she stopped.

Dusk was falling when the witch-child finally managed to tear herself away from the cottage, and she suddenly realized how late it must be. With one last backward glance she hastened towards the forest.

Next morning, instead of taking her usual route to the hollow oak on the edge of the forest, Necromancy altered course as soon as she knew that she was out of sight, and flew towards the south-east.

Lest she should be seen she flew very low, just skimming over the hedges, and in quite a short while she caught sight of the cottage chimney directly ahead of her.

The path outside the cottage was smooth and wide; with its springy turf it made an ideal landing-place, and Necromancy touched down very gently. For a few minutes she stood and stared with shining eyes at the little house, still hardly able to believe in its existence. Then she climbed over the broken door and propped her broomstick up inside.

'This evening,' she said aloud, addressing the kitchen stove, 'I shall sweep all the floors and move the cobwebs. The spiders will just have to go somewhere else, though

I don't mind the birds: they can stay if they don't make too much noise. The mice can stay too, only they mustn't make the place untidy. But I won't have rats.'

She walked through the door to the inner room and inspected it briefly.

'Tomorrow I'll scrub the floors,' she decided. 'Then I suppose I had better start mending everything. And I'll polish you' – she called up the stairs to the bedstead – 'as soon as I've done the dirty jobs. And now I really must go or I'll be late for school, but I'll be back this evening! I'll be back!'

chapter 10

Enter Mr Ebenezer

It never occurred to Necromancy that the cottage might actually belong to someone, for it was quite clear that nobody had lived in it for many a long year. But of course, like almost everything else in the world, it did have an owner – a fat old farmer called Mr Ebenezer, who spent a lot of his time sitting on the bench outside the Barley Mow Inn with a mug of ale in his hand. Necromancy knew him well by sight, for the Barley Mow was just opposite the school; and although she did not know it, he also knew her. He had often wondered who she was and where she came from, in her ragged black dress and odd-looking shoes; with her sunburnt face and tangle of brown hair she stood out from all the other children, and there was something about her that intrigued him.

In time he learned that she was the daughter of a man called Gumblethrush, a marvellously handy man who could mend anything that happened to be broken, and charged next to nothing for it; but nobody seemed to know where he actually lived.

Mr Ebenezer determined to find out. He had a great many things that badly needed mending: all his gates had fallen off their hinges, the roofs of his barns all leaked, his ditches were all choked with weeds, and none of his men was any use. Or so he thought; but the truth was that Mr Ebenezer had become very mean and tight-fisted since his wife died, and his men would not work well for a master who didn't pay them. So his farm, which had once been thriving, had fallen into neglect.

But if he were able to get hold of the Gumblethrush fellow, he might be able to set the place to rights, and very cheaply too, so it seemed.

So, one afternoon when Necromancy came out of school, Mr Ebenezer waited until she had turned the corner by the church, then he got to his feet and followed her. He had to walk fast to keep her in sight as she skipped and hopped along in front of him. Snatches of song reached his ears; the words seemed to be her own:

> 'When I first went to school
> I was, oh! such a fool –
> I couldn't add up or subtract!
> But now I do sums
> Without fingers or thumbs.
> (I'm Top, as a matter of fact!)'

He wished she wouldn't go so fast, it was such a hot afternoon. To make matters worse she had now turned off the road and was bounding away down a cart-track, hopping over the sun-baked ruts like a rabbit, still singing.

> 'Art was a mystery,
> Ditto with History,
> Geography, Grammar as well;
> I had no notions
> But Philtres and Potions
> And all I could do was to Spell!'

Mr Ebenezer gave up. His feet hurt dreadfully on the hard uneven ground and his breath was coming in painful gasps. Thankfully he leaned against a tree and fanned himself with his hat.

By this time the child had disappeared round a bend in the lane, but being still too much out of breath to move any further, Mr Ebenezer continued to gaze after her in a vacant sort of way. After a while he was puzzled to see what he thought was a huge bird with a spreading tail soar up into the sky above the forest. He stared at it, mystified, until it had vanished in the distance. Suddenly he slapped himself on the thigh and exclaimed aloud: 'Why, dash me! Well, I'll be dashed! A *broomstick*! No *wonder* they say her father's a magician!'

As he turned and began to trudge wearily homewards a new and better idea occurred to Mr Ebenezer. If the child could ride on a broomstick, then she must be a witch, and if she were indeed a witch, there would be no need to bother about the wizard! All he need do now was to capture her.

But capturing Necromancy turned out to be rather more difficult than he expected, for the next day was the day on which she discovered the cottage, and after that, of course, she did not use the old path any more.

Three more evenings Mr Ebenezer waited in vain for the witch-child, sitting on his camp stool in the shade of a clump of ilex trees that grew beside the cart-track, but as each day passed without a sign of her he grew more and more convinced that she must be a fully qualified witch. How else could she have known that he was lying in ambush for her? And why else should she have stopped using her habitual route?

It was with some surprise that the regulars in the Barley Mow learned that old Bill Ebenezer had taken up bird-watching. But there could be no doubt of it: hadn't he been seen, three evenings in a row, perched on top of his tallest haystack, peering through a spy-glass? And what could he have been looking at, pray, if not birds?

chapter 11

Kidnapped

Necromancy continued to work in the cottage every evening after school, and soon it began to look very different.

She beat the stinging-nettles down with a stick, and when they were dead she carried them to the end of the garden and made a heap of them. She could not mend the front door by herself, but she propped it up so that it looked all right, and she chipped all the broken glass out of the windows, which made them much tidier.

She made tight little bundles of dry twigs and grasses and stuffed them into the holes in the roof, balancing precariously on the bottomless bucket; then she swept the cobwebs from the walls and with the aid of a pot of flour-and-water paste borrowed from school, stuck the peeling wallpaper back again. Soon the rooms lost their sorrowful appearance.

She scoured the stove with earth, and when all the rust had come off she filled the fire-box with kindling and put a match to it. As she waited for the sound of the flames roaring up the chimney her heart thumped with excitement.

But there was no sound of roaring, and in a little while smoke began to pour out of every crack in the old range, filling the room so that Necromancy had to run, choking and spluttering, into the garden.

She looked up at the chimney, wondering why no

smoke came out of it, and at that moment a sleek, speckled starling alighted on it, carrying something in its beak, and loud delighted chirpings came from within the chimney-pot.

'Bother!' said Necromancy. 'Now I shan't be able to light the fire until you've all flown away, I suppose!'

She worked in the cottage for a whole week, and at the end of that time there was no more that she could do without help, so she decided that on the following day she would show it to her parents.

She worked feverishly all the evening, dusting and polishing, putting jam-jars of roses in all the rooms and fresh green bracken on the floors; the brass knobs of the old bedstead shone like gold. When she had finished she gazed with deep satisfaction at the results of her labours. No one, she thought, could ever have lived in a more perfectly beautiful, dear little, sweet little house.

When she came to the front door she turned round for one last glance at her handiwork, and stepping backwards over the sill, walked straight into the waiting arms of – Mr Ebenezer.

That evening Abigail sat outside the cave sewing in the late sunlight.

'Drat this cobweb! That's the third time it's broken,' she grumbled. 'I don't know what spiders make it of nowadays.'

'I'm hungry,' said Zachary, stumbling down the steep side of the dell. 'Isn't that child back yet? She's always back by frog-croak even with this house-keeping class she talks of.'

Abigail laid down her mending. 'She'll be home in a

minute. Perhaps she's bringing back some work. Come, I'll give you your broth! No sense in starving.'

She ladled the thin green liquid into two striped china bowls and put a third in the ashes to warm. These bowls were a new acquisition, lately bought by Necromancy with some of her father's earnings, and Abigail spent a lot of time washing them in the stream and arranging them on the ledge in the cave. They were much more convenient to eat out of than the pewter mug, and she was very proud of them. They ate in silence, their ears straining for the sound of a broomstick. Zachary grew more and more fidgety.

'What ever can have become of the child?' he said at last, pushing his empty bowl away from him. 'I do hope she hasn't crashed.'

'Necromancy crashed? Why, you are an old worrier! She's as safe on a broomstick as you are. She'll be back any minute, you'll see.'

But in spite of these reassuring remarks Abigail was beginning to be worried herself, and when the moon rose above the tree-tops and Necromancy still did not return, she became really alarmed.

'Zachary, love,' she said at length, 'perhaps you'd better go and look for her. 'Tis a fine clear night and you'd see her easily from the air.'

So Zachary put on his cloak, for even in summer it can be chilly flying, and mounted his broomstick.

Two hours later he returned, cold and downcast.

'Not a sign,' he said, warming his hands in front of the fire. 'Unless she's crashed in the forest I don't know where she is. I've covered every inch of the ground between the village and the forest, five miles east and five miles west

– not a sign. And I received no indication from the broomstick whatever: it never lost height or flew off course, or I should have known at once that she was somewhere around. It's remarkable how they seek each other out – remember that time when she ran away to school and left her broomstick in a yew tree? Found it at once, that time. But now . . . Blessed if I know what to do next . . .'

Abigail thought for a moment.

'How about sending Isaac? If she's crashed in the forest he's the only one who could find her. Have you got a searching spell?'

He went to look for one. Isaac, with an air of great importance, rose slowly to his feet, and arching his back, paced majestically to and fro in front of the fire until Zachary returned.

'Weave your net like web of spider – '

began the wizard, panting rather from the exertion of scrambling up and down the side of the dell –

'Round in circles ever wider,
Hither, thither, to and fro,
Up above and down below –
Find her, Isaac – off you go!'

Obediently Isaac slid away between the trees, black and silent as a shadow. When he had quite vanished Abigail went into the cave, to reappear a few moments later staggering under the weight of an enormous spinning-wheel.

'There's nothing like it for soothing the nerves,' she said; and sitting down on a log she began to move her foot

75

up and down on the treadle. Softly she hummed the lilting, age-old tune of the spinning-song that her grand-mother had taught her:

> 'Man shall exploring go, wenching and
> warring-O,
> Man shall adventuring go, far and wide;
> Woman shall spin and sew, sniffing and
> blowing-O,
> Sighing and sorrowing by the fire-side ...'

'Fiddlesticks!' said Zachary irritably. 'Sing something sensible, for goodness' sake!'

He could not sit still. Every five minutes he would leave the fire and, climbing up to the edge of the dell, peer intently into the darkness.

By first light Isaac returned, alone and bedraggled, his coat badly torn by brambles. He glanced disdainfully at the bowl of broth which Abigail offered him, and, lying down in the ashes, immediately went to sleep. A faint smell of scorching arose from him.

Abigail was distraught.

'Something terrible must have happened,' she moaned, wringing her hands. 'Oh, Zachary, what ever shall we do now? If she's not in the forest, nor yet out of it, what ever can have become of her?'

'There now,' Zachary comforted her, 'don't take on so! We'll just have to wait till daylight. Perhaps she's spend-ing the night with a school-friend. Anyway,' he went on, 'there's nothing we can do until daybreak. Except ... except ...'

'Except what?'

'I was going to say,' said Zachary very gently, 'except the crystal.'

'Oh!' Abigail's voice was sharp, her breath indrawn. 'The crystal! Oh, Zachary, must I? I'm so scared of what I might see. I've never gazed in that great glass ball but I've seen some terrible thing, for there's nothing but death and sadness to be found in it! Oh, Zachary, love, don't make me . . .' She looked at him beseechingly.

But Zachary spoke firmly, for it was their last hope of discovering Necromancy's whereabouts, and he knew it would not fail. He did not possess the seer's gift himself, but he understood Abigail's fear, for it was true that she had sometimes seen tragedies mirrored in its magic depths; but that did not mean that it would always reveal disaster.

'Don't be so foolish, woman,' he said roughly. 'If the child is in trouble, you want to help her, don't you? Go now, and fetch the crystal.'

So Abigail fetched the crystal, carefully wrapped in its cloth of blue velvet, and, setting it on the ground, sat down cross-legged before it. Zachary gave her a reassuring smile. As always when she was afraid, Abigail felt the hot prick of tears behind her eyes, but she smiled bravely back and, with a great effort of will, turned her whole concentration on the crystal.

At first it was as clear as spring water, flawless in its transparency, a miracle of perfection: colourless as ice, lifeless as a stone, yet holding in its compass all colours and the reflection of all life – love, hate, fear and sorrow. To Abigail it seemed a frozen ball of tears.

As she gazed, the diamond-bright translucence softened, clouding into a pearly milkiness which swirled and eddied, then split into jewel-colours – topaz and amethyst, emerald, amber, sapphire, ruby. The colours spun and whirled and now no power on earth could have

forced Abigail's eyes away from the crystal; then slowly,
as she watched, spell-bound, the kaleidoscope settled.

She found herself looking into a dark room with a tiny
window high up on one wall; an iron bedstead stood in
a corner of the gaunt chamber and huddled upon it was
the forlorn figure of a little girl, her face hidden by a mass
of dark hair.

An anguished cry broke suddenly from Abigail's lips:
'Necromancy! Oh, my little one!'

With both arms she reached towards the crystal . . .

chapter 12

Captivity

Necromancy awoke with a start: it seemed to her that she heard her mother calling – a strange cry full of sadness – and sitting up she searched the darkness for Abigail's familiar figure.

The faint light from the window above her head made her look up, and in an instant she realized where she was: the memory of yesterday with all its fear and anger and bitter disappointment came flooding back, and she remembered furiously how Mr Ebenezer – the horrible old man – had watched her and spied upon her and then, on the very day when everything was finished, when the cottage was ready and the surprise complete, he had lain in wait for her and captured her.

Captured her! Ambushed her, kidnapped her! Necromancy's blood boiled with rage. And all for his own selfish purpose, too, so that he could have his socks darned and his shirts washed and pay never so much as a farthing for any of it.

And if she were to refuse: if she were to object to spending the rest of her days shut up in Mr Ebenezer's murky old house scrubbing and sewing, then he would tell all the village that she was a witch – that was what he had said. He would tell everyone he knew: he would raise a hue and cry and have her ducked in the pond and she would never be able to show her face again, or go to school, or to tea with her friends or ... or ... *anything* ...

Tears of anger stung her eyes and rolled, hot and salty, into the corners of her mouth; they came so fast that they formed little rivers, and as she lay down again on the damp and lumpy flock mattress small tributaries branched off and flowed into her ears.

Poor Necromancy! Her plight was indeed a sorry one.

For a long time she wept, but at last it seemed that there were no more tears left, and gradually she grew calmer.

Above her head the grey square slowly lightened, until it was possible to make out the sparse details of the room: the rails of the bed, the wooden chair beside it, the bare floor and the heavy oak door.

She knew that it was useless to try to open the door. With a fresh surge of anger she remembered how Mr Ebenezer had laughed at her when, the evening before, she had wrenched desperately at the iron handle.

He had stood there with his great stomach shaking, and laughed and laughed. 'Save your strength, my little witch-baby,' he had said mockingly, 'save your strength! That door's quite a job for a fully-grown man to open, and anyways, I've locked it!' And he had dangled the huge key tantalizingly just beyond her reach.

It was then that she had bitten him.

With deep satisfaction she recalled his yell of pain as her sharp white teeth sank into his wrist. He had shaken her off, though, hurling her viciously against the wall. Ruefully she rubbed the bump on her head and vowed that she would get even with Mr Ebenezer if it were to take her a month of witches' sabbaths.

She began to make a plan.

*

Mr Ebenezer slept heavily, his snores reverberating through the old house, and the square of grey sky in Necromancy's bedroom had turned to forget-me-not blue by the time he came to let her out. His wrist, beneath its dirty bandage, still throbbed painfully, and he opened the door with caution.

He was not a little relieved to find his prisoner sitting in a docile fashion on the edge of her bed, her hands primly folded together. It was hard to believe that this was the same child as the little spitfire of the night before.

'C'mon,' he said roughly. 'Don't dawdle! There's work to be done.'

Necromancy rose obediently and followed him out of the room. He led the way down the stairs and along a flagged stone passage in which there were many doors painted chocolate brown; high up under the ceiling a row of rusty bells dangled crookedly on broken springs. The whole place was thick with dust.

He pushed open one of the doors and Necromancy saw that they were in a huge kitchen, as dirty and gloomy as the rest of the house. One wall was almost entirely occupied by an enormous fireplace full of strange wheels and spikes and pulleys; there were bread-ovens on either side and a great iron pot hung above the dead embers, reminding her painfully of her mother's dear old cauldron. Over the whole fireplace was a kind of tent-shaped canopy to draw the smoke and steam up the chimney.

'Light the fire and make the porridge,' said Mr Ebenezer in a commanding tone.

'Yes, sir,' answered Necromancy. 'What with?'

'There's the oats and here's the matches,' he said grumpily, throwing a match-box on to the table. 'And don't use them all up or you'll catch it, good and proper.

Johnny-up-the-Orchard is what you'll get, and if you
don't know what that means you'll soon find out. When
you've made the porridge, scrub the floor.'

'Yes, sir. Please, sir, what with?'

'What with? What with?' bellowed Mr Ebenezer in a
voice of thunder. 'By heaven, miss, I'll give you what
with! Elbow-grease, of course – that's what with! And
when you've scrubbed the floor you'll clean me boots –
with spit-and-polish. I don't go wasting good money on
fancy cakes of soap and boot-polish, and no more will
you. Work's what you're here for, and work's what you'll
do, and you'll not eat till you've done it, so you'd best get
on with it, quick and sharp. I want me breakfast,' he
added querulously and stumped out of the room.

'Whew!' said Necromancy as she watched the door
close behind him. 'Cross old hippopotamus!'

She turned and looked about her: in one corner of the
kitchen was a pile of firewood consisting for the most part
of rotten gate-posts; as far as she could see there was no
kindling or straw or anything with which to start a fire,
and even if there had been, all the matches seemed to be
wet. She sighed despairingly, wondering what in the
world she was going to do.

Luckily, however, the ashes proved to be still faintly
warm, and with much perseverance and puffing she
eventually managed to blow a tiny spark of life into a
piece of charcoal, and presently a flame appeared.

When the fire was burning brightly she took the smallest of the great iron pots that stood on the dresser and
put into it a double handful of oatmeal; then she pumped
a stream of rusty water on to it and hung it on the hook
above the fire. Shutting her eyes tightly she began to stir,
reciting in a low voice:

'Greasy dishes, bones of fishes,
Let him think this stuff delicious.'

She pronounced the last word 'delishes' to make it rhyme and with all her strength she willed the spell to work: it was very, very important that the old man should find her so good a cook that he would do anything rather than lose her.

By the time the porridge was done she had scrubbed the floor and cleaned the boots and was beginning to feel quite pleased with herself. If only she could keep it up she felt sure that her plan would succeed, but it was going to mean a lot of hard work.

Meanwhile, in the forest, a gloom as dense and impenetrable as a November fog had settled over the dell.

Hardly a word had passed between the witch and the wizard for three days and the only sounds which broke the silence were Abigail's incessant sniffs, and from time to time a loud, mournful blow. Her tears soaked her aprons as fast as the sun could dry them and they hung dismally on the clothes-line together with half-a-dozen of Zachary's largest black handkerchiefs.

Zachary was beginning to lose patience with his wife; indeed he almost doubted whether she ever would stop crying. She'd been at it now for a day and a half and he only had two more handkerchiefs left.

'*Sniff* sniff, sniff, *sniff* sniff sniff, *sniff* sniff sniff. What will happen if I catch a cold, I'd like to know?' he inquired irritably. Receiving no answer he shrugged and, stuffing his fingers into his ears, turned back to the *Encyclopaedia of Witchcraft*. Many of the spells dated from the Dark Ages and were consequently rather hard to understand. It was a long time before he found anything at all hopeful. 'P,' he read. 'Property, Lost, Finding of. Charm for. Ingredients: Half a gill Snayle-Watter, Three oz. Powdered Turmericke, Blood of ye large ladye Ratte, newly slayne, Salt-petre one gramme. Methodde: Pound ye drye ingredients fynely . . .'

No good, anyway, he thought, turning the page almost without hope. The child wasn't lost, she was stolen. Captured, kidnapped . . . Kidnapped . . .

Wearily he turned the thick leaves of parchment back to K.

Down below in the dell Abigail stirred the cauldron with the great iron ladle, round and round, east to west, north to south, round and slowly round until at length her hand was still ...

She gazed unseeingly into the greenish-black soup, and her tears, dripping into it, made it saltier and more watery than ever and sent small ripples out to the edge of the old iron pot like little waves on a miniature lake.

'Like waves on a lake ...' she thought musingly; and then suddenly she shuddered and stared intently into the cauldron – into depths that seemed suddenly awful, bottomless ... Into the depths of a lake as black as pitch.

'The Black Lake!' The words broke from her lips in a thin cry of fear as she realized the full meaning of what she had seen.

Far away on the other side of the forest, in a part to which Abigail had never been, lived a very powerful Black witch known as the Weir-Woman, who was feared and hated by all who knew her.

Nothing short of despair ever drove people to her, for her price was so high and her reputation so terrible. Like some great, evil spider she sat waiting, night and day, until fear or sorrow drove some poor creature into her net; then there would be no escape for him until she had bled him white – until there was not a penny, or a sheep, or a hen, or even a child, so Zachary said, left to him. And if he had none of these things he would be forced to serve her for perhaps as long as seven years, or until his health gave out, or he died of misery. So Zachary said; but then he hated the Weir-Woman with a professional as well as a personal hatred, for she stood for everything that was abhorrent to him in the ancient art of witchcraft. But Abigail knew that if there was anyone on earth who could bring her daughter back it was the Weir-Woman, and to the Black Lake she would have to go.

As she stared into the cauldron the image slowly faded, until she found herself gazing once more into a gallon and a half of wild-garlic soup. To her surprise she found that she had stopped crying.

She looked up to the edge of the dell where Zachary sat at his stone, deep in concentration. She knew what she had to do: there was no time to be lost. She slipped quietly into the cave and emerged stuffing something heavy into her deep pocket.

Zachary was not looking at her; he still seemed to be busy with his spell-binding. Quickly Abigail took her broomstick from the cleft branch of the broomstick-tree. Behind her she could hear Zachary's melancholy intonation growing fainter as she rose into the air:

> 'Lure of Bait or pull of Magnet,
> Nose of Bloodhound, Mesh of Drag-net,
> Spike of Pick or Blow of Axe, or
> Turn of Key or Blade of Hacksaw . . .'

chapter 13

The Bargaining

Mr Ebenezer smacked his lips and rubbed his hands together happily. He tucked his napkin under his chin and pulling his chair up to the table, stuck his knife and fork into the soggy pastry covering Necromancy's pie.

'Scrumptioush,' he said, his mouth full. 'Perf'ly shcrumptioush. Get on with your shcrubbing, my girl. I'll call when I'm ready for me pudding.' And he stuffed another large forkful into his already full mouth.

For the first time since his wife died, thought Mr Ebenezer, as he watched the door close behind Necromancy, he was being really well looked after: the house was clean, the water was hot, even his socks were mended – not very well, it was true, but still mended. His little witch was really a marvel – a perfect treasure! And he did feel – although of course he couldn't be sure – but he did feel that *perhaps* she was beginning to grow a little bit fond of him. Just a *little*, perhaps. Feeling very happy he helped himself to another slice of pie.

In the great kitchen Necromancy sat, deep in thought, her elbows on the table and her chin in her hands.

For three days now she had worked like a beaver, scrubbing and cooking and washing and mending, tending the fires and airing the bedding, and Mr Ebenezer undoubtedly wanted to keep her for ever. She was beginning to doubt whether she would ever make much of a cook, but she cast the spell fervently on every dish, and the old man seemed delighted with her efforts. So far her plan had succeeded.

There were four parts to this plan: the first was to lull Mr Ebenezer into an unsuspecting frame of mind and to make him think that he could not possibly bear to part with her; the second, which depended on the success of the first, was to get possession, by hook or by crook, of the cottage. The third was to blackmail him into silence regarding the Gumblethrush profession, and the fourth was to escape. How she was to do all this Necromancy had no idea at all, but she hoped for an inspiration.

Her thoughts were interrupted by loud cries of 'Pudding!' echoing down the stone passage, followed by a great banging and thumping and jangling of bells.

'Dash my whiskers!' cried the old man in delight as Necromancy set the dish before him. 'Roly-poly!' And helping himself to an enormous slice he began to stuff it into his mouth.

Necromancy watched him disgustedly. His table-manners, she thought, were worse than any wizard's, but all the same she could not help being a little bit flattered at the success of her cooking. In a remarkably short time the pale and greasy roll of suet had disappeared.

'Fetch me 'baccy, there's a good girl,' said the old man presently, pushing away his plate. 'It's on the mantel-piece and I don't feel like moving. Matches are up there too.'

Soon great clouds of smoke arose, so that Necromancy could hardly breathe, and Mr Ebenezer's face wore a look of perfect felicity.

After a while the pleasant thought came to Mr Ebenezer that he would rather fancy a little elderberry port, and as he watched the ruby liquid flowing into the largest glass that Necromancy, seizing her opportunity, could find, his heart fairly brimmed over with affection for his little witch.

'Come and sit here, lass,' he said, patting the seat of the chair beside him. 'We'll have a little chat ...'

'Well,' he went on, when she was seated; 'not so bad working for me, is it?' He took a large gulp of port.

'I like it very much, thank you, sir,' said Necromancy, hastily crossing the fingers of her left hand, for she never remembered telling such a dreadful lie in all her life; with her right she quietly filled his glass up to the top again, earnestly whispering as she did so:

> 'Ere he's taken seven sips, he
> Shall be absolutely tipsy!'

Sure enough, before the glass was half empty Mr Ebenezer's behaviour was becoming rather odd: his voice sounded thick and sentimental and he kept spilling his glass of port.

'You're the best little witch in all the world,' he said, putting an arm round her shoulders and squeezing painfully. 'Not going to leave old Ebenezer, are you? Going to stay with me for ever and ever, aren't you? Stay and look after me ...'

'I'm afraid I can't stay much longer,' said Necromancy. 'Father wouldn't like it. I shall have to go soon.'

'You can't,' said Mr Ebenezer. 'I've got you! You're locked in, me li'l witch, and you can't get out!'

'But if Father gets angry,' said Necromancy, 'he'll do the most terrible things. Turn you into a pumpkin or porpoise or something ...'

'A *pumpkin*!' shouted Mr Ebenezer, going purple in the face. 'A *porpoise*! I wouldn't let him!'

'You wouldn't be able to stop him,' said Necromancy. 'He's a *terrifically* powerful wizard. He's already turned the milk sour twice.' She sighed deeply. 'It'd be all right, of course, if I lived at home. He wouldn't mind that a bit. He might even do some of the biggest jobs for you himself, but it's much too far to come every day. What a *pity* we couldn't live in the cottage ...'

'Cottage!' said Mr Ebenezer. 'What cottage? You can't go living in other people's cottages. Pass the port.'

Necromancy passed the port, and Mr Ebenezer sloshed some more into his glass and quite a lot all over the table. He was certainly becoming very tipsy indeed and it seemed more than likely that he would fall into a drunken slumber at any moment, and when he awoke he would probably have forgotten their entire conversation. Necromancy would have to act quickly.

'Father could buy it from you,' she said. 'He's got piles and piles of money.'

At the mention of the word 'money' Mr Ebenezer's

head, which had dropped on to his chest, jerked upward. 'Money?' he said. 'How much?'

'Oh, lots and lots,' said Necromancy. 'He never spends any of it, you see.'

'Fifty pound?' asked Mr Ebenezer, his little pig eyes narrowing with greed. 'Has he got fifty pound?'

Necromancy did not think he had. She thought perhaps there might be as much as twenty; hurriedly she tried to calculate her father's earnings from the work she had brought home: nine shoe repairs, fifty pence each, four – no, five broken cups, twenty pence each, two broken umbrellas, forty pence ... It was no use, she couldn't remember half of them. She wasn't at all sure that her father would want her to squander the lot on a cottage, either, but it seemed to be her only chance.

'Ten,' she said.

'Ten pounds!' said Mr Ebenezer. 'Ten pounds for that good stone house! That fine solid cottage with a roof and a chimney and – and ...' And his voice trailed away as he tried in vain to remember what else the fine solid cottage could boast.

'Oh, dear,' thought Necromancy, 'that's done it. He's not going to sell it at all. And ten pounds is a lot of money, and a very fair price for a ruin.'

''Sworth a hundred,' said Mr Ebenezer.

'Twelve,' said Necromancy.

'Forty-five!'

'Well, twelve pounds fifty, then.'

And so they wrangled and haggled and argued, and at times it seemed that they were never going to reach an agreement; but by the time Mr Ebenezer had finished the bottle of port a bargain had been struck.

'Go and fetch the ink, girl!' he cried. 'We'll have it in

writing, signed and sealed. I'll send a message to your father in the morning.'

And as Necromancy went off in search of paper and ink he rubbed his hands together gleefully. Twenty pounds for that old hovel! Not bad! Twenty pounds!

chapter 14

The Weir-Woman

'That'll be twenty pounds,' said the Weir-Woman, licking up the flap of a mauve scented envelope.

Her voice was soft and low and purring, and so different from what Abigail had expected that she still was not sure that she had come to the right place. But broomsticks don't make mistakes, and it had flown straight as a die to this rickety wooden house by the weir, where the river ran into the lake. There were no other houses anywhere near, and anyway there was that brass plate on the door saying:

'Madame Asphyxia. Clairvoyante'

And Madame Asphyxia or whatever she called herself had certainly been expecting her. It was just that it was all so ... so different from what she had imagined.

And then, the Weir-Woman herself. After all, Black or White, you did expect a witch to look like a witch. But this – this lady, all dressed in grey and pink and mauve cobwebby stuff, and no proper witch's hat, but only that cloth thing tied round her head, and as many necklaces and bracelets as the Pedlar would sell in a year, and those great rings hanging from her ears ... And the way she kept eating chocolates, if that was what they were in that box labelled Black Magic. It was not what you would expect of a witch, somehow.

The room was stiflingly hot, and Abigail leaned back

amongst the cushions and fanned herself with her hat, whilst her eyes wandered round and round, fascinated, for she had never been in such a place before. Lace curtains over the windows filtered the daylight to a misty dusk, softening the outlines of ornaments and furniture. There were cushions everywhere, and cats everywhere, orange and blue and white, with long silky hair like caterpillars, unlike any witch's cats that she had ever seen. Everything in the room seemed to be covered with something else: lace mats lay on the tables, antimacassars covered the chair-backs; a velvet cloth edged with bobbles draped the mantelpiece. There seemed to be so many objects in the room that Abigail wondered how so fat a woman as Madame Asphyxia ever managed to steer her way between the potted palms and the Chinese vases.

'Twenty pounds, if you please,' repeated the Weir-Woman in rather a nasty tone.

'Twenty pounds!' exclaimed Abigail, sitting up with a jerk and holding the money-bag tightly with both hands. 'Oh, my goodness gracious, that's far too much! Why, I doubt whether I've got half that sum!'

The Weir-Woman said nothing. Her thick, pale hand stroked and stroked the blue Persian cat that lay half-submerged in the cloudy chiffon nest of her lap, while her hard black eyes bored into Abigail's, drawing them, forcing them to meet her own, holding them ... And suddenly Abigail knew that nothing could be hidden from this woman once you were in her power, and that those eyes could see through the tough goat-skin of the money-bag as if it were made of cobweb.

Then there *is* that much money, she thought, for she had never troubled to count it. Twenty pounds! All earned by Zachary – every penny of it. Bit by bit over the long months ... What would he say if he knew what she was going to do with it?

All at once she felt overcome with shame for having ever doubted her husband's powers. Of *course* he would bring Necromancy back! Of *course* he would ... Was there a wart or a hare-lip in all England that he could not charm away? She would have nothing to do with the Weir-Woman's spell. Nothing, nothing ...

The sound of that voice, low and menacing, broke in on Abigail's thoughts.

'... this little daughter of yours, this sweet rosy child, your only one, your baby – how long has she been shut up like an animal behind bars, in this dark, gloomy place? I wonder how much longer you mean to leave her there, till her cheeks grow pale and her eyes are blurred with weeping? One month, perhaps, or two? How much longer will she be able to stand captivity ...?' She helped herself to another chocolate.

Abigail fidgeted miserably in her chair. She turned her head this way and that, but she could not draw her eyes from the Weir-Woman's face.

'A small price to pay for the life of a child, don't you think? Some people, now, would do anything to save the life of someone they love; but then again, some are different. Some would rather keep their money ...'

On and on went the Weir-Woman's voice, heavy with sarcasm, monotonous and evil.

Zachary will do it, said Abigail to herself, over and over again, repeating it like a charm, shutting her mind to everything but this one thought. He *will* do it, he *will*, he *will* ...

'Perhaps even now she is feeling weak and ill, forsaken

by her mother, tired out with crying ... Come, we will have a look. Move, my precious.'

There was a soft thud as the Persian cat landed on the carpet. Without taking her eyes from Abigail's the Weir-Woman stretched out an arm and pulled a small table towards her; a large round object covered with a cloth stood on top, and suddenly Abigail's heart went cold with terror as she realized what was happening.

'Oh, no!' she begged. 'Please don't! I can't bear it.' But her voice was no more than a whisper, and Madame Asphyxia appeared not to hear. Slowly she lifted the cloth from the crystal.

Abigail began to feel faint; the room was hotter and more airless than ever, and her head was swimming. Before her eyes the colours in the crystal had already started to melt and swirl, and from a great distance she seemed to hear the Weir-Woman's voice:

'Soon we shall see ... ah! soon ... soon ...'

On either side of the table they sat, gazing at the crystal, the Black witch and the White, drawn together by its strange power, oblivious of the stuffy room, the purring cats and the minutes ticking loudly away.

All at once an astonishing thing happened: there was a fearful oath from the Weir-Woman's lips, and at the same instant Abigail leapt to her feet with a victorious cry, rocking the little table perilously.

'Did you see that? Did you see?' she cried in triumph. '*There's* magic for you! Magic to be proud of! I'll not be wanting your spell now, thank you. Twenty pounds, indeed! Good *afternoon*!' And she fled down the stairs, seized her broomstick from the umbrella-stand in the hall and wrenched open the front door.

'It's a trick!' fumed the Weir-Woman, struggling to get

out of her arm-chair. 'You've upset the crystal, that's what you've done, you and your White magic! Mixing the two, it's enough to turn any crystal – they're delicate things, you know. You'd no business to go gazing into it! You'll have to pay for the damage ... Come back!' She coughed asthmatically.

With a final grunt and heave she managed at last to prise herself out of the chair, just as the front door slammed behind Abigail. Realizing that she was too late to catch her visitor she waddled over to the window and wrestled furiously with the latch, which had not been moved for half a century and was very stiff. Finally it broke, and pushing the window wide open the Weir-Woman called after Abigail in a voice intended to make

the flesh creep, but which was, in fact, no more than a
wheezy croak:

> 'White as a Corpse, White as a Bone,
> White as a Shroud, White as a Stone,
> Curséd shall you be this day –
> White you'll grow and White you'll stay!
> Every Black hair in your head
> White as Death shall be instead!'

chapter 15

In which Mr Ebenezer is Spell-bound

All the port that Mr Ebenezer had drunk made him very drowsy, and when he had signed the agreement with Necromancy he fell fast asleep on the dining-room table. Several hours later he awoke, feeling thoroughly out of sorts: his face was sore from lying on the hard wood and he had a nasty headache.

'Necromancy!' he bellowed.

He had to call several times before Necromancy, up-stairs in her bedroom, heard him. She had spent a fruit-less afternoon searching for her broomstick, which seemed to have disappeared from the face of the earth, or at any rate from Mr Ebenezer's house, for she had explored every cranny and was hot, tired and covered in dust and cobwebs. She had finally abandoned the search and was now busy composing a spell to cast upon the old man at the moment of her escape. It would not work, of course, but Mr Ebenezer would not know that, and she hoped that he would be sufficiently frightened by it to keep silent on the subject of her witch-hood.

'Necromancy!' came Mr Ebenezer's voice, louder and crosser than ever. 'I want me tea!'

In the kitchen the fire had burnt low and Necromancy had to blow hard to get it going again. As she knelt by the hearth her mind went back to another fireplace in another house, and she smiled as she remembered the starling's nest that had blocked the cottage chimney. It was strange to think that all that had been less than a week ago – it seemed half a lifetime.

Suddenly she was struck by a wonderful idea. She stopped blowing the fire and leaned forward, peering up the chimney: far, far up was a little patch of blue . . .

A muffled thumping came to her ears through the thick wall separating the kitchen from the dining-room. Soon Mr Ebenezer would be getting really impatient. She must hurry!

She started to dash round the kitchen . . .

Mr Ebenezer was just about to go and see what had become of his tea when there was a frantic knocking on the door and Necromancy burst into the room. She was coughing and tears were running down her face; she seemed in great distress.

'Oh, quick, sir, quick!' she cried, between sobs and chokes. 'There's smoke all over the kitchen, and the fire won't draw at all and I don't know what's gone wrong with it – perhaps the chimney's on fire or something. Oh, please, sir, come and see!'

Annoyed, Mr Ebenezer shuffled along the passage and into the kitchen, coughing and spluttering through the smoke.

'Must be a bird's nest fallen down the chimney,' he said crossly, raking out the fire. 'You'll have to sweep it out. Look sharp and get on with it, or I'll never get me tea, I can see.'

'What shall I sweep it with, sir?'

'Why, the broom, of course, you stupid girl.'

'Please, sir, the head's come off.'

'Well, stick the handle up, then.'

'I have, sir. It didn't do any good.'

'Climb up, then, you idle skivvy!' shouted Mr Ebenezer, losing all patience, 'and fetch it down yourself!'

Necromancy stared at him in mock horror.

'Up the chimney, sir? Oh, please, sir, I couldn't! It needs the sweep really, sir, and he only charges a pound a chimney. He's got proper brushes and all.'

'Get up there, and no argument!' said Mr Ebenezer fiercely. 'A pound indeed! He'll not be getting a pound out of me, I can tell you! Get on with your work, miss, and be a little less free with other people's money!'

The smoke from the fire had thinned a bit, and Necromancy, with a great show of reluctance, began to climb slowly and awkwardly up the greasy, soot-encrusted road to freedom.

'I can't quite reach it, sir, it's too narrow,' she called presently. 'It does really need the chimney-sweep, with his proper brushes. I don't see how it can be done without a proper brush.'

'I'm not paying a pound to any sweep for sticking a brush up a chimney! You wait where you are!'

Necromancy, wedged between the rough bricks far up the chimney, could hear a sound of retreating footsteps. Doors opened and shut. Then there was silence.

After a while the footsteps returned; the kitchen door opened and a moment later something hard hit her on the ankle.

'Here you are!' came Mr Ebenezer's voice up the shaft. 'Now get on with it. I do want my tea!'

Necromancy's heart thumped wildly as she tried to reach the object that the old man was handing to her. Supposing it was not her broomstick at all, but something else – a pitchfork, perhaps, or a clothes-prop? But at last her fingers closed round a smooth piece of wood and she gave a great sigh of relief as she felt the place where she had carved her initials: N.G. There was no mistaking it – it was her own broomstick.

And what a mercy the old fool had handed it to her stick first! She could never have turned it round inside the chimney, and it was going to be awkward enough flying out of the tiny hole at the top without having to do it backwards.

Clutching the broomstick with one hand she climbed up until she reached the place where, not ten minutes since, she had blocked the shaft with a wet sack.

'Come on! Get on with it!' shouted Mr Ebenezer, peering up into the darkness. 'You've not fetched down more than a handful yet, and that chimney hasn't been swept sin—'

The sentence remained unfinished, for Necromancy dislodged the sack and quietly dropped it on to the pale moon of Mr Ebenezer's upturned face. There came a muffled sound of swearing.

When it stopped she took a deep breath, and in the most menacing tone she could produce, began to recite:

> 'If ever you say
> That I'm a Witch
> You'll gather no Hay
> And your Nose will Twitch,
> Your Head will Itch
> And your Hens won't lay;
> So you'll never be Rich
> If a Word you Say!'

Her voice echoed weirdly in the deep shaft, and as her words came down to Mr Ebenezer a prickle of fear ran over his bald head.

She stopped for a moment when she reached the top of the chimney to shout one last word of advice and farewell:

> 'And pay your men, you mean old geezer!
> GOODBYE, Mr Ebenezer!'

Then with a cry of joy she flew out into the pink and gold of the summer evening.

For a few seconds Mr Ebenezer remained standing where he was; and then, in a fit of uncontrollable rage, he snatched up the paraffin can that stood by the dresser and threw its contents on to the fire.

'I'll get you!' he screamed. Quickly he stepped back, expecting a mighty flame to leap up the chimney, searing everything with its terrible heat.

But the fire was almost out, and the paraffin only spread in a great pool over the kitchen floor, while thick smoke and a horrible smell began to rise from the hot ashes. Flinging down the empty can in disgust he stumped out of the kitchen, defeated.

Abigail and Necromancy reached home at almost the same moment, and with loud cries of rejoicing fell into each other's arms.

Zachary, who, until a moment ago, had been peacefully thumbing through the *Encyclopaedia* in search of a spell for Whole Families, The Return Of, found himself quite confused by the noise and vehemence of their embraces.

His daughter, he was glad to see, appeared none the worse for her adventures beyond a thick coating of soot, out of which her eyes and teeth shone like stars on a frosty night. She seemed thoroughly over-excited and would not keep still for a second, but must needs run harum-scarum all over the dell, bothering the toads and disturbing the cats. He called to her sharply.

'Come along now, Necromancy, and have your soup. I've kept it hot for you. And you too, Mrs Gumblethrush. Where have you been all afternoon? I called and called. I wish you'd tell me when you're going to go off and leave me for half the day. And what *have* you done to your hair?'

'My hair?'

'Yes, Mother. It's quite different! It's all white!'

'Oh, my goodness ...' said Abigail, remembering the sound of that window opening. She *thought* the Weir-Woman had called something after her ... It must have been a sp—

'Must have been the strain,' said Zachary. 'But it certainly is an improvement. You look almost handsome.'

'It's *beautiful*, Mother!' said Necromancy. 'Look!'

Abigail peered apprehensively into the cauldron at her steamy reflection. It was quite true: in place of the lank, black, witch's locks that had hung round her face like wet seaweed all these years, there was a wild cloud of milk-white hair, silky and soft as thistle-down. It certainly was very becoming, though unsuitable, perhaps, for a witch.

'Come *along*, Mrs Gumblethrush, your soup will be quite spoiled.'

After a while, when the soup was finished, Necromancy related all her adventures, beginning with the finding of the cottage and ending with her escape from Mr Ebenezer's chimney, which Abigail had seen in the Weir-Woman's crystal.

'And tomorrow,' she cried excitedly, her story finished, 'tomorrow I'll show you the cottage!'

There was a long silence. Abigail drew patterns in the wood-ash with the handle of the ladle, while Zachary took his father's spectacles off and put them on again several times.

'It's so *sweet*,' went on Necromancy, 'and it's got proper stairs and a proper chimney just like the ones we used to talk about, and – Why, Mother, what is it? Why ever are you crying?'

'Oh, child,' sobbed Abigail, wiping her eyes on Zachary's sleeve, 'it isn't any good – We couldn't take the risk again. It'd be far, far too dangerous . . .'

'Your mother's right,' said Zachary. 'She's been worried clean out of her wits, and there's been nothing to eat for the past three days but cold roast puffball, and I'm not putting up with it any longer. You're not going back, my girl, and that's the end of that.'

chapter 16

The Pedlar's Return

Zachary and Abigail stood firm. Their minds were made up: their daughter was far too precious and they refused to run any risks with her; they would never again have a moment's peace with her out of their sight. She must stay at home.

It was a great sacrifice for them, for they had come to rely on the money brought in by the work from the village, and the small articles that they were now able to buy they had come to look upon as necessities. It was hard indeed to go back to their old way of life, with never so much as a chitterling to make a change from witch's-brew.

But for Necromancy herself it proved hardest of all. She missed her friends and the lessons in school, and she missed the satisfaction of bringing work home to her father and collecting payment for it when it was done. Life in the forest, that once had seemed so sweet to her in its timelessness and freedom, she now found very dull.

To pass the time she collected wild flowers and pressed them between strips of silver-birch bark, but she had soon collected all the flowers there were. She watched the birds, but she already knew their habits as well as her own, and could whistle their songs better than they could themselves, with far more feeling and expression. She climbed trees, but to one brought up in a forest this pastime was not very amusing, and she could not go for a walk, for her mother would not let her out of sight for five minutes. There was nothing at all to do.

She grew more bored and despondent and cross every day; often and often her mind went back to the vanished dream of the cottage, and she felt very bitter.

Slowly the weeks went by, and the delicate flickering canopy that had covered the forest in spring darkened and thickened until it had become a dense green roof through which even the air penetrated with difficulty. In the dell it was as hot and damp and still as a greenhouse and there seemed to be no sign of a change in the weather; each day was hotter than the last.

On a day of suffocating heat the Pedlar came, dragging his heavy boots through the deep soft leaves. His legs felt as if they were made of candle-grease, and his suitcase seemed to weigh more with every step. He longed to set it down.

The witch-child came to meet him. She was pleased enough to see him and laughed politely at his jokes and his teasing, but he sensed that all was not well with her. Perhaps it was the heat . . .

'How's school, then?' he asked after a while. 'Top o' the form, are you? I bet you've made a lot of friends. I heard all about it in the Barley Mow, last night, and of all the work your dad's been doing, repairs and that. Pity you don't live a bit nearer, though.'

At this, much to his surprise, she suddenly flung her arms round his neck and burst into tears.

'Oh, Pedlar . . . oh, Pedlar . . .' she wept, but was quite unable to continue, what with the sniffs and the sobs.

'There, there, now,' said the Pedlar comfortingly. 'Let's sit down in the shade a minute, and I'll show you what I've got in my pack.' And collapsing thankfully on to the cool, fungus-smelling floor of the forest he started to open his suitcase.

'They won't let – let – let me *go* any more,' sobbed Necromancy, when at last she had recovered sufficient breath to say anything. 'They've sto—sto—stopped me *going*! And we *could* have gone to live nearer the village – we *could* have, but they *wouldn't*, and they wouldn't even come to *see* it, and it was such a swee—a swee—a *sweet* little cottage . . .'

Bit by bit the Pedlar managed to unravel her story, and little by little she grew calmer. He lent her his red spotted handkerchief to mop up her tears, and he unpacked his suitcase and showed her the carved ivory elephant, all the way from Karachi, and the electric torch all the way from Birmingham that shone red or green or yellow, and all sorts of other treasures.

'We'd better go now,' said Necromancy after a while. 'They'll be wondering where we are.' So they got to their feet and wandered on towards the dell, carrying the suitcase between them.

'You leave it to me,' said the Pedlar, with a wink.

Late that evening, when their purchases had been made, they all lay on the bank of the stream, idly watching the tiny trickle of water that threaded its way between the caked banks of mud. If they did not have some rain soon it would dry up altogether, and then the frogs might die . . . Necromancy decided that she would have to make a reservoir for them in case of emergencies; soon, lost in schemes of dams and culverts, she fell asleep.

'I must say,' said the Pedlar presently, clasping his

hands behind his head and stretching his legs comfortably, 'it's very pleasant here, of a summer evening. Very pleasant.'

'It's not such a bad place,' agreed Zachary, pleased. 'Of course, you're seeing it at its best.'

' 'Tis a different place in the winter, I can tell you,' said Abigail.

'Ah,' said the Pedlar, shaking his head sympathetically.

' 'Tis bitter when the wind is in the east,' went on Abigail; 'and when the snow comes – oh, my! 'Tis hard to bear.'

'Oh, I don't know,' said Zachary loyally. 'I rather like

the winter. With a good fire burning and the bearskin pulled up round you, and a bowl of good hot brew in your hands . . . I dare say there are worse places!'

'Oh, come now, Zachary,' said his wife, 'you know you feel the cold as much as anyone. Many's the time you've come down from your Stone half-perished with the cold and I've had to rub the life back into your feet with horse-radish. And as for the child, poor little mite . . .!'

'Ah, yes,' said the Pedlar, 'it must be hard on her. Lucky she's as strong and healthy as she is or she'd never get through the winter. When you look at those children in the village with their warm dry houses and hot baths and woollen blankets on their beds . . . Doesn't seem fair, somehow, does it?' He smiled and shook his head sadly. 'But luckily she's strong, as you say. Be a bad business, though, if she got ill.'

'Gumblethrushes are never ill,' said Zachary, a trifle hotly. He did not quite like the way the conversation was going: his wife might get Ideas. He wished the Pedlar would talk about something else. 'Travelled far, have you, Pedlar, since your last visit?' he asked.

'Up the hills and down the valleys,' answered the Pedlar. 'I don't cross the seas now like I used to, and I like to come back to the places that I know. And there's no nicer village in all the land than your village, you know. Not that you live in it exactly, but with Necro-mancy going to school there – '

Zachary suddenly gave a loud splutter as if something had choked him, but the Pedlar continued unperturbed:

' – and you being so well thought of by everyone. Why, they were saying in the Barley Mow, only last night, what a pity 'twas that you didn't live a bit closer. "They oughter move into old Bill Ebenezer's cottage," one of the lads was saying. Seems it's been lying empty these last ten years.'

Out of the corner of his eye the Pedlar looked to see what effect all this was having on his host and hostess. Abigail was drinking in every word, but Zachary was going to be a bit harder to convince.

'Of course,' went on the Pedlar, twiddling a grass stem, 'I knew it wouldn't be any good to you. After all, you've never lived in a proper house, have you? Be a bit like putting a donkey into a house and expecting him to like it. No offence meant!'

However, by the look on Zachary's face it was clear that some had been taken, and the Pedlar thought it was time to be on his way. He stood up, bade them all goodbye and started up the side of the dell with his suitcase. Suddenly he stopped.

'Oh, by the way,' he said, turning round, 'I nearly forgot to tell you: old Ebenezer's getting married again! And you'll never guess who his bride is to be – your old friend Mrs Pennyfeather!'

chapter 17

In which Abigail and Necromancy gather Hemlock

As the first low rays of the morning sun came glancing and glittering through the forest Abigail rose quietly from her mossy bed, taking care not to rouse Zachary, who lay on his back beside her, still fast asleep. Cautiously she pulled his cloak right over his face so that he should not be awakened by the sun.

Beneath the cloak it was as dark and stuffy as the cave and Zachary, dreaming that he was a newly-hatched blackbird half-smothered by the hot black feathers of his vigilant mother, wheezed and grunted.

Abigail regarded him anxiously for a moment, then, satisfied that he was sleeping soundly, began to bustle silently about her work. She blew on the fire, which was soon burning brightly; then she gathered several large fungi from a nearby tree and, throwing them into the cauldron, stirred them thirteen times. With a piece of charcoal she wrote a message on a large flat stone, and propped it up where Zachary would see it. It said:

'Gatheringe Hemlocke. Breakfaste in Cauldron. Back by Froggecroake. A. Gumblethrush.'

Then she woke up Necromancy.

'Ssh-sh, child, don't make a sound! We mustn't wake your father.'

'Why not?' asked Necromancy, thick with sleep. 'What's happened?'

'Quick!' whispered Abigail, handing her a yellowish

chunk of warm, but still raw, fungus. 'Eat this. We're going to see your cottage!'

'You – lead – the – way!' shouted Abigail as she sailed over the tree-tops; with each word the air rushed down her throat, making her gasp for breath.

Necromancy nodded in reply and turning her broomstick to the south-east began to fly steadily above the green roof of the forest towards the cottage.

It was a beautiful morning for flying – clear and still, with the first breath of autumn in the air. A low mist lay over the countryside, making the tops of trees and distant spires look as if they were half-submerged in a calm silver sea.

When she reached the edge of the forest Necromancy dropped to within about two metres of the ground, as she had done every morning on her way to school, and Abigail followed her down; but because of the mist it proved to be highly dangerous, for they nearly hit a haystack in the corner of a field. A little farther on they were puzzled by what appeared to be the leafless branches of a blighted willow, but turned out to be the horns belonging to a herd of cows.

'We'll have to fly a little higher,' shouted Necromancy as she swished over a hawthorn hedge, 'or we might crash into the cottage!'

Abigail was breathless with excitement, and the slight tingle of fear that came when she thought of Zachary only added to the sense of adventure; the exhilaration of flying through the keen morning air, of skimming over hedges and streaking across meadows, filled her with joy and she burst into song.

'If you should offer
    Me gold in a coffer
Or riches to make a man swoon –
    Or if I were given
    A palace to live in
I'd count it no very great boon:

    For a Millionaire
    Cannot sail through the air
As free as a skylark in June;
    But a Witch on a Broomstick,
    A Witch on a Broomstick
Can fly thirteen times round the moon!

Oh, a witch on a witch on a witch on a broomstick
Can fly thirteen times round the m—'

'There it is, Mother! Just ahead!' cried Necromancy in great excitement, disappearing behind a hazel thicket.

Too late Abigail saw the tall brick chimney rising crookedly out of the mist: there was a sudden dull, scrunching, crackling thud and a cloud of startled birds rose into the air ...

'Mother?' Necromancy picked herself up off the green sward and looked round, puzzled. She was sure her mother had been just behind her; she had heard her singing a moment ago. She called again.

A faint sound that might almost have been laughter came to her ears. It seemed to be coming from upstairs.

'Mother!' called Necromancy again, running into the cottage. The laughter was louder now: it sounded rather hysterical. What on earth was her mother up to? Hurriedly she climbed up the stairs.

On reaching the top the first things that met her eyes were Abigail's legs dangling from a large hole in the roof; the rest of her was invisible.

'Oh, Mother!' she cried, in a voice of horrified reproach. 'How in the world did you get up there? Just *look* what you've done to the roof!' She bent and picked up a large armful of thatch.

'Oh, ha ha ha!' came Abigail's voice, slightly muffled. 'Oh, dear me, he he! Oh, ha ha ha!' Her legs in their long black stockings thrashed backwards and forwards helplessly, the Pedlar's pink elastic garters – a present from Zachary – plainly visible.

'Oh, Mother, stop it, for goodness' sake!' said Necromancy crossly. 'How ever am I going to mend a hole as big as that? You should have come down in the garden, like me!'

'Don't be so silly, child!' said Abigail, stopping at last. 'Come on, get me down! Fetch a log or something!'

'Can't you get down the way you came in?' asked Necromancy, thinking that her mother had done quite enough damage as it was.

'No,' said Abigail. 'I'm stuck.'

'Oh, all right.' Angrily Necromancy clattered downstairs and returned with the bottomless bucket. It was really too bad of her mother not to look where she was going – making a great hole in the roof like that. 'I could almost hit her on the head – the silly old thing,' she thought irritably.

Standing on the bucket she grasped her mother by the ankles. 'Now!' she shouted through the thatch, 'one, two, three, *heave!*'

There was a great splintering and groaning, followed by a fearful crash, and Abigail, Necromancy, the broom-

stick and the bucket landed on the floor. A choking,
suffocating cloud of dust and sticks and straw and feathers
filled the room.

Spluttering and gasping they at last managed to dis-
entangle their limbs and, picking themselves up, stumbled down the dark stairs and out into the sun.

When they had brushed the thatch out of each other's
hair and clothes and had filled their lungs once more with
fresh air, Abigail and Necromancy sat down on the
smooth grass in happy wonderment and gazed at the

cottage. But they had not been sitting for five minutes before a familiar sound came to their ears, and glancing quickly upwards they were horrified to perceive Zachary, his gown billowing behind him, coming in to land at a quite alarming speed.

'Mercy!' cried Abigail. 'He's followed us! We forgot to hide the broomsticks! Oh, my Thursday hat, whatever will he say?'

chapter 18

The Moving of the Gumblethrushes

Well, whatever the wizard said, his wife and his daughter got their way in the end. To Necromancy it seemed little short of magical, only this time it was not her father's magic or her mother's, and certainly not her own, but some special sorcery of the Pedlar's that had wrought this extraordinary change in their fortunes. From the day of his yearly visit, all her dreams had begun to turn into realities, with everything working out in a way that was almost miraculous. Surely it must have been some sort of magic that had made her mother go and look at the cottage; magic too, that had made her father agree to talk to Mr Ebenezer. And wasn't it magic, again, that had led Mr Ebenezer to become engaged to Mrs Pennyfeather? Mrs Pennyfeather, her mother's friend, now a widow, who had written that kind and interesting letter, and who remembered them all so well; how lucky that *she* had been there at Mr Ebenezer's house when they all turned up on his doorstep feeling so nervous. How pleased she had been to see them, and how warmly she had welcomed them, and how cross she had been with Mr Ebenezer about the price of the cottage!

'William!' she had scolded, 'oh, shame on you, William Ebenezer! Fancy asking such a price for that broken-down old hovel not fit for a goat! You're a sinful old devil to play such a trick on an innocent child. The very idea!'

And so in the end Mr Ebenezer had had to give them

the cottage for nothing, in exchange for a bit of help from Zachary with repairs and things. But if it hadn't been for the Pedlar none of it would have happened ...

And now they were actually moving. Necromancy could scarcely believe it, and had to pinch herself more than once to make sure she wasn't dreaming. She was beginning to feel extremely hungry, but no one had had time to think about the cooking; moving house seemed to make her parents very bad-tempered. She thought it was just as well they did not do it often. She went and sat down beside the cats, who were keeping well out of the way.

'Burn the rubbish!' she could hear her mother shouting. 'Throw it on the fire! You'll not be wanting these old things!'

'Foolish, extravagant, spendthrift creature!' cried her father, making a dive towards the flames. 'Will you never learn economy? What is the use of burning a perfectly serviceable mattress, even though we have got a bed? I thought you said it was rubbish we wanted to burn – these old rags, for instance ...' and he threw them on to the fire.

'Why, you – you careless old buzzard!' shrieked Abigail, rescuing the bundle just in time. 'That's my grandmother's top petticoat that she wore when she was head of the Coven! Rags, indeed! But we'll burn these old books – they're too heavy to carry ...'

Until they came to do the packing the Gumblethrushes had had no idea of the number of their possessions, and it almost began to seem that they would never manage to move at all. Zachary had already made nine journeys to and from the cottage.

But at last everything was packed and, with heavily laden broomsticks, Abigail and Necromancy took off for the last time from the edge of the dell.

In a few moments Zachary, too, would fly out of the forest. Out of the forest – *his* forest, where Gumblethrushes had lived since time immemorial: out of it for ever, never to return.

With a heavy heart he turned down towards the cave and, picking up one leg of the tripod, prised the sign from the face of the rock; then he hung another, carefully etched in poker-work, in its place. It said:

For Sale
This Desirable Wizard's Cave
Every Amenity
Apply ... Gumblethrush
Nettlebed Cottage.
(Viewing by appointment)

For a full minute he surveyed it; then, tucking the old

sign under his arm he turned and walked quickly away up the side of the dell. Loudly he blew his nose.

Late on the evening of the same day Abigail and Necromancy sat outside the cottage, gazing at the view.

'Your father should be back with the cauldron soon,' said Abigail. 'He'll be tired, poor man, after so many journeys. I do hope he managed to take off all right – it's such a heavy old pot.'

Just then, however, they heard the swishing of a broomstick, followed by a tremendous crash on the other side of the cottage. Leaping to their feet they hastened to Zachary's assistance.

He had come down rather heavily, owing to the cauldron, but was fortunately unhurt.

'That's the lot!' he said, straightening himself and brushing the dust out of his beard. 'Where's that Inventory?'

After a thorough search of all his pockets the Inventory was discovered in the crown of his hat; he propped himself against the apple tree and started to read it.

' 1 Crystal,' he began, pushing his spectacles on to his forehead. 'Check it, will you, Mrs Gumblethrush? 1 Spinning-wheel, 1 *Encyclopaedia* (3 Vols.), 7 Books, Writing Materials, 1 Witch-Child – that's Necromancy – 13 Shoe Repairs, 4 Love Potions, 2 doz. Wart Charms, 7 Cough-cures, 5 Various – '

'What's Various?' inquired Necromancy.

'Labels missing. We'll sell 'em cheap. Don't interrupt. 8 Frogs,' he continued, '3 Toads, 1 Cauldron, 1 Witch, 1 Bearskin, 1 Tripod, 1 Leather Bag, 3 Broomsticks, Father's Spectacles, Grandfather's Hat, Wife's Grandmother's Top Petticoat, Grandfather's best Robes, 3 striped Mugs, 1 Pewter Mug, 1 Pestle, 1 Mortar, 3 Cats, 3 Broomsticks –'

'You've said broomsticks.'

' – 4 Wands, 2 Mattresses, 1 Hammock, 1 Ladle, 1 Wizard ... There!' He stuffed the list back into his pocket. 'And I'm not going back for anything.' Tenderly he picked the frogs and toads out of the cauldron in which they had travelled and wandered off with them towards the pond.

Zachary was very tired after so much flying and went to bed while it was still daylight, firmly taking his bracken-filled mattress with him; but Abigail and Necromancy worked far into the night arranging and rearranging their belongings.

'There, Mother!' said Necromancy proudly, pointing to the witch-ball which she had just hung on a rafter. 'Doesn't that make it look like home?'

Abigail nodded approvingly: in the cave it had always hung from a stalactite and she had never felt very happy about it. It had always looked as if it might slip off and break, which would undoubtedly have brought seven years' misfortune upon them all; it looked much safer on the beam.

At last everything was put away and they started to climb the stairs to bed, when Abigail paused.

'There's one more thing, love, before we go: those spells your father said he'd sell off cheap – I don't really like it. There might be the most unfortunate results! Run and throw them into the pond, there's a good girl, then we'll be rid of them. He'll have forgotten all about them in the morning.'

So Necromancy took the five nameless bottles and ran through the moonlit garden until she reached the pond.

As she emptied the spells into the water it began to bubble and hiss in the most remarkable way, and turned first green and then a sulphurous yellow; phosphorescent ripples swirled across it like the glittering tentacles of some great silver octopus. Then slowly the colour of the water turned a deep purple, and as the widening circles reached the bank a small puff of smoke rose into the air.

'Goodness!' exclaimed Necromancy; then, feeling suddenly cold, she turned and ran back to the cottage as fast as she could.

*

The Moving of the Gumblethrushes

The next morning the witch-child awoke to find herself in a world so strange that for a moment she could not think where she was. Instead of the black roof of the cave or the green leaves under which she so often slept in summer, there was above her head a dusty, dirty, cobwebby mass of old grey straw, supported at intervals by wooden rafters. Sunshine streamed through dozens of little holes in the thatch, giving the place a curious striped appearance.

Sleepily she turned over in her hammock; through the little window she could just see the topmost branches of the apple tree. In a flash she jumped out of the hammock and ran down the stairs and through the house and out into the dew-drenched garden ...

'Mother! Come quickly!'

Abigail grunted and pulled her cloak up over her ears: it was the first night in the whole of her life that she had spent in a bed and – dream or no dream – she wasn't going to wake up yet.

'Mother!'

Slowly the urgent insistence of Necromancy's whisper roused her and she opened her eyes.

'What's the matter?' she asked, her voice thick with drowsiness. 'Couldn't you let your poor dear mother sleep a little while?'

'Ssh-sh, Mother!' hissed Necromancy in an agony; 'don't wake Father! It's the frogs – they've *changed* ...'

'*Changed*?'

'Yes. They aren't frogs any more – it must have been those spells. Oh, do come, Mother. *Hurry!*'

At last, by dint of much shaking and pulling, Necromancy succeeded in getting her mother out of bed, and a few minutes later they were both scurrying through the long wet grass down to the pond.

'Oh, Zachary, dear,' began Abigail, directly after breakfast; 'don't be alarmed – it's nothing to worry about – they're really quite all right, it's nothing serious – '

'What ever are you talking about? *Who* is all right? *What* isn't serious? Come to the point, Mrs Gumble-thrush.'

'Well, love, 'tis just – 'tis just that something peculiar has happened to the – well, to the frogs. They're really quite all right – 'tis just peculiar, that's all.'

'What d'you mean, *peculiar*?' asked Zachary. He was not in a very good humour: he kept knocking his head on the ceiling, and the porridge had been full of lumps; also they had had watercress for breakfast. He hated watercress. And now something had happened to his frogs . . .

'You'd better come and see for yourself, Father. In any case they'll be wondering where you are,' said Necromancy tactfully.

In the garden the air was sweet with the smell of apples; birds sang as if it were spring, and once outside the unfamiliar confinement of the cottage Zachary began to feel happier. He stood on the edge of the pond and looked about anxiously for his frogs.

'There they are!' cried Necromancy suddenly. 'Aren't they *beautiful*?'

On the opposite bank stood two white nanny-goats and three brown hens. They were all gazing sorrowfully into the water where the three remaining frogs gambolled and splashed, delighted to have so much room to themselves. One by one the toads hopped out of the reeds, unaltered.

'*Isn't* that nice?' said Abigail brightly, while Zachary, speechless with amazement, stared at his erstwhile frogs. 'Things have really turned out very well after all,' she went on, 'but it wouldn't have done to have sold them off cheap – you can't be too careful with spells. We don't want our customers turning into goats! Oh, dear me, that would never do, that would never do at all!' And throwing her apron over her head she went off into peals of laughter.

chapter 19

In which Zachary does some Mending and some Making, too

After this everything seemed to go well for the witch-family. With eggs from the hens, milk from the goats, fish from the pond and apples from the apple tree they enjoyed a better diet than they had ever known before; the cats grew fat on the families of mice that lived beneath the floorboards, and even Abigail began to grow a little plump.

They all worked furiously to set the cottage to rights before the winter, and while Abigail and Necromancy clipped and cut and dug and hoed the garden, Zachary set about mending the roof. He spent long hours thumbing through the great *Encyclopaedia of Witchcraft* in search of a spell, but the only thing that sounded at all possible was a charm against leaks:

> 'Nettle-sting and Thistle-prickle,
> Mushy Plum and Apple-bruise:
> Dry for evermore this trickle!
> Stop this seep and drip and ooze!
> Mildew gangrenous and green,
> Vanish! and no more be seen ...'

Clearly this was no good: when it rained there would be rather more than a trickle coming through the hole made by his wife ... Despondently he flicked over the pages until he came to F, in the hope that he might find something under Flood, but this was evidently outside the scope even of so complete a work as the *Encyclopaedia*. There was nothing for it – he would have to mend it by hand, for to make a new spell strong enough to repair such extensive damage was, he feared, beyond his powers.

Luckily he was able to discover a spell for glazing windows which was simple, effective and cheap:

> 'Clear as Crystal, Bright as Brass,
> White as Water, Green as Grass,
> Window-frames be filled with Glass!'

Soon all the windows were twinkling with a pretty mixture of green and white panes, and the place was considerably less draughty. Zachary was very pleased with the result. Indeed, he seemed to be so happy nowadays that quite often he forgot to grumble at all, although from time to time, out of loyalty, he would still say that this new life was in no way to be compared with their life in the forest, with its low cost of living and proximity to nature. But Necromancy noticed that he talked less and less about the old days.

One day a quite unexpected visitor appeared at the cottage in the shape of the Postman, very hot and rather cross from pushing his bicycle over the ruts and bumps of the bridle-path. He wished very much that he had left it in the village.

'Totally unfit for Postmen,' he said, addressing his bicycle. 'If these Nettlebed Cottage folks are likely to be having any more letters they'd best make a good stout box with a padlock, and screw it to a tree at the end of the lane, where it can be reached without inconvenience.'

But he did not suppose that they would have very many: from what he'd heard it was surprising that they should have been sent this one; but then there had been one for every house in the village, and Mrs Pennyfeather was like that – such a good-hearted lady. She wouldn't want anyone to feel left out . . .

He was rapturously received by the entire Gumblethrush family, who had never before, so it appeared, had a letter by post, and Mrs Gumblethrush offered him a mug of something-or-other, he couldn't quite catch what she said. He could have done with a cup of tea, but these people made him feel nervous, somehow, what with the man nearly standing on his head to look at the cogwheels on his bicycle, and all of them dressed in those queer-looking black clothes. Of course, he'd seen the child often enough, but still . . . He couldn't really say he liked the look of them.

'No, thanks,' he said, turning his bicycle sharply round. 'I must be getting along. I'm all behind as it is, coming out here. Contrary to regulations, it is, too. Roads like that!' He jerked his head disapprovingly in the direction of the bridle-path, and gripping his bicycle firmly by the handlebars, wheeled it away, quoting the Post Office Regulations to himself as he went.

Necromancy turned impatiently:

'Do *open* it, Mother! I can't wait any longer! What can it be?'

Abigail handed the stiff white envelope to Zachary, who, with much deliberation and ceremony, slit it open with his great-grandfather's knife: out fell a thick double sheet of paper, printed in a beautiful copper-plate and embellished with silver horse-shoes and wedding-bells in the corners.

'Oh, my!' sighed Abigail. 'It must be an invitation to Mrs Pennyfeather's wedding! I've never been asked to a wedding before ...' And much to the surprise of her husband and daughter she burst into tears.

Several times during the next few days Necromancy found her mother gazing wistfully at Mrs Pennyfeather's invitation, while large tears coursed slowly down her cheeks; and although she always pretended that she had just bumped her nose, or had been peeling onions, or feared that it was hay-fever coming on, Necromancy nevertheless grew more and more suspicious, until in the end she decided that she must discuss it with her father.

She found him in the shed.

'Father,' she said, 'I must talk to you. It's about Mother ...'

One evening about a week later, when Necromancy was working in the garden, she heard a loud hissing noise coming from the apple tree, and on going to investigate was surprised to find her father perched in its branches.

'I've done it!' he whispered. 'Come here. Quickly, child! I don't want your mother to see.'

Necromancy scrambled up the rough bark of the twisted old tree-trunk and sat down beside her father.

'There!' said Zachary proudly, holding out a length of mauve material. 'What do you think of it?'

Necromancy surveyed it in silence, uncertain what to say.

'Well?'

'It's very nice, Father.'

'Certainly it's nice!' said Zachary indignantly; 'it's taken me half the afternoon. But do you think it will fit?'

Necromancy looked at him apologetically.

'I'm not really sure, Father. What exactly is it?'

'Why, you stupid girl! D'you mean to tell me you don't know what it is? It's a dress for your mother. What else could it be?'

'Oh, how *lovely*!' cried Necromancy aloud, clapping her hands.

Zachary sh-sh'd furiously.

'For the wedding,' he whispered. His throat was getting rather dry; he wished the apples had been ripe. 'I couldn't have her going dressed like an old witch – wouldn't be to my credit – so I thought I had better do something about it.'

Necromancy shifted herself on the apple-tree branch and considered her father's creation.

'Let's see it again.'

Zachary shook out its folds and held it up. 'There wasn't a dressmaking spell in the *Encyclopaedia*, so I had to make one. Quite straightforward really – didn't take long. I've got it here somewhere ...' He fumbled in his pocket and produced a small bit of paper.

'Witchery Stitchery Needle and Thread, Round the Middle and Over the Head,' he read rapidly, and stuffed it back into his pocket. 'Takes a man to do a job properly.'

'It's rather a funny shape, Father,' said Necromancy, holding up the curious-looking garment. 'And you've forgotten to leave a hole for her to get in! Oh, Father you haven't done it properly at all! It's most *peculiar*. There's no trimming or anything, and it's not at *all* in fashion!'

'Pah!' said Zachary with scorn. 'Trimming! Fashion! You don't find men bothering about fashion. Silly feminine fiddle faddle! And women look much better in simple clothes. She's very lucky to have any new ones at all ... Let me tell you something, young lady! There hasn't been a new pair of breeches in the Gumblethrush family since my great-grandfather's day!' He shook a long bony forefinger at his daughter.

'It's different with men,' said Necromancy. 'But all the same, she's got to get into it. You've done all the difficult part, Father. Why don't you let me just finish it off?'

Somewhat mollified, Zachary agreed. He was really getting rather tired of dressmaking anyway, and an afternoon up the apple tree had given him pins and needles in his legs. Thankfully he climbed down, leaving Necromancy with the bundle of material, and went off to finish a ticklish job on a second-hand television set.

Necromancy stood in the middle of the field, her arms outstretched and her eyes tightly shut; the mauve stuff and an assortment of herbs and roots and various oddments lay at her feet. With bated breath she recited:

> 'Cuckoo-pint leaves
> And Queen-Anne's-Lace,
> Ribbons and Sleeves
> And pretty, neat Waist
> Missel-Thrush Speck
> And a rain-wet Rose,
> From the Middle of her Neck
> Till her Shin-bone shows.'

'Look, Father, look! Don't you think it's *beautiful*?'

'Milocycles, Kilocycles, Cathode Ray –' mumbled Zachery, jotting things down on a piece of paper. 'Whatever is it now, child? Can't you see I'm busy?' He looked worried.

'Oh, but, Father, just look at it! Isn't it a lovely dress?'

Zachary pushed his father's spectacles up on to his forehead and looked at the dress.

'Well,' he said at length, 'I suppose it's not bad. As dresses go. But I must say, I can't see your mother in it – can't see her in it at all, in fact.' He shook his head disapprovingly and turned back to the bits of television. 'B.B.C. and I.T.A. . . .'

'*Men!*' said Necromancy.

chapter 20

The Day of the Wedding

And so the day of Mrs Pennyfeather's wedding came at last, and with it – just to complete the happiness of the witch-family – came the Pedlar.

The wind was buffeting the high white clouds across the sky and the air was loud with bird-song, and as he walked along the Pedlar wondered about the Gumble-thrushes, whether they would have become 'very mortal', as they put it, and how they might have fared during the winter. Perhaps they might have been disappointed with civilization and have returned to the forest.

But as he rounded the bend in the lane and the cottage came into view he saw at once that all was well: smoke puffed hospitably from the chimney, the windows twinkled, the door shone brightly with buttercup-yellow paint and primroses bordered the little brick path. He strode up it and raised the gleaming door-knocker – a miniature witch on a broomstick. He put down his suit-case and gazed about him in admiration.

'Why, *Pedlar*!'

He swung round. There in the open doorway stood Necromancy, looking very neat and clean in a new blue dress and wearing proper leather shoes; her face was shiny with scrubbing and her hair with brushing, and on her head she wore a wreath of woodbine. Even her nails were clean.

'Oh, Pedlar!' she cried again, 'we weren't expecting you at all! Are you coming to the wedding? We can all go together. How *lovely*! Oh, please come in,' she added, remembering her manners.

She held the door open and the Pedlar bent his head and stepped inside. He put his suitcase down beside the door.

'Father and Mother aren't ready yet,' said Necromancy. 'I *know* they'll be late! I do wish they'd hurry. Mother!' she called, opening the inner door. 'Father! Guess who's here!'

'There's plenty of time,' said the Pedlar, looking at his watch. 'It's only eleven. Wedding's not till half past twelve. Plenty of time.'

The cottage was certainly much cosier than the cave. There were rosy-patterned curtains, very pretty and bright, and chairs, too – one quite comfortable-looking one in a faded chintz cover, and another that did not look quite so inviting.

'Father made that one out of an old tree-trunk,' said Necromancy proudly, seeing the direction of his gaze. 'It's Mother's. And I made these,' and she pointed to two padded boxes covered with more of the curtain stuff. 'You can put things inside them too, you see. They're very useful.'

'I see you still use the cauldron, then,' said the pedlar, pointing to where it stood in one corner of the room. 'Can't I have some infusion? Or don't you brew it any more?'

'Not very often,' said Necromancy. 'Tea's easier. The cauldron's really only used for spells and potions and things nowadays. Won't you sit down?'

'Spells?' said the Pedlar in surprise, seating himself in the comfortable chair. 'Do you still brew spells?'

'Oh, my goodness me, we never stop,' answered Necromancy, riddling the fire. She opened the damper and put the kettle on. 'Today's early-closing day, of course – I expect you saw the sign on the gate as you came in. Father will show you everything when he comes in. We do an awful lot of business – much more than in the forest.'

'Well,' mused the Pedlar, 'it's strange how things work out ...'

'Mother's kept very busy,' went on Necromancy. 'We did keep her stock in here, on the mantelpiece, but she had to brew so much that there wasn't room any more, so Father gave her half the den. She does all the old stuff – corn-cures, teething syrup – you know, and quite a lot of new ones as well. There's a very good Slimming Draught she does – people are always asking for it. It's very quick-acting, but it doesn't last long. They generally buy it on Fridays to slim them down for the weekend, then in the week they let themselves spread again. Then she's got a whole line in Hair-Colour Restorers – you know, dyes really. There's Spring Enchantment – that's a very popular one, bright yellow; then there's Midsummer Magic, rich gold, and Autumn Tints and Winter Wizardry. She'll do others to order, of course. Winter Wizardry is blue. That goes down best with the older people.

'Father sticks more to the repair side of the business, and then of course there's Mr Ebenezer's dilapidations two evenings a week regularly, apart from emergencies.'

'And you, my little witch,' said the Pedlar, when

Necromancy paused for breath, ' – or aren't I allowed to call you that, now that you've got a smart new dress and all? Are you busy at school all day? Or don't you go any more?'

'Oh, yes, I still go to school, but it's holidays at the moment,' said Necromancy. 'And you can call me a witch as much as you like. Do you know, it's all finished, all that nonsense! Nobody seems to mind at all. Oh, good, here they come!'

The Pedlar looked round and got to his feet as Abigail came into the room. At least he supposed it must be Abigail, though he could scarcely recognize the skinny, dishevelled, black-clad creature he had known for years in this – this lady who stood in the doorway, looking as fine as any lady he had ever met, in her crisp lavender gown and her wavy white hair. (Was there perhaps just a *hint* of Winter Wizardry about it, he wondered?)

'Oh, Pedlar!' cried Abigail, stepping forward with both hands outstretched. 'Oh, I'm that glad to see you. I've been feeling so nervous all day I can scarce pull up my stockings, and Zachary's just as bad, though he won't admit it. Oh, my, I'm glad you're here to take us ...'

At that moment Zachary himself burst into the room in a blaze of planets and meteors, the gorgeous folds of his grandfather's gown swirling round him. The Pedlar was speechless with admiration.

'My dear fellow!' said Zachary, clasping him warmly by the hand, 'so glad you could come with us. Mrs Gumblethrush was feeling somewhat apprehensive, but now that you're here she'll be much happier. Come, I must show you round the place ...' and with that he swept the Pedlar out into the garden.

*

'Here,' said Zachary, peering intently at a patch of brown earth, 'here we have broad beans. I *think*,' he added doubtfully. 'They should be coming along well soon. And over there are leeks . . .'

'Time's getting on,' said the Pedlar. 'Perhaps we'd better be going. Mustn't be late for the wedding!'

'. . . and these are my artichokes. Early potatoes look well, don't you think?'

At last the tour of the garden came to an end and they went back into the cottage, where Necromancy and Abigail were discovered tidying themselves in front of, or rather, beneath, the witch-ball, which gave them a rather distorted idea of what they looked like. Then the wedding presents were remembered, and at last the little procession set off down the grassy path in the direction of the village. Necromancy skipped ahead, clutching the tea-cosy she had knitted at school; next came Abigail, escorted by the Pedlar. (Her present was a kettle-holder,

crocheted out of wool-gatherings.) Lastly came Zachary, an awe-inspiring figure in his marvellous robes, carrying the blackthorn stick he had cut for Mr Ebenezer in the forest.

Suddenly Abigail, unable to contain her excitement any longer, burst into song:

'I'm a wicked old witch of a-hundred-and-five,
With a bonfire and broomstick and cauldron and cat:
    If I'm not dead by doomsday I'll still be alive,
A-wearing my dear old great-grandmother's hat!

    Cheerio, tra-la,
    Cheeriay, tra-lay,
A-wearing my dear old great-grandmother's hat!'

There were a great many verses and they had all joined in the chorus with enthusiasm, dancing as they went, Abigail leading them.

'I'm a wicked old witch of a-hundred-and-six,
With a bonfire and broomstick and cauldron and cat:
    If I'm not in my coffin I'll be on two sticks,
A-wearing my dear old great-grandmother's hat!'

By the time they reached the wicked old witch of a-hundred-and-eleven – 'If I'm not on this earth you won't find me in heaven!' – they had come in sight of the village. Abigail straightened Necromancy's wreath and Necromancy straightened Abigail's dress, which seemed to have a tendency to turn itself back to front; Zachary straightened his hat, and the Pedlar mopped his forehead with his spotted handkerchief; and with proper decorum they proceeded towards the church.

And long afterwards, long after Mrs Pennyfeather's wedding-bells had ceased to ring in their ears, the witch-family still remembered it all. And each time the Pedlar came to see them – and as the years went by he seemed to come more and more often – they would relive every minute of that memorable day, sitting beside the kitchen range if it were winter, or under the apple tree in summer.

How Abigail had danced! And how Necromancy had *eaten!* Such cakes! And such ices! And Zachary – how splendid he had looked! And wasn't Mrs Penny–– that is, Mrs Ebenezer's hat a picture? And how handsome they had both looked coming down the aisle? And oh, the bridesmaids, and the music, and the flowers and the dancing . . .!

And at last, just as in the old days in the forest, tired and happy, they would drop off to sleep one by one. Then the Pedlar would get quietly to his feet and arrange a little pile of presents – tobacco for Zachary, needles and a thimble for Abigail, a lollipop for Necromancy – as a token of his gratitude, and picking up the battered old suitcase that held so many treasures, walk away down the garden path, the curlew-call of his whistle floating behind him like a pennant.

The Anonymous Vene

Donna Leon is a prof... y near
Venice and visits Er... *tian* is
her third novel to fe... *Death*
at La Fenice and *De*... d by *A*
Venetian Reckoning, ...

'This series is one of the adornments of current detective fiction . . . Written with cool lucidity. Ms Leon has created a gem of a book.' Gerald Kaufman, *The Scotsman*

'Slips along like a motorized gondola.' *Oxford Times*

'Venice is the perfect backdrop for a crime novel and there can rarely have been one so compulsively readable.' Frances Fyfield

'Like Dibdin's, this is a Venice unknown to tourists . . . a finely organized, stylishly told story about how crime gets done in Venice. No travel agent will recommend it.' Julian Symons

'Commissario Brunetti, most charismatic current Euro-cop, uncovers deadly ants' nest of corruption. Highly accomplished scary read.' *Guardian*

'Intriguing – with an excellent denouement.' *Mail on Sunday*

'Venice, that eerie, beauteous city where things are rarely what they seem . . . First class.' *Ms London*

'One of the most ingenious and absorbing stories I have read in a lifetime of addiction to mysteries. Brunetti's Venice is my Venice as well, and I am fascinated to find it intimately portrayed in these pages. I can hardly wait for his next investigation.' Marcella Hazan

'Highly atmospheric Venetian whodunnits with exceptionally beautiful covers.' Sarah Broadhurst, *Bookseller*

The Anonymous Venetian

Donna Leon

PAN BOOKS

First published 1994 by Macmillan

This edition published 1995 by Pan Books
an imprint of Macmillan Publishers Ltd
25 Eccleston Place, London SW1W 9NF
Basingstoke and Oxford
Associated companies throughout the world
www.macmillan.com

ISBN 0 330 34412 9

11 13 15 17 19 18 16 14 12

A CIP catalogue record for this book is available from
the British Library.

Phototypeset by Intype, London
Printed and bound in Great Britain by
Mackays of Chatham PLC, Chatham, Kent

To the memory of Arleen Auger
a perished sun

Ah forse adesso
Sul morir mio delusa
Priva d'ogni speranza, e di consiglio
Lagrime di dolor versa dal ciglio.

Ah, perhaps already
Deceived by my death
Deprived of every hope and counsel
Tears of pain flow from her eyes.

Mozart, *Lucio Silla*

Chapter One

The shoe was red, the red of London phone booths, New York fire engines, although these were not images that came to the man who first saw the shoe. He thought of the red of the Ferrari Testarossa on the calendar in the butchers' showers, the one with the naked blonde draped across it, seeming to make fevered love to the left headlight. He saw the shoe lying drunkenly on its side, its toe barely touching the edge of one of the pools of oil that lay like a spotted curse upon the land beyond the abattoir. He saw it there and, of course, he also thought of blood.

Somehow, years before, permission had been given to put the slaughterhouse there, long before Marghera had blossomed, though that is perhaps an inopportune choice of verb, into one of the leading industrial centres of Italy, before the petroleum refineries and the chemical plants had spread themselves across the acres of swampy land that lay on the other side of the *laguna* from Venice, pearl of the Adriatic. The cement building lay, low and feral, within the enclosure of a high mesh fence. Had the fence been built in the early days, when sheep and cattle could still be herded down dusty roads towards the

1

building? Was its original purpose to keep them from escaping before they were led, pushed, beaten up the ramp towards their fate? The animals arrived in trucks now, trucks which backed directly to the high-sided ramps, and so there was no chance that they could escape. And surely no one would want to come near that building; hence the fence was hardly necessary to keep them away. Perhaps because of this, the long gaps in it went unmended, and stray dogs, drawn by the stench of what went on inside, sometimes came through the fence at night and howled with longing for what they knew was there.

The fields around the slaughterhouse stood empty; as if obeying a taboo as deep as blood itself, the factories stood far off from the low cement building. The buildings maintained their distance, but their ooze and their run-off and those deadly fluids that were piped into the ground knew nothing of taboo and seeped each year closer to the slaughterhouse. Black slime bubbled up around the stems of marsh grass, and a peacock-bright sheen of oil floated on the surface of the puddles that never disappeared, however dry the season. Nature had been poisoned here, outside, yet it was the work that went on inside that filled people with horror.

The shoe, the red shoe, lay on its side about a hundred metres to the rear of the slaughterhouse, just outside the fence, just to the left of a large clump of tall seagrass that seemed to thrive on the poisons that percolated around its roots. At eleven-thirty on a hot Monday morning in August, a thickset man in a blood-soaked leather apron flung back the metal door at the rear of the slaughter-

house and emerged into the pounding sun. From behind him swept waves of heat, stench, and howls. The sun made it difficult to feel that it was cooler here, but at least the stench of offal was less foul, and the sounds came from the hum of traffic, a kilometre away, as the tourists poured into Venice for Ferragosto, not from the shrieks and squeals that filled the air behind him.

He wiped a bloody hand on his apron, stooping to find a dry spot down by the hem, then reached into his shirt pocket and pulled out a package of Nazionale. With a plastic lighter, he lit the cigarette and pulled at it greedily, glad of the smell and acrid taste of the cheap tobacco. A deep-throated howl came from the door behind him, pushing him away from the building, over towards the fence and the shade that was to be found under the stunted leaves of an acacia that had managed to grow to a height of four metres.

Standing there, he turned his back on the building and looked out across the forest of smokestacks and industrial chimneys that swept off towards Mestre. Flames spurted up from some of them; grey, greenish clouds spilled out of others. A light breeze, too weak to be felt on his skin, brought the clouds back towards him. He pulled at his cigarette and looked down at his feet, always careful, here in the fields, where he stepped. He looked down and saw the shoe, lying on its side beyond the fence.

It was made out of some sort of cloth, that shoe, not out of leather. Silk? Satin? Bettino Cola didn't know that sort of thing, but he did know that his wife had a pair made out of the same sort of stuff, and she had spent

more than a hundred thousand lire on them. He'd have to kill fifty sheep or twenty calves to earn that much money, yet she'd spend it on a pair of shoes, wear them once, then stuff them in the back of the closet and never look at them again.

Nothing else in the blasted landscape deserved his attention, so he studied the shoe, pulling at his cigarette. He moved to the left and looked at it from another angle. Though it lay close to a large pool of oil, it appeared to rest on a patch of dry land. Cola took another step to the left, one that drew him out into the full violence of the sun, and studied the area around the shoe, looking for its mate. There, under the clump of grass, he saw an oblong shape that seemed to be the sole of the other one, it too lying on one side.

He dropped his cigarette and crushed it into the soft earth with his toe, walked down the fence a few metres, then bent low and crept through a large hole, careful of the jagged, rusty barbs of metal that encircled him. Straightening up, he walked back towards the shoe, now a pair of them and perhaps salvageable because of that.

'*Roba di puttana*,' he muttered under his breath, seeing the heel on the first shoe, taller than the pack of cigarettes in his pocket: only a whore would wear such things. He reached down and picked up the first shoe, careful to keep from touching the outside. As he had hoped, it was clean, had not fallen into the oily puddle. He took a few steps to the right, reached down and wrapped two fingers around the heel of its mate, but it appeared to be caught on a tuft of grass. He lowered himself to one knee, careful to see where he knelt, and

4

gave the shoe a sharp tug. It came loose, but when Bettino Cola saw that what he had pulled it loose from was a human foot, he leaped back from the bush and dropped the first shoe into the black puddle from which it had survived the night.

Chapter Two

The police arrived on the scene twenty minutes later, two blue and white sedans from the Squadra Mobile of Mestre. By then, the field at the back of the slaughter-house was filled with men from inside the building, brought out into the sun by curiosity about this different kind of slaughter. Cola had run drunkenly back inside as soon as he saw the foot and the leg to which it was attached and gone into the foreman's office to tell him there was a dead woman in the field beyond the fence.

Cola was a good worker, a serious man, and so the foreman believed him and called the police immediately without going outside himself to check and see that Cola was telling the truth. But others had seen Cola come into the building and came to ask what it was, what had he seen? The foreman snarled at them to get back to work: the refrigerated trucks were waiting at the loading docks, and they didn't have time to stand around all day and gabble about some whore who got her throat cut.

He didn't mean this literally, of course, for Cola had told him only about the shoe and the foot, but the fields between the factories were well-known territory to the men who worked in the factories – and to the women

6

who worked in those fields. If she'd got herself killed there, then she was probably one of those painted wrecks who spent the late afternoon standing at the side of the road that led from the industrial zone back into Mestre. Quitting time, time to go home, but why not a quick stop at the side of the road and a short walk back to a blanket spread beside a clump of grass? It was quick, they expected nothing of you except ten thousand lire, and they were, more and more often now, blondes come in from Eastern Europe, so poor that they couldn't make you use anything, not like the Italian girls on Via Cappuccina, and since when did a whore tell a man what to do or where to put it? She probably did that, got pushy, and the man had pushed back. Plenty more of them and plenty more coming across the border every month.

The police cars pulled up and a uniformed officer got out of each. They walked towards the front of the building, but the foreman reached them before they got to the door. Behind him stood Cola, feeling important to be the centre of all this attention, but still faintly sick from the sight of that foot.

'Is it you who called?' the first policeman asked. His face was round, glistening with sweat, and he stared at the foreman from behind dark glasses.

'Yes,' the foreman answered. 'There's a dead woman in the field behind the building.'

'Did you see her?'

'No,' the foreman answered, stepping aside and motioning Cola to step forward. 'He did.'

After a nod from the first one, the policeman from the second car pulled a blue notebook out of his jacket

pocket, flipped it open, uncapped his pen, and stood with the pen poised over the page.

'Your name?' asked the first policeman, the dark focus of his glance now directed at the butcher.

'Cola, Bettino.'

'Address?'

'What's the use of asking his address?' interrupted the foreman. 'There's a dead woman out there.'

The first officer turned away from Cola and tilted his head down a little, just enough to allow him to peer at the foreman over the tops of his sun-glasses. 'She's not going anywhere.' Then, turning back to Cola, he repeated, 'Address?'

'Castello 3453.'

'How long have you worked here?' he asked, nodding at the building that stood behind Cola.

'Fifteen years.'

'What time did you get here this morning?'

'Seven-thirty. Same as always.'

'What were you doing in the field?' Somehow, the way he asked the questions and the way the other one wrote down the answers made Cola feel they suspected him of something.

'I went out to have a cigarette.'

'The middle of August, and you went out into the sun to have a cigarette?' the first officer asked, making it sound like lunacy. Or a lie.

'It was my break time,' Cola said with mounting resentment. 'I always go outside. I like to get away from the smell.' The word made it real to the policemen, and they looked towards the building, the one with the

notebook incapable of disguising the contraction of his nostrils at what they met.

'Where is she?'

'Just beyond the fence. She's under a clump of bushes, so I didn't see her at first.'

'Why did you go near her?'

'I saw a shoe.'

'You what?'

'I saw a shoe. Out in the field, and then I saw the second one. I thought they might be good, so I went through the fence to get them. I thought maybe my wife would want them.' That was a lie: he had thought he could sell them, but he didn't want to tell this to the police. It was a small lie, and entirely innocent, but it was only the first of many lies that the police were going to be told about the shoe and the person who wore it.

'Then what?' the first policeman prompted when Cola added nothing to this.

'Then I came back here.'

'No, before that,' he said with an irritated shake of his head. 'When you saw the shoe. When you saw her. What happened?'

Cola spoke quickly, hoping that would get him through and rid of it. 'I picked up one shoe, and then I saw the other one. It was under the bush. So I pulled on it. I thought it was stuck. So I pulled again, and it came off.' He swallowed once. Twice. 'It was on her foot. That's why it wouldn't come off.'

'Did you stay there long?'

This time it was Cola who suspected lunacy. 'No. No.

No, I came back into the building and told Banditelli, and he called you.'

The foreman nodded to confirm this.

'Did you walk around back there?' the first policeman asked Cola.

'Walk around?'

'Stand around? Smoke? Drop anything near her?'

Cola shook his head in a strong negative.

The second one flipped the pages of his notebook and the first said, 'I asked you a question.'

'No. Nothing. I saw her and I dropped the shoe, and I went into the building.'

'Did you touch her?' the first one asked.

Cola looked at him with eyes wide with amazement. 'She's dead. Of course I didn't touch her.'

'You touched her foot,' the second policeman said, looking down at his notes.

'I didn't touch her foot,' Cola said, though he couldn't remember now if he had or had not. 'I touched the shoe, and it came off her foot.' He couldn't keep himself from asking, 'Why would I want to touch her?'

Neither policeman answered this. The first one turned and nodded to the second, who flipped his notebook closed. 'All right, show us where she is.'

Cola stood rooted to the spot and shook his head from side to side. The sun had dried the blood that spattered down the front of his apron, and flies buzzed around him. He didn't look at them. 'She's at the back, out beyond the big hole in the fence.'

'I want you to show us where she is,' the first police-man said.

'I just told you where she is,' Cola snapped, voice rising up sharply.

The two policemen exchanged a glance that somehow managed to suggest that Cola's reluctance was significant, worth remembering. But they turned away from him and from the foreman and walked around the side of the building, saying nothing.

It was noon and the sun beat down on the flat tops of the officers' uniform caps. Beneath them, their hair was sopping, their necks running with sweat. At the back of the building, they saw the large hole in the fence and made towards it. Behind them, filtering through the death squeals that still came from the building, they heard human sounds and turned towards them. Clustered around the back entrance of the building, their aprons as red with gore as Cola's, five or six men huddled in a tight ball. Used to this curiosity, the policemen turned back to the fence and headed towards the hole. Bowing low, they went through it in single file and then off to the left, towards a large spiky clump of bush that stood beyond the fence.

The officers stopped a few metres from it. Knowing to look for the foot, they easily found it, saw its sole peering out from beneath the low branches. Both shoes lay just in front of it.

The two of them approached the foot, walking slowly and looking at the ground where they walked, as careful to avoid the malevolent puddles as to keep from stepping in anything that might be another footprint. Just beside the shoes, the first one knelt down and pushed the waist-high grass aside with his hand.

The body lay on its back, the outer side of the ankles pressed into the earth. The policeman reached forward and pushed at the grass, exposing a length of hairless calf. He removed his sun-glasses and peered into the shadows, following with his eyes the legs, long and muscular, following across the bony knee, up to the lacy red underpants that showed under the bright red dress that was pulled back over the face. He stared a moment longer.

'*Cazzo*,' he exclaimed and let the grass spring back into place.

'What's the matter?' the other one asked.

'It's a man.'

Chapter Three

Ordinarily, the news that a transvestite prostitute had been found in Marghera with his head and face beaten in would have created a sensation even among the jaded staff at the Venice Questura, especially during the long Ferragosto holiday, when crime tended to drop off or take on the boring predictability of burglaries and break-ins. But today it would have taken something far more lurid to displace the spectacular news that ran like flame through the corridors of the Questura: Maria Lucrezia Patta, wife of Vice-Questore Giuseppe Patta, had that weekend left her husband of twenty-seven years to take up residence in the Milano apartment of – and here each teller of the tale paused to prepare each new listener for the bombshell – Tito Burrasca, the founding light and prime mover of Italy's pornographic film industry.

The news had dropped from heaven upon the place beneath just that morning, carried into the building by a secretary in the Ufficio Stranieri, whose uncle lived in a small apartment on the floor above the Pattas and who claimed to have been passing the Pattas' door just at the moment when terminal hostilities between the Pattas had erupted. Patta, the uncle reported, had shouted

Burrasca's name a number of times, threatening to have him arrested if he ever dared come to Venice; Signora Patta had returned fire by threatening not only to go and live with Burrasca, but to star in his next film. The uncle had retreated up the steps and spent the next half hour trying to open his own front door, during which time the Pattas continued to exchange threats and recriminations. Hostilities ceased only with the arrival of a water taxi at the end of the *calle* and the departure of Signora Patta, who was followed down the steps of the building by six suitcases, carried by the taxi driver, and by the curses of Patta, carried up to the uncle by the funnel-like acoustics of the staircase.

The news had arrived at eight on Monday morning; Patta followed it into the Questura at eleven. At one-thirty, the call came in about the transvestite, but by then most of the staff had already left for lunch, during which meal some employees of the Questura engaged in quite wild speculation about Signora Patta's future film career. An indication of the Vice-Questore's popularity was the bet that was made at one table, offering a hundred thousand lire to the first person who dared to enquire of the Vice-Questore as to his wife's health.

Guido Brunetti first heard about the murdered transvestite from Vice-Questore Patta himself, who called Brunetti into his office at two-thirty.

'I've just had a call from Mestre,' Patta said after telling Brunetti to take a seat.

'Mestre, sir?' Brunetti asked.

'Yes, that city at the end of the Ponte della Libertà,' Patta snapped. 'I'm sure you've heard of it.'

14

Brunetti thought of what he had learned about Patta that morning and decided to ignore his remark. 'Why did they call you, sir?'

'They've got a murder over there and no one to investigate.'

'But they've got more staff than we have, sir,' Brunetti said, never quite certain just how much Patta knew about the workings of the police force in either city.

'I know that, Brunetti. But two of their commissarios are on vacation. Another broke his leg in an automobile accident this weekend, so that leaves only one, and she' – Patta managed to give a snort of disgust at such a possibility – 'leaves for maternity leave on Saturday and won't be back until the end of February.'

'What about the two who are on vacation? Surely they can be called back.'

'One of them is in Brazil, and no one seems able to find the other one.'

Brunetti started to say that a commissario had to leave word where he could be reached, no matter where he went on vacation, but then he looked at Patta's face and decided, instead, to ask, 'What did they tell you about the murder, sir?'

'It's a whore. A transvestite. Someone beat his head in and left his body in a field out in Marghera.' Before Brunetti could object, Patta said, 'Don't even ask. The field is in Marghera, but the slaughterhouse that owns it is in Mestre, just by a few metres, so Mestre gets it.'

Brunetti had no desire to waste time on the details of property rights or city boundaries, so he asked, 'How do they know it's a prostitute, sir?'

'I don't know how they know it's a prostitute, Brunetti,' Patta said, his voice going up a few notes. 'I'm telling you what they told me. A transvestite prostitute, in a dress, with his head and face beaten in.'

'When was he found, sir?'

It was not Patta's habit to take notes, so he had not bothered to make any record of the call he had received. The facts hadn't interested him – one whore more, one whore less – but he was bothered by the fact that it would be his staff doing Mestre's work. That meant any success they met with would go to Mestre. But then he thought of recent events in his personal life and came to the decision that this might well be the sort of case he should let Mestre take any and all credit for – and publicity.

'I had a call from their Questore, asking if we could handle it. What are you three doing?'

'Mariani is on vacation and Rossi's still going through the papers on the Bortolozzi case,' Brunetti explained.

'And you?'

'I'm scheduled to begin my vacation this weekend, Vice-Questore.'

'That can wait,' Patta said with a certainty that soared above things like hotel reservations or plane tickets. 'Besides, this has got to be a simple thing. Find the pimp, get a list of customers. It's bound to be one of them.'

'Do they have pimps, sir?'

'Whores? Of course they have pimps.'

'Male whores, sir? Transvestite whores? Assuming, of course, that he was a prostitute.'

'Why would you expect me to know a thing like that,

Brunetti?' asked Patta, suspicious with more than usual irritation, again forcing Brunetti to remember that morning's first news and quickly to change the subject.

'How long ago did the call come in, sir?' Brunetti asked.

'A few hours ago. Why?'

'I wondered if the body's been moved?'

'In this heat?' Patta asked.

'Yes, there is that,' Brunetti agreed. 'Where was it taken?'

'I have no idea. One of the hospitals. Umberto Primo, probably. I think that's where they do the autopsies. Why?'

'I'd like to have a look,' Brunetti said. 'And at the place where it happened.'

Patta wasn't a man to be interested in details. 'Since this is Mestre's case, make sure you use their drivers, not ours.' Some details.

'Was there anything else, sir?'

'No. I'm sure this will be a simple thing. You'll have it wrapped up by the weekend and be free to go on vacation.' It was like Patta that he asked nothing about where Brunetti planned to go or what sort of reservations he might have to cancel. More details.

Leaving Patta's office, Brunetti noticed that, while he was inside, furniture had suddenly appeared in the small anteroom that stood directly outside Patta's office. A large wooden desk stood on one side, and a small table had been placed below the window. Ignoring this, he went downstairs and into the office where the uniformed branch worked. Sergeant Vianello looked up from some

17

papers on his desk and smiled at Brunetti. 'Even before you ask, Commissario, yes, it's true. Tito Burrasca.'

Hearing the confirmation, Brunetti was no less astonished than he had been, hours before, when he first heard the story. Burrasca was a legend, if that was the proper word, in Italy. He had begun making films during the sixties, blood and guts horrors that were so patently artificial that they became unconscious parodies of the genre. Burrasca, not at all foolish, no matter how inept he might have been at making horror films, answered the popular response to his films by making the films even more false: vampires with wrist-watches that the actors seemed to have forgotten to remove; telephones that brought the news of Dracula's escape; actors of the semaphore school of dramatic presentation. After a very short time, he had become a cult figure and people flocked to his films, eager to detect the artifice, to spot the howlers.

In the seventies, he gathered up all those masters of semaphoric expression and turned them to the making of pornographic films, at which they turned out to be no more adept. Costuming no problem, he soon realized that plot, similarly, presented no obstacle to the creative mind: he merely dusted off the plots of his old horror films and turned the ghouls, vampires, and werewolves into rapists and sex maniacs, and he filled the theatres, though smaller theatres this time, with a different audience, one that seemed not at all interested in the spotting of anachronism.

The eighties presented Italy with scores of new private television stations, and Burrasca presented those

stations with his latest films, somewhat toned down in deference to the supposed sensibilities of the TV audience. And then he discovered the video cassette. His name quickly became part of the small change of Italian daily life: he was the butt of jokes on TV game shows, a figure in newspaper cartoons, but close consideration of his success had caused him to move to Monaco and become a citizen of that sensibly taxed principality. The twelve-room apartment he maintained in Milano, he told the Italian tax authorities, was used only for entertaining business guests. And now, it would appear, Maria Lucrezia Patta.

'Tito Burrasca, in fact,' Sergeant Vianello repeated, keeping himself, Brunetti knew not with what force, from smiling. 'Perhaps you're lucky to be spending the next few days in Mestre.'

Brunetti couldn't keep himself from asking, 'Didn't anyone know about it before?'

Vianello shook his head. 'No. No one. Not a whisper.'

'Not even Anita's uncle?' Brunetti asked, revealing that even the higher orders knew the source of this one.

Vianello began to answer but was interrupted by the buzzer on his desk. He picked up the phone, pressed a button, and asked, 'Yes, Vice-Questore?'

He listened for a moment, said, 'Certainly, Vice-Questore,' and hung up.

Brunetti gave him an inquisitive glance.

'The immigration people. He wants to know how long Burrasca can stay in the country, now that he's changed his citizenship.'

Brunetti shook his head. 'I suppose you have to feel sorry for the poor devil.'

Vianello's head shot up. He couldn't disguise his astonishment, or wouldn't. 'Sorry? For him?' With evident effort, he stopped himself from saying more and turned his attention back to the folder on his desk.

Brunetti left him and went back to his own office. From there he called the Questura in Mestre, identified himself, and asked to be put through to whoever was in charge of the case of the murdered transvestite. Within minutes, he was speaking to a Sergeant Gallo, who explained that he was handling the case until a person of higher rank took over from him. Brunetti identified himself and said that he was that person, then asked Gallo to send a car to pick him up at Piazzale Roma in a half an hour.

When Brunetti stepped outside the dim entryway of the Questura, the sun hit him like a blow. Momentarily blinded by the light and the reflection from the canal, he reached into the breast pocket of his jacket and pulled out his sun-glasses. Before he had taken five steps, he could feel the sweat seeping into his shirt, crawling down his back. He turned right, deciding in that instant to go up to San Zaccaria and get the No. 82, though it would mean walking in the sun a good part of the way to get there. Though the *calli* that led to Rialto were all shaded from the sun by high houses, it would take him twice as long to get there, and he dreaded even so little as an extra minute spent outside.

When he emerged at Riva degli Schiavoni, he looked off to the left and saw that the vaporetto was tied to

the landing stage, people streaming from it. He was confronted with one of those peculiarly Venetian decisions: run and try to get the boat or let it go and then spend ten minutes in the trapped heat of the bobbing *embarcadero*, waiting for the next one. He ran. As he pounded across the wooden boards of the landing stage, he was presented with another decision: pause a moment to stamp his ticket in the yellow machine at the entrance and thus perhaps lose the boat, or run on to the boat and pay the five hundred lire supplement for failing to stamp the ticket. But then he remembered that he was on police business and, consequently, could ride at the expense of the city.

Even the short run had flooded his face and chest with sweat, and so he chose to remain on deck, body catching what little breeze was created by the boat's stately progress up the Grand Canal. He glanced around him and saw the half-naked tourists, the men and women with their bathing suits, shorts, and scoop necked T-shirts, and for a moment he envied them, even though he knew the impossibility of his appearing like that any place other than a beach.

As his body dried, the envy fled, and he returned to his normal state of irritation at seeing them dressed like this. If they had perfect bodies and perfect clothing, perhaps he would find them less annoying. As it was, the shabby materials of the clothing and the even shabbier state of too many of the bodies left him thinking long-ingly of the compulsory modesty of Islamic societies. He was not what Paola called a 'beauty snob', but he did believe that it was better to look good than bad. He

turned his attention from the people on the boat to the *palazzi* that lined the canal, and immediately he felt his irritation evaporate. Many of them, too, were shabby, but it was the shabbiness of centuries of wear, not that of laziness and cheap clothing. The city had grown old, but Brunetti loved the sorrows of her changing face.

Though he hadn't specified where the car was to meet him, he walked to the Carabinieri station at Piazzale Roma and saw, parked in front of it, motor running, one of the blue and white sedans of the Squadra Mobile of Mestre. He tapped on the driver's window. The young man inside rolled it down, and a wave of cold air flowed across the front of Brunetti's shirt.

'Commissario?' the young man asked. At Brunetti's nod, the young man got out, saying, 'Sergeant Gallo sent me,' and held open the rear door for him. Brunetti got into the car and rested his head for a moment against the back of the seat. The sweat on his chest and shoulders grew cold, but Brunetti couldn't tell if its evaporation brought him pleasure or pain.

'Where would you like to go, sir?' the young officer asked as he slipped the car into gear.

On vacation. On Saturday, he said, but only in his mind and only to himself. And to Patta. 'Take me to where you found him,' Brunetti directed.

At the other end of the causeway that led from Venice to the mainland, the young man pulled off in the direction of Marghera. The *laguna* disappeared, and soon they were riding down a straight road blocked with traffic and with a light at every intersection. Progress was slow. 'Were you there this morning?' The young

22

man turned and glanced back at Brunetti, then looked again at the road. The back of his collar was crisp and clean. Perhaps he spent his entire day in this air-conditioned car.

'No, sir. That was Buffo and Rubelli.'

'The report I got says he's a prostitute. Did someone identify him?'

'I don't know about that, sir. But it makes sense, doesn't it?'

'Why is that?'

'Well, sir, that's where the whores are, at least the cut-rate ones. Out there by the factories. There's always a dozen or so of them, on the side of the road, in case anyone wants a quickie on the way home from work.'

'Even men?'

'I beg your pardon, sir? Who else would use a whore?'

'I mean even a male whore. Would they be likely to be out there, where the men who use them could be seen stopping on the way home from work? It doesn't sound like the sort of thing too many men would want their friends to know about.'

The driver thought about that for a while.

'Where do they usually work?' Brunetti asked.

'Who?' the young man asked cautiously. He didn't want to be caught again by another trick question.

'The male whores.'

'They're usually along Via Cappuccina, sir. Sometimes at the train station, but we try to stop that sort of thing during the summer when so many tourists pass through the station.'

'Was this one a regular?'

23

'I don't know about that, sir.'

The car pulled off to the left, cut down a narrow road, then turned right on to a broad road lined with low buildings on either side. Brunetti glanced down at his watch. Almost five.

The buildings on either side of them were further and further apart from one another now, the spaces between them filled with low grass and the occasional bush. A few abandoned cars stood at crazy angles, their windows shattered and their seats ripped out and flung beside them. Each building appeared to have once been surrounded by a fence, but most of these now hung drunkenly from the posts that had forgotten about holding them up.

A few women stood at the side of the road; two of them stood in the shade created by a beach umbrella sunk into the dirt at their feet.

'Do they know what happened here today?' Brunetti asked.

'I'm sure they do, sir. Word about something like that spreads quickly.'

'And they're still here?' Brunetti asked, unable to conceal his surprise.

'They've got to live, haven't they, sir? Besides, if it was a man who got killed, then there's no risk to them, or I suppose that's the way they'd look at it.' The driver slowed and pulled to the side of the road. 'This is it, sir.'

Brunetti opened his door and got out. Heat and humidity slid up and embraced him. Before him stood a long low building; on one side, four steep cement ramps led up to double metal doors. A blue and white police

sedan was parked at the bottom of one of the ramps. No name was visible on the building, and no sign of any sort identified it. The smell that surged towards them made that unnecessary.

'I think it was at the back, sir,' the driver volunteered.

Brunetti walked to the right of the building, towards the open fields that he could see stretching out behind it. When he came around to the back of the building, he saw yet another lethargic fence, an acacia tree that had survived only by a miracle, and, in its shade, a policeman asleep in a wooden chair, head nodding forward on his chest.

'Scarpa,' the driver called out before Brunetti could say anything. 'Here's a commissario.'

The policeman's head shot up and he was instantly awake, then as quickly on his feet. He looked at Brunetti and saluted. 'Good afternoon, sir.'

Brunetti saw that the man's jacket was draped over the back of the chair and that his shirt, plastered to his body with sweat, seemed to be a faint pink, no longer white. 'How long have you been out here, Officer Scarpa?' Brunetti asked when he approached the man.

'Since the lab people left, sir.'

'When was that?'

'About three, sir.'

'Why are you still here?'

'The sergeant in charge told me to stay here until a team came out to talk to the workers.'

'What are you doing out here in the sun?'

The man made no attempt to avoid the question or to embellish his answer. 'I couldn't stand it inside, sir. The

smell. I came out here and was sick, and then I knew I couldn't go back inside. I tried standing for the first hour, but there's only this little place where there's any shade, so I went back and got a chair.'

Instinctively, Brunetti and the driver had crowded into that small patch of shade while the other man spoke. 'Do you know if the team has come out to question them?' Brunetti asked.

'Yes, sir. They got here about an hour ago.'

'Then what are you still doing out here?' Brunetti asked.

The officer gave Brunetti a stony look. 'I asked the sergeant if I could go back to town, but he wanted me to help with the questioning. I told him I couldn't, not unless the workers came outside to talk to me. He didn't like that, but I couldn't go back inside.'

A playful breeze reminded Brunetti of the truth of that.

'So what are you doing out here? Why aren't you in the car?'

'He told me to wait here, sir.' The man's face didn't change when he spoke. 'I asked if I could sit in the car – it's got air-conditioning – but he told me to stay out here if I wouldn't help with the questioning.' As if anticipating Brunetti's next question, he said, 'The next bus isn't until quarter to eight, to take people back into the city after work.'

Brunetti considered this and then asked, 'Where was he found?'

The policeman turned and pointed to a long clump of

26

grass on the other side of the fence. 'He was under that, sir.'

'Who found him?'

'One of the workers inside. He'd come outside to have a cigarette, and he saw one of the guy's shoes lying on the ground – red, I think – so he went to have a closer look.'

'Were you here when the lab team was?'

'Yes, sir. They went over it, taking photos and picking up anything that was on the ground for about a hundred metres around the bush.'

'Footprints?'

'I think so, sir, but I'm not sure. The man who found him left some, but I think they found others.' He paused a moment, wiped some sweat from his forehead, and added, 'And the first police who were on the scene left some.'

'Your sergeant?'

'Yes, sir.'

Brunetti glanced off at the clump of grass then back at the policeman's sweat-soaked shirt. 'Go on back to our car, Officer Scarpa. It's air-conditioned.' Then to the driver, 'Go with him. You can both wait for me there.'

'Thank you, sir,' the policeman said gratefully and reached down to pull his jacket from the back of the chair.

'Don't bother,' Brunetti said when he saw the man start to put one arm in a sleeve.

'Thank you, sir,' he repeated and bent to pick up the chair. The two men walked back towards the building. The policeman set the chair down on the cement outside

the back door of the building then joined the other man. They disappeared round the side of the building, and Brunetti went towards the hole in the fence.

Ducking low, he passed through it and walked over towards the bush. The signs left by the lab team were all around: holes in the earth where they had driven rods into the earth to measure distance, dirt scuffed into small piles by pivoting footsteps, and, nearer to the clump, a small pile of clipped grass placed neatly to the side: apparently, they'd had to cut down the grass to get to the body and remove it without scratching it on the sharp edges of the leaves.

Behind Brunetti, a door slammed shut, and then a man's voice called, 'Hey, you, what are you doing? Get the hell away from there.'

Brunetti turned and, as he knew he would, saw a man in police uniform coming quickly towards him from the back of the building. As Brunetti watched but didn't move away from the bush, the man drew his revolver from his holster and shouted at Brunetti, 'Put your hands in the air and come over to the fence.'

Brunetti turned and walked back towards the fence; he moved like a man on a rocky surface, hands held out at his sides to maintain balance.

'I told you to put them in the air,' the policeman snarled as Brunetti reached the fence.

He had a gun in his hand, so Brunetti did not try to tell him that his hands were in the air; they just weren't over his head. Instead, he said, 'Good afternoon, Sergeant. I'm Commissario Brunetti from Venice. Have you been taking the statements of the people inside?'

28

The man's eyes were small, and there wasn't much in the way of intelligence to be read in them, but there was enough there for Brunetti to realize that the man saw the trap opening at his feet. He could ask to see proof, ask a commissario of police for his warrant card, or he could allow a stranger claiming to be a police official to go unquestioned.

'Sorry, Commissario, I didn't recognize you with the sun in my eyes,' the sergeant said, though the sun shone over his left shoulder. He could have got away with it, earning Brunetti's grudging respect, had he not added, 'It's hard, coming out into the sun like this, from the darkness inside. Besides, I wasn't expecting anyone else to come out here.'

The name tag on his chest read 'Buffo'.

'It seems that Mestre is out of police commissari for the next few weeks, so I was sent out to handle the investigation.' Brunetti bent down and walked through the hole in the fence. By the time he stood up on the other side, Buffo's revolver was back in its holster, the flap snapped securely closed.

Brunetti started towards the back door of the slaughterhouse, Buffo walking beside him. 'What did you learn from the people inside?'

'Nothing more than what I got when I answered the first call this morning, sir. A butcher, Bettino Cola, found the body at a little past eleven this morning. He had gone outside to have a cigarette, and he went over to the bush to have a look at some shoes he said he saw lying on the ground.'

'Weren't there any shoes?' Brunetti asked.

29

'Yes. They were there when we got here.' From the way he spoke, anyone hearing him would believe that Cola had placed them there to divert suspicion from himself. As much as any civilian or criminal, Brunetti hated Tough Cops. 'The call we got said there was a whore in a field out here, a woman. I answered the call and took a look, but it was a man.' Buffo spat.

'The report I received said he's a prostitute,' Brunetti said in a level voice. 'Has he been identified?'

'No, not yet. We're having the morgue people take pictures, though he was beat up pretty badly, and then we'll have an artist make a sketch of what he must have looked like before. We'll show that around, and sooner or later someone will recognize him. They're pretty well known, those boys,' Buffo said with something between a grin and a grimace, then continued, 'If he's one of the locals, we'll have an ID on him pretty soon.'

'And if not?' Brunetti asked.

'Then it will take longer, I guess. Or maybe we won't find out who he is. Small loss, in either case.'

'And why is that, Sergeant Buffo?' Brunetti asked softly, but Buffo heard only the words and not the tone.

'Who needs them? Perverts. They're all full of AIDS, and they think nothing about passing it on to decent working men.' He spat again.

Brunetti stopped, turned, and faced the sergeant. 'As I understand it, Sergeant Buffo, these decent working men about whom you are so concerned get AIDS passed on to them because they pay these "perverts" to let them ram their cocks up their asses. Let us try not to forget that. And let us try not to forget that, whoever the

dead man is, he's been murdered, and it is our duty to find the murderer. Even if it was a decent working man.' Saying that, Brunetti opened the door and went into the slaughterhouse, preferring the stench there to the one he left outside.

Chapter Four

Inside, he learned little more: Cola repeated his story, and the foreman verified it. Sullenly, Buffo told him that none of the men who worked in the factory had seen anything strange, not that morning and not the day before. The whores were so much a part of the landscape that no one now paid any real attention to them or to what they did. No one could remember that particular area behind the slaughterhouse ever being used by the whores: the smell alone would explain that. But had one of them been seen in that area, no one was likely to have noticed.

After learning all of this, Brunetti went back to his car and asked the driver to take him to the Questura in Mestre. Officer Scarpa, who had put his jacket back on, got out of the car and joined Sergeant Buffo in the other. As the two cars headed back towards Mestre, Brunetti opened his window half-way to let some air, however hot, into the car and dilute the smell of the slaughterhouse that still clung to his clothing. Like most Italians, Brunetti had always scoffed at the idea of vegetarianism, scorning it as yet another of the many self-indulgences

of the well-fed, but today the idea made complete sense to him.

At the Questura, his driver took him to the first floor and introduced him to Sergeant Gallo, a cadaverous man with sunken eyes who looked like the years spent in pursuit of the criminal had eaten into his flesh from the inside.

When Brunetti was seated at the side of Gallo's desk, the sergeant told him there was little else to add to what Brunetti had been told, though he did have the initial, verbal report from the pathologist: death had resulted from a series of blows to the head and face and had taken place from twelve to eighteen hours before the body was found. The heat made it difficult to tell. From pieces of rust found in some of the wounds and from their shape, the pathologist guessed that the murder weapon had been a piece of metal, most probably a length of pipe, but surely something cylindrical. The lab analysis of stomach contents and blood wouldn't be back until Wednesday morning at the earliest, so it was impossible to say yet whether he had been under the influence of drugs or alcohol when he was killed. Since many of the prostitutes in the city and almost all of the transvestites were confirmed drug users, this was likely, though there seemed to be no sign on the body of intravenous drug use. The stomach was empty, though there were signs that he had eaten a meal within the twenty-four hours before he was killed.

'What about his clothing?' he asked Gallo.

'Red dress, some sort of cheap synthetic material.

Red shoes, barely worn, size forty-one. I'll have them checked to see if we can find the manufacturers.'

'Are there any photos?' Brunetti asked.

'They won't be ready until tomorrow morning, sir, but from the reports of the men who brought him in, you might not want to see them.'

'That bad, eh?' Brunetti asked.

'Whoever did it to him must really have hated him or been out of his mind when he did it. There's no nose left.'

'Will you get an artist to make a sketch?'

'Yes, sir. But most of it's going to be guesswork. All he'll have is the shape of the face, the eye colour. And the hair.' Gallo paused for a moment and added, 'It's very thin, and he's got a large bald spot, so I'd guess he wore a wig when, ah, when he worked.'

'Was a wig found?' Brunetti asked.

'No, sir, there wasn't. And it looks like he was killed somewhere else and carried there.'

'Footprints?'

'Yes. The technical team said they found a set of them going towards the clump of grass and coming away from it.'

'Deeper when going?'

'Yes, sir.'

'So he was carried out there and dumped under that clump of grass. Where did the footprints come from?'

'There's a narrow paved road that runs along the back of the field behind the slaughterhouse. It looks like he came from there.'

'And on the road?'

'Nothing, sir. It hasn't rained in weeks, so a car, or

34

even a truck, could have stopped there, and there'd be no sign of it. There's just those footprints. A man's. Size forty-three.' Brunetti's size.

'Do you have a list of the transvestite prostitutes?'

'Only those who have been in trouble, sir.'

'What sort of trouble do they get into?'

'The usual. Drugs. Fights among themselves. Occasionally, one of them will get into a fight with a client. Usually over money. But none of them has ever been mixed up in anything serious.'

'What about the fights? Are they ever violent?'

'Nothing like this, sir. Never anything like this.'

'How many of them are there?'

'We've got files on about thirty of them, but I'd guess that's just a small fraction of them. A lot of them come down from Pordenone or in from Padova. It seems business is better for them there, but I don't know why.' The first place was the nearest big city to both American and Italian military installations: that would account for Pordenone. But Padova? The university? If so, things had changed since Brunetti took his law degree.

'I'd like to take a look at those files tonight. Can you make me copies of them?'

'I've already had that done, sir,' Gallo said, handing him a thick blue file that lay on his desk.

As he took the folder from the sergeant, Brunetti realized that, even here in Mestre, less than twenty kilometres from home, he was likely to be treated as a foreigner, so he sought for some common ground that would establish him as a member of a working unit, not the commissario come in from out of town. 'But you're

Venetian, aren't you, Sergeant?' Gallo nodded and Brunetti added, 'Castello?' Again, Gallo nodded, but this time with a smile, as if he knew the accent would follow him, no matter where he went.

'What are you doing out here in Mestre?' Brunetti asked.

'You know how it is, sir,' he began. 'I got tired of trying to find an apartment in Venice. My wife and I looked for two years, but it's impossible. No one wants to rent to a Venetian, afraid you'll get in and they'll never be able to get you out. And the prices if you want to buy – five million a square metre. Who can afford that? So we came out here.'

'You sound like you regret it, Sergeant.'

Gallo shrugged. It was a common enough fate among Venetians, driven out of the city by skyrocketing rents and prices. 'It's always hard to leave home, Commissario,' he said, but it seemed to Brunetti that his voice, when he said it, was somewhat warmer.

Returning to the issue at hand, Brunetti tapped a finger on the file. 'Do you have anyone here they talk to, that they trust?'

'We used to have an officer, Benvenuti, but he retired last year.'

'No one else?'

'No, sir.' Gallo paused for a moment, as if considering whether he could risk his next statement. 'I'm afraid many of the younger officers, well, I'm afraid they treat these guys as something of a joke.'

'Why do you say that, Sergeant Gallo?'

'If any of them makes a complaint, you know, about

being beat up by a client – not about not being paid, you understand. That's not something we have any control over – but about being beat up, well, no one wants to be sent to investigate it, even if we have the name of the man who did it. Or if they do go to question him, usually nothing happens.'

'I got a taste of that, even something stronger, from Sergeant Buffo,' Brunetti said.

At the name, Gallo compressed his lips but said nothing.

'What about the women?' Brunetti asked.

'The whores?'

'Yes. Is there much contact between them and the transvestites?'

'There's never been any trouble, not that I know of, but I don't know how well they get on. I don't think they're in competition over clients, if that's what you mean.'

Brunetti wasn't sure what he meant and realized that his questions would have no clear focus until he read the files in the blue folder or until someone could identify the body of the dead man. Until they had that, there could be no talk of motive and, until that, there could be no understanding what had happened.

He stood, glanced at his watch. 'I'd like your driver to pick me up at eight-thirty tomorrow morning. And I'd like the artist to have the sketch ready by then. As soon as you have it, even if it's tonight, get at least two officers to start making the rounds of the other transvestites, to see if any of them know who he is or if they've heard that anyone from Pordenone or Padova is missing. I'd

also like your men to ask the whores – the women, that is, if the transvestites use the area where he was found or if they know of any of them who ever has in the past.' He picked up the file. 'I'll read through this tonight.'

Gallo had been taking notes of what Brunetti said, but now he stood and walked with him to the door.

'I'll see you then tomorrow morning, Commissario.' He headed back towards his desk and reached for the phone. 'When you get downstairs, there'll be a driver waiting to take you back to Piazzale Roma.'

As the police car sped back over the causeway towards Venice, Brunetti looked out to the right, at the clouds of grey, white, green, yellow smoke billowing up from the forest of smokestacks in Marghera. As far as the eye could see, the pall of smoke enveloped the vast industrial complex, and the rays from the declining sun turned it all into a radiant vision of the next century. Saddened by the thought, he turned away and looked off towards Murano and, beyond it, the distant tower of the basilica of Torcello, where, some historians said, the whole idea of Venice had begun more than a thousand years ago, when the people of the coast fled into the marshes to avoid the invading Huns.

The driver swerved wildly to avoid an immense camper-van with German plates that suddenly cut in front of them then swerved off to the parking island of Tronchetto, and Brunetti was pulled back to the present. More Huns, and now no place to hide.

He walked home from Piazzale Roma, paying little attention to what or whom he passed, his mind hovering over that bleak field, still seeing the flies that swarmed

around the spot under the grass where the body had been. Tomorrow, he would go and see the body, talk to the pathologist, and see what secrets it might reveal.

He got home just before eight, still early enough for it to seem like he was returning from a normal day. Paola was in the kitchen when he let himself into the apartment, but there were none of the usual smells or sounds of cooking. Curious, he went down the corridor and stuck his head into the kitchen; she was at the counter, slicing tomatoes.

'*Ciao*, Guido,' she said, looking up and smiling at him.

He tossed the blue folder on the kitchen counter, walked over to Paola, and kissed the back of her neck.

'In this heat?' she asked, but she leaned back against him as she said it.

He licked delicately at her skin.

'Salt depletion,' he said, licking again.

'I think they sell salt pills in the pharmacies. Probably more hygienic,' she said, leaning forward, but only to take another ripe tomato from the sink. She cut it into thick slices and added them to the ones already arranged in a circle around the edge of a large ceramic plate.

He opened the refrigerator, took out a bottle of *acqua minerale*, and reached for a glass from the cabinet above his head. He filled the glass, drank it down, drank another, then capped the bottle and replaced it in the refrigerator.

From the bottom shelf, he removed a bottle of Prosecco. He ripped the silver foil from the cap, then slowly pushed the cork up with both thumbs, moving it slowly and working it back and forth gently. As soon as the cork

popped from the bottle, he tilted it to one side to prevent the bubbles from spilling out. 'How is it that you knew how to keep champagne from spilling when I married you and I didn't?' he asked as he poured some of the sparkling wine into his glass.

'Mario taught me about it,' she explained, and he knew immediately that, from the twenty or so Marios they knew, she was talking about her cousin, the vintner.

'Want some?' he asked.

'Just give me a sip of yours. I don't like to drink in this heat; it goes right to my head.' He reached his arm around her and held his glass to her lips while she took a small sip. '*Basta*,' she said. He took the glass and sipped at the wine.

'Good,' he murmured. 'Where are the kids?'

'Chiara's out on the balcony. Reading.' Did Chiara ever do anything else? Except maths problems and beg for a computer?

'And Raffi?' He'd be with Sara, but Brunetti always asked.

'With Sara. He's eating dinner at her house, and then they're going to a movie.' She laughed with amusement at Raffi's doglike devotion to Sara Paganuzzi, the girl two floors down. 'I hope he's going to be able to pry himself away from her for two weeks to come to the mountains with us,' Paola said, not meaning it at all: two weeks in the mountains above Bolzano, an escape from the grinding heat of the city, were enough to lure even Raffi away from the delights of new love. Besides, Sara's parents had said she could join Raffaele's family for a weekend of that vacation.

Brunetti said nothing to this, poured himself another half glass of wine. '*Caprese*?' he asked, nodding at the ring of tomatoes on the plate in front of Paola.

'Oh, supercop,' Paola said, reaching for another tomato. 'He sees a ring of tomatoes with spaces left between each slice, pieces just big enough to allow a slice of mozzarella to be slipped in between them, and then he sees the fresh basil standing in a glass to the left of his fair wife, right beside the fresh mozzarella that lies on a plate. And he puts it all together and guesses, with lightning-like induction, that it's *insalata caprese* for dinner. No wonder the man strikes fear into the heart of the criminal population of the city.' She turned and smiled at him when she said this, gauging his mood to see if she had perhaps pushed too far. Seeing that, somehow, she had, she took the glass from his hand and took another slip. 'What happened?' she asked as she handed the glass back to him.

'I've been assigned to a case in Mestre.' Before she could interrupt, he continued. 'They've got two commissari out on vacation, one in hospital with a broken leg, and another one on maternity leave.'

'So Patta's given you away to Mestre?'

'There's no one else.'

'Guido, there's always someone else. For one, there's Patta himself. It wouldn't hurt him to do something else but sit around in his office and sign papers and fondle the secretaries.'

Brunetti found it difficult to imagine anyone allowing Patta to fondle her, but he kept that opinion to himself.

'Well?' she asked when he said nothing.

'He's got problems,' Brunetti said.

'Then it's true?' she asked. 'I've been dying to call you all day and ask you if it was. Tito Burrasca?'

When Brunetti nodded, she put her head back and made an indelicate noise that might best be described as a hoot. 'Tito Burrasca,' she repeated, turned back to the sink and grabbed another tomato. 'Tito Burrasca.'

'Come on, Paola. It's not all that funny.'

She whipped around, knife still held in front of her. 'What do you mean, it's not that funny? He's a pompous, sanctimonious, self-righteous bastard, and I can think of no one who deserves something like this better than he does.'

Brunetti shrugged and poured more wine into his glass. So long as she was fulminating against Patta, she might forget Mestre, though he knew this was only a momentary deviation.

'I don't believe this,' she said, turning around and apparently addressing this remark to the single tomato remaining in the sink. 'He's been hounding you for years, making a mess of any work you do, and now you defend him.'

'I'm not defending him, Paola.'

'Sure sounds like it to me,' she said, this time to the ball of mozzarella she held in her left hand.

'I'm just saying that no one deserves this. Burrasca is a pig.'

'And Patta's not?'

'Do you want me to call Chiara?' he asked, seeing that the salad was almost ready.

42

'Not before you tell me how long this thing in Mestre is likely to take.'

'I have no idea.'

'What is it?'

'A murder. A transvestite was found in a field in Mestre. Someone beat in his face, probably with a pipe, then carried him out there.' Did other families, he wondered, have pre-dinner conversations as uplifting as his own?

'Why beat in the face?' she asked, centring on the question that had bothered him all afternoon.

'Rage?'

'Um,' she said, slicing away at the mozzarella and then interspersing the slices with the tomato. 'But why in a field?'

'Because he wanted the body far away from wherever he killed him.'

'But you're sure he wasn't killed there?'

'Doesn't seem so. There were footprints going up to the place where the body was, then lighter ones going away.'

'A transvestite?'

'That's all I know. No one has told me anything about age, but everyone seems sure he was a prostitute.'

'Don't you believe it?'

'I have no reason not to believe it. But I also have no reason to believe it.'

She took some basil leaves, ran them under cold water for a moment, and chopped them into tiny pieces. She sprinkled them on top of the tomato and mozzarella,

added salt, then poured olive oil generously over the top of everything.

'I thought we'd eat on the terrace,' she said. 'Chiara's supposed to have set the table. Want to check?' When he turned to leave the kitchen, he kept the bottle and glass with him. Seeing that, Paola set the knife down in the sink. 'It's not going to be finished by the weekend, is it?'

He shook his head. 'Not likely.'

'What do you want me to do?'

'We've got the reservations at the hotel. The kids are ready to go. They've been looking forward to it since school got out.'

'What do you want me to do?' she repeated. Once, about eight years ago, he had managed to evade her questions about something; he couldn't remember what it was. He'd got away with it for a day.

'I'd like you and the kids to go to the mountains. If this finishes on time, I'll come up and join you. I'll try to come up next weekend at any rate.'

'I'd rather have you there, Guido. I don't want to spend my vacation alone.'

'You'll have the kids.'

Paola didn't deign to grace this with rational opposition. She picked up the salad and walked towards him. 'Go see if Chiara has set the table.'

Chapter Five

He read through the files that night before going to sleep and found in them evidence of a world he had perhaps known existed but about which he had known nothing either detailed or certain. To the best of his knowledge, there were no transvestites in Venice who worked as prostitutes. There was, however, at least one transsexual, and Brunetti knew of this person's existence only because he had once had to sign a letter attesting that Emilio Marcato had no criminal record, this before Emilia could have the sex listed on her *carta d'identità* changed to accord with the physical changes already made to her body. He had no idea of what urges or passions could lead a person to make a choice so absolutely final; he remembered, though, being disturbed and moved to an emotion he had chosen not to analyse by that mere alteration of a single letter on an official document: Emilio – Emilia.

The men in the file had not been driven to go so far and had chosen to transform only their appearance: face, clothing, make-up, walk, gesture. The photos attached to some of the files attested to the skill with which some of them had done this. Half of them were utterly

unrecognizable as men, even though Brunetti knew that was what they were. There was a general softness of cheek and fineness of bone that had nothing of the masculine about them; even under the merciless lights and lens of the police camera, many of them appeared beautiful, and Brunetti searched in vain for a shadow, a jut of chin, for anything that would mark them as men and not as women.

Sitting beside him in bed and reading the pages as he handed them to her, Paola glanced through the photos, read one of the arrest reports, this one for the sale of drugs, and handed the pages back to him with no comment.

'What do you think?' Brunetti asked.

'About what?'

'All of this.' He raised the file in his hand. 'Don't you find these men strange?'

Her look was a long one and, he thought, replete with distaste. 'I find the men who hire them much stranger.'

'Why?'

Pointing to the file, Paola said, 'At least these men don't deceive themselves about what they're doing. Unlike the men who use them.'

'What do you mean?'

'Oh, come on, Guido. Think about it. These men are paid to be fucked or fuck, depending on the taste of the men paying them. But they have to dress up as women before the other men will pay them or use them. Just think about that for a minute. Think about the hypocrisy there, the need for self deceit. So they can say, the next morning, "Oh, *Gesù Bambino*, I didn't know it was a

46

man until it was too late," or, "Well, even if it turned out to be a man, I'm still the one who stuck it in." So they're still real men, macho, and they don't have to confront the fact that they prefer to fuck other men because to do that would compromise their masculinity.' She gave him a long look. 'I suspect sometimes that you don't really bother to think about a lot of things, Guido.'

That, loosely translated, generally meant that he didn't think in the same way she did. But this time Paola was right: this was something he hadn't ever thought about. Once he had discovered them, women had conquered Brunetti, and he could never understand the sexual appeal of any – well, there really was only one – other sex. Growing up, he had assumed that all men were pretty much like him; when he had learned that they were not, he was too convinced in his own delight to give anything other than an intellectual acknowledgement to the existence of the alternative.

He remembered, then, something Paola had told him soon after they met, something he had never noticed: that Italian men were constantly touching, fondling, almost caressing their own genitals. He remembered laughing in disbelief and scorn when she told him, but the next day he had begun to pay attention, and, within a week, had realized just how right she was. Within another week, he had become fascinated by it, overwhelmed by the frequency with which men on the street brought that hand down to give an inquisitive pat, a reassuring touch, as if afraid they had fallen off. Once, walking with him, Paola had stopped and asked him what he was thinking about, and the fact that she was the

47

only person in the world he would not be embarrassed to tell just what it was he had been thinking about at that moment convinced him, though a thousand things had already done so, that this was the woman he wanted to marry, had to marry, would marry.

To love and want a woman had seemed absolutely natural to him then, as it continued to do now. But the men in this file, for reasons he could read about and know, but which he could never hope to understand, had turned from women and sought the bodies of other men. They did so in return for money or drugs or, no doubt, sometimes in the name of love. And one of them, in what wild embrace of hatred had he met his violent end? And for what reason?

Paola slept peacefully beside him, a curved lump in which rested his heart's delight. He placed the file on the table beside the bed, turned off the light, wrapped his arm around Paola's shoulder and kissed her neck. Still salty. He was soon asleep.

When Brunetti arrived at the Mestre Questura the following morning, he found Sergeant Gallo at his desk, another blue folder in his hand. As Brunetti sat, the policeman passed the folder to him, and Brunetti saw for the first time the face of the murdered man. On top lay the artist's reconstruction of what he might have looked like, and, below that, he saw the photos of the shattered reality from which the artist had made his sketch.

There was no way of estimating the number of blows the face had suffered. As Gallo had said the night before, the nose was gone, driven into the skull by one

especially ferocious blow. One cheekbone was entirely crushed, leaving a shallow indentation on that side of the face. The photos of the back of the head showed a similar violence, but these would have been blows that killed rather than disfigured.

Brunetti closed the file and handed it back to Gallo. 'Have you had copies of the sketch made?'

'Yes, sir, we've got a stack of them, but we didn't get it until about half an hour ago, so none of the men has been out on the street with it.'

'Fingerprints?'

'We took a perfect set and sent them down to Rome and to Interpol in Geneva, but we haven't had an answer yet. You know what they're like.' Brunetti did know. Rome could take weeks; Interpol was usually a bit faster.

Brunetti tapped on the cover of the folder with the tip of his finger. 'There's an awful lot of damage to the face, isn't there?'

Gallo nodded but said nothing. In the past, he had dealt with Vice-Questore Patta, if only telephonically, so he was wary of whoever would come his way from Venice.

'Almost as if the person who did it didn't want the face to be recognizable,' Brunetti added.

Gallo shot him a quick glance from under thick eyebrows and nodded again.

'Do you have any friends in Rome who could speed things up for us?' Brunetti asked.

'I've already tried that, sir, but he's on vacation. You?'

Brunetti shook his head in quick negation. 'The

person I knew there has been transferred to Brussels to work with Interpol.'

'Then we'll have to wait, I suppose,' Gallo said, making it clear from his tone that he was not at all pleased with this.

'Where is he?'

'The dead man? In the morgue at Umberto Primo. Why?'

'I'd like to see him.'

If Gallo thought this a strange request, he gave no indication of it. 'I'm sure your driver could take you over there.'

'It's not very far, is it?'

'No, only a few minutes,' Gallo answered. 'Might be a bit longer, with the morning traffic.'

Brunetti wondered if these people ever walked any- where, but then he remembered the blanket of tropical heat that lay like a shroud across the whole Veneto area. Perhaps it was wiser to travel in air-conditioned cars to and from air-conditioned buildings, but he doubted that it was a method with which he would ever feel comfort- able. He said nothing about this, however, but went downstairs and had his driver – he seemed to rate his own driver and his own car – take him to the Hospital of Umberto Primo, the major of the many hospitals of Mestre.

At the morgue, he found the attendant at a low desk, with a copy of the *Gazzettino* spread out in front of him. Brunetti showed his warrant card and asked to see the murdered man who had been found in the field the day before.

The attendant, a short man with a substantial paunch and bowed legs, folded his paper closed and got to his feet. 'Ah, him, I've got him over on the other side, sir. No one's been to see him except that artist, and all he wanted to do was see the hair and eyes. Too much flash on the pictures, so he couldn't get them right. He just took a look at him, peeled back the lid and had a look at the eye. Didn't like looking at him, I'd say, but, Jesus, he should have seen him before the autopsy, with all that make-up on him, mixed in with the blood. It took for ever to clean him up. Looked like a clown before we did, I'll tell you. He had that eye stuff all over his face. Well, over what was left of his face. It's funny how some of that stuff is so hard to wash off. Must take women the devil's own time to clean themselves up, don't you think?'

During all of this, he led Brunetti across the chilly room, stopping occasionally to address Brunetti directly. He finally stopped in front of one of the many metal doors that formed the walls of the room, bent down and turned a metal handle, then pulled out the low drawer in which the body lay. 'Is he good enough for you here, sir, or would you like me to raise him up for you? Nothing to it. Just take a minute.'

'No, this is good enough,' Brunetti said, looking down. Unasked, the attendant pulled back the white sheet that covered the face, then looked up at Brunetti to see if he should continue. Brunetti nodded, and the attendant pulled the sheet from the body and folded it quickly into a neat rectangle.

Though Brunetti had seen the photos, nothing had

prepared him for the wreckage in front of him. The pathologist had been interested only in exploration and cared nothing for restoration; if a family were ever found, they could pay someone to attend to that.

No attempt had been made to restore the man's nose, and so Brunetti looked down at a concave surface with four shallow indentations, as if a retarded child had made a human face with clay but instead of a nose had simply punched a hole. Without the nose, recognizable humanity had fled.

He looked at the body, seeing if it could give him an idea of age or physical condition. Brunetti heard his own intake of breath when he realized that the body looked frighteningly like his own: the same general build, a slight thickening around the waist, and the scar from a childhood appendectomy. The only difference seemed to be a general hairlessness, and he leaned down closer to study the chest, brutally bisected by the long incision of the autopsy. Instead of the wiry, grizzled hair that grew on his own chest, he saw faint stubble. 'Did the pathologist shave his chest before the autopsy?' Brunetti asked the attendant.

'No, sir. It's not heart surgery he did on him, only an autopsy.'

'But his chest has been shaved.'

'His legs, too, if you look.'

Brunetti did. They were.

'Did the pathologist say anything about that?'

'Not while he was working, sir. Might be something in his report. You had enough?'

Brunetti nodded and stepped back from the corpse.

52

The attendant flung the sheet out in front of him, waved it in the air as though it were a tablecloth, and floated it perfectly in place over the body. He slid the body back inside, closed the door, and quietly turned the handle.

As they started back towards the desk, the attendant said, 'He didn't deserve that, whoever he was. The word here is that he was on the street, one of those fellows who dress up as women.'

For a moment, Brunetti thought the man was being sarcastic, but then he heard the tone under the words and realized he was serious.

'You the one who's going to try to find out who killed him, sir?'

'Yes.'

'Well, I hope you do. I suppose I can understand if you want to kill someone, but I can't understand killing him like that.' He stopped and looked up inquisitively at Brunetti. 'Can you, sir?'

'No, I can't.'

'As I said, sir, I hope you get the man who did it. Whore or no whore, no one deserves to die like that.'

Chapter Six

'You saw him?' Gallo asked when Brunetti returned to the Questura.

'Yes.'

'Not at all pretty, is it?'

'You saw him, too?'

'I always try to see them,' Gallo said, voice uninflected. 'It makes me more willing to work to get the person who killed them.'

'What do you think, Sergeant?' Brunetti asked, lowering himself into the chair at the side of the sergeant's desk and laying down the blue folder as if he meant it to serve as a physical sign of the murder.

Gallo thought for almost a full minute before he answered. 'I think it could have been done in the midst of tremendous rage.' Brunetti nodded at this possibility. 'Or, as you suggested earlier, Dottore, in an attempt to disguise his identity.' After a second, Gallo amended this, perhaps recalling what he had seen in the morgue, 'Or to destroy it.'

'That's pretty impossible in today's world, wouldn't you say, Sergeant?'

'Impossible?'

'Unless a person is entirely alien to a place or lives without any family or friends, their disappearance will be noticed in a few days – a few hours in most cases. Nobody manages to disappear any more.'

'Then perhaps rage makes more sense,' Gallo said. 'He could have said something to a client, done something that set him off. I don't know much about the men in the file I gave you yesterday. I'm not a psychologist or anything like that, so I don't know what drives them, but my guess is that the men who, ah, who pay them are far less stable than the men they pay. So rage?'

'What about carrying him out to a part of the city where whores are known to work?' Brunetti asked. 'That suggests intelligence and planning rather than rage.'

Gallo responded quickly to the testing that was being given him by this new commissario. 'Well, after he did it, he could have come to his senses. Maybe he killed him in his own place or a place where one of them was known, so he'd have to move the body. And if he's the sort of man – the killer, I mean – if he's the sort of man who uses these transvestites, then he'd know where the whores go. So maybe that would seem the logical place to leave him, so other people who use them would be suspected.'

'Yes . . .' Brunetti agreed slowly, and Gallo waited for the 'but' that the commissario's tone made inevitable. 'But that's to suggest that whores are the same as whores.'

'I beg your pardon, sir.'

'That male whores are the same as female whores, or

that, at least, they work in the same place. From what I heard and saw yesterday, it looks like that area out by the slaughterhouse is a place the female whores use.' Gallo considered this, and Brunetti added, prodding, 'But this is your city, so you'd know more about that than I would, coming in as something of a foreigner.' Complimenting, as well.

Gallo nodded. 'It's usually the girls who work those fields out by the factories. But we're getting more and more boys – a lot of them are Slavs and North Africans – so maybe they've been forced to move into new territory.'

'Have you heard any rumours about this?'

'I haven't personally, sir. But I usually don't have much to do with the whores, not unless they're involved in violent crimes.'

'Does that happen very often?'

Gallo shook his head. 'Usually, if it does happen, the women are afraid to tell us about it, afraid they'll end up in jail, no matter who's responsible for the violence. A lot of them are illegals, so they're afraid of coming to us, afraid of being deported if they get in any sort of trouble. And there are a lot of men who like to beat them up. I guess they learn how to spot those, or the other girls pass the word and they try to avoid them.

'I'd guess that the men are better able to protect themselves. If you read that file, you saw how big some of them are. Pretty, even beautiful, some of them, but they're still men. I'd imagine they'd have less of that sort of trouble. Or if they had it, they'd at least know how to defend themselves.'

'Have you got the autopsy report yet?' Brunetti asked.

Gallo picked up a few pieces of paper and handed them to him. 'It came in while you were at the hospital.'

Brunetti began to read through it quickly, familiar with the jargon and technical terms. No puncture wounds on the body, so the deceased wasn't an intra-venous drug user. Height, weight, general physical con-dition: all those things that Brunetti had seen were listed here, but in exact, measured detail. Mention was made of the make-up the attendant had talked about but no more than to say that there had been significant traces of lipstick and eyeliner. There was no evidence of recent sexual activity, either active or passive. Examination of the hands suggested a sedentary occupation; the nails were trimmed bluntly, and there was no callousing on the palms. Patterns of bruising on the body confirmed the supposition that he had been killed somewhere else and carried to the place where he was found, but the intense heat in which he had lain made it impossible to determine how much time had elapsed between his murder and his discovery, more than to say it could have been anywhere from twelve to twenty hours.

Brunetti looked up at Gallo and asked, 'Have you read this?'

'Yes, sir.'

'And what do you think?'

'We still have to decide between rage and cunning, I suppose.'

'But first we have to find out who he is,' Brunetti said. 'How many men have been detailed to this?'

'There's Scarpa.'

'The man who was out in the sun yesterday?'

Gallo's calm 'Yes, sir,' told Brunetti that he had heard about the incident, and the way he said it suggested that he didn't like it. 'He's the only officer who's been assigned. The death of a prostitute isn't a high priority, especially during the summer when we're short-staffed.'

'No one else?' Brunetti asked.

'I was assigned the case provisorily because I was here when the call came in, so I sent the Squadra Mobile to the scene. The Vice-Questore has suggested that it be handed over to Sergeant Buffo, since he's the one who answered the original call.'

'I see,' Brunetti said, considering this. 'Is there an alternative?'

'Do you mean, is there an alternative to Sergeant Buffo?'

'Yes.'

'You could request that, as your original contact was with me, and we have discussed the case at great length . . .' Here Gallo paused, as if to make that length even greater, then continued, 'It might save time if I were to continue to be assigned to the case.'

'Who is the vice-questore in charge of this?'

'Nasci.'

'Is she liable to . . . I mean, will she think this a good idea?'

'I'm sure that if the request came from a commissario, she'd agree, sir. Especially as you're coming out here to give us a hand.'

'Good. Get someone to write up a request, and I'll

sign it before lunch.' Gallo nodded, made a note on a piece of paper in front of him, then looked up at Brunetti and nodded again. 'And get your people working on the clothing and shoes he was wearing.' Gallo made another note.

Brunetti flipped open the blue file that he had studied the night before and pointed to the list of names and addresses stapled to the inside cover. 'I think the best thing we can do is to begin asking these men questions about the victim, if they know who he is or if they recognize him or know anyone who might have known him. The pathologist said he must be in his early forties. None of the men in the file are that old, few of them are even in their thirties, so if he's a local, he'd stand out because of his age, and people would certainly know about him.'

'How do you want to do this, sir?'

'I think we should divide the list into three, and then you and I and Scarpa can start showing them the picture and asking them what they know.'

'They aren't the sort of people who are willing to talk to the police, sir.'

'Then I suggest we take along a second picture, one of the photos of what he looked like when we found him out in the field. I think if we convince these men that the same thing could happen to them, they might be less reluctant to talk to us.'

'I'll get Scarpa up here,' Gallo said and reached for the phone.

Chapter Seven

They decided, even though it was still morning – probably more like the middle of the night to the men on the list – to talk to them now. Brunetti asked the other men, because they were familiar with Mestre, to arrange the addresses into some sort of geographic order, so they wouldn't have to traverse the city repeatedly as they went through the names.

When this was done, Brunetti took the list he was given and went downstairs to find his driver. He doubted the wisdom of arriving to question the men on this particular list in a blue and white police car with a uniformed policeman at the wheel, but he had only to step out into the mid-morning air of Mestre to decide that mere survival overrode any consideration of caution.

The heat wrapped itself around him, and the air seemed to nibble at his eyes. There was no breeze, not the slightest current; the day lay like a filthy blanket upon the city. Cars snaked past the Questura, their horns bleating in futile protest against changing lights or crossing pedestrians. Whirls of dirt and cigarette packages flying back and forth across the street marked their

passing. Brunetti, seeing it, hearing it, and breathing it, felt as though someone had come from behind and wrapped tight arms around his chest. How did human beings live like this?

Brunetti fled into the cool cocoon of the police car and emerged from it a quarter of an hour later in front of an eight-storey apartment building on the western edge of the city. He looked up and saw that lines of washing hung extended between it and the building on the opposite side of the street. A faint breeze blew here, so the particoloured strata of sheets, towels, and underwear undulated above him and, for a moment, raised his spirits.

Inside, the *portiere* sat in his cage-like office, arranging papers and envelopes on a desk, sorting the mail that must just have been delivered for the inhabitants of the building. He was an old man with a thin beard and silver-framed reading glasses hovering on the end of his nose. He raised his eyes over the tops of the lenses and said good morning. The humidity intensified the sour smell of the room, and a fan on the floor, blowing across the old man's legs, did no more than shove the smell around the room.

Brunetti said good-morning and asked where he could find Giovanni Feltrinelli.

At the mention of the name, the *portiere* shoved his chair back and got to his feet. 'I've warned him not to have any more of you come to this building. If he wants to do his job, then he can go do it in your cars or in the open fields, with the other animals, but he's not going to do his filthy work here, or I'll call the police.' As he said

61

it, his right hand reached out for the telephone on the wall behind him, his fiery eyes running up and down Brunetti with disgust he did nothing to disguise.

'I am the police,' Brunetti said softly and pulled his warrant card from his wallet, holding it out for the old man to see. He took it roughly from Brunetti, as if to suggest that he, too, knew where these things could be faked, and pushed his glasses up on his nose to read it.

'It looks real,' he finally admitted and handed it back to Brunetti. He took a dirty handkerchief from his pocket, removed his glasses, and began to rub at the lenses, first one and then the other, carefully, as though he had spent his life doing this. He put them back on, careful to hook them behind each ear, put the handkerchief back in his pocket, and asked Brunetti, in a different voice, 'What's he done now?'

'Nothing. We need to question him about someone else.'

'One of his faggot friends?' the old man asked, returning to his aggressive tone.

Brunetti ignored the question. 'We'd like to speak to Signor Feltrinelli. Perhaps he can give us some information.'

'Signor Feltrinelli? Signor?' the old man asked, repeating Brunetti's words but turning the formality into an insult. 'You mean Nino the Pretty Boy, Nino the Cocksucker?'

Brunetti sighed tiredly. Why couldn't people learn to be more discriminating in whom they chose to hate, a bit more selective? Perhaps even a bit more intelligent?

Why not hate the Christian Democrats? Or the Socialists? Or why not hate people who hated homosexuals?

'Could you tell me Signor Feltrinelli's apartment number?'

The ld man retreated behind his desk and sat back down to his task of sorting the mail. 'Fifth floor. The name's on the door.'

Brunetti turned and left without saying anything further. When he was at the door, he thought he heard the old man mutter, 'Signor,' but it could have been only an angry noise. On the other side of the marble-floored hallway, he pushed the button for the elevator and stood waiting for it. After a few minutes, the elevator still had not come, but Brunetti refused to go back to ask the *portiere* if it was working. Instead, he moved over to the left, opened a door to the stairs, and climbed to the fifth floor. By the time he reached it, he had to loosen his tie and pull the cloth of his trousers away from his thighs, where it clung wetly. At the top, he pulled out his handkerchief and wiped at his face.

As the old man had said, the name was on the door: 'Giovanni Feltrinelli – Architetto'.

He glanced at his watch: 11.35. He rang the bell. In immediate response, he heard quick footsteps approach the door. It was opened by a young man who bore a faint resemblance to the police photo Brunetti had studied the night before: short blond hair, a squared and masculine jaw, and soft dark eyes.

'*Si*?' he said, looking up at Brunetti with a friendly smile of enquiry.

'Signor Giovanni Feltrinelli?' Brunetti asked, holding out his warrant card.

The young man barely glanced at the card, but he seemed to recognize it immediately, and that recognition wiped the smile from his face.

'Yes. What do you want?' His voice was as cool as his smile had become.

'I'd like to talk to you, Signor Feltrinelli. May I come in?'

'Why bother to ask?' Feltrinelli said tiredly and opened the door wider, stepping back to let Brunetti enter.

'*Permesso*,' Brunetti said and stepped inside. Perhaps the title on the door didn't lie: the apartment had the symmetrical look of a living space that had been planned with skill and precision. The living-room into which Brunetti walked was painted a flat white, the floor a light herring-bone parquet. A few kelims, colours muted with age, lay on the floor, and two other woven pieces – Brunetti thought they might be Persian – hung on the walls. The sofa was long and low, set back against the far wall, and appeared to be covered in beige silk. In front of it stood a long glass-topped table with a wide ceramic platter placed on one side. One wall was covered with a bookshelf, another with framed architectural renderings of buildings and photographs of completed buildings, all of them low, spacious, and surrounded by wide expanses of rough terrain. In the far corner stood a high draughting table, surface tilted to face the room and covered with outsized sheets of tissue paper. A cigarette

burned in an ashtray which perched at a crazy angle on the slanted surface of the draughting table.

The symmetry of the room kept pulling the viewer's eye back to its centre, to that simple ceramic platter. Brunetti sensed strongly that this was being done, but he didn't understand how it had been achieved.

'Signor Feltrinelli,' he began, 'I'd like to ask you to help us, if you can, in an investigation.'

Feltrinelli said nothing.

'I'd like you to look at a picture of a man and tell us if you know him or recognize him.'

Feltrinelli walked over to the draughting table and picked up the cigarette. He drew hungrily at it, then crushed it out in the ashtray with a nervous gesture. 'I don't give names,' he said.

'Excuse me?' Brunetti asked, understanding him but not wanting to show that he did.

'I don't give the names of my clients. You can show me all the pictures you want, but I won't recognize any of them, and I don't know any names.'

'I'm not asking you about your clients, Signor Feltrinelli,' Brunetti said. 'And I'm not interested in who they are. We have reason to believe that you might know something about this man, and we'd like you to take a look at the sketch and tell us if you recognize him.'

Feltrinelli walked away from the table and went to stand beside a small window in the wall on the left, and Brunetti realized why the room had been constructed the way it had: the whole purpose was to draw attention

65

away from that window and from the bleak brick wall that stood only two metres from it. 'And if I don't?' Feltrinelli asked.

'If you don't what, recognize him?'

'No. If I don't look at the picture?'

There was no air-conditioning and no fan in the room, and it reeked of cheap cigarettes, an odour which Brunetti imagined he could feel sinking into his damp clothing, into his hair. 'Signor Feltrinelli, I am asking you to do your duty as a citizen, to help the police in the investigation of a murder. We are seeking merely to identify this man. Until we do, there is no way we can begin that investigation.'

'Is he the one you found out in that field yesterday?'

'Yes.'

'And you think he might be one of us?' There was no need for Feltrinelli to explain who 'us' were.

'Yes.'

'Why?'

'It's not necessary for you to know that.'

'But you think he's a transvestite?'

'Yes.'

'And a whore?'

'Perhaps,' Brunetti answered.

Feltrinelli turned away from the window and came across the room towards Brunetti. He extended his hand. 'Let me see the picture.'

Brunetti opened the folder in his hand and drew a Xerox copy of the artist's sketch from it. He noticed that the damp palm of his hand had been stained a bright

66

blue by the dye of the paper cover of the folder. He handed the sketch to Feltrinelli, who looked at it carefully for a moment, then used his other hand to cover the hairline and study it again. He handed it back to Brunetti and shook his head. 'No, I've never seen him before.'

Brunetti believed him. He put the photo back into the folder. 'Can you think of anyone who might be able to help us find out who this man is?'

'I assume you're checking through a list of those of us with arrest records,' Feltrinelli said, voice no longer so confrontational.

'Yes. We don't have a way to get anyone else to look at the picture.'

'You mean the ones who haven't been arrested yet, I suppose,' Feltrinelli said and then asked, 'Do you have another one of those drawings?'

Brunetti pulled one from the folder and handed it to him and then handed him one of his cards. 'You'll have to call the Questura in Mestre, but you can ask for me. Or for Sergeant Gallo.'

'How was he killed?'

'It will be in this morning's papers.'

'I don't read the papers.'

'He was beaten to death.'

'In the field?'

'I'm not at liberty to tell you that, Signore.'

Feltrinelli went and placed the drawing face up on the draughting table and lit another cigarette.

'All right,' he said, turning back to Brunetti. 'I've got

the drawing. I'll show it to some people. If I find out anything, I'll let you know.'

'Are you an architect, Signor Feltrinelli?'

'Yes. I mean I have the *laurea d'architettura*. But I'm not working. I mean I have no job.'

Nodding towards the tissue paper on the drawing-board, Brunetti asked, 'But are you working on a project?'

'Just to amuse myself, Commissario. I lost my job.'

'I'm sorry to hear that, Signore.'

Feltrinelli put both hands in his pockets and looked up at Brunetti's face. Keeping his voice absolutely neutral, he said, 'I was working in Egypt, for the government, designing public-housing projects. But then they decided that all foreigners had to have an AIDS test every year. I failed mine last year, so they fired me and sent me back.'

Brunetti said nothing to this, and Feltrinelli continued, 'When I got back here, I tried to find a job, but, as you surely know, architects are as easily found as grapes at harvest time. And so . . .' He paused here, as if in search of a way to put it. 'And so I decided to change my profession.'

'Are you referring to prostitution?' Brunetti asked.

'Yes, I am.'

'You're not concerned about the hazard?'

'Hazard?' Feltrinelli asked, and came close to repeating the smile he had given Brunetti when he opened the door. Brunetti said nothing. 'You mean AIDS?' Feltrinelli asked, unnecessarily.

'Yes.'

'There's no hazard for me,' Feltrinelli said and turned away from Brunetti. He went back to the draughting table and picked up his cigarette. 'You can let yourself out, Commissario,' he said, taking his place at the table and bending down over his drawing.

Chapter Eight

Brunetti emerged into the sun, the street, the noise and turned into a bar that stood to the right of the apartment building. He asked for a glass of mineral water, then for a second one. When he had almost finished that, he poured the water at the bottom of the glass on to his handkerchief and wiped futilely at the blue dye on his hand.

Was it a criminal act for a prostitute with AIDS to have sex? Unprotected sex? It was so long since policemen had treated prostitution as a crime that Brunetti found it difficult to consider it as such. But surely, for anyone with AIDS knowingly to have unprotected sex, surely that was a crime, though it was entirely possible that the law lagged behind the truth in this, and it was not illegal. Seeing the moral quicksand that distinction created ahead of him, he ordered a third glass of mineral water and looked at the next name on the list.

Francesco Crespo lived only four blocks from Feltrinelli, but it might as well have been a world away. The building was sleek, a tall glass-fronted rectangle which must have seemed, when it was built ten years ago, right on the cutting edge of urban design. But Italy is a country

where new ideas in design are never prized for much longer than it takes to put them into effect, by which time the ever-forward-looking have abandoned them and gone off in pursuit of gaudy new banners, like those damned souls in the vestibule of Dante's *Inferno*, who circle round for all eternity, seeking a banner they can neither identify nor name.

The decade that had elapsed since the construction of this building had carried fashion away with it, and now the building looked like nothing so much as an upended box of *spaghettini*. The glass in the windows gleamed, and a small patch of land between it and the street was manicured with precision, but none of that could save it from looking entirely out of place among the other lower, more modest buildings amidst which it had been erected with such futile confidence.

He had the apartment number and was quickly carried to the seventh floor by the air-conditioned elevator. When the door opened, Brunetti stepped out into a marble corridor, also air-conditioned. He walked to the right and rang the bell of apartment D.

He heard a sound inside, but no one came to the door. He rang again. The sound wasn't repeated, but still no one came to the door. He rang the bell a third time, keeping his finger pressed to it. Even through the door he could hear the shrill whine of the bell and then a voice calling, '*Basta. Vengo.*'

He took his finger off the bell, and a moment later the door was yanked open by a tall, heavy-set man in linen slacks and what looked like a cashmere turtle neck. Brunetti glanced at the man for an instant, saw two dark

eyes, angry eyes, and a nose that had been broken a number of times, but then his eyes fell again to the high neck of the sweater and found themselves imprisoned there. The middle of August, people collapsing on the street from the heat, and this man wore a cashmere turtle neck. He pulled his eyes back to the man's face and asked, 'Signor Crespo?'

'Who wants him?' the man asked, making no attempt to disguise both anger and menace.

'Commissario Guido Brunetti,' he answered, again showing his warrant card. This man, like Feltrinelli, needed only the slightest of glances to recognize it. He suddenly stepped a bit closer to Brunetti, perhaps hoping to force him back into the corridor with the offensive presence of his body. But Brunetti didn't move, and the other man stepped back. 'He's not here.'

From another room, both of them heard the sound of something heavy falling to the floor.

This time it was Brunetti who took a step forward, backing the other man away from the door. Brunetti continued into the room and walked over to a throne-like leather chair beside a table on which stood an immense spray of gladioli in a crystal vase. He sat in the chair, crossed his legs, and said, 'Then perhaps I'll wait for Signor Crespo.' He smiled. 'If you have no objection, Signor . . .?'

The other man slammed the front door, wheeled towards a door that stood on the other side of the room, and said, 'I'll get him.'

He disappeared into the room beyond, closing the door behind him. His voice, deep and angry, resounded

through it. Brunetti heard another voice, a tenor to the
bass. But then he heard what seemed to be a third
voice, another tenor, but a full tone higher than the last.
Whatever conversation went on behind the door took a
number of minutes, during which Brunetti looked
around the room. It was all new, it was all visibly expensive, and Brunetti would have wanted none of it, neither
the pearl grey leather sofa nor the sleek mahogany table
that stood beside it.

The door to the other room opened, and the heavy-
set man came out, followed closely by another man a
decade younger and at least three sizes smaller than him.

'That's him,' the one in the sweater said, pointing
to Brunetti.

The younger man wore loose pale-blue slacks and an
open-necked white silk shirt. He walked across the room
towards Brunetti, who stood and asked, 'Signor Francesco Crespo?'

He came and stood in front of Brunetti, but then
instinct or professional training seemed to exert itself in
the presence of a man of Brunetti's age and general
appearance. He took a small step closer, raised a hand
in a delicate, splay-fingered gesture, and placed it at the
base of his throat. 'Yes, what would you like?' It was
the higher tenor voice Brunetti had heard through the
door, but Crespo tried to make it deeper, as if that would
make it more interesting or seductive.

Crespo was a bit shorter than Brunetti and must have
weighed ten kilos less. Either through coincidence or
design, his eyes were the same pale grey as the sofa; they
stood out sharply in the deep tan of his face. Had his

73

features appeared on the face of a woman, they would have been judged no more than conventionally pretty; the sharp angularity conveyed by his masculinity made them beautiful.

This time it was Brunetti who took a small step away from the other man. He heard the other one snort at this and turned to pick up the folder, which he had placed on the table beside him.

'Signor Crespo, I'd like you to look at a picture of someone and tell me if you recognize him.'

'I'd be glad to look at anything you chose to show me,' Crespo said, putting heavy emphasis on 'you' and moving his hand inside the collar of his shirt to caress his neck.

Brunetti opened the folder and handed Crespo the artist's drawing of the dead man. Crespo glanced down at it for less than a second, looked up at Brunetti, smiled, and said, 'I haven't an idea of who he could be.' He held the picture out to Brunetti, who refused to take it.

'I'd like you to take a better look at the picture, Signor Crespo.'

'He told you he didn't know him,' the other one said from across the room.

Brunetti ignored him. 'The man was beaten to death, and we need to find out who he was, so I'd appreciate it if you'd take another look at him, Signor Crespo.'

Crespo closed his eyes for a moment and moved his hand to brush a wayward curl behind his left ear. 'If you insist,' he said, looking down at the picture again. He bowed his head down over the drawing and, this time, looked at the face pictured there. Brunetti couldn't see

his eyes, but he did watch his hand suddenly move away from his ear and move towards his neck again, this time with no attempt at flirtatiousness.

A second later, he looked up at Brunetti, smiled sweetly, and said, 'I've never seen him before, officer.'

'Are you satisfied?' the other one asked and took a step towards the door.

Brunetti took the drawing that Crespo held out to him and slipped it back into the folder. 'That's only an artist's guess of what he looked like, Signor Crespo. I'd like you to look at a photograph of him, if you don't mind.'

Brunetti smiled his most seductive smile, and Crespo's hand flew, with a swallow-like flutter, back to the soft hollow between his collar bones. 'Of course, officer. Anything you suggest. Anything.'

Brunetti smiled and reached to the bottom of the thin pile of photos in the folder. He took one out and studied it for an instant. One would serve as well as the next. He looked at Crespo, who had again closed the distance between them. 'There is a possibility that he was killed by a man who was paying for his services. That means men like him might be at risk from the same person.' He offered the photo to Crespo.

The young man took the photo, managing to touch Brunetti's fingers with his own as he did so. He held it in the air between them, gave Brunetti a long smile, and then bowed his smiling face over the photo. His hand left his neck and slid up to cover his gasping mouth. 'No, no,' he said, eyes still on the photo. 'No, no,' he repeated and looked up at Brunetti with eyes gone wide with

75

horror. He thrust the picture away from him, jammed it into Brunetti's chest, and backed away from him, as though Brunetti had carried pollution into the room with him. 'They can't do that to me. That won't happen to me,' he said, backing away from Brunetti. His voice rose with every word, teetered on the edge of hysteria, and then fell over into it. 'No, that won't happen to me. Nothing will ever happen to me.' His voice rose up into a high-pitched challenge to the world he lived in. 'Not to me, not to me,' he shouted, backing further and further away from Brunetti. He bumped into a table in the middle of the room, panicked at finding himself blocked in his attempt to get away from the photo and the man who had shown it to him, and lashed out at it with his arm. A vase identical to the one near Brunetti crashed to the floor.

The door to the other room opened, and a fourth man came quickly into the room. 'What's wrong?' he asked. 'What's going on?'

He looked towards Brunetti, and they recognized one another instantly. Giancarlo Santomauro was not only one of the best known lawyers in Venice, often serving as legal counsel to the Patriarch at no cost, but he was also the president and moving light of the Lega della Moralità, a society of lay Christians dedicated to the 'preservation and perpetuation of faith, home, and virtue'.

Brunetti did no more than nod. If by any chance these men didn't know the identity of Crespo's client, it was better for the lawyer that it remain that way.

'What are you doing here?' Santomauro demanded

76

angrily. He turned to the older of the two men, now standing above Crespo, who had ended on a sofa, both hands over his face, sobbing. 'Can't you shut him up?' Santomauro shouted. Brunetti watched as the older man bent over Crespo. He said something to him, then put both hands on his shoulders and shook him till his head wove back and forth. Crespo stopped crying, but his hands remained over his face.

'What are you doing in this apartment, Commissario? I'm Signor Crespo's legal representative, and I refuse to permit the police to continue to brutalize him.'

Brunetti didn't answer but continued to study the pair at the sofa. The older man moved to sit beside Crespo and put a protective arm around his shoulders, and Crespo gradually grew quiet.

'I asked you a question, Commissario,' Santomauro said.

'I came to ask Signor Crespo if he could help us identify the victim of a crime. I showed him a photo of the man. You see his response. Rather strong way to respond to the death of a man he didn't recognize, wouldn't you say?'

The man in the sweater looked at Brunetti but it was Santomauro who spoke. 'If Signor Crespo has said he didn't recognize him, then you have your answer and can leave.'

'Of course,' Brunetti said, tucking the folder under his right arm and taking a step towards the door. Glancing back at Santomauro, voice easy and conversational, Brunetti said, 'You forgot to tie your shoes, Avvocato.'

Santomauro looked down and saw immediately that

77

they were both tied neatly. He gave Brunetti a look that would have etched glass but said nothing.

Brunetti stopped in front of the sofa and looked down at Crespo. 'My name is Brunetti,' he said. 'If you remember anything, you can call me at the Questura in Venice.'

Santomauro started to speak but cut himself short. Brunetti let himself out of the apartment.

Chapter Nine

The rest of the day was no more productive, neither for Brunetti nor for the two other policemen working their way down the list. When they met back at the Questura late in the afternoon, Gallo reported that three of the men on his part of the list said they had no idea of who the man was. They were probably telling the truth, two others weren't home, and another said he thought the man looked familiar but couldn't remember why or how. Scarpa's experience had been much the same; all of the men he spoke to were sure they had never seen the dead man.

They agreed that they would try the same approach the next day, trying to finish up the names on the list. Brunetti asked Gallo to prepare a second list of the female whores who worked both out by the factories and on Via Cappuccina. Though he didn't have much hope that these women would help, there was always the possibility that they had paid attention to the competition and would recognize the man.

As Brunetti climbed the steps to his apartment, he fantasized about what would happen when he opened the door. Magically, elves would have come in during the

day and air-conditioned the entire place; others would have installed one of those showers he had seen only in brochures from spas and on American soap operas: twenty different shower heads would direct needle-thin streams of scented water at his body, and when he finished with the shower, he would wrap himself in a thick towel of imperial size. And then there would be a bar, perhaps the sort set at the end of a swimming pool, and a white-jacketed barman would offer him a long, cool drink with a hibiscus floating on its surface. His immediate physical needs attended to, he passed to science fiction and conjured up two children both dutiful and obedient and a devoted wife who would tell him, the instant he opened the door, that the case had been solved and they were all free to leave for vacation the following morning.

Reality, as is ever its wont, was discovered to be somewhat different. His family had retreated to the terrace which was filled with the first cool of early evening. Chiara looked up from her book, said '*Ciao*, Papà,' tilted her chin to receive his kiss, and then dived back into the pages. Raffi looked up from that month's issue of *Gente Uomo*, repeated Chiara's greeting, and then himself dived back to a consideration of the compelling need for linen. Paola, seeing his state, got to her feet, put her arms around him, and kissed him on the lips.

'Guido, go take a shower, and I'll get you something to drink.' A bell pealed out, somewhere to the left of them, Raffi flipped a page, and Brunetti reached up to loosen his tie.

'Put a hibiscus in it,' he said and turned to go take his shower.

Twenty minutes later, he sat, dressed in loose cotton pants and a linen shirt, with his bare feet up on the railing of the terrace, and told Paola about the day. The children had disappeared, no doubt off in pursuit of some dutiful and obedient activity.

'Santomauro?' she asked. 'Giancarlo Santomauro?'

'The very one.'

'How delicious,' she said, voice rich with real delight. 'I wish I'd never had to promise you I wouldn't talk about what you tell me; this one is wonderful.' And she repeated Santomauro's name.

'You don't tell people, do you, Paola?' he asked, though he knew he shouldn't.

She started to shoot back an angry answer, but then she leaned over and put her hand on his knee. 'No, Guido. I've never repeated anything. And never will.'

'I'm sorry I asked,' he said, looking down and sipping at his Campari soda.

'Do you know his wife?' she asked, veering back to the original topic.

'I think I was introduced to her once, at a concert somewhere, a couple of years ago. But I don't think I'd remember her if I saw her again. What's she like?'

Paola sipped at her drink, then placed the glass on the top of the railing, something she was repeatedly forbidding the children to do. 'Well,' she began, considering how most acidly to answer the question. 'If I were Signor, no, Avvocato Santomauro and I were given the choice between my tall, thin, impeccably well-

dressed wife, she of the Margaret Thatcher *coiffure*, to make no mention of disposition, and a young boy, regardless of his height, hair or disposition, there is no doubt that my arms would reach out and embrace that boy.'

'How do you know her?' Brunetti asked, as ever ignoring the rhetoric and attending to the substance.

'She's a client of Biba's,' she said, naming a friend of hers who was a jeweller. 'I've met her a few times in the shop, and then I met them at my parents' place at one of those dinners you didn't go to.' Figuring that this was a way of getting back at him for having asked if she told people what he said to her, Brunetti let it pass.

'What are they like together?'

'She does all the talking, and he just stands around and glowers, as if there were nothing and no one within a radius of ten kilometres who could ever possibly measure up to his high standards. I always thought they were a pair of sanctimonious, self-important bigots. All I had to do was listen to her talk for five minutes, and I knew it: she's like a minor character in a Dickens novel, one of the pious, malevolent ones. Because she did all the talking, I was never sure about him, had to go on instinct, but I'm very pleased to learn that I was right.'

'Paola,' he cautioned, 'I have no reason to believe he was there for any other reason than to give Crespo legal advice.'

'And he had to take his shoes off to do that?' she asked with a snort of disbelief. 'Guido, please come back to this century, all right? Avvocato Santomauro was there for one reason only, and it had nothing to do with

his profession, not unless he has worked out a very interesting payment plan for Signor Crespo.'

Paola, he had learned over the course of more than two decades, had the tendency to Go Too Far. He was uncertain, even after all this time, whether this was a vice or a virtue, but there was no doubt that it was an irremovable part of her character. She even got a certain wild look in her eye when she was planning to Go Too Far, which look he saw there now. He had no idea what form it would take, but he knew it was coming.

'Do you think he's arranged the same payment plan for the Patriarch?'

In those same decades, he had also learned that the only way to deal with her tendency was to ignore her completely. 'As I was saying,' Brunetti continued, 'the fact that he was in the apartment proves nothing.'

'I hope you're right, or I'd have to worry every time I saw him coming out of the Patriarchal Palace or the Basilica, wouldn't I?'

He did no more than glance in her direction.

'All right, Guido, he was there on business, legal business.' She allowed a few moments to pass and then added, in a completely different voice, so as to alert him that she was now going to behave and treat this seriously, 'But you said that Crespo recognized the man in the picture.'

'I think he did, the first time, but by the time he looked up at me, he'd had a second to recover, so his expression was perfectly natural.'

'Then the man in the picture could be anyone, couldn't he? Another whore, even a client? Have you

thought about that, Guido, that he might be a client who likes to dress up as a woman when he, well, when he goes to see these other men?'

In the sexual supermarket that was modern society, Brunetti knew, the man's age made him far more likely to be a shopper than a seller. 'That means we'd be looking for a man who used male prostitutes, rather than a man who was one,' he said.

Paola took her drink, swirled it around a few times, and finished it. 'Well, that would surely be a longer list. And, considering what you've just told me about l'Avvocato del Patriarcato, a far more interesting one.'

'Is this another one of your conspiracy theories, Paola, that the city is filled with seemingly happily married men who can't wait to sneak off into the bushes with one of these transvestites?'

'For God's sake, Guido, what do you men talk about when you're together? Soccer? Politics? Don't you ever hunker down and gossip?'

'About what? The boys on Via Cappuccina?' He put his glass down with unnecessary force and scratched at his ankle, where one of the night's first mosquitoes had just bit him.

'I guess it's because you don't have gay friends,' she said equably.

'We have lots of gay friends,' he said, conscious of the fact that it was only in an argument with Paola that he could be forced to make that statement as a claim to honour.

'Of course we have, but you don't talk to them, Guido, really talk to them.'

'What am I supposed to do, swap recipes or divulge my beauty secrets?'

She started to speak, stopped, gave him a long look, and then said, voice absolutely level, 'I'm not sure if that remark is more offensive than stupid.'

He scratched at his ankle, thought about what they had both just said. 'I suppose it was more stupid, but it was pretty offensive, too.' She gave him a suspicious glance. 'I'm sorry,' he added. She smiled.

'All right, tell me what I ought to know about this,' he asked, scratching again at his ankle.

'What I was trying to tell you was that some of the gays I know say that a lot of the men here are perfectly willing to have sex with them: family men, married men, doctors, lawyers, priests. I imagine there's a great deal of exaggeration in what they tell me, and not a little vanity, but I also imagine there's a great deal of truth, as well.' He thought she was finished, but she added, 'As a policeman, you've probably heard something about this, but I'd suspect that most men wouldn't want to hear it. Or, if they hear it, not want to believe it.' She seemed not to be including him in this list, but, of course, there was no way of being sure about that.

'Who is your chief source of information in all of this?' he asked.

'Ettore and Basilio,' she said, naming two of her colleagues at the university. 'And some of Raffi's friends have said the same thing.'

'What?'

'Two of Raffi's friends at the *liceo*. Don't look so surprised, Guido. They're both seventeen.'

'They're both seventeen and *what*?'

'And gay, Guido. Gay.'

'Are they close friends?' he asked before he could prevent himself.

Suddenly, Paola got to her feet. 'I'm going to put the water on for the pasta. I think I might want to wait until after dinner to continue this discussion. That might give you some time to think about some of the things you've said and some of the assumptions you seem to be making.' She picked up her glass, took his from his hand, and went back into the house, leaving him to think about his assumptions.

Dinner was far more peaceful than he had thought it would be, given the abruptness with which Paola had departed to prepare it. She had made a sauce with fresh tuna fish, tomatoes, and peppers, something he was sure she had never made before, and had used the thick Martelli spaghetti he liked so much. After that, there was salad, a piece of *pecorino* that Raffi's girlfriend's parents had brought back from Sardinia, and then fresh peaches. Responding to his fantasy, the children offered to do the dishes, no doubt in preparation for their planned depredations upon his wallet before their departure for the mountains.

He retreated to the terrace, a small glass of chilled vodka in his hand, and resumed his seat. In the air above and all around him, bats swirled, cutting the sky with their jagged flight. Brunetti liked bats: they gobbled up mosquitoes. After a few minutes, Paola joined him. He

offered her the glass and she took a small sip. 'Is that the bottle in the freezer?' she asked.

He nodded.

'Where'd you get it?'

'I suppose you could call it a bribe.'

'From whom?'

'Donzelli. He asked me if I could arrange the vacation schedule so that he could go to Russia – ex-Russia – on leave. He brought me a bottle when he came back.'

'It's still Russia.'

'Hm?'

'It's the ex-Soviet Union, but it's still plain old Russia.'

'Oh. Thank you.'

She nodded in acknowledgement.

'Do you think they eat anything else?' he asked.

'Who?' Paola asked, for once at a loss.

'The bats.'

'I don't know. Ask Chiara. She generally knows things like that.'

'I've been thinking about what I said before dinner,' he said, sipping again at his glass.

He expected a sharp retort from her, but all she said was, 'Yes?'

'I think you might be right.'

'About what?'

'That he might be a client and not one of the whores. I saw his body. I don't think it's a body that a man would want to pay to use.'

'What sort of body was it?'

He took another sip. 'This is going to sound strange, but when I saw him, I thought how much he looked like

87

me. We're about the same height, same general build, probably the same age. It was very strange, Paola, to see him lying there, dead.'

'Yes, it must have been,' she said, but she didn't say any more than that.

'Are those boys good friends of Raffi's?'

'One of them is. He helps him with his Italian homework.'

'Good.'

'Good what, that he helps him with his homework?'

'No, good that he's Raffi's friend, or that Raffi's his.'

She laughed out loud and shook her head. 'I will never figure you out, Guido. Never.' She placed a hand on the back of his neck, leaned forward, and took the drink from his hand. She took another sip and then handed it back to him. 'You think when you're finished with this, you could think about letting me pay to use your body?'

Chapter Ten

The next two days were much the same, only hotter. Four of the men on Brunetti's list were still not at the addresses listed for them, nor did the neighbours of either have any idea of where they might be or when they might return. Two knew nothing. Gallo and Scarpa had as little luck, though one of the men on Scarpa's list did say that the man in the drawing looked faintly familiar, only he wasn't sure why or where he might have seen him.

The three men had lunch together in a trattoria near the Questura and discussed what they did and didn't know.

'Well, he didn't know how to shave his legs,' Gallo said, when they seemed to have run out of things to list. Brunetti didn't know if the sergeant was attempting humour or grasping at straws.

'Why do you say that?' Brunetti asked, finishing his wine and looking around for the waiter so he could ask for the bill.

'His corpse. There were lots of little nicks on his legs, as if he wasn't too accustomed to shaving them.'

'Would any of us be?' Brunetti asked, and then clarified the pronoun, 'Men, I mean.'

Scarpa smiled into his glass. 'I'd probably cut my kneecap off. I don't know how they do it,' he said, and shook his head at yet another of the wonders of women.

The waiter came up then with the bill. Sergeant Gallo took it before Brunetti could, pulled out his wallet, and laid some money on top of the bill. Before Brunetti could object, he explained, 'We've been told you're a guest of the city.' Brunetti wondered how Patta would feel about such a thing, aside from believing that he didn't deserve it.

'We've exhausted the names on the list,' Brunetti said. 'I think that means we've got to talk to the ones who aren't on the list.'

'Do you want me to bring some of them in, sir?' Gallo asked.

Brunetti shook his head: that was hardly the best way to encourage them to co-operate. 'No, I think the best thing is to go and talk to them—'

Scarpa interrupted. 'But we haven't got names and addresses for most of them.'

'Then I suppose I'll have to go visit them where they work,' Brunetti explained.

Via Cappuccina is a broad, tree-lined street that runs from a few blocks to the right of the Mestre train station into the commercial heart of the city. It is lined with shops and small stores, offices and some blocks of apartment buildings; by day, it is a normal street in an entirely normal small Italian city. Children play under the trees

and in the small parks that are to be found along its length. Their mothers are generally with them, to warn them about the cars and the traffic, but they are also there to warn them about and keep them safe from some of the other people who gravitate towards Via Cappuccina. The shops close at twelve-thirty, and Via Cappuccina rests for a few hours in the early afternoon. Traffic decreases, the children go home for lunch and a nap; businesses close, and the adults go home to eat and rest. There are fewer children playing in the afternoon, though the traffic returns, and Via Cappuccina fills up with life and motion, as shops and offices reopen.

Between seven-thirty and eight o'clock in the evening, the shops, offices, and stores close down; the merchants and owners pull down metal shutters, lock them securely, and go home for their evening meal, leaving Via Cappuccina to those who work along it after they leave.

During the evening, there is still traffic on Via Cappuccina, but no one seems any longer to be in much of a hurry. Cars move along slowly, but parking is no longer a problem, for it is not parking spaces that the drivers are seeking. Italy has become a wealthy nation, so most of the cars are air-conditioned. Because of this, the traffic is even slower, for the windows must now be lowered before a price can be called out or heard, and thus things take more time.

Some of the cars are new and slick: BMWs, Mercedes, the occasional Ferrari, though they are oddities on Via Cappuccina. Most of the cars are sedate, well-fed sedans, cars for families, the car that takes the children to school

91

in the morning, the car that takes the family to church on Sunday and then out to the grandparents' house for dinner. They are generally driven by men who feel more comfortable wearing a suit and tie than anything else, men who have done well as a result of the economic boom that has been so generous to Italy during the last decades.

With increasing frequency, doctors who deliver babies in the private wards and clinics of Italy, those used by people wealthy enough to avail themselves of private medical care, have had to tell new mothers that both they and their babies are infected with the AIDS virus. Most of these women respond with stupefaction, for these are women faithful to their marriage vows. The answer, they believe, must lie in some hideous error in the medical treatment they have received. But perhaps the answer is more easily to be found on Via Cappuccina and the dealings that take place between the drivers of those sober cars and the men and women who crowd the sidewalks.

Brunetti turned into Via Cappuccina at eleven-thirty that night, walking down from the train station, where he had arrived a few minutes before. He had gone home for dinner, slept for an hour, then dressed himself in what he thought would make him look like something other than a policeman. Scarpa had had smaller copies made of both the drawing and the photographs of the dead man, and Brunetti carried some of these in the inner pocket of his blue linen jacket.

From behind him and off to his right, he could hear the faint hum of traffic as cars continued to stream past

on the *tangenziale* of the autostrada. Though he knew it was unlikely, Brunetti felt as though their fumes were all being blown down here, so dense and tight was the breezeless air. He crossed a street, another, and then another, and then he began to notice the traffic. There were the cars, gliding along slowly, windows raised, heads turned to the kerb as the drivers inspected the other traffic.

Brunetti saw that he was not the only pedestrian here, but he was one of very few wearing a shirt and tie, and he seemed to be the only one not standing still.

'*Ciao, bello.*'

'*Cosa vuoi, amore?*'

'*Ti faccio tutto che vuoi, caro.*'

The offers came at him from almost every form he passed, offers of delight, joy, bliss. The voices suggested undreamed of pleasures, promised him the realization of every fantasy. He paused under a street light and was immediately approached by a tall blonde in a white miniskirt and very little else.

'Fifty thousand,' she said. She smiled, as if that would serve as greater inducement. The smile showed her teeth.

'I want a man,' Brunetti said.

She turned away without a word and walked towards the kerb. She leaned towards a passing Audi and called out the same price. The car kept moving. Brunetti stayed where he was, and she turned back towards him. 'Forty,' she said.

'I want a man.'

'They cost a lot more, and there's nothing they can do

93

for you that I can't, *bello*.' She showed him her teeth again.

'I want them to look at a picture,' Brunetti said.

'*Gesù Bambino*,' she muttered under her breath, 'not one of those.' Then, louder, 'It'll cost you extra. With them. I do everything for one price.'

'I want them to look at the picture of a man and tell me if they recognize him.'

'Police?' she asked.

He nodded.

'I thought so,' she said. 'They're up the street, the boys, on the other side of Piazzale Leonardo da Vinci.'

'Thank you,' Brunetti said and continued walking up the street. At the next kerb, he looked back and saw the blonde climbing into the passenger seat of a dark blue Volvo.

Another few minutes brought him to the open Piazzale. He crossed it, having no trouble making his way between the crawling cars, and saw a cluster of forms leaning up against a low wall on the other side.

As he drew near, he heard more voices, tenor voices, call out the same offers and promise the same pleasures. So much bliss to be had here.

He approached the group and saw much that he had seen while walking from the station: mouths made larger by red lipstick and all turned up in smiles meant to be inviting; clouds of bleached hair; legs, thighs, and bosoms which looked every bit as real as those he had seen before.

Two of them came and fluttered around him, moths to the flame of his power to pay.

'Anything you want, sweetie. No rubbers. Just the real thing.'

'My car's around the corner, *caro*. You name it, I'll do it.'

From the pack leaning against the low wall that ran along one side of the Piazzale, a voice called out to the second one, 'Ask him if he'd like you both, Paolina.' Then, to Brunetti directly, 'They're fabulous if you take them together, *amore*; make you a sandwich you'll never forget.' That was enough to set the others off into peals of laughter, laughter that was deep and had nothing of the feminine in it.

Brunetti spoke to the one called Paolina. 'I'd like you to look at a picture of a man and tell me if you recognize him.'

Paolina turned back to the group and shouted, 'It's a cop, little girls. And he wants me to look at some pictures.'

A chorus of shouts came back: 'Tell him the real thing's better than dirty pictures, Paolina.' 'Cops don't even know the difference.' 'A cop? Make him pay double.'

Brunetti waited until they had run out of things to say and asked, 'Will you look at the picture?'

'What's in it for me if I do?' Paolina asked, and his companion laughed to see his friend being so tough with a policeman.

'It's a picture of the man we found out in the field on Monday.' Before Paolina could pretend ignorance, Brunetti added, 'I'm sure you all know about him and what happened to him. We'd like to identify him so we

can find the person who killed him. I think you men can understand why that's important.'

He noticed that Paolina and his friend were dressed almost identically, each in tight tube tops and short skirts that showed sleek, muscular legs. Both wore high-heeled shoes with needle toes; neither could ever hope to outrun an assailant.

Paolina's friend, whose daffodil-yellow wig cascaded to his shoulders, said, 'All right, let's see it,' and held out his hand. Though the man's feet were disguised in those shoes, nothing could disguise the breadth and thickness of his hand.

Brunetti pulled the drawing from his pocket and handed it to him. 'Thank you, Signore,' Brunetti said. The man gave him an uncomprehending look, as though Brunetti had begun to speak in tongues. The two men bent over the drawing, talking together in what Brunetti thought might be Sardinian dialect.

The blonde held the drawing out towards Brunetti. 'No, I don't recognize him. This the only picture you've got of him?'

'Yes,' Brunetti answered, then asked, 'Would you mind asking your friends if they recognize him?' He nodded towards the group that still hung back against the wall, tossing occasional remarks at passing cars but keeping their eyes on Brunetti and the two men.

'Sure. Why not?' Paolina's friend turned back towards the group. Paolina followed him, perhaps nervous at the risk of spending time alone in the company of a policeman.

The group peeled itself away from the wall to walk

towards them. The one with the drawing stumbled and caught himself from falling only by clutching on to Paolina's shoulder. He swore viciously. The group of bright-coloured men crowded round them, and Brunetti watched as they handed the drawing round. One of them, a tall, gangly boy in a red wig, let the picture go, then suddenly grabbed it back and looked at it again. He pulled at another man, pointed down towards the picture, and said something to him. The second one shook his head, and the redhead jabbed at the picture again. The other one still did not agree, and the redhead dismissed him with an angry flip of his hand. The picture was passed around to a few more of them, and then Paolina's friend came back to Brunetti with the redhead walking at his side.

'*Buona sera*,' Brunetti said as the redhead came up. He held out his hand and said, 'Guido Brunetti.'

The two men stood as if rooted to the spot by their high heels. Paolina's friend glanced down at his skirt and wiped his hand nervously across its front. The redhead put his hand to his mouth for a moment and then extended it to Brunetti. 'Roberto Canale,' he said. 'Pleased to meet you.' His grip was firm, his hand warm.

Brunetti held out his hand to the other, who glanced nervously back to the group and, hearing nothing, took Brunetti's hand and shook it. 'Paolo Mazza.'

Brunetti turned back to the redhead. 'Do you recognize the man in the photo, Signor Canale?' Brunetti asked.

The redhead looked off to the side until Mazza said,

'He's talking to you, Roberta, don't you even remember your name?'

'Of course I remember my name,' the redhead said, turning angrily to Mazza. Then, to Brunetti, 'Yes, I recognize the man, but I can't tell you who he is. I can't even tell you why I recognize him. He just looks like someone I know.'

Realizing how inadequate this must sound, Canale explained, 'You know how it is when you see the man from the cheese store on the street, and he's not wearing his apron: you know him but you don't know how you know him, and you can't remember who he is. You know that you know him, but he's out of place, so you can't remember who he is. That's how it is with the man in the drawing. I know I know him, or I've seen him, the same way you see the man in the cheese store, but I can't remember where he's supposed to be.'

'Is he supposed to be here?' Brunetti asked. When Canale gave him an empty look, he explained, 'Here on Via Cappuccina? Is this where you'd expect to see him?'

'No, no. Not at all. That's what's so strange about it. Wherever it was I saw him, it didn't have anything to do with all of this.' He waved his hands in the air, as if seeking the answer there. 'It's like I saw one of my teachers here. Or the doctor. He's not supposed to be here. It's just a feeling, but it's very strong,' Then, seeking confirmation, he asked Brunetti, 'Do you understand what I mean?'

'Yes, I do. Perfectly. I once had a man stop me on the street in Rome and say hello to me. I knew I knew him,

but I didn't know why.' Brunetti smiled, risking it. 'I'd arrested him two years before. But in Naples.'

Luckily, both men laughed. Canale said, 'May I keep the picture? Maybe it will come back to me if I can, you know, look at it every once in a while. Maybe that will surprise me into remembering.'

'Certainly. I appreciate your help,' Brunetti said.

It was Mazza's turn to risk. 'Was he very bad? When you found him?' He brought his hands together in front of him, one clutching at the other.

Brunetti nodded.

'Isn't it enough they want to fuck us?' Canale broke in. 'Why do they want to kill us, too?'

Though the question was addressed to powers well beyond those for whom Brunetti worked, he still answered it. 'I have no idea.'

Chapter Eleven

The next day, Friday, Brunetti thought he had better make an appearance at the Venice Questura to see what paperwork and mail had accumulated for him. Furthermore, he admitted to Paola over coffee that morning, he wanted to see if there was anything new on 'Il Caso Patta'.

'Nothing in *Gente* or *Oggi*,' she contributed, naming the two most famous gossip magazines, then added, 'though I'm not sure that Signora Patta rates the attention of either.'

'Don't let her hear you say that,' Brunetti warned, laughing.

'If I'm a lucky woman, Signora Patta will never hear me say anything.' More amiably, she asked, 'What do you think Patta will do?'

Brunetti finished his coffee and set his cup down before he answered. 'I don't think there's very much he can do except wait for Burrasca to get tired of her or for her to get tired of Burrasca and come back.'

'What's he like, Burrasca?' Paola didn't waste time asking if the police had a file on Burrasca. As soon as

anyone in Italy made enough money, someone would have a file.

'From what I've heard, he's a pig. He's part of that Milano world of cocaine, cars with fast engines, and girls with slow brains.'

'Well, he's got half of one of them this time,' Paola said.

'What do you mean?'

'Signora Patta. She's not a girl, but she's certainly got a slow brain.'

'Do you know her that well?' Brunetti was never sure whom Paola knew. Or what.

'No, I'm simply inferring it from the fact that she married Patta and stayed married to him. I imagine it would be difficult to put up with a pompous ass like that.'

'But you put up with me,' Brunetti said, smiling, in search of a compliment.

Her look was level. 'You're not pompous, Guido. At times you're difficult, and sometimes you're impossible, but you are not pompous.' No compliments here.

He pushed himself back from the table, feeling that it was perhaps time to go to the Questura.

When he got to his office, he looked through the papers waiting for him on his desk, disappointed to find nothing about the dead man in Mestre. He was interrupted by a knock on the door. '*Avanti*,' he called, thinking it might be Vianello with something from Mestre. Instead of the sergeant, a dark-haired young woman walked in, a sheaf of files in her right hand. She smiled across the room at him and approached his desk,

looking down at the papers in her hand and paging through them.

'Commissario Brunetti?' she asked.

'Yes.'

She pulled a few papers from one of the files and placed them on the desk in front of him. 'The men downstairs said you might want to see these, Dottore.'

'Thank you, Signorina,' he said, pulling the papers across the desk towards him.

She remained standing in front of his desk, clearly waiting to be asked who she was, perhaps too shy to introduce herself. He looked up, saw large brown eyes in an appealing full face and an explosion of bright lipstick. 'And you are?' he asked with a smile.

'Elettra Zorzi, sir. I started work last week as secretary to Vice-Questore Patta.' That would explain the new desk outside Patta's office. Patta had been going on for months, insisting that he had too much paperwork to handle by himself. And so he had managed, like a particularly industrious truffle pig, to root around in the budget long enough to find the money for a secretary.

'I'm very pleased to meet you, Signorina Zorzi,' Brunetti said. The name rang familiarly in his ear.

'I believe I'm to work for you, as well, Commissario,' she said, smiling.

Not if he knew Patta, she wouldn't. But still he said, 'That would certainly be very nice,' and glanced down at the papers she had placed on the desk.

He heard her move away and glanced up to follow her out of the door. A skirt, neither short nor long, and very, very nice legs. She turned at the door, saw him

looking at her, and smiled again. He looked down at the papers. Who would name a child Elettra? How long ago? Twenty-five years? And Zorzi; he knew lots of Zorzis, but none of them was capable of naming a daughter Elettra. The door closed behind her, and he returned his attention to the papers, but there was little of interest in them; crime seemed to be on holiday in Venice.

He went down to Patta's office but stopped in amazement when he entered the anteroom. For years, the room had held only a chipped porcelain umbrella stand and a desk covered with outdated copies of the sort of magazines generally found in dentists' offices. Today, the magazines had vanished, replaced by a computer console attached to a printer that stood on a low metal table to the left of the desk. In front of the window, in place of the umbrella stand, stood a small table, this one of wood, and on it rested a glass vase holding an enormous bouquet of orange and yellow gladioli.

Either Patta had decided to give an interview to *Architectural Digest*, or the new secretary had decided that the opulence Patta believed fitting for his office should trickle out to where worked the lower orders. As if summoned by Brunetti's thoughts, she came into the office.

'It looks very nice,' he said, smiling and gesturing around the small area with a wave of his hand.

She crossed the room and set an armful of folders on her desk, then turned to face him. 'I'm glad you like it, Commissario. It would have been impossible to work in here the way it was. Those magazines,' she added with a delicate shudder.

'The flowers are beautiful. Are they to celebrate your arrival?'

'Oh, no,' she replied blandly. 'I've given a permanent order to Fantin; they'll deliver fresh flowers every Monday and Thursday from now on.' Fantin: the most expensive florist in the city. Twice a week. A hundred times a year? She interrupted his calculations by explaining, 'Since I'm also to prepare the Vice-Questore's expense account, I thought I'd add them in as a necessary expense.'

'And will Fantin bring flowers for the Vice-Questore's office, as well?'

Her surprise seemed genuine. 'Good heavens, no. I'm certain the Vice-Questore could afford them himself. It wouldn't be right to spend the taxpayers' money like that.' She walked around the desk and flipped on the computer. 'Is there anything I can do for you, Commissario?' she asked, the issue of the flowers, apparently, settled.

'Not at the moment, Signorina,' he said as she bent over the keys.

He knocked on Patta's door and was told to enter. Though Patta sat where he always did, behind his desk, little else was the same. The surface of the desk, usually clear of anything that might suggest work, was covered with folders, reports; even a crumpled newspaper lay to one side. It was not Patta's usual *L'Osservatore Romano*, Brunetti noticed, but the just-short-of-scurrilous *La Nuova*, a paper whose large readership numbers seemed to rest on the joint proposition that people not only would do base and ignoble things but that they would

also want to read about them. Even the air-conditioning, this one of the few offices to have it, seemed not to be working.

'Sit down, Brunetti,' the Vice-Questore commanded.

As if Brunetti's glance were contagious, Patta looked at the papers on his desk and began to gather them up. He piled them one on top of the other, edges every which way, pushed them aside, and sat, his hand forgotten on top of them.

'What's happening in Mestre?' he finally asked Brunetti.

'We haven't identified the victim yet, sir. His picture has been shown to many of the transvestites who work there, but none of them has been able to recognize him.' Patta said nothing. 'One of the men I questioned said that the man looked familiar, but he couldn't give a definite identification, so it could mean anything. Or nothing. I think another one of the men I questioned, a man named Crespo, recognized him, but he insisted that he didn't. I'd like to talk to him again, but there might be problems in doing that.'

'Santomauro?' Patta asked and, for the first time in the years they had worked together, succeeded in surprising Brunetti.

'How do you know about Santomauro?' Brunetti blurted out and then added, as if to correct his sharp tone, 'sir.'

'He's called me three times,' Patta said, and then added in a voice he made lower but which was definitely intended for Brunetti to hear, 'the bastard.'

Immediately on his guard at Patta's unwonted, and

carefully planned, indiscretion, Brunetti, like a spider on its web, began to run his memory over the various strands that might connect these two men. Santomauro was a famous lawyer, his clients the businessmen and politicians of the entire Veneto region. That, if nothing else, would ordinarily have Patta grovelling at his feet. But then he remembered it: Holy Mother Church and Santomauro's Lega della Moralità, the women's branch of which was under the patronage and direction of none other than the absent Maria Lucrezia Patta. What sort of sermon about marriage, its sanctity, and its obligations had accompanied Santomauro's phone calls to the Vice-Questore?

'That's right,' Brunetti said, deciding to admit to half of what he knew, 'he's Crespo's lawyer.' If Patta chose to believe that a commissario of police found nothing strange in the fact that a lawyer of the stature of Giancarlo Santomauro was the lawyer of a transvestite whore, then it was best to allow him that belief. 'What has he told you, sir?'

'He said you harassed and terrified his client, that you were, to use his words, "unnecessarily brutal" in trying to force him to divulge information.' Patta ran one hand down the side of his jaw, and Brunetti realized it looked as though the vice-questore had not shaved that day.

'I told him, of course, that I would not listen to this sort of criticism of a commissario of police, that he could come in and file an official complaint if he wanted to.' Ordinarily a complaint of this sort, from a man of Santomauro's importance, would have Patta promising to have the offending officer disciplined, if not demoted

and transferred to Palermo for three years. And Patta would usually have done this even before asking for details. Patta continued in his role as defender of the principle that all men are equal before the law. 'I will not tolerate civilian interference with the workings of the agencies of the state.' That, Brunetti was sure, could loosely be translated to read that Patta had a private axe to grind with Santomauro and would be a willing partner to any attempt to see the other man lose face.

'Then do you think I ought to go ahead and question Crespo again, sir?'

No matter how great his immediate anger at Santomauro might be, it was too much to expect Patta to overcome the habit of decades and order a policeman to perform an action that opposed the will of a man with important political connections. 'Do whatever you think is necessary, Brunetti.'

'Is there anything else, sir?'

Patta didn't answer, so Brunetti got to his feet. 'There is one other thing, Commissario,' Patta said before Brunetti had turned to walk away.

'Yes, sir?'

'You have friends in the publishing world, don't you?' Oh, good lord, was Patta going to ask him to help? Brunetti looked past his superior's head and nodded vaguely. 'I wonder if you would mind getting in touch with them.' Brunetti cleared his throat and looked at his shoes. 'I find myself in an embarrassing situation at the moment, Brunetti, and I would prefer that it go no further than it has already.' Patta said no more than that.

'I'll do what I can, sir,' Brunetti said lamely, thinking

of his 'friends in the publishing world', two writers on financial affairs and one political columnist.

'Good,' Patta said and paused. 'I've asked that new secretary to try to get some information on his taxes.' It was not necessary for Patta to explain whose taxes he meant. 'I've asked her to give you anything she finds.' Brunetti was too surprised by this to do anything but nod.

Patta bent his head over the papers and Brunetti, reading this as a dismissal, left the office. Signorina Elettra was no longer at her desk, so Brunetti wrote a note and left it on her desk. 'Could you see what your computer tells you about the dealings of Avvocato Giancarlo Santomauro?'

He went back upstairs to his office, conscious of the heat, which he felt expanding, seeking out every corner and crevice of the building, ignoring the thick walls and the marble floors, bringing thick humidity with it, the sort that caused sheets of paper to turn up at the corners and cling to any hand that touched them. His windows were open, and he went to stand by them, but they did no more than bring new heat and humidity into the room, and, now that the tide was at its lowest, the penetrating stench of corruption that always lurked beneath the water, even here, close to the broad expanse of open water in front of San Marco. He stood by the window, sweat soaking through his slacks and shirt to his belt, and he thought of the mountains above Bolzano and of the thick down comforters under which they slept during August nights.

He went to his desk and called down to the main

office, told the officer who answered to ask Vianello to come up. A few minutes later, the older man came into the office. Usually tanned by this time of year to the ruddy brown of *bresaola*, the air-dried beef fillet that Chiara loved so much, Vianello was still his normal pale, winter self. Like most Italians of his age and background, Vianello had always believed himself immune to statistical probability. Other people died from smoking, other people's cholesterol rose from eating rich food, and it was only they who died of heart attacks because of it. He had, every Monday for years, read the 'Health' section in the *Corriere della Sera*, even though he knew that all those horrors were consequent upon the behaviour of other people only.

This spring, however, five precancerous melanomas had been dug out from his back and shoulders, and he had been warned to stay out of the sun. Like Saul on the road to Damascus, Vianello had experienced conversion, and, like Paul, he had tried to spread his particular gospel. Vianello had not, however, counted on one of the qualities basic to the Italian character: omniscience. Everyone he spoke to knew more than he did about this issue, knew more about the ozone layer, about chlorofluorocarbons and their effects upon the atmosphere. What is more, all of them, and this to a man, knew that this talk of danger from the sun was just another *bidonata*, another swindle, another trick, though no one was quite certain just what this swindle was in aid of.

When Vianello, still filled with Pauline zeal, had attempted to argue from the scars on his back, he was

told his particular case proved nothing, that all of the statistics were false; besides, it wouldn't happen to them. And he had then come to realize that most remarkable of truths about Italians: no truth existed beyond personal experience, and all evidence that contradicted personal belief was to be dismissed. And so Vianello had, unlike Paul, abandoned his mission, and had, instead, bought a tube of Protection 30, which he wore on his face all year long.

'Yes, Dottore?' he asked when he came into the office. Vianello had left his tie and jacket downstairs and wore a short-sleeved white shirt and his dark blue uniform pants. He had lost weight since the birth of his third child last year and had told Brunetti that he was trying to lose more weight and get into better shape. A man in his late forties with a new baby, he explained, had to be careful, take better care of himself. In this heat and this humidity, with the memory of those down comforters fresh in his mind, Brunetti didn't want to think about health in any way, not his own and not Vianello's.

'Have a seat, Vianello.' The officer took his usual chair, and Brunetti went around to sit behind his desk.

'What do you know about this Lega della Moralità?' Brunetti asked.

Vianello looked up at Brunetti, narrowed his eyes in an inquisitive glance but, getting no further information, sat and thought about the question for a moment, then answered.

'I don't know all that much about them. I think they meet at one of the churches: Santi Apostoli? No, that's the *catecumeni*, those people who have guitars and too

many babies. La Lega meets in private homes, I think, and in some of the parish houses and meeting rooms. They're not political, so far as I've heard. I'm not sure what they do, but from their name, it sounds like they probably sit around and talk about how good they are and how bad everyone else is.' His tone was dismissive, indicative of the contempt he would have for such foolishness.

'Do you know anyone who's a member, Vianello?'

'Me, sir? I should certainly hope not.' He smiled at this, then saw Brunetti's face. 'Oh, you're serious, eh, sir? Well, then, let me think for a minute.' He did this for the minute he named, hands clasped around one knee and face raised towards the ceiling.

'There's one person, sir, a woman in the bank. Nadia knows her better than I do. That is, she has more to do with her than I do since she takes care of the banking. But I remember one day Nadia said that she thought it was strange that such a nice woman would have anything to do with something like that.'

'Why do you think she said that?' Brunetti asked.

'What?'

'Assume that they weren't good people?'

'Well, just think about the name, sir. Lega della Moralità, as if they'd invented the stuff. They've got to be a bunch of *basibanchi* if you ask me.' With that word, Veneziano at its most pure, scoffing at people who knelt in church, bowed so low as to kiss the pew in front of them, Vianello gave yet more proof of their dialect's genius and his own good sense.

111

'Do you have any idea of how long she's been a member or how she came to join?'

'No, sir, but I could ask Nadia to find out. Why?'

Brunetti quickly explained about Santomauro's presence at Crespo's apartment and his subsequent phone calls to Patta.

'Interesting, isn't it, sir?' Vianello asked.

'Do you know him?'

'Santomauro?' Vianello asked, unnecessarily. Crespo was hardly someone he'd be likely to know.

Brunetti nodded.

'He used to be my cousin's lawyer, before he became famous. And expensive.'

'What did your cousin say about him?'

'Not all that much. He was a good lawyer, but he was always willing to push the law, to make it do what he wanted it to do.' A common enough type in Italy, Brunetti thought, where law was often written but was seldom clear.

'Anything else?' Brunetti asked.

Vianello shook his head. 'Nothing I can remember. It was years ago.' Before Brunetti could ask him to do it, Vianello said, 'I'll call my cousin and ask. He might know other people Santomauro worked for.'

Brunetti nodded his thanks. 'I'd also like to see what we can find out about this Lega: where they meet, how many of them there are, who they are, and what it is they do.' When he stopped to think about it, Brunetti found it strange that an organization so well known that it had become a common reference point for humour should, in truth, have managed to reveal so little about itself.

People knew about the Lega, but if Brunetti's own experience was anything to go by, no one had a clear idea what the Lega did.

Vianello had his notebook in his hand now and took this all down. 'Do you want me to ask questions about Signora Santomauro, as well?'

'Yes, anything you can find.'

'I think she's from Verona originally. A banking family.' He looked across at Brunetti. 'Anything else, sir?'

'Yes, that transvestite in Mestre, Francesco Crespo. I'd like you to put the word out here and see if anyone knows him or if the name means anything.'

'What has Mestre got on him, sir?'

'Nothing more than that he was arrested twice for drugs, trying to make a sale. The boys in Vice have him on their list, but he lives in an apartment on Viale Ronconi now, a very nice apartment, and I suppose that means he's moved beyond Via Cappuccina and the public gardens. And see if Gallo has come up with names for the manufacturers of the dress and the shoes.'

'I'll see what I can find out,' Vianello said, making notes for himself. 'Anything else, sir?'

'Yes. I'd like you to keep an eye on any missing person reports that come in for a man in his early forties, same description as the dead man. It's in the file. Maybe the new secretary can do something about it on her computer.'

'From what region, sir?' Vianello asked, pen poised over the page. The fact that he didn't ask about the

secretary was enough to tell Brunetti that word of her arrival had already spread.

'If she can do it, for the entire country. Also missing tourists.'

'You don't like the idea of a prostitute, sir?'

Brunetti remembered that naked body, so terribly like his own. 'No, it's not a body anyone would pay to use.'

Chapter Twelve

On Saturday morning, Brunetti accompanied his family to the train station, but it was a subdued group that got on to the Number One vaporetto at the San Silvestro stop: Paola was angry that Brunetti would not leave what she had taken to calling 'his transvestite' to come up to Bolzano at least for the first weekend of the vacation; Brunetti was angry that she wouldn't understand; Raffaele regretted leaving the virginal charms of Sara Paganuzzi behind, though he took some comfort from the fact that they would be reunited in one week's time – besides, until then, there would be fresh mushrooms to hunt for in the woods; Chiara, as was so often the case, was entirely unselfish in her regret, for she wished that her father, who always worked too hard, could get away and have a real vacation.

Family etiquette dictated that everyone carry their own bag, but since Brunetti would be going only as far as Mestre, and hence had no bag, Paola took advantage of him to carry her large suitcase while she carried only her handbag and *The Collected Letters of Henry James*, a volume so formidable in size as to convince Brunetti that she wouldn't have had time for him, anyway.

Because Brunetti carried Paola's suitcase, the domino theory was immediately made manifest, and Chiara stuffed some of her books into her mother's suitcase, thus leaving space in her own for Raffi's second pair of mountain boots. Whereupon his mother insisted that he use that space to carry her copy of *The Sacred Fount*, having decided that this was the year she would finally have enough time to read it.

They all climbed into the same compartment of the 8.35, a train that would get Brunetti to Mestre in ten minutes and themselves to Bolzano in time for lunch. No one had much to say during the short trip across the *laguna*: Paola made sure he had the phone number of the hotel in his wallet, and Raffaele reminded him that this was the same train Sara was to take next Saturday, leaving Brunetti to wonder if he was supposed to carry her bag, too.

At Mestre, he kissed the children, and Paola walked down the corridor to the door with him. 'I hope you can come up next weekend, Guido. Even better, that you get this settled and can come up even sooner.'

He smiled, but he didn't want to tell her how unlikely that was: after all, they didn't even know who the dead man was yet. He kissed her on both cheeks, got down from the train, and walked back towards the compartment where the children were. Chiara was already eating a peach. As he stood on the platform, gazing at them through the window, he saw Paola come back into the compartment and, almost without glancing at her, pull out a handkerchief and hand it to Chiara. The train began to move just as Chiara turned to wipe her mouth

and, turning, saw him on the platform. Her face, half of it still gleaming with peach juice, lit up with pure delight and she leaped to the window. '*Ciao*, Papà, *ciao*, *ciao*,' she shouted over the sound of the engine. She stood on the seat of the train and leaned out, waving Paola's handkerchief at him madly. He stood on the platform and waved until the tiny white flag of love disappeared in the distance.

When he got to Gallo's office at the Mestre Questura, the sergeant met him at the door. 'We've got someone coming out to take a look at the body,' he said with no prelude.

'Who? Why?'

'Your people had a call this morning. From a,' and here he looked down at a piece of paper in his hand, 'from a Signora Mascari. Her husband is the director of the Venice office of the Bank of Verona. He's been gone since Saturday.'

'That's a week ago,' Brunetti said. 'What's taken her this long to notice he's missing?'

'He was supposed to go on a business trip. To Messina. He left Sunday afternoon, and that's the last she heard of him.'

'A week? She let a week go before she called us?'

'I didn't speak to her,' Gallo said, almost as if Brunetti had been accusing him of negligence.

'Who did?'

'I don't know. All I have is a piece of paper that was put on my desk, telling me that she's going to Umberto Primo this morning to take a look at him and hoped to get there by nine.'

The men exchanged a look; Gallo pushed up his sleeve and glanced at his watch.

'Yes,' Brunetti said. 'Let's go.'

There ensued a muddle that was almost cinematic in its idiocy. Their car found itself in heavy early-morning traffic; the driver decided to cut round it and come at the hospital from the rear, only to meet even heavier traffic, which got them to the hospital after Signora Mascari had not only identified the body as that of her husband, Leonardo, but had left in the same taxi that had brought her out from Venice, heading towards the Mestre Questura, where, she was told, the police would answer her questions.

All of this meant that Brunetti and Gallo got back to the Questura to find that Signora Mascari had been waiting for them for more than quarter of an hour. She sat, upright and entirely alone, on a wooden bench in the corridor outside Gallo's office. She was a woman whose dress and manner suggested, not that her youth had fled, but that it had never existed. Her suit, a midnight-blue raw silk, was conservative in cut, the skirt a bit longer than was then fashionable. The colour of the cloth contrasted sharply with her pallid skin.

She looked up as the two men approached, and Brunetti noticed that her hair was that standard red so popular to women of Paola's age. She wore little make-up, and so he was able to see the small lines at the corners of the eyes and mouth, lines brought on either by age or worry, Brunetti couldn't tell which. She stood and took a step towards them. Brunetti stopped in front

of her and held out his hand. 'Signora Mascari, I'm Commissario Brunetti from the Venice police.'

She took his hand and gave it no more than the quickest of light touches. He noticed that her eyes seemed very bright, but he couldn't tell if this was caused by unshed tears or the reflection from the glasses she wore.

'I extend my condolences, Signora Mascari,' he said. 'I understand how painful and shocking this must be for you.' She still made no acknowledgement that he had spoken. 'Is there someone you would like us to call and have come here to be with you?'

She shook her head at this. 'Tell me what happened,' she said.

'Perhaps we could step into Sergeant Gallo's office,' Brunetti said, reaching down to open the door. He allowed the woman to pass in front of him. He glanced backwards at Gallo, who raised his eyebrows in interrogation; Brunetti nodded, and the sergeant came into the office with them. Brunetti held a chair for Signora Mascari, who sat and looked up at him.

'Is there something we could get you, Signora? A glass of water? Tea?'

'No. Nothing. Tell me what happened.'

Sergeant Gallo took his place quietly behind his desk; Brunetti sat in a chair not far from Signora Mascari.

'Your husband's body was found in Mestre on Monday morning. If you've spoken to the people at the hospital, you know that the cause of death was a blow to the head.'

She interrupted him. 'There were blows to the face,

119

as well.' After she said this, she looked away and stared down at her hands.

'Do you know of anyone who might have wanted to harm your husband, Signora? Can you think of anyone who has ever menaced him or with whom he had a serious argument?'

She shook her head in immediate negation. 'Leonardo had no enemies,' she said.

Brunetti's experience suggested that a man did not get to be the director of a bank without making enemies, but he said nothing.

'Did your husband ever mention difficulties at his work? Perhaps an employee he had to fire? Someone who was turned down for a loan and who held him responsible?'

Again, she shook her head. 'No, nothing like that. There's never been any trouble.'

'And your family, Signora? Has your husband ever had difficulties with anyone in your family?'

'What is this?' she demanded. 'Why are you asking me these questions?'

'Signora,' Brunetti began, making what he hoped was a calming gesture with his hands. 'The manner of your husband's death, the very violence of it, suggests that whoever did it had reason to hate your husband a great deal, and so, before we can begin to look for that person, we have to have some idea of why he might have done what he did. So it is necessary that these questions be asked, painful as I know them to be.'

'But I can't tell you anything. Leonardo had no enemies.' After repeating this, she looked across at Gallo, as if

to ask him to verify what she said or to help her persuade Brunetti to believe her.

'When your husband left the house last Sunday, he was on his way to Messina?' Brunetti asked. She nodded. 'Do you know the purpose of his trip, Signora?'

'He told me it was for the bank and that he would be back on Friday. Yesterday.'

'But he didn't mention what the trip was about?'

'No, he never did. He always said his work wasn't very interesting, and he seldom discussed it with me.'

'Did you hear anything from him after he left, Signora?'

'No. He left for the airport on Sunday afternoon. He had a flight to Rome, where he had to change planes.'

'Did your husband call you after that, Signora? Did he call you from Rome or from Messina?'

'No, but he never did. Whenever he went on a business trip, he'd simply go wherever he was going and then come home, or he'd call me from his office in the bank if he went directly there when he got back to Venice.'

'Was this usual, Signora?'

'Was what usual?'

'That he would go away on business and not get in touch with you?'

'I just told you,' she said, her voice going a bit sharp. 'He travelled a bit for the bank, six or seven times a year. Sometimes he would send me a postcard or bring me a gift, but he never called.'

'When did you begin to become alarmed, Signora?'

'Last night. I thought he would go to the bank in the afternoon, when he got back, and then come home. But

121

when he wasn't home by seven, I called the bank, but it was closed. I tried to call two of the men he worked with, but they weren't home.' She paused here, took a deep breath, and then continued, 'I told myself I'd got the day wrong or the time, but by this morning, I couldn't fool myself any more, so I called one of the men who works at the bank, and he called a colleague in Messina, and then he called me back.' She stopped talking here.

'What did he tell you, Signora?' Brunetti asked in a low voice.

She put one knuckle to her mouth, hoping, perhaps, to keep the words from coming out, but she had seen the body in the morgue, and so there was no use in that. 'He told me that Leonardo had never been to Messina. And so I called the police. Called you. They told me . . . when I gave them a description of Leonardo . . . they told me that I should come out here. So I did.' Her voice had grown increasingly ragged as she explained all of this, and when she finished, her hands were clutched desperately together in her lap.

'Signora, are you sure there's no one you'd like to call or have us call to come here to be with you? Perhaps you shouldn't be alone at this time,' Brunetti said.

'No. No, there's no one I want to see.' Abruptly, she stood. 'I don't have to stay here, do I? Am I free to leave?'

'Of course, Signora. You've been more than kind to answer these questions.'

She ignored this.

Brunetti made a small gesture to Gallo as he stood

and followed Signora Mascari to the door. 'We'll have a car take you back to Venice, Signora.'

'I don't want anyone to see me arrive in a police car,' she said.

'It will be an unmarked car, Signora, and the driver won't be in uniform.'

She made no acknowledgement to this, and the fact that she didn't object probably meant that she would accept the ride to Piazzale Roma.

Brunetti opened the door and accompanied her to the stairs at the end of the corridor. He noticed that her right hand had a death grip on her purse, and the left was jammed into the pocket of her jacket.

Downstairs, Brunetti went out on to the steps of the Questura with her, out into the heat that he had forgotten. A dark blue sedan waited at the foot of the steps, motor running. Brunetti bent down and opened the door for her, held her arm as she stepped into the car. Once seated, she turned away from him and looked out of the window on the other side, though all she saw was traffic and the bleak façade of office buildings. Brunetti closed the door softly and told the driver to take Signora Mascari back to Piazzale Roma.

When the car disappeared into the flow of traffic, Brunetti went back to Gallo's office. As he went in, he asked the sergeant, 'Well, what did you think?'

'I don't believe in people who have no enemies.'

'Especially middle-aged bank managers,' Brunetti added.

'And so?' Gallo asked.

'I'll go back to Venice and see if there's anything I can

123

find out there, from my people. Now that we've got a name, we at least have a place to begin to look.'

'For what?' Gallo asked.

Brunetti's answer was immediate. 'First, we've got to do what we should have been doing from the beginning, find out where the clothing and the shoes he was wearing came from.'

Gallo took this as a reproach and answered just as quickly, 'Nothing on the dress yet, but we've got the name of the manufacturer of the shoes and should have a list by this afternoon of the stores that sold them.'

Brunetti had not intended his remark as a criticism of the Mestre branch, but he let it stand. It could do no harm to spur Gallo and his men into finding out where Mascari's clothing had come from, for surely those shoes and that dress were not the sort of thing a middle-aged banker wore to the office.

Chapter Thirteen

If Brunetti thought he was going to find people working on a Saturday morning in August, the staff of the Questura thought otherwise: there were guards at the door, even a cleaning woman on the stairs, but the offices were empty, and he knew there was no hope of getting anything done until Monday morning. For a moment, he thought of getting on a train to Bolzano, but he knew it would be after dinner before he got there, just as he knew he would spend all the next day eager to be back in the city.

He let himself into his office and opened the windows, though he was aware there was no good to be done by that. The room became more humid, perhaps even minimally hotter. No new papers lay on his desk, no report from Signorina Elettra.

He reached down into his bottom drawer and pulled out the telephone book. He flipped it open and turned to the L's, but there was no listing for Lega della Moralità, though that didn't surprise him. Under the S's, he found Santomauro, Giancarlo, *avv.* and an address in S. Marco. The late Leonardo Mascari, he learned by using the same system, lived in Castello. This surprised him:

Castello was the least prestigious *sestiere* of the city, a zone primarily inhabited by solid working-class families, an area where children could still grow up speaking nothing but dialect and remain entirely ignorant of Italian until they began elementary school. Perhaps it was the Mascari family home. Or perhaps he had made a lucky deal on an apartment or house. Apartments in Venice were so hard to find, and those found so outrageously priced, either to buy or to rent, that even Castello was becoming fashionable. Spending enough money on restoration could perhaps provide respectability, if not for the entire *quartiere*, then at least for the individual address.

He checked the listings in the yellow pages for banks, and found that the Bank of Verona was listed in Campo San Bartolomeo, the narrow *campo* at the foot of the Rialto where many banks had their offices; this surprised him, for he could not remember ever having seen it. More out of curiosity than anything else, he dialled the number. The phone was picked up on the third ring, and a man's voice said, '*Si?*' as though he were expecting a call.

'Is this the Bank of Verona?' Brunetti asked.

There was a moment's pause, and then the man said, 'I'm sorry, you've reached a wrong number.'

'Sorry to trouble you,' Brunetti said.

The other man replaced the phone without saying anything else.

The vagaries of SIP, the national telephone service, were such that having reached a wrong number would strike no one as in any way strange, but Brunetti was

certain he had dialled the number correctly. He dialled the number again, but this time it rang unanswered twelve times before Brunetti replaced the receiver. He looked at the listing again and made a note of the address. Then he checked the phone book for Morelli's pharmacy. The addresses were only a few numbers apart. He tossed the phone book back into the drawer and kicked it shut. He closed the windows, went downstairs, and left the Questura.

Ten minutes later, he walked out from the *sottoportico* of Calle della Bissa and into Campo San Bartolomeo. His eyes went up to the bronze statue of Goldoni, perhaps not his favourite playwright, but certainly the one who could make him laugh the hardest, especially when the plays were presented in their original Veneziano dialect, as they always were here, in the city that swarmed to his plays and loved him enough to put up this statue. Goldoni was in full stride, which made this *campo* the perfect place for him to be, for here, everyone rushed, always on their way somewhere: across the Rialto Bridge to go to the vegetable market; from Rialto to either the San Marco or the Cannaregio district. If people lived anywhere near the heart of the city, its geography would pull them through San Bartolomeo at least once a day.

When Brunetti got there, foot traffic was at its height as people rushed to the market before it closed, or they hurried home from work, the week finally over. Casually, he walked along the east side of the *campo*, looking at the numbers painted above the doors. As he had expected, the number was painted above an entrance-

way two doors to the right of the pharmacy. He stood for a moment in front of the panel of bells beside the door and studied the names. The Bank of Verona was listed, as were three other names with bells beside them, probably private apartments.

Brunetti rang the first bell above the bank. There was no answer. The same happened with the second. He was about to ring the top bell when he heard a woman's voice behind him, asking in purest Veneziano, 'May I help you? Are you looking for someone who lives here?'

He turned away from the bells and found himself looking down at a small old woman with an enormous shopping trolley leaning against her leg. Remembering the name on the first bell, he said, answering in the same dialect, 'Yes, I'm here to see the Montinis. It's time for them to renew their insurance policy, and I thought I'd stop by and see if they wanted to make any changes on the coverage.'

'They're not here,' she said, looking into an enormous handbag, hunting for her keys. 'Gone to the mountains. Same with the Gasparis, except they're at Jesolo.' Abandoning her hope of touching or seeing the keys, she took the bag and shook it, bent on locating them by sound. It worked, and she pulled out a bunch of keys as large as her hand.

'That's what all this is,' she said, holding the keys up to Brunetti. 'They've left me their keys, and I go in and water the plants, see the place doesn't fall down.' She looked up from the keys and at Brunetti's face. Her eyes were a faded pale-blue, set in a round face covered with a tracery of fine lines. 'Do you have children, Signore?'

'Yes, I do,' he responded immediately.

'Names and ages?'

'Raffaele's sixteen, and Chiara's thirteen, Signora.'

'Good,' she said, as though he had passed some sort of test. 'You're a strong young man. Do you think you could carry that cart up to the third floor for me? If you don't, then I'll have to make at least three trips to get it all up there. My son and his family are coming to lunch tomorrow, so I've had to get a lot of things.'

'I'd be very glad to help you, Signora,' he said, bending down to pick up the cart, which must have weighed fifteen kilos. 'Is it a big family?'

'My son and his wife and their children. Two of them are bringing the great-grandchildren, so there'll be, let's see, there'll be ten of us.'

She opened the door and held it open while Brunetti slipped past her with the cart. She pushed on the timed light and started up the steps ahead of him. 'You wouldn't believe what they charged me for peaches. Middle of August, and they're still charging three thousand lire a kilo. But I got them anyway; Marco likes to cut his up in red wine before lunch and then have it as dessert. And fish. I wanted to get a *rombo*, but it cost too much. Everyone likes a good boiled *bosega*, so that's what I got, but he still wanted ten thousand lire a kilo. Three fish and it cost me almost forty thousand lire.' She stopped at the first landing, just outside the door to the Bank of Verona, and looked down at Brunetti. 'When I was a girl, we gave *bosega* to the cat, and here I am, paying ten thousand lire a kilo for it.'

She turned and started up the next flight. 'You're carrying it by the handles, aren't you?'

'Yes, Signora.'

'Good, because I have a kilo of figs right on the top, and I wouldn't want them to be crushed.'

'No, they're all right, Signora.'

'I went to Casa del Parmigiana and got some *prosciutto* to go with the figs. I've known Giuliano since he was a boy. He's got the best *prosciutto* in Venice, don't you think?'

'My wife always goes there, Signora.'

'Costs *l'ira di dio*, but it's worth it, don't you think?'

'Yes, Signora.'

They were at the top. She still carried the keys, so she didn't have to hunt for them again. She opened the single lock on the door and pushed it open, letting Brunetti into a large apartment with four tall windows, closed and shuttered now, that opened on to the *campo*.

She led the way through the living-room, a room familiar from Brunetti's youth: fat armchairs and a sofa with horsehair stuffing that scratched at whoever sat down; massive dark brown credenzas, their tops covered with silver candy bowls and silver-framed photos; the floor of poured Venetian pavement that glistened, even in the dim light. He could have been in his grandparents' house.

The kitchen was the same. The sink was stone, and an immense cylindrical water-heater sat in one corner. The kitchen table had a marble surface, and he could see her both rolling out pasta and ironing on the surface.

'Just put it there, by the door,' she said. 'Would you like a glass of something?'

'Water would be nice, Signora.'

As he knew she would, she reached down a small silver salver from the top of the cabinet, placed a small round lace doily on it, then set a Murano wineglass on top of it. From the refrigerator, she took a bottle of mineral water and filled the glass.

'*Grazie infinite*,' he said before he drank the water. He set it carefully down on the centre of the doily and refused her offer of more. 'Would you like me to help you unpack it all, Signora?'

'No, I know where everything is and where it all goes. You've been very kind, young man. What's your name?'

'Brunetti, Guido.'

'And you sell insurance?'

'Yes, Signora.'

'Well, thank you very much,' she said, placing his glass in the sink and reaching into the trolley.

Remembering what his real job was, he asked, 'Signora, do you always let people into the apartment with you like this? Without knowing who they are?'

'No, I'm not a fool. I don't let just anyone in,' she replied. 'I always see if they have children. And, of course, they have to be Veneziano.'

Of course. When he thought about it, her system was probably better than a lie detector or a security check. 'Thank you for the water, Signora. I'll let myself out.'

'Thank you,' she said, bent over her trolley, hunting for the figs.

He went down the first two flights of stairs and stood

on the landing above the door of the Bank of Verona. He heard nothing at all, though occasionally a voice or a shout would float up from the *campo*. In the dim light that filtered in through the small windows of the staircase, he looked at his watch. A little after one. He stood for another ten minutes and still heard nothing except odd, disjointed sounds from the *campo*.

He walked slowly down the stairs and stood outside the door to the bank. Feeling not a little ridiculous, he bent his head and put his eye against the horizontal keyhole of the metal *porta blindata*. From behind it, he could make out the faintest trace of light, as if someone had forgotten to turn off a light when they closed the shutters on Friday afternoon. Or as if someone were working inside on this Saturday afternoon.

He went back up the steps and leaned against the wall. After about ten minutes, he took his handkerchief from his pocket and spread it on the second step above him, hiked up his trousers, and sat down. He leaned forward, put his elbows on his knees and his chin on his fists. After what seemed a long time, he got up, moved the handkerchief closer to the wall, and sat down again, now leaning against the wall. No air circulated, he had eaten nothing all day, and the heat battered at him. He glanced down at his watch and saw that it was after two. He determined that he would stay there until three and not a minute later.

At 3.40, still there but now determined to leave at four, he heard a sharp sound from below. He stood and backed up on to the second step. Below him, a door opened, but he remained where he was. The door closed,

a key turned in the lock, and footsteps sounded on the stairs. Brunetti stuck his head out and looked down after the retreating figure. In the dim light, he made out only a tall man in a dark suit, carrying a briefcase. Short dark hair, a starched white collar just visible at the back of his neck. The man turned and started down the next flight of stairs, but the dim light of the stairwell revealed little about him. Brunetti moved silently down behind him. At the door to the bank, Brunetti glanced in through the keyhole, but it was now dark inside.

From below, he heard the sound of the front door being opened and closed, and at the sound Brunetti ran down the remaining steps. He paused at the door, opened it quickly, and stepped out into the *campo*. For a moment, the bright sun blinded him, and he covered his eyes with his hand. When he took it away, he swept his eyes across the *campo*, but all he saw were pastel sports clothes and white shirts. He walked to the right and looked down Calle della Bissa, but there was no dark-suited man there. He ran across the *campo* and looked down the narrow *calle* that led to the first bridge, but he didn't see the man. There were at least five other *calli* that led off the *campo*, and Brunetti realized the man would be long gone before he could check them all. He decided to try the Rialto *embarcadero*: perhaps he had taken a boat. Dodging past people and pushing others out of his way, he ran to the water's edge and then up towards the *embarcadero*. When he got there, a boat was just leaving, heading towards him in the direction of San Marcuola and the train station.

He pushed his way through a gaggle of Japanese

tourists until he got to the edge of the canal. The boat sailed past him, and he ran his eyes over the passengers standing on deck and those sitting inside. The boat was crowded, and most of the people on it wore casual clothing. Finally Brunetti saw, on the other side of the deck, a man in a dark suit and white shirt. He was just lighting a cigarette and turned aside to flip the match into the canal. The back of his head looked the same, but Brunetti knew he couldn't be certain about this. When the man turned back, Brunetti stared at his profile, trying to memorize it. And then the boat slipped under the Rialto Bridge, and the man was gone.

Chapter Fourteen

Brunetti did what any sensible man will do when he has known defeat: he went home and called his wife. When he was put through to Paola's room, Chiara answered the phone.

'Oh, *ciao*, Papà; you should have been on the train. We got stuck outside Vicenza and had to sit there for almost two hours. No one knew what happened, but then the conductor told us that a woman had thrown herself under a train between Vicenza and Verona, so we had to wait and wait. I guess they had to clean it up, eh? When we finally got going, I stayed right at the window all the way to Verona, but I didn't see anything. You think they got it cleaned up so fast?'

'I suppose so, *cara*. Is your mother there?'

'Yes, she is, Papà. But maybe I was looking out the wrong side of the train and all the mess was on the other side. Do you think that might be it?'

'Perhaps, Chiara. Could I talk to Mamma?'

'Oh, sure, Papà. She's right here. Why do you think someone would do that, throw themselves under a train?'

'Probably because someone wouldn't let them talk to the person they wanted to, Chiara.'

'Oh, Papà, you're always so silly. Here she is.'

Silly? Silly? He thought he had sounded entirely serious.

'*Ciao*, Guido,' Paola said. 'You've just heard? Our child is a ghoul.'

'When did you get there?'

'About half an hour ago. We had to have lunch on the train. Disgusting. What have you been doing? Did you find the *insalata di calamari*?'

'No, I just got in.'

'From Mestre? Did you have lunch?'

'No, there was something I had to do.'

'Well, there's *insalata di calamari* in the refrigerator. Eat it today or tomorrow; it won't keep very long in this heat.' He heard Chiara's voice in the background, and then Paola asked, 'Are you coming up tomorrow?'

'No, I can't. We've identified his body.'

'Who is he?'

'Mascari, Leonardo. He's the director of the Banca di Verona here. Do you know him?'

'No, never heard of him. Is he Venetian?'

'I think so. The wife is.'

Again, he heard Chiara's voice. It went on for a long time. Then Paola was back. 'Sorry, Guido. Chiara's going for a walk and couldn't find her sweater.' The very word made Brunetti more conscious of the heat that simmered in the apartment, even with all the windows open.

'Paola, do you have Padovani's number? I looked in the phone book here, but it's not listed.' He knew she

wouldn't ask why he wanted the number, so he explained, 'He's the only person I could think of to answer questions about the gay world here.'

'He's been in Rome for years, Guido.'

'I know, I know, Paola, but he's got a house here for when he comes up every couple of months to review art shows, and his family's still here.'

'Well, maybe,' she said, managing to sound not at all convinced. 'Wait a second while I get my address book.' She set down the phone and was gone long enough to convince Brunetti that the address book was in another room, perhaps another building. Finally she was back. 'Guido, his Venice number is 5224404. If you talk to him, please say hello for me.'

'Yes, I will. Where's Raffi?'

'Oh, he was gone the minute we set down the bags. I don't expect to see him until dinner-time.'

'Give him my love. I'll call you this week.' With mutual promises of calls and another admonition about the *insalata di calamari*, they hung up, and Brunetti thought about how strange it was for a man to go away for a week and not call his wife. Perhaps if there were no children, it made a difference, but he thought not.

He rang Padovani's number and got, as was increasingly the case in Italy these days, a machine telling him that Professore Padovani was not able to come to the phone at the moment but would return the call as soon as possible. Brunetti left a message asking Padovani to ring, and hung up.

He went into the kitchen and pulled the now-famous *insalata* from the refrigerator. He peeled back the plastic

wrap from the top and picked out a piece of squid with his fingers. Chewing on it, he pulled a bottle of Soave from the refrigerator and poured himself a glass. Wine in one hand, *insalata* in the other, he went out on to the terrace and set them both down on the low glass table. He remembered bread, went back into the kitchen to grab a *panino*, and while there, remembering civilization, he took a fork from the top drawer.

Back on the terrace, he broke off a piece of the bread, put another piece of squid on top of it, and popped them into his mouth. Certainly, banks had work to be done on Saturday – no holiday for money. And certainly whoever was working on the weekend wouldn't want to be disturbed by a phone call, so he'd say it was a wrong number and then not answer the next call. So as not to be disturbed.

The salad had rather more celery than he liked, so he pushed the tiny cubes to the side of the bowl with his fork. He poured himself more wine, and he thought of the Bible. Somewhere, he thought it was in *Mark*, there was a passage about Jesus' disappearance when he was going back to Nazareth after he'd first been taken up to Jerusalem. Mary thought he was with Joseph, travelling with the men, and that sainted man believed the boy to be with his mother and the women. It wasn't until their caravan stopped for the night that they spoke to one another and discovered that Jesus was nowhere to be found: he turned out to be back in Jerusalem, teaching in the Temple. The Bank of Verona believed Mascari to be in Messina; hence, the office in Messina must have

believed him to be somewhere else, or they surely would have called to check.

He went back into the living-room and found one of Chiara's notebooks on the table, left there in a muddle of pens and pencils. He flipped through the notebook; finding it empty and liking the picture of Mickey Mouse on the cover, he took it and one of the pens out to the terrace.

He began to jot down a list of things to do on Monday morning. Check the Bank of Verona to see where Mascari was supposed to go and then call that bank to see what reason they'd been given for his failure to arrive. Find out why there had been no progress on finding where the shoes and dress came from. Start digging into Mascari's past, both personal and financial. And take another look at the autopsy report for any mention of those shaved legs. He also had to see what Vianello had managed to learn about the Lega and about Avvocato Santomauro.

He heard the phone ring and, hoping it would be Paola but knowing it couldn't be, he went inside to answer it.

'*Ciao*, Guido, it's Damiano. I got your message.'

'What are you a professor of?' Brunetti asked.

'Oh, that,' the journalist answered dismissively. 'I liked the sound of it, so I'm trying it on my message machine this week. Why? Don't you like it?'

'Of course I like it,' Brunetti found himself saying. 'It sounds wonderful. But what are you a professor of?'

A long silence emanated from Padovani's end of the phone. 'I once gave a series of classes in painting in a

139

girls' school, back in the seventies. Do you think that counts?'

'I suppose so,' Brunetti admitted.

'Well, perhaps it's time to change the message. How do you think Commendatore would sound? Commendatore Padovani? Yes, I think I like that. Would you like me to change the message, and you call me back?'

'No, I don't think so, Damiano. I'd like to talk to you about something else.'

'Just as well. It takes me forever to change the message. So many buttons to push. The first time I did it, I recorded myself swearing at the machine. No one left a message for a week, until I thought the thing wasn't working and called myself from a phone booth. Shocking, the language the machine used. I dashed home and changed the message immediately. But it's still very confusing. Are you sure you don't want to call me back in twenty minutes?'

'No, I don't think so, Damiano. Do you have time to talk to me now?'

'For you, Guido, I am, as an English poet says in an entirely different context, "as free as the road, as loose as the wind".'

Brunetti knew he was supposed to ask, but he didn't. 'It might take a long time. Would you be willing to meet me for dinner?'

'What about Paola?'

'She's taken the kids up to the mountains.'

There was a moment's silence from Padovani, a silence which Brunetti could not help but interpret as entirely speculative. 'I've got a murder case here, and

the hotel's been reserved for months, so Paola and the kids have gone up to Bolzano. If I get through with this on time, I'll go up, as well. That's why I called you. I thought you might be able to help me.'

'With a murder case? Oh, how very exciting. Since this AIDS business, I've had so little to do with the criminal classes.'

'Ah, yes,' Brunetti said, momentarily at a loss for a suitable rejoinder. 'Would you like to meet for dinner? Any place you like.'

Padovani considered this for a minute then said, 'Guido, I'm leaving to go back to Rome tomorrow, and I've got a house full of food. Would you mind coming here to help me finish it up? It won't be anything fancy, just pasta and whatever else I find.'

'That would be fine. Tell me where you live.'

'I'm down in Dorsoduro. Do you know the Ramo degli Incurabili?'

It was a small *campo* with a running fountain, just back from the Zattere. 'Yes, I do.'

'Stand with your back to the fountain looking at the little canal, and it's the first door on the right.' Far clearer than giving a number or street name, this would get any Venetian to the house with no difficulty.

'Good, what time?'

'Eight.'

'Can I bring anything?'

'Absolutely not. Anything you bring, we just have to eat, and I've already got enough here for a football team. Nothing. Please.'

'All right. I'll see you at eight. And thanks, Damiano.'

'My pleasure. What is it you want to ask me about? Or would I say, "whom"? This way, I can sort through my memory, or I might even have time to make a few phone calls.'

'Two men. Leonardo Mascari—'

'Never heard of him,' Padovani interrupted.

'And Giancarlo Santomauro.'

Padovani whistled. 'So you people finally tumbled to the saintly Avvocato, eh?'

'I'll see you at eight,' Brunetti said.

'Tease,' Padovani said with a laugh and hung up.

At eight that evening, Brunetti, freshly showered and shaved and carrying a bottle of Barbera, rang the bell to the right of the small fountain in the Ramo degli Incurabili. The front of the building, which had only one bell and which, consequently, was probably that greatest of all luxuries, a separate house owned by only one person, was covered by jasmine plants which trailed up from two terracotta pots on either side of the door and filled the air around them with perfume. Padovani opened the door almost immediately and extended his hand to Brunetti. His grip was warm and firm and, still holding Brunetti's hand, he pulled him inside. 'Get out of the heat. I've got to be out of my mind to go back to Rome in the midst of this, but at least my apartment there is air-conditioned.'

He released Brunetti's hand and stepped back. Inevitably, like any two people who have not seen one another for a long time, they tried, without being obvious about it, to see what changes had taken place. Was he thicker, thinner, greyer, older?

Brunetti, seeing that Padovani still appeared to be the thickset ruffian he very clearly was not, turned his eyes to the room in which they stood. The central part of it soared up two floors to a roof inset with skylights. This open space was surrounded on three sides by an open loggia reached by an open wooden staircase. The fourth side was closed in and must hold the bedroom.

'What was it, a boathouse?' Brunetti asked, remembering the little canal that ran just outside the door. Boats brought for repair could easily have been dragged inside.

'Good for you. Yes. When I bought it, they were still working on boats in here, and there were holes in the roof the size of watermelons.'

'How long have you had it?' Brunetti asked, looking around and giving a rough estimate of the quantity of work and money that must have gone into the place to make it look the way it did now.

'Eight years.'

'You've done a lot. And you're lucky not to have neighbours.' Brunetti handed him the bottle, wrapped in white tissue paper.

'I told you not to bring anything.'

'It won't spoil,' Brunetti said with a smile.

'Thank you, but you shouldn't have,' Padovani said, though he knew it was as impossible for a dinner guest to show up without a gift as it was for the host to serve chaff and nettles. 'Make yourself at home and look around while I go and take a look at the dinner,' Padovani said, turning towards a door with a stained-

glass panel that led to the kitchen. 'I put ice in the bucket in case you'd like a drink.'

He disappeared behind the door, and Brunetti heard the familiar noises of pots and lids and running water. He glanced down and saw that the floor was a dark oak parquet; the sight of a charred semicircle of floor that stood in front of the fireplace made Brunetti uncomfortable because he couldn't decide whether he approved of the placing of comfort over caution or disapproved of the ruining of such a perfect surface. A long wooden beam had been set into the plaster above the fireplace, and along it danced a multicoloured parade of ceramic Commedia dell'Arte figurines. Paintings filled two walls; there was no attempt to order them into styles or schools: they hung on the walls and fought for the viewer's eye. The keenness of the competition gave evidence of the taste with which they had been selected. He spotted a Guttoso, a painter he had never liked much, and a Morandi, whom he did. There were three Ferruzzis, all giving joyous testimony to the beauty of the city. Then, a little to the left of the fireplace, a Madonna, clearly Florentine and probably fifteenth-century, looked adoringly down at yet another ugly baby. One of the secrets Paola and Brunetti never revealed to anyone was their decades-long search for the ugliest Christ Child in western art. At the moment, the title was held by a particularly bilious infant in Room 13 of the Pinacoteca di Siena. Though the baby in front of Brunetti was clearly no beauty, Siena's title was not at risk. Along one wall ran a long shelf of carved wood that must have once been part of a wardrobe or cabinet. On top of it rested a

row of brightly coloured ceramic bowls whose strict geometric designs and swirling calligraphy clearly marked them as Islamic.

The door opened and Padovani came back into the room. 'Don't you want a drink?'

'No, a glass of wine would be good. I don't like to drink when it's so hot.'

'I know what you mean. This is the first summer I've been here in three years, and I'd forgotten how awful it can be. There are some nights, when the tide is low, and I'm anywhere on the other side of the Canal, that I think I'll be sick with the smell.'

'Don't you get it here?' Brunetti asked.

'No, the Canale della Giudecca must be deeper or move more quickly, or something. We don't get the smell here. At least not yet. If they continue to dig up the channels to let in those monster tankers – what are they called, supertankers? – then God alone knows what will happen to the *laguna*.'

Still talking, Padovani walked over to the long wooden table, set for two, and poured out two glasses from a bottle of Dolcetto that stood there, already opened. 'People think the end of the city will come in some major flood or natural disaster. I think the answer is much easier,' he said, coming back to Brunetti and handing him a glass.

'And what is that?' Brunetti asked, sipping at the wine, liking it.

'I think we've killed the seas, and it's only a question of time before they begin to stink. And since the *laguna* is just a gut hanging off the Adriatic, which is itself a gut

hanging from the Mediterranean, which . . . well, you get the idea. I think the water will simply die, and then we'll be forced either to abandon the city or else fill in the canals, in which case there will no longer be any sense in living here.'

It was a novel theory and certainly no less bleak than many he had heard, than many he himself half believed. Everyone talked, all the time, of the imminent destruction of the city, and yet the price of apartments doubled every few years, and the rents for those available continued to soar ever higher above what the average worker could pay for one. Venetians had bought and sold real estate through the Crusades, the Plague, and various occupations by foreign armies, so it was probably a safe bet that they would continue to do so through whatever ecological holocaust awaited them.

'Everything's ready,' Padovani said, sitting in one of the deep armchairs. 'All I've got to do is throw the pasta in. But why don't you give me an idea of what you want so I'll have something to think about while I'm stirring?'

Brunetti sat on the sofa facing him. He took another sip of his wine and, choosing his words carefully, began. 'I have reason to believe that Santomauro is involved with a transvestite prostitute who lives and, apparently, works in Mestre.'

'What do you mean by "involved with"?' Padovani asked, voice level.

'Sexually,' Brunetti said simply. 'But he also claims to be his lawyer.'

'One does not necessarily exclude the other, does it?'

'No. Hardly. But since I found him in the company

of this young man, he has tried to prevent me from investigating him.'

'Which him?'

'The young man.'

'I see,' Padovani said, sipping at his wine. 'Anything else?'

'The other name I gave you, Leonardo Mascari, is the name of the man who was found in the field in Mestre on Monday.'

'The transvestite?'

'So it would seem.'

'And what's the connection here?'

'The young man, Santomauro's client, denied recognizing Mascari. But he knew him.'

'How do you know that?'

'You'll have to believe me here, Damiano. I know. I've seen it too many times not to know. He recognized his picture and then pretended he didn't.'

'What was the young man's name?' Padovani asked.

'I'm not at liberty to say.' Silence fell.

'Guido,' Padovani finally said, leaning forward, 'I know a number of those boys in Mestre. In the past, I knew a large number of them. If I'm to serve as your gay consultant in this' – he said it entirely without irony or rancour – 'then I'm going to have to know his name. I assure you that nothing you tell me will be repeated, but I can't make any connection unless I know his name.' Brunetti still said nothing. 'Guido, you called me. I didn't call you.' Padovani got to his feet. 'I'll just put the pasta in. Fifteen minutes?'

While he waited for Padovani to come back from the

kitchen, Brunetti looked at the books that filled one wall. He pulled down one on Chinese archaeology and took it back to the sofa, glanced through it until he heard the door open and looked up to see Padovani come back into the room.

'*A tavola, tutti a tavola. Mangiamo*,' Padovani called. Brunetti closed the book, set it aside, and went over to take his place at the table. 'You sit there, on the left,' Padovani said. He set the bowl down and started immediately to heap pasta on to the plate in front of Brunetti.

Brunetti looked down, waited until Padovani had served himself, and began to eat. Tomato, onion, cubes of *pancetta*, and perhaps a touch of *pepperoncino*, all poured over *penne rigate*, his favourite dried pasta.

'It's good,' he said, meaning it. 'I like the *pepperoncino*.'

'Oh, good. I never know if people are going to think it's too hot.'

'No, it's perfect,' Brunetti said and continued to eat. When he had finished his helping and Padovani was putting more on to his plate, Brunetti said, 'His name's Francesco Crespo.'

'I should have known,' said Padovani with a tired sigh. Then, sounding far more interested, he asked, 'You sure there's not too much *pepperoncino*?'

Brunetti shook his head and finished his second portion, then held out his hands to cover his plate when Padovani reached for the serving spoon.

'You better. There's hardly anything else,' Padovani insisted.

'No, really, Damiano.'

'Suit yourself, but Paola's not to blame me if you starve to death while she's away.' He picked up their two plates, set them inside the serving bowl, and went back into the kitchen.

He was to emerge twice before he sat down again. The first time, he carried a small roast of ground turkey breast wrapped in *pancetta* and surrounded by potatoes, and the second a plate of grilled peppers soaked in olive oil and a large bowl of mixed salad greens. 'That's all there is,' he said when he sat down, and Brunetti suspected that he was meant to read it as an apology.

Brunetti helped himself to the roast meat and potatoes and began to eat.

Padovani filled their glasses and helped himself to both turkey and potatoes. 'Crespo came originally from, I think, Mantova. He moved to Padova about four years ago, to study pharmacy. But he quickly learned that life was far more interesting if he followed his natural inclination and set himself up as a whore, and he soon discovered that the best way to do that was to find himself an older man who would support him. The usual stuff: an apartment, a car, plenty of money for clothes, and in return all he had to do was be there when the man who paid the bills was able to get away from the bank, or the city council meeting, or his wife. I think he was only about eighteen at the time. And very, very pretty.' Padovani paused with his fork in the air. 'In fact, he reminded me then of the Bacchus of Caravaggio: beautiful, but too knowing and just on the edge of corruption.'

Padovani offered some peppers to Brunetti and took

some himself. 'The last thing I know about him at first hand was that he was mixed up with an accountant from Treviso. But Franco could never keep himself from straying, and the accountant threw him out. Beat him up, I think, and threw him out. I don't know when he started with the transvestism; that sort of thing has never interested me in the least. In fact, I suppose I don't understand it. If you want a woman, then have a woman.'

'Maybe it's a way to deceive yourself that it is a woman,' Brunetti suggested, using Paola's theory and thinking, now, that it made sense.

'Perhaps. But how sad, eh?' Padovani moved his plate to the side and sat back. 'I mean, we deceive ourselves all the time, about whether we love someone, or why we do, or why we tell the lies we do. But you'd think we could at least be honest with ourselves about who we want to go to bed with. It seems little enough, that.' He picked up the salad and sprinkled salt on it, poured olive oil liberally over the leaves, then added a large splash of vinegar.

Brunetti handed him his plate and accepted the clean salad plate he was given in its place. Padovani pushed the bowl towards him. 'Help yourself. There's no dessert. Only fruit.'

'I'm glad you didn't have to go to any trouble,' Brunetti said, and Padovani laughed.

'Well, I really did have all of this in the house. Except for the fruit.'

Brunetti took a very small portion of salad; Padovani took even less.

'What else do you know about Crespo?' Brunetti asked.

'I heard that he was dressing up, calling himself Francesca. But I didn't know he'd finished on Via Cappuccina. Or is it the public parks in Mestre?' he asked.

'Both,' Brunetti answered. 'And I don't know that he has finished there. The address he gave is a very nice one, and his name is outside the door.'

'Anyone's name can be on the door. Depends on who pays the rent,' Padovani said, apparently more practised in these things.

'I suppose you're right,' Brunetti said.

'I don't know much more about him. He's not a bad person, at least he wasn't when I knew him. But sneaky and easily led. Things like that don't change, so he's likely to lie to you if he sees any advantage in doing so.'

'Like most of the people I deal with,' Brunetti said.

Padovani smiled and added, 'Like most of the people we all deal with all of the time.'

Brunetti had to laugh at the grim truth of this.

'I'll get the fruit,' Padovani said, stacking their salad plates and taking them from the table. He was back quickly with a pale-blue ceramic bowl that held six perfect peaches. He passed Brunetti another of the small plates and set the bowl in front of him. Brunetti took one of the peaches and began to peel it with his knife and fork.

'What can you tell me about Santomauro?' he asked as he peeled the peach, keeping his eyes on that.

'You mean the president, or whatever he calls himself,

151

of the Lega della Moralità?' Padovani asked, making his voice richly sombre as he pronounced the last words.

'Yes.'

'I know enough about him to assure you that, in certain circles, the announcement of the Lega and its purpose was met with the same sort of peals of delight with which we used to watch Rock Hudson make his assault upon the virtue of Doris Day or with which we now watch some of the more belligerent film appearances of certain living actors, both our own and American.'

'You mean it's common knowledge?'

'Well, it is and it isn't. To most of us, it is, but we still respect the rules of gentlemen, unlike the politicians, and we do not tell tales out of school about one another. If we did, there'd be no one left to run the government or, for that fact, the Vatican.'

Brunetti was glad to see the real Padovani resurfacing, well, the airy chatterer that he had been led to believe was the real Padovani.

'But something like the Lega? Could he get away with something as blatant as that?'

'That's an excellent question. But, if you look back into the history of the Lega, I believe you will find that, in the days of its infancy, Santomauro was no more than the *éminence grise* of the movement. In fact, I don't think his name was associated with it, not in any official capacity, until two years ago, and he didn't become prominent until last year, when he was elected hostess or governess, or whatever their leader is called. *Gran priore*? Something pretentious like that.'

'But why didn't anyone say something then?'

'I think it's because most prefer to treat the Lega as a joke. I think that's a very serious mistake.' There was a note of uncharacteristic seriousness in his voice.

'Why do you say that?'

'Because I think the political wave of the future is groups like the Lega, groups which aim at fragmenting larger groups, breaking larger units into smaller. Just look at Eastern Europe and Yugoslavia. Look at our own political *leghe*, wanting to chop Italy back up into a lot of smaller, independent units.'

'Could you be making too much of this, Damiano?'

'Of course, I could be. The Lega della Moralità could just as easily be a bunch of harmless old ladies who like to meet together and talk about how good the old times were. But who has an idea of how many members they have? What their real goal is?'

In Italy, conspiracy theories are sucked in with mother's milk, and no Italian is ever free of the impulse to see conspiracy everywhere. Consequently, any group that is in any way hesitant to reveal itself is immediately suspected of all manner of things, as had been the Jesuits, as are the Jehovah's Witnesses. As the Jesuits still are, Brunetti corrected himself. Conspiracy certainly bred secrecy, but Brunetti was not willing to buy the proposition that it worked the other way, and secrecy necessitated conspiracy.

'Well?' Padovani prodded him.

'Well what?'

'How much do you know about the Lega?'

'Very little,' Brunetti admitted. 'But if I had to be

suspicious of them, I wouldn't look to their goals; I'd look to their finances.' During twenty years of police work, Brunetti had come to form few rules, but one of them was surely that high principles or political ideals seldom motivated people as strongly as did the desire for money.

'I doubt that Santomauro would be interested in anything as prosaic as money.'

'Dami, everyone is interested in money, and most people are motivated by it.'

'Regardless of motive or goal, you can be sure that if Giancarlo Santomauro is interested in running it, it stinks. That's little enough, but it's certain.'

'What do you know about his private life?' Brunetti asked, thinking of how much more subtle 'private' sounded than 'sexual', which is what it meant.

'All I know is what has been suggested, what has been implied in remarks and comments. You know the way it is.' Brunetti nodded. He certainly did. 'Then what I know, which, I repeat, I don't really *know* – though I know – is that he likes little boys, the younger the better. If you check his past, you'll see that he used to go to Bangkok at least once a year. Without the ineffable Signora Santomauro, I hasten to add. But for the last few years, he has not done so. I have no explanation for this, but I do know that tastes such as his do not change, they do not disappear, and they cannot be satisfied in any way other than by what they desire.'

'How much of that is, um, available here?' Why was it so easy to talk to Paola about some things, so difficult with other people?

154

'A fair bit, though the real centres are Rome and Milano.'

Brunetti had read about this in police reports. 'Films?'

'Films, certainly, but the real thing, as well, for those who are prepared to pay. I was about to add, and who are willing to take the risk, but there really cannot be said to be any risk, not today.'

Brunetti looked down at his plate and saw that his peach lay there, peeled but untouched. He didn't want it. 'Damiano, when you say, "little boys", is there an age you have in mind?'

Padovani suddenly smiled. 'You know, Guido, I have the strangest sensation that you are finding all of this terribly embarrassing.' Brunetti said nothing. ' "Little" can be twelve, but it can also be ten.'

'Oh.' There was a long pause, and then Brunetti asked, 'Are you sure about Santomauro?'

'I'm sure that's his reputation, and it's not likely to be wrong. But I have no proof, no witnesses, no one who would ever swear to it.'

Padovani got up from the table and went across the room to a low sideboard with bottles crowded together on one side of its surface. 'Grappa?' he asked.

'Please.'

'I've got some lovely pear-flavoured. Want to try it?'

'Yes.'

Brunetti joined him on that side of the room, took the glass Padovani offered him, and went to sit again on the sofa. Padovani went back to his chair, taking the bottle with him.

Brunetti tasted it. Not pears: nectar.

'It's too weak,' Brunetti said.

'The grappa?' Padovani asked, confused.

'No, no, the connection between Crespo and Santomauro. If Santomauro likes little boys, then Crespo could just be his client and nothing more.'

'Entirely possible,' Padovani said in a voice that said he thought it wasn't.

'Do you know anyone who could give you more information about either of them?' Brunetti asked.

'Santomauro and Crespo?'

'Yes. And Leonardo Mascari, as well, if there's some connection between them.'

Padovani looked down at his watch. 'It's too late to call the people I know.' Brunetti looked at his watch and saw that it was only ten-fifteen. Nuns?

Padovani had noticed his glance and laughed. 'No, Guido, they'll all have gone out for the evening, the night. But I'll call them from Rome tomorrow and see what they know or can find out.'

'I'd prefer that neither of the men know that questions are being asked about them.' It was polite, but it was stiff and awkward.

'Guido, it will be as if gossamer had been floated in the air. Everyone who knows Santomauro will be delighted to spread whatever they know or have heard about him, and you can be equally certain that none of this will get back to him. The very thought that he might be mixed up in something nasty will be a source of tingly delight to the people I'm thinking of.'

'That's just it, Damiano. I don't want there to be any talk, especially that he might be mixed up in anything,

especially something nasty.' He knew he sounded severe when he said it, so he smiled and held out his glass for another grappa.

The fop disappeared and the journalist took his place. 'All right, Guido. I won't play around with it, and perhaps I'll call different people, but I ought to be able to have some information about him by Tuesday or Wednesday.'

Padovani poured himself another glass of grappa and sipped at it. 'You should look into the Lega, Guido, at least into its membership.'

'You're really worried about it, aren't you?' Brunetti asked.

'I'm worried about any group that assumes its own superiority, in any way, to other people.'

'The police?' Brunetti asked with a smile, trying to lighten the other man's mood.

'No, not the police, Guido. No one believes they're superior, and I suspect that most of your boys don't believe it, either.' He finished his drink but poured himself no more. Instead, he put both glass and bottle on the floor beside his chair. 'I always think of Savonarola,' he said. 'He started by wanting to make things better, but the only way he could think of to do that was to destroy anything he disapproved of. In the end, I suspect zealots are all like him, even the *ecologisti* and the *femministi*. They start out wanting a better world, but they end up wanting to get it by removing anything in the world around them that doesn't correspond to their idea of what the world should be. Like Savonarola, they'll all end up on the pyre.'

'And then what?' Brunetti asked.

'Oh, I guess the rest of us will somehow manage to muddle through.'

It wasn't much in the way of philosophical affirmation, but Brunetti took it as a sufficiently optimistic note on which to end the evening. He got to his feet, said the necessary things to his host, and went home to his solitary bed.

Chapter Fifteen

Another reason Brunetti had been reluctant to go to the mountains was that this was his Sunday to visit his mother: he and his brother Sergio alternated weekends or went in the other's place when necessary. But this weekend, Sergio and his family were in Sardinia, so there was no one but Brunetti to go. It made no difference, of course, whether he went or not, but still he went, or Sergio went. Because she was in Mira, about ten kilometres from Venice, he had to take a bus and then either a taxi or a long walk to get to the Casa di Riposo.

Knowing that he was to go, he slept badly, kept awake by memory, heat, and the mosquitoes. He finally woke at about eight, woke to the same decision that he had to make every second Sunday: whether to go before or after lunch. Like the visit itself, this made no difference whatsoever and today was influenced only by the heat. If he waited until the afternoon, it would only be more infernal, so he decided to go immediately.

He left the house before nine, walked to Piazzale Roma and was lucky to get there only minutes before the bus for Mira left. Because he was one of the last people to get on, he stood, rocked from side to side as

the bus crossed the bridge and entered on to the maze of overpasses that carried traffic above or around Mestre.

Some of the faces on the bus were familiar to him; often some of them would share a taxi from the station in Mira or, in better weather, walk together from the station, seldom talking about anything more than the weather. Six people climbed down from the bus at the main station; two of them were women familiar to him, and the three of them quickly agreed to share a taxi. Because the taxi was not air-conditioned, they could talk about the weather, all of them glad of that distraction.

In front of the Casa di Riposo, each pulled out five thousand lire. The driver used no meter; everyone who made the trip knew the fare.

They went inside together, Brunetti and the two women, still expressing hope that the wind would change or that rain would come, all protesting that they had never known a summer like this one, and what would happen to the farmers if it didn't rain soon?

He knew the way, walked to the third floor, the two women going their separate way on the second floor, where the men were kept. At the top of the stairs, he saw Suor'Immacolata, his favourite of the sisters who worked here.

'*Buon giorno*, Dottore,' she said, smiling and coming across the corridor towards him.

'*Buon giorno*, Sister,' he said. 'You look very cool, as if the heat doesn't bother you at all.'

She smiled at this, as she did every time he joked with her about it. 'Ah, you Northerners, you don't know what real heat is. This is nothing, just a taste of springtime in

the air.' Suor'Immacolata was from the mountains of Sicily, had been transferred here by her community two years before. In the midst of the agony, madness, and misery which engulfed her days, the only thing she minded was the cold, but her remarks about it were always wry and casually dismissive as if to say that, exposed to real suffering, it was absurd to discuss her own. Seeing her smile, he saw again how beautiful she was: almond-shaped brown eyes, a soft mouth, and a thin, elegant nose. It made no sense. Worldly, believing himself to be a man of the flesh, Brunetti could see only the renunciation and could make nothing of the desires that might have animated it.

'How is she?' he asked.

'She's had a good week, Dottore.' That could, to Brunetti, mean only negative things: she hadn't attacked anyone, she hadn't destroyed anything, she had done no violence to herself.

'Is she eating?'

'Yes, Dottore. In fact, on Wednesday, she went and had lunch with the other ladies.' He waited to learn what disaster that might have brought, but Suor'Immacolata said nothing more.

'Do you think I could see her?' he asked.

'Oh, certainly, Dottore. Would you like me to come with you?' How beautiful, the grace of women; how soft their charity.

'Thank you, Sister. Perhaps she would be more comfortable if she could see you with me, at least when I first went in.'

'Yes, that might take away the surprise. Once she gets

161

accustomed to another person, she's usually all right. And once she senses that it's you, Dottore, she's really quite happy.'

This was a lie. Brunetti knew it, and Suor'Immacolata knew it. Her faith told her it was a sin to lie, and yet she told this lie to Brunetti and his brother each and every week. Later, on her knees, she prayed to be forgiven for a sin she could not help committing and knew she would commit again. In the winter, after she prayed and before she slept, she would open the window of her room and remove from her bed the single blanket she was allowed. But, each week, she told the same lie.

She turned and led the way, the well-known way, down towards room 308. On the right side of the corridor, three women sat in wheelchairs pushed up against the wall. Two of them beat rhythmically against the arms of their wheelchairs, muttering nonsense, and the third rocked back and forth, back and forth, a mad human metronome. As he passed, the one who always smelled of urine reached out and grabbed at Brunetti. 'Are you Giulio? Are you Giulio?' she asked.

'No, Signora Antonia,' Suor'Immacolata said, leaning down and stroking back the old woman's short white hair. 'Giulio was just here to see you. Don't you remember? He brought you this lovely little animal?' she said, taking a small chewed teddy bear from the woman's lap and putting it into her hands.

The old woman looked at her with puzzled, eternally confused eyes, eyes from which only death could remove the confusion, and asked, 'Giulio?'

'That's right, Signora. Giulio gave you the little

162

orsetto. Isn't he beautiful?' She held out the tiny bear to the old woman, who took it from her and asked Brunetti, 'Are you Giulio?'

Suor'Immacolata took his arm and led him away, saying, 'Your mother took Communion this week. That seemed to help her a great deal.'

'I'm sure it did,' Brunetti said. When he thought about it, it seemed to Brunetti that what he did when he came here was similar to what a person who was going to experience physical pain – an injection, exposure to sharp cold – did with his body: he tensed his muscles and concentrated, to the exclusion of all other sensation, on resisting that anticipated pain. But, instead of tightening his muscles, Brunetti found himself, if such a thing could be said to be, tightening his soul.

They stopped at the door of his mother's room, and memories of the past crowded around and beat at him like the Furies: glorious meals filled with laughter and singing, his mother's clear soprano rising up above them all; his mother breaking into angry, hysterical tears when he told her he wanted to marry Paola, then coming into his room that same night to give him her gold bracelet, her only remaining gift from Brunetti's father, saying that it was for Paola, for the bracelet was always supposed to belong to the wife of the eldest son.

A twist of his will, and all memory fled. He saw only the door, the white door, and the white back of Suor'Immacolata's habit. She opened the door and went in, leaving the door open.

'Signora,' she said, 'Signora, your son is here to see

163

you.' She moved across the room and went to stand near the bent old woman sitting by the window. 'Signora, isn't that nice? Your son's come to visit you.'

Brunetti stood by the door. Suor'Immacolata nodded to him, and he stepped inside, leaving the door open behind him, as he had learned to do.

'Good morning, Dottore,' the nun said loudly, enunciating clearly. 'I'm so glad you could come to see your mother. Isn't she looking well?'

He came a few more steps into the room and stopped, holding his hands well away from his body. '*Buon dì*, Mamma,' he said. 'It's Guido. I've come to see you. How are you, Mamma?' He smiled.

The old woman grabbed at the nun's arm and pulled her down, whispered something into her ear, never taking her eyes off Brunetti.

'Oh, no, Signora. Don't say such things. He's a good man. It's your son, Guido. He's come to see you and see how you are.' She stroked the old woman's hand, knelt down to be closer to her. The old woman looked at the nun, said something else to her, then looked back at Brunetti, who hadn't moved.

'He's the man who killed my baby,' she suddenly shouted. 'I know him. I know him. He's the man who killed my baby.' She pushed herself from side to side in her chair. She raised her voice and began to shout, 'Help, help, he's come back to kill my babies.'

Suor'Immacolata put her arms around the old woman, held her tight, and whispered in her ear, but nothing could contain the woman's fear and wrath. She

pushed the nun away with such force that she fell sprawling on the ground.

Suor'Immacolata quickly pushed herself to her knees and turned to Brunetti. She shook her head and made a gesture to the door. Brunetti, keeping his hands clearly visible in front of him, backed slowly out of the room and closed the door. From inside, he heard his mother's voice, screaming wildly for long minutes, then gradually growing calmer. Under it, in soft counterpoint, he heard the softer, deeper voice of the young woman as she soothed, calmed, and gradually removed the old woman's fear. There were no windows in the corridor, and so Brunetti stood outside the door and looked at it.

After about ten minutes, Suor'Immacolata came out of the room and stood beside him. 'I'm sorry, Dottore. I really thought she was better this week. She's been very quiet, ever since she took the Communion.'

'That's all right, Sister. These things happen. You didn't hurt yourself, did you?'

'Oh, no. Poor thing, she didn't know what she was doing. No, I'm all right.'

'Is there anything she needs?' he asked.

'No, no, she has everything she needs.' To Brunetti, it seemed like his mother had nothing she needed, but maybe that was only because there was nothing she needed any longer, and never would again.

'You're very kind, Sister.'

'It's the Lord who is kind, Dottore. We merely do His service.'

Brunetti found nothing to say. He put out his hand

and shook hers, kept her hand in his for long seconds, and then wrapped his other hand around it. 'Thank you, Sister.'

'God bless you and give you strength, Dottore.'

Chapter Sixteen

A week had passed, so the story of Maria Lucrezia Patta was no longer the sun around which the Questura of Venice revolved. Two more cabinet ministers had resigned over the weekend, each vociferous in his protestations that his decision had nothing whatsoever to do with and was in no way related to his having been named in the most recent scandals about bribery and corruption. Ordinarily, the staff of the Questura, like all of Italy, would yawn over this and turn to the sports page, but as one of them happened to be the Minister for Justice, the staff took a special interest, if only to speculate about what other heads would soon be seen rolling down the steps of the Quirinale.

Even though this was one of the biggest scandals in decades – and when had there ever been a small scandal? – popular opinion held that it would all be *insabbiata*, buried in sand, hushed up, just as had happened with all of the other scandals in the past. Once any Italian got this particular bit between his teeth, he was virtually unstoppable, and there usually followed a list of the cases that had been effectively covered up: Ustica, PG2, the death of Pope John Paul I, Sindona. Maria Lucrezia

Patta, no matter how dramatic her exit from the city had been, could hardly be expected to keep company at such dizzy heights, and so life drifted back to normal, the only news being that the transvestite found in Mestre last week had turned out to be the director of the Banca di Verona, and who would have expected that, a bank director, for God's sake?

One of the secretaries in the passport office up the street had heard in her bar that morning that this Mascari was pretty well known in Mestre and that it had been an open secret for years what he did when he went away on his business trips. Furthermore, it was learned at another bar, his marriage wasn't a real marriage, just a cover for him because he worked in a bank. Here someone interjected that he hoped his wife had at least worn the same size clothing; why else marry her? One of the fruit vendors at Rialto had it on very good authority that Mascari had always been like that, even when he was at school.

By late morning, it was necessary for public opinion to pause for breath, but by the afternoon, common knowledge had it that Mascari was dead as a result of the 'rough trade' he pursued, even against the warnings of those few friends who knew of his secret vice, and that his wife was refusing to claim his body and give it Christian burial.

Brunetti had an appointment with the widow at eleven and went to it ignorant of the rumours that were swirling around the city. He called the Banca di Verona and learned that, a week before, their office in Messina had received a phone call from a man identifying himself

as Mascari, explaining that his visit would have to be delayed, perhaps for two weeks, perhaps a month. No, they had not bothered to confirm this call, having no reason to suspect its validity.

The Mascari apartment was on the third floor of a building one block back from Via Garibaldi, the main thoroughfare of Castello. When she opened the door for Brunetti, the widow looked much the same as she had two days before, save that her suit today was black, and the signs of weariness around her eyes were more pronounced.

'Good morning, Signora. It's very kind of you to speak to me today.'

'Come in, please,' she said and stepped back from the door. He asked permission, then walked into the apartment and, for a moment, had a strange sense of complete dislocation that he had already been here. It was only after he looked around that he realized the source of this feeling: the apartment was almost identical to the apartment of the old woman in Campo San Bartolomeo and had the look of a place in which the same family had lived for generations. An identical heavy credenza stood against the far wall, and the velvet upholstery on the two chairs and sofa was the same vaguely patterned green. Curtains were also pulled closed in front of these windows, either to keep out the sun or the eyes of the curious.

'Can I get you something to drink?' she asked, an offer that was clearly formulaic.

'No, please, nothing, Signora. I would like only a bit

169

of your time. There are some questions we have to ask you.'

'Yes, I know,' she said and moved back into the room. She sat in one of the overstuffed chairs, and Brunetti took the other. She removed a small piece of thread from the arm of the chair, rolled it into a ball, and put it carefully in the pocket of her jacket.

'I don't know how much you've heard of the rumours surrounding your husband's death, Signora.'

'I know he was found dressed as a woman,' she said in a small, choking voice.

'If you know that, then you must realize that certain questions must be asked.'

She nodded and looked down at her hands.

He could make the question sound either brutal or awkward. He chose the latter. 'Do you have any or did you have any reason to believe that your husband was involved in such practices?'

'I don't know what you mean,' she said, though it must have been clear what he meant.

'That your husband was involved in transvestism.' Why not just say the word, 'transvestite', and have done with it?

'That's impossible.'

Brunetti didn't say anything, waiting for her.

All she did was repeat, stolidly, 'That's impossible.'

'Signora, has your husband ever received strange phone calls or letters?'

'I don't know what you mean.'

'Has anyone ever called and spoken to him, after

170

which he seemed worried or preoccupied? Or perhaps a letter? Or had he seemed worried lately?'

'No, nothing like that,' she said.

'If I might return to my original question, Signora, did your husband ever give any indication that he might have been drawn in that direction?'

'Towards men?' she asked, voice high with disbelief, and with something else. Disgust?

'Yes.'

'No, nothing. That's a horrible thing to say. Revolting. I won't let you say that about my husband. Leonardo was a man.' Brunetti noticed that her hands were drawn into tight fists.

'Please be patient with me, Signora. I am merely trying to understand things, and so I need to ask you these questions about your husband. That does not mean that I believe them.'

'Then why ask them?' she asked, voice truculent.

'So that we can find out the truth about your husband's death, Signora.'

'I won't answer any questions about that. It's not decent.'

He wanted to tell her that murder wasn't decent, either, but, instead, he asked, 'During the last few weeks, had your husband seemed different in any way?'

Predictably, she said, 'I don't know what you mean.'

'For example, did he say anything about his trip to Messina? Did he seem eager to go? Reluctant?'

'No, he seemed like he always did.'

'And how was that?'

'He had to go. It was part of his job, so he had to do it.'

'Did he say anything about it?'

'No, just that he had to go.'

'And he wouldn't call you during these trips, Signora?'

'No.'

'Why was that, Signora?'

She seemed to sense that he wasn't going to let this one go, so she answered, 'The bank wouldn't allow Leonardo to put personal calls on his expense account. Sometimes he'd call a friend at the office and ask him to call me, but not always.'

'Ah, I see,' Brunetti said. Director of a bank, and he wouldn't pay for a phone call to his wife.

'Do you and your husband have any children, Signora?'

'No,' she answered quickly.

Brunetti dropped that and asked, 'Did your husband have any special friends at the bank? You mentioned a friend you called; could you give me his name?'

'Why do you want to talk to him?'

'Perhaps your husband said something at work, or perhaps he gave some indication of how he felt about the trip to Messina. I'd like to speak to your husband's friend and see if he noticed anything unusual about your husband's behaviour.'

'I'm sure he didn't.'

'I'd nevertheless like to speak to him, Signora, if you could give me his name.'

'Marco Ravanello. But he won't be able to tell you anything. There was nothing wrong with my husband.' She shot Brunetti a fierce glance and repeated, 'There was nothing wrong with my husband.'

'I don't want to trouble you any more, Signora,' Brunetti said, getting to his feet and taking a few steps towards the door. 'Have the funeral arrangements been made?'

'Yes, the Mass is tomorrow. At ten.' She didn't say where it was to be held, and Brunetti didn't ask. That information was easily enough obtained, and he would attend.

At the door, he paused. 'Thank you very much for your help, Signora. I'd like to extend my personal condolences, and I assure you that we will do everything in our power to find the person responsible for your husband's death.' Why did 'death' always sound better than 'murder'?

'My husband wasn't like that. You'll find out. He was a man.'

Brunetti did not extend his hand, merely bowed his head and let himself out of the door. As he went down the steps, he remembered the last scene of *The House of Bernarda Alba*, the mother standing on stage, screaming at the audience and at the world that her daughter had died a virgin, died a virgin. To Brunetti, only the fact of their deaths mattered; all else was vanity.

At the Questura, he asked Vianello to come up to his office. Because Brunetti's was two floors higher, it was more likely to catch whatever wisp of breeze was available. When they got inside and Brunetti had opened the windows and taken off his jacket, he asked Vianello, 'Well, did you get anything on the Lega?'

'Nadia expects to be put on the payroll for this,

173

Dottore,' Vianello said as he sat down. 'She spent more than two hours on the phone this weekend, talking to friends all over the city. Interesting, this Lega della Moralità.'

Vianello would tell the story in his own way, Brunetti knew, but he thought he'd sweeten the process and said, 'I'll stop at Rialto tomorrow morning and get her some flowers. Will that be enough, do you think?'

'She'd rather have me home next Saturday,' Vianello said.

'What are you scheduled for?' Brunetti asked.

'I'm supposed to be on the boat that brings the Minister of the Environment in from the airport. We all know he's not going to come to Venice, that he's going to cancel at the last minute. You think he'd dare come here in August, with the algae stinking up the city, and talk about their great, new environmental projects?' Vianello laughed scornfully; interest in the new Green Party was another result of his recent medical experiences. 'But I'd like not to have to waste the morning going out to the airport, only to get there and be told he isn't coming.'

His argument made complete sense to Brunetti. The Minister, to use Vianello's words, wouldn't dare present himself in Venice, not in the same month when half the beaches on the Adriatic coast were closed to swimming because of high levels of pollution, not in a city that had recently learned that the fish that made up a major part of its diet contained dangerously high levels of mercury and other heavy metals. 'I'll see what I can do,' Brunetti said.

Pleased with the prospect of something better than flowers, though he knew Brunetti would bring them as well, Vianello pulled out his notebook and began to read the report compiled by his wife.

'The Lega was started about eight years ago, no one quite knows by whom or for what purpose. Because it's supposed to do good works, things like taking toys to orphanages and meals to old people in their homes, it's always had a good reputation. Over the years, the city and some of the churches have let it take over and administer vacant apartments: it uses them to give cheap, sometimes free, housing to the elderly and, in some cases, to the handicapped.' Vianello paused for a moment, then added, 'Because all of its employees are volunteers, it was allowed to organize itself as a charitable organization.'

'Which,' Brunetti interrupted him, 'means that it is not obliged to pay taxes and that the government will extend the usual courtesy to it, and its finances will not be examined closely, if at all.'

'We are two hearts that beat as one, Dottore.' Brunetti knew Vianello's politics had changed. But his rhetoric, as well?

'What is very strange, Dottore, is that Nadia wasn't able to find anyone who actually belonged to the Lega. Not even the woman at the bank, as it turns out. Lots of people said they knew someone who they thought was a member, but, after Nadia asked, it turned out that they weren't sure. Twice, she spoke to the people who were said to be members, and it turned out that they weren't.'

'And the good works?' Brunetti asked.

'Also very elusive. She called the hospitals, but none of them had ever had any contact with the Lega. I tried the social service agency that takes care of old people, but they've never heard of anyone from the Lega doing anything for the old people.'

'And the orphanages?'

'She spoke to the mother superior of the order that runs the three largest ones. She said she had heard of the Lega but had never had any help from them.'

'And the woman in the bank. Why did Nadia think she was a member?'

'Because she lives in an apartment the Lega administers. But she's never been a member, and she said she didn't know anyone who was. Nadia's still trying to find someone who is.' If Nadia put this time down, as well, Vianello would probably end up asking for the rest of the month off.

'And Santomauro?' Brunetti asked.

'Everyone seems to know he's the boss, but no one seems to know how he became it. Nor, interestingly enough, does anyone have an idea of what it means to be boss.'

'Don't they have meetings?'

'People say they do. In parish houses or private homes. But, again, Nadia couldn't find anyone who had ever actually been to one.'

'Have you spoken to the boys in Finance?'

'No, I thought Elettra would take care of that.' Elettra? What was this, the informality of the converted?

'I've asked Signorina Elettra to put Santomauro into her computer, but I haven't seen her yet this morning.'

176

'She's down in the archives, I think,' Vianello explained.

'What about his professional life?' Brunetti asked.

'Success and success and nothing else. He represents two of the biggest building firms in the city, two city councillors, and at least three banks.'

'Is one of them the Bank of Verona?'

Vianello looked down at his notebook and flipped back a page. 'Yes. How did you know that?'

'I didn't know it. But that's where Mascari worked.'

'Two plus two makes four, doesn't it?' Vianello asked.

'Political connections?' Brunetti asked.

'With two city councillors as clients?' Vianello asked by way of answering the question.

'And his wife?'

'No one seems to know much about her, but everyone seems to believe she's the real power in the family.'

'And is there a family?'

'Two sons. One's an architect, the other a doctor.'

'The perfect Italian family,' Brunetti observed, then asked, 'And Crespo? What did you find out about him?'

'Have you seen his record from Mestre?'

'Yes. Usual stuff. Drugs. Trying to shake down a customer. Nothing violent. No surprises. Did you find out anything else?'

'Not much more than that,' Vianello answered. 'He was beaten up twice, but both times he said he didn't know who did it. The second time, in fact—' he flipped a few pages ahead in his notebook '—here it is. He said he was "set upon by thieves".'

' "Set upon?" '

'That's what it said in the report. I copied it down just like it was.'

'He must read a lot of books, Signor Crespo.'

'More than is good for him, I'd say.'

'Did you find out anything else about him? Whose name is on the contract for the apartment where he lives?'

'No. I'll check and see.'

'And see if you can get Signorina Elettra to find anything there might be about the finances of the Lega, or Santomauro, or Crespo, or Mascari. Tax returns, bank statements, loans. That sort of information should be available.'

'She'll know what to do,' Vianello said, noting it all down. 'Will there be anything else?'

'No. Let me know as soon as you hear anything or if Nadia finds someone who's a member.'

'Yes, sir,' Vianello said, getting to his feet. 'This is the best thing that could have happened.'

'What do you mean?'

'Nadia's getting interested in this. You know how she's been for years, not liking it when I have to work late or on the weekends. But once she got a taste of it, she was off like a bloodhound. And you should have heard her on the phone. She could get people to tell her anything. It's too bad we don't hire free lance.'

Chapter Seventeen

If he hurried, Brunetti could get to the Bank of Verona before it closed, that is, if an office that functioned from the second floor and appeared to have no place in which to fulfil the public functions of a bank bothered to observe regular hours. He arrived at 12.20 and, finding the downstairs door closed, rang the bell next to the simple brass plate that bore the bank's name. The door snapped open, and he found himself back in the same small lobby where he had stood with the old woman on Saturday afternoon.

At the top of the stairs, he saw that the door to the bank's office was closed, so he rang a second bell at its side. After a moment, he heard steps approach the door, and then it was pulled open by a tall blond man, clearly not the one he had seen go down the steps on Saturday afternoon.

He took his warrant card from his pocket and held it out to him. '*Buon giorno*, I'm Commissario Guido Brunetti from the Questura. I'd like to speak to Signor Ravanello.'

'Just one moment, please,' the man said and closed the door so quickly that Brunetti didn't have time to

stop him. At least a full minute passed before the door was opened again, this time by another man, neither tall nor blond, though neither was he the man Brunetti had seen on the stairs. 'Yes?' he asked Brunetti, as though the other man had been a mirage.

'I'd like to speak to Signor Ravanello.'

'And who shall I say is here?'

'I just told your colleague. Commissario Guido Brunetti.'

'Ah, yes, just a moment.' This time, Brunetti was ready, had his foot poised above the ground, ready to jam it into the door at the first sign the man might try to close it, a trick he had learned from reading American murder mysteries but which he had never had the chance to try.

Nor was he to get the chance to try it now. The man pulled the door back and said, 'Please come in, Signor Commissario. Signor Ravanello is in his office and would be happy to see you.' It seemed a lot for the man to assume, but Brunetti allowed him the right to his own opinion.

The main office appeared to occupy the same area as did the old woman's apartment. The man led him across a room that corresponded to her living-room: the same four large windows looked out on the *campo*. Three men in dark suits sat at separate desks, but none of them bothered to look up from his computer screen as Brunetti crossed the room. The man stopped in front of a door that would have been the door to the old woman's kitchen. He knocked and entered without waiting for an answer.

The room was about the same size as the kitchen, but where the old woman had a sink, this room had four rows of filing cabinets. In the space where she had her marble-topped table, there was a broad oak desk, and behind it sat a tall, dark-haired man of medium build who wore a white shirt and dark suit. He did not have to turn round and show the back of his head for Brunetti to recognize him as the man who had been working in the office on Saturday afternoon and whom he had seen on the vaporetto.

He had been at some distance, and he had been wearing dark glasses when Brunetti saw him, but it was the same man. He had a small mouth and a long patrician nose. This, coupled with narrow eyes and heavy dark eyebrows, succeeded in pulling all attention to the centre of his face so that the viewer tended at first to ignore his hair, which was very thick and tightly curled.

'Signor Ravanello,' Brunetti began. 'I'm Commissario Guido Brunetti.'

Ravanello stood behind his desk and extended his hand. 'Ah, yes, I'm sure you've come about this terrible business with Mascari.' Then, turning to the other man, he said, 'Thank you, Aldo. I'll speak to the commissario.' The other man left the office and closed the door.

'Please, have a seat,' Ravanello offered and came around the desk to turn one of the two straight-backed chairs that stood there so that it was more directly facing his own. When Brunetti was seated, Ravanello went back to his own chair and sat down. 'This is terrible, terrible. I've been speaking to the directors of the bank

in Verona. None of us has the least idea what to do about this.'

'About replacing Mascari? He was the director here, wasn't he?'

'Yes, he was. But, no, our problem isn't about who will replace him. That's been taken care of.'

Though Ravanello clearly meant this as a pause before he got to the real business of the bank's concern, Brunetti asked, 'And who replaced him?'

Ravanello looked up, surprised by the question. 'I have, as I was Assistant Director. But, as I said, this is not the reason for the bank's concern.'

To the best of Brunetti's knowledge – and experience had never interfered to prove him wrong – the only reason for a bank's concern about anything was how much money it made or lost. He smiled a curious smile and asked, 'And what is that, Signor Ravanello?'

'The scandal. The awful scandal. You know how discreet we have to be, bankers, you know how careful.'

Brunetti knew they couldn't be seen in a *casino*, couldn't write a bad cheque, or they could be fired, but these hardly seemed onerous demands to place upon someone who, after all, had in trust the money of other people.

'Which scandal are you talking about, Signor Ravanello?'

'If you're a police commissario, then you know the circumstances in which Leonardo's body was found.'

Brunetti nodded.

'That, unfortunately, has become common knowledge here, and in Verona. We have already had a number

of calls from our clients, from people who dealt with Leonardo for a number of years. Three of them have asked to transfer their funds from this bank. Two of those represent substantial losses for the bank. And today is only the first day.'

'And you believe these decisions are the result of the circumstances in which Signor Mascari's body was found?'

'Obviously. I should think that would be self-evident,' Ravanello said, but he sounded worried, not angry.

'Do you have reason to believe that there will be more withdrawals as a result of this?'

'Perhaps. Perhaps not. In those cases, the real losses, we can trace them directly to Leonardo's death. But we are far more worried about the immeasurable loss to the bank.'

'Which would be?'

'People who choose not to invest with us. People who hear about this or read about this and, as a result, choose to entrust their finances to another bank.'

Brunetti thought about this for a while, and he also thought about the way bankers always avoided the use of the word 'money', thought of the broad panoply of words they'd invented to replace that crasser term: funds, finances, investments, liquidity, assets. Euphemism was usually devoted to crasser things: death and bodily functions. Did that mean there was something fundamentally sordid about money and that the language of bankers attempted to disguise or deny this fact? He pulled his attention back to Ravanello.

'Have you any idea of how much this might be?'

'No,' Ravanello said, shaking his head as at the mention of death or serious illness. 'There's no way to calculate it.'

'And what you call the real losses, how great have they been?'

Ravanello's look became more guarded. 'Could you tell me why you want that information, Commissario?'

'It's not a case of my wanting that information, Signor Ravanello, not specifically. We are still in the opening stages of this investigation, and so I want to acquire as much information as possible, from as many sources as possible. I'm not sure which of it will prove important, but we won't be able to make that determination until we have acquired all of the information there is to be had regarding Signor Mascari.'

'I see, I see,' Ravanello said. He reached out and pulled a folder towards him. 'I have those figures here, Commissario. I was just looking at them.' He opened the folder and ran his finger down a computer printout of names and numbers. 'The combined worth of the liquidated assets, just from the two depositors I mentioned – the third hardly matters – is roughly eight billion lire.'

'Because he was wearing a dress?' Brunetti said, intentionally exaggerating his response.

Ravanello disguised his distaste at such levity, but just barely. 'No, Commissario, not because he was wearing a dress. But because that sort of behaviour is suggestive of a profound lack of responsibility, and our investors, perhaps rightly, are concerned that this same lack of

responsibility might have characterized his professional as well as his personal life.'

'So people are bailing out before it's discovered that he's bankrupted the bank by spending it all on stockings and lace underwear?'

'I see no reason to treat this as a joke, Commissario,' Ravanello said in a voice that must have brought countless creditors to their knees.

'I am merely attempting to suggest that this is an excessive response to the man's death.'

'But his death is very compromising.'

'For whom?'

'For the bank, certainly. But far more so for Leonardo himself.'

'Signor Ravanello, however compromising Signor Mascari's death may seem to be, we have no definite facts regarding the circumstances of that death.'

'Is that supposed to mean that he was not found wearing a woman's dress?'

'Signor Ravanello, if I dress you in a monkey suit, that does not mean you are a monkey.'

'What's that supposed to mean?' Ravanello asked, no longer attempting to disguise his anger.

'It's supposed to mean exactly what it does mean: the fact that Signor Mascari was wearing a dress at the time of his death does not necessitate the fact that he was a transvestite. In fact, it does not necessitate the fact that there was the least irregularity in his life.'

'I find that impossible to believe,' Ravanello said.

'Apparently so do your investors.'

'I find it impossible to believe for other reasons,

Commissario,' Ravanello said and looked down at the folder, closed it, and set it to the side of the desk.

'Yes?'

'This is very difficult to talk about,' he said, took the folder and shifted it to the other side of the desk.

When he said nothing more, Brunetti urged in a softer voice, 'Go on, Signor Ravanello.'

'I was a friend of Leonardo's. Perhaps his only close friend.' He looked up at Brunetti, then down again at his hands. 'I knew about him,' he said in a soft voice.

'Knew what, Signor Ravanello?'

'About the dressing-up. And about the boys.' His colour rose as he said this, but he kept his eyes steadily on his hands.

'How did you know it?'

'Leonardo told me.' He paused here and took a deep breath. 'We've worked together for ten years. Our families know each other. Leonardo is my son's godfather. I don't think he had other friends, not close ones.' Ravanello stopped talking, as if this was all he could say.

Brunetti allowed a moment to pass and then asked, 'How did he tell you? And what did he tell you?'

'We were here, working on a Sunday, just the two of us. The computers had been down on Friday and Saturday, and we couldn't begin to work on them until Sunday. We were sitting at the terminals in the main office, and he just turned to me and told me.'

'What did he say?'

'It was very strange, Commissario. He just looked over at me. I saw that he had stopped working, thought he wanted to tell me something or ask me something

about the transaction he was recording, so I stopped and looked at him.' Ravanello paused, conjuring up the scene. 'He said, "You know, Marco, I like boys." Then he bent down over the computer and continued to work, just as if he'd given me a transaction number or the price of a stock. It was very strange.'

Brunetti allowed silence to emanate out from this for a while, and then he asked, 'Did he ever explain the remark or add to it?'

'Yes. When we were finished work that afternoon, I asked him what he meant, and he told me.'

'What did he say?'

'That he liked boys, not women.'

'Boys or men?'

'*Ragazzi*. Boys.'

'Did he say anything about the dressing?'

'Not then. But he did about a month later. We were on the train, going out to the main office in Verona, and we passed a few of them on the platform in Padova. He told me then.'

'How did you respond to what he told you?'

'I was shocked, of course. I never suspected Leonardo was that way.'

'Did you warn him?'

'About what?'

'His position at the bank?'

'Of course. I told him that if anyone learned about it, his career would be ruined.'

'Why? I'm sure many homosexuals work in banks.'

'No, it's not that. It was the dressing-up. And the whores.'

'He told you that?'

'Yes. He told me that he used them and that he would do the same, sometimes.'

'Do what?'

'Whatever you call it – solicit? He would take money from men. I told him that this could destroy him.' Ravanello paused for a moment and then added, 'And it did destroy him.'

'Signor Ravanello, why haven't you told the police any of this?'

'I've just told you, Commissario. I've told you everything.'

'Yes, but I came here to question you. You didn't contact us.'

Ravanello paused and finally said, 'I saw no reason to destroy his reputation.'

'It would seem, from what you've told me about your clients, that there isn't much left to destroy.'

'I didn't think it was important.' Seeing Brunetti's look, he said, 'That is, everyone seemed to believe it already. So I saw no reason in betraying his confidence.'

'I suspect there's something you aren't telling me, Signor Ravanello.'

The banker met Brunetti's gaze and looked quickly away. 'I also wanted to protect the bank. I wanted to see if Leonardo had been . . . if he had been indiscreet.'

'Is that banker's language for "embezzle"?'

Again, Ravanello's lips expressed his opinion of Brunetti's choice of words. 'I wanted to be sure that the bank had been in no way affected by his indiscretions.'

'Meaning what?'

'All right, Commissario,' Ravanello said, leaning forward and speaking angrily. 'I wanted to see that his accounts were in order, that nothing was missing from any of the clients or institutions whose funds he handled.'

'You've had a busy morning, then.'

'No, I came in this weekend to do it. I spent most of Saturday and Sunday at the computer, checking through his files, going back three years. That's all I had time to check.'

'And what did you find?'

'Absolutely nothing. Everything is perfectly as it should be. However disorderly Leonardo's private life might have been, his professional life is perfectly in order.'

'And if it had not been?' Brunetti asked.

'Then I would have called you.'

'I see. Can copies of these records be made available to us?'

'Of course,' Ravanello agreed, surprising Brunetti by the speed with which he did so. In his experience, banks were even more reluctant to disclose information than to give money. Usually, it was available only with a court order. What a pleasant, accommodating gesture for Signor Ravanello to make.

'Thank you, Signor Ravanello. One of our finance people will be down to get them from you, perhaps tomorrow.'

'I'll have them ready.'

'I'd also like you to think of anything else Signor

Mascari might have confided in you about his other, his secret, life.'

'Of course. But I think I've told you everything.'

'Well, perhaps the emotion of the moment might be preventing you from remembering other things, minor things. I'd be very grateful if you'd make a note of anything that comes to mind. I'll be in touch with you in a day or two.'

'Of course,' Ravanello repeated, perhaps made amiable by the clear sense that the interview was soon to end.

'I think that will be all for today,' Brunetti said, getting to his feet. 'I appreciate both your time and your candour, Signor Ravanello. I'm sure this time is very difficult for you. You've lost not only a colleague, but a friend.'

'Yes, I have,' Ravanello said, nodding.

'Again,' Brunetti said, extending his hand, 'let me thank you for your time and your help.' He paused a moment and then added, 'And your honesty.'

Ravanello looked up sharply at this but said, 'You're welcome, Commissario,' and came round the desk to accompany Brunetti to the door of the main office. They shook hands again, and Brunetti let himself out on to those same steps down which he had followed Ravanello on Saturday afternoon.

Chapter Eighteen

Because he was near Rialto, it would have been easy for Brunetti to go home for lunch, but he neither wanted to cook for himself nor risk the rest of the *insalata di calamari*, now in its third day and hence suspect. Instead, he walked down to Corte dei Milion and had an adequate lunch in the small trattoria that crouched in one corner of the tiny *campo*.

He got back to his office at three and thought it might be wise to go down and talk to Patta without having to be summoned. Outside the Vice-Questore's office, he found Signorina Elettra standing by the table that stood against the wall of her tiny office, pouring water from a plastic bottle into a large crystal vase that held six tall calla lilies. The lilies were white, but not so white as the cotton of the blouse she wore with the skirt of her purple suit. When she saw Brunetti, she smiled and said, 'It's remarkable how much water they drink.'

He could think of no adequate rejoinder, so he contented himself with returning her smile and asking, 'Is he in?'

'Yes. He just got back from lunch. He's got an

appointment at four-thirty, so if you want to talk to him, you better do it now.'

'Do you know what kind of appointment it is?'

'Commissario, are you asking me to reveal a confidence about the Vice-Questore's private life?' she asked, managing to sound properly shocked, then continued, 'The fact that his appointment is with his lawyer is one I do not feel myself at liberty to reveal.'

'Ah, yes,' Brunetti said and looked down at her shoes, the same purple as her skirt. 'Then perhaps I better see him now.' He stepped a bit to the side and knocked on Patta's door, waited for the '*Avanti*' that answered his knock, and went in.

Because he sat behind the desk in Patta's office, the man had to be Vice-Questore Giuseppe Patta. But the man Brunetti saw sitting there resembled the Vice-Questore in much the same way a police photo resembled the person it depicted. Usually bronzed to a light mahogany by this time of the summer, Patta was still pale, but it was a strange kind of paleness that had been laid down under a superficial coating of tanned skin. The massive chin, which Brunetti could not glimpse without calling to mind photos of Mussolini seen in history books, had lost its jutting firmness and had grown soft, as if it needed only another week to begin to sag. Patta's tie was neatly knotted, but the collar of the suit under which it sat looked as though it needed to be brushed. The tie was just as bare of tie-pin as the lapel was of flower, creating the strange impression that the Vice-Questore had come to his office in a state of undress.

'Ah, Brunetti,' he said when he saw the other man come in. 'Have a seat. Please have a seat.' In the more than five years Brunetti had worked for Patta, this, he was certain, was the first time he had heard the Vice-Questore say 'please', other than to strain the word through tightly clenched teeth.

Brunetti did as he was asked and waited to see what new marvels were in store.

'I wanted to thank you for your help,' Patta began, looking at Brunetti for a second and then glancing away, as if following a bird that had flown across the room behind Brunetti's shoulder. Because Paola was gone, no copies of *Gente* or *Oggi* were in the house, so Brunetti could not be sure of the absence of stories about Signora Patta and Tito Burrasca, but he assumed that this was the reason for Patta's gratitude. If Patta wanted to credit that fact to Brunetti's supposed connections with the world of publishing rather than to the relative inconsequence of his wife's behaviour, Brunetti saw no sense in disillusioning the man.

'It was nothing, sir,' he said, quite truthfully.

Patta nodded. 'What about this business in Mestre?'

Brunetti gave him a brief account of what he had learned so far, concluding with his visit to Ravanello that morning and the man's assertion that he knew of Mascari's inclinations and tastes.

'Then it would seem that his murderer has got to be one of his, what do you call them, "tricks"?' Patta said, showing his unerring instinct for the obvious.

'That is, sir, if you think men of our age are sexually attractive to other men.'

'I don't know what you're talking about, Commissario,' Patta said, returning to a tone with which Brunetti was more familiar.

'We're all assuming that he was either a transvestite or a whore and was killed as a result of that, yet the only evidence we have is the fact that he was found in a dress and the statement of the man who took his job.'

'That man is also the director of a bank, Brunetti,' Patta said, with his usual reverence for such titles.

'Which job he has as a result of the other man's death.'

'Bankers do not kill one another, Brunetti,' Patta said with the rock-solid certainty so characteristic of him.

Too late, Brunetti realized the danger here. Patta had only to see the advantage of attributing Mascari's death to some violent episode in his deviant private life, and he would be justified in leaving it to the Mestre police to search for the person responsible and thus effectively remove Brunetti from any involvement with the case.

'You're probably right, sir,' Brunetti conceded, 'but this is not the time when we can risk a suggestion in the press that we have not explored every possible avenue in this case.'

Like a bull at the slightest flip of the cape, Patta responded to this reference to the media. 'What are you suggesting, then?'

'I think we should, of course, concentrate all efforts on an examination of the world of the transvestites in Mestre, but I think we should at least go through the motions of examining the possibility of some connection to the bank, however remote we both know that to be.'

Almost with dignity, Patta said, 'Commissario, I'm

not that far gone yet. If you want to pursue this idea that there might be some connection between his death and the bank, you are free to do so, but I want you to bear in mind whom you are dealing with and treat them with the respect due to their position.'

'Certainly, sir.'

'I'll leave it to you, then, but I don't want you to do anything involving the bank without checking with me first.'

'Yes, sir. Will that be all?'

'Yes.'

Brunetti got to his feet, pushed the chair closer to the desk, and left the office without another word. He found Signorina Elettra in the outer office, leafing through the papers in a file.

'Signorina,' he began, 'have you managed to get any of that financial information?'

'About which one?' she asked with a small smile.

'Eh?' Brunetti asked, entirely at a loss.

'Avvocato Santomauro or Signor Burrasca?' So pre-occupied had Brunetti been by his involvement with Mascari's death that he had forgotten that Signorina Elettra had been given the task of finding out everything she could about the film director as well.

'Oh, I'd forgotten all about that,' Brunetti admitted. The fact that she mentioned Burrasca made it clear to Brunetti that she wanted to talk about him. 'What did you find out about him?'

She laid the file to one side of her desk and looked up at Brunetti as if surprised by his question. 'That his apartment in Milano is for sale, that his last three films

lost money, and that the villa in Monaco has already been taken over by his creditors.' She smiled. 'Would you like more?'

Brunetti nodded. How on earth had she done it?

'Criminal charges have been brought against him in the United States for using children in pornographic films. And all copies of his last film have been confiscated by the police in Monaco; I can't find out why.'

'And his taxes? Are those copies of his returns you're looking through?'

'Oh, no,' she answered, voice heavy with disapproval. 'You know how difficult it is to get any information from the tax people.' She paused and added, as he suspected she might, 'Unless you know someone who works there. I won't have them until tomorrow.'

'And then will you give it all to the Vice-Questore?'

Signorina Elettra favoured him with a fierce look. 'No, Commissario. I'm going to wait at least a few more days before I do that.'

'Are you serious?'

'I do not joke about the Vice-Questore.'

'But why make him wait?'

'Why not?'

Brunetti wondered what minor indignities Patta had heaped on this woman's head during the last week to have made him be so soon repaid in this way. 'And what about Santomauro?' he asked.

'Ah, the Avvocato is an entirely different case. His finances couldn't possibly be in better condition. He's got a portfolio of stocks and bonds that must be worth more than half a billion lire. His yearly income is

declared at two hundred million lire, which is at least double what a man in his position would normally declare.'

'What about taxes?'

'That's what's so strange. It seems that he declares it all. There's no evidence that he's cheating in any way.'

'You sound like you don't believe it,' Brunetti said.

'Please, Commissario,' she said, giving him another reproachful look, though less fierce than the last. 'You know better than to believe that anyone tells the truth on their taxes. That's what's so strange. If he's declaring everything he earns, then he's got to have another source of money that makes his declared income so insignificant he doesn't have to cheat on it.'

Brunetti thought about it for a moment. Given the tax laws, no other interpretation was possible. 'Does your computer give you any indication of where that money might be coming from?'

'No, but it does tell me that he's the president of the Lega della Moralità. So that would seem the logical place to look.'

'Can you,' he asked, speaking in the plural and nodding at the screen in front of her, 'see what you can find out about the Lega?'

'Oh, I've already begun that, Commissario. But the Lega, so far, has been even more elusive than have Signor Burrasca's tax returns.'

'I have confidence you'll see your way clear of every obstacle, Signorina.'

She bowed her head, taking it as no more than her due.

He decided to ask, 'How is it that you're so familiar with the computer network?'

'Which one?' she asked, looking up.

'Financial.'

'Oh, I worked with it at my last job,' she said and glanced back down at the screen.

'And where was that, if I might ask?' he said, thinking of insurance agencies, perhaps an accountant's office.

'For the Banca d'Italia,' she said, as much to the screen as to Brunetti.

He raised his eyebrows. She glanced up and, seeing his expression, explained. 'I was an assistant to the president.'

One didn't have to be a banker or a mathematician to work out the drop in salary that a change like this meant. Further, for most Italians, a job in a bank represented absolute security; people waited years to be accepted on the staff of a bank, any bank, and Banca d'Italia was certainly the most desirable. And she was now working as a secretary for the police? Even with flowers twice a week from Fantin, it made no sense. Given the fact that she would work, not just for the police, but for Patta, it seemed an act of sovereign madness.

'I see,' he said, though he didn't. 'I hope you'll be happy with us.'

'I'm sure I will be, Commissario,' Signorina Elettra said. 'Is there any other information you'd like me to find?'

'No, not at the moment, thank you,' Brunetti said and left her to go back to his office. Using the outside line,

198

he dialled the number of the hotel in Bolzano and asked to speak to Signora Brunetti.

Signora Brunetti, he was told, had gone for a walk and was not expected to be back at the hotel before dinner. He left no message, merely identified himself and hung up.

The phone rang almost immediately. It was Padovani, calling from Rome, apologetic about the fact that he had succeeded in learning nothing further about Santomauro. He had called friends, both in Rome and in Venice, but everyone seemed to be away on vacation, and he had done no more than leave a series of messages on answering machines, requesting that his friends call him but not explaining why he wanted to speak to them. Brunetti thanked him and asked him to call if he did learn anything further.

After he hung up, Brunetti pushed the papers on his desk around until he found the one he wanted, the autopsy report on Mascari, and read through it carefully again. On the fourth page he found what he was looking for. 'Some scratches and cuts on the legs, no sign of epidermal bleeding. Scratches no doubt caused by the sharp edges on – ' and here the pathologist had done a bit of showing off by giving the Latin name of the grass in which Mascari's body had been hidden.

Dead people can't bleed; there is no pressure to carry the blood to the surface. This was one of the simple truths of pathology that Brunetti had learned. If those scratches had been caused by, and here he repeated out loud the orotund syllables of the Latin name, then they would not have bled, for Mascari was dead when his

body was shoved under those leaves. But if his legs had been shaved by someone else, after he was dead, then they would not have bled, either.

Brunetti had never shaved any part of his body except his face, but he had, for years, been witness to this process as performed by Paola, as she attempted to run a razor over calf, ankle, knee. He had lost count of the times that he had heard muttered curses from the bathroom, only to see Paola emerge with a piece of toilet paper sticking to some segment of her limb. Paola had been shaving her legs regularly since he knew her; she still cut herself when she did it. It seemed unlikely that a middle-aged man could achieve this feat with greater success than Paola and shave his legs without cutting them. He tended to believe that, to a certain degree, most marriages were pretty similar. Hence, if Brunetti were suddenly to begin to shave his legs, Paola would know it immediately. It seemed to Brunetti unlikely that Mascari could have shaved his legs and not have his wife notice, even if he didn't call her while away on business trips.

He glanced at the autopsy report again: 'No evidence of bleeding on any of the cuts on victim's legs or traces of wax.' No, Signor Mascari, regardless of the red dress and the red shoes, regardless of the make-up and the underwear, had not shaved or waxed his own legs before he died. And so that must mean that someone had done it for him after he was dead.

Chapter Nineteen

He sat in his office, hoping that a late afternoon breeze would spring up and bring some relief, but the hope proved to be as futile as his hope that he would begin to see some connection between all the random factors of the case. It was clear to him that the whole business of the transvestism was an elaborate posthumous charade, designed to pull attention away from whatever the real motive had been for Mascari's death. That meant that Ravanello, the only person to have heard Mascari's 'confession', was lying and probably knew something about the murder. But, though Brunetti found no difficulty in believing that bankers did, in fact, kill people, he couldn't bring himself to believe that they would do it merely as a short cut to promotion.

Ravanello had been in no way reluctant to admit to having been in the bank's office that weekend; in fact, he had volunteered the information. And with Mascari just identified, his reason made sense – what any good friend would do. Moreover, what any loyal employee would do.

Still, why hadn't he identified himself on the phone

on Saturday, why kept secret, even from some unknown caller, that he was in the bank that afternoon?

His phone rang and, still musing on this, still dulled with the heat, he gave his name. 'Brunetti.'

'I need to talk to you,' a man's voice said. 'In person.'

'Who is this?' Brunetti asked calmly.

'I'd rather not say over the phone,' answered the voice.

'Then I'd rather not talk to you,' Brunetti said and hung up.

This response usually stunned callers so much that they felt they had no option but to call back. Within minutes, the phone rang again, and Brunetti answered in the same way.

'It's very important,' the same voice said.

'So is it that I know who I'm talking to,' Brunetti said quite conversationally.

'We talked last week.'

'I talked to a lot of people last week, Signor Crespo, but very few of them have called me and said they wanted to see me.'

Crespo was silent for a long time, and Brunetti feared for a moment that it might be his turn to be hung up on, but instead, the young man said, 'I want to meet you and talk to you.'

'We are talking, Signor Crespo.'

'No, I have some things I want to give you, some photos and some papers.'

'What sort of papers and what sort of photos?'

'You'll know when you see them.'

'What does this have to do with, Signor Crespo?'

'With Mascari. The police got it all wrong about him.'

Brunetti was of the opinion that Crespo was correct about this, but he thought he'd keep that opinion to himself.

'What have we got wrong?'

'I'll tell you when I see you.'

Brunetti could tell from Crespo's voice that he was running out of courage or whatever other emotion had led him to make the call. 'Where do you want to meet me?'

'How well do you know Mestre?'

'Well enough.' Besides, he could always ask Gallo or Vianello.

'Do you know the parking lot at the other side of the tunnel to the train station?'

It was one of the few places where someone could park for free in the vicinity of Venice. All anyone had to do was park in the lot or along the tree-lined street that led to the tunnel and then duck into the entrance and up on to the platforms for the trains to Venice. Ten minutes by train, no parking fee, and no waiting in line to park or pay at Tronchetto.

'Yes, I know it.'

'I'll meet you there, tonight.'

'What time?'

'Not until late. I've got something to do first, and I don't know when I'll be finished.'

'What time?'

'I'll be there by one this morning.'

'Where will you be?'

'When you come up out of the tunnel, go down to the

first street and turn left. I'll be parked on the right side in a light blue Panda.'

'Why did you ask about the parking lot?'

'Nothing. I just wanted to know if you knew about it. I don't want to be in the parking lot. It's too well lit.'

'All right, Signor Crespo, I'll meet you.'

'Good,' Crespo said and hung up before Brunetti could say anything more.

Well, Brunetti wondered, who had put Signor Crespo up to making that particular call? He did not for an instant believe that Crespo had made the call for his own purposes or designs – someone like Crespo would never have called back – but that in no way diminished his curiosity to know what the call had really been about. The most likely conclusion was that someone wanted to deliver a threat, or perhaps something stronger, and what better way to do that than to lure him out on to a public street at one in the morning?

He phoned the Mestre Questura and asked to speak to Sergeant Gallo, only to be told that the sergeant had been sent to Milan for a few days to give evidence in a court case. Did he want to speak to Sergeant Buffo, who was handling Sergeant Gallo's work? Brunetti said no and hung up.

He called Vianello and asked him to come up to his office. When the sergeant came in, Brunetti asked him to sit down and told him about Crespo's call and his own to Gallo. 'What do you think?' Brunetti asked.

'I'd say they're, well, somebody's trying to get you out of Venice and into an open space where you're not well

protected. And if there's any protecting to be done, it's going to have to be done by our boys.'

'What means would they use?'

'Well, it could be someone sitting in a car, but they'd know we'll have people there. Or it could be a car or a motorcycle that came by, either to run you down or to take a shot at you.'

'Bomb?' Brunetti asked, shivering involuntarily at the memory of the photos he'd seen of the wreckage left by the bombs that had destroyed politicians and judges.

'No, I don't think you're that important,' Vianello said. Cold comfort, but comfort nevertheless.

'Thanks. I'd say it will probably be someone who will drive by.'

'So what do you want to do?'

'I'd like people in at least two of the houses, one at the beginning and one at the end of the street. And, if you can get someone to volunteer for it, someone in the back seat of a car. It'll be hell, being inside a closed car in this heat. That's already three people. I don't think I can assign more than that.'

'Well, I won't fit in a back seat, and I don't think I'd much like just sitting in a house and having to watch, but I think I might park around the corner, if I can get one of the women officers to come with me, and make love for a while.'

'Perhaps Signora Elettra would be willing to volunteer,' Brunetti said and laughed.

Vianello's voice was sharp, as sharp as it had ever been. 'I'm not joking, Commissario. I know that street; my aunt from Treviso always leaves her car there when

she comes to visit, and I always take her back. I often see people in cars there, so one or two more won't make any difference.'

Brunetti had it on his lips to ask how Nadia would view this, but he thought better of it and, instead, said, 'All right, but she has to be a volunteer for this. If there's any danger, I don't like the idea of a woman being involved.' Before Vianello could object, Brunetti added, 'Even if she is a police officer.'

Did Vianello raise his eyes to the ceiling at that? Brunetti thought so but didn't ask. 'Anything else, Sergeant?'

'You have to be there at one?'

'Yes.'

'There's no train that late. You'll have to take the bus out and walk down from the station and through the tunnel.'

'What about getting back to Venice?' Brunetti asked.

'Depends on what happens, I suppose.'

'Yes, I suppose.'

'I'll see if I can find anyone who wants to be in the back of the car,' Vianello said.

'Who's on night duty this week?'

'Riverre and Alvise.'

'Oh,' Brunetti said simply, but the sound spoke volumes.

'That's who's on the roster.'

'I guess you better put them in the houses.' Neither one of them wanted to say that, put in the back of a car, either one of them would simply fall asleep. Of course, there was equal possibility of that if they were put in a

house, but perhaps the owners would be sufficiently curious to help keep them awake.

'What about the others? Do you think you'll be able to get volunteers?'

'There'll be no trouble,' Vianello assured him. 'Rallo will want to come, and I'll ask Maria Nardi. Her husband is on some sort of training programme in Milano for a week, so she might like to do it. Besides, it's overtime. Isn't it?'

Brunetti nodded, then added, 'Vianello, make it clear to them that there might be some danger involved.'

'Danger? In Mestre?' Vianello asked with a laugh, dismissing the idea, then added, 'Do you want to carry a radio?'

'No, I don't think so, not with four of you so close.'

'Well, two of us, at any rate,' Vianello corrected him, saving Brunetti the embarrassment of having to speak slightingly of the lower orders.

'If we're going to be up all night with this, then I suppose we ought to be able to go home for a while,' Brunetti said, looking at his watch.

'Then I'll see you there, sir,' Vianello said and stood.

Just as Vianello had said, there was no train that would get Brunetti to the Mestre station at that hour, so he contented himself with taking the Number One bus and getting out, the only passenger at that hour, across from the Mestre train station.

He walked up the steps into the station then down again through the tunnel that cut under the train tracks and came up on the other side. He emerged on a quiet, tree-lined street, behind him the well-lit parking lot,

filled now with cars parked there for the night. The street in front of him was lined on both sides with parked cars; light filtered down on to them from the few street lights above. Brunetti stayed on the right side of the street, where there were fewer trees and, consequently, more light. He walked up to the first corner and paused, looking all round him. About four cars down, on the other side of the street, he saw a couple in a fierce embrace, but the man's head was obscured by the woman's, so he could not tell if it was Vianello or some other married man having a stolen hour.

He looked down the street to the left, studying the houses that lined it on both sides. At the front of one, about half-way down the block, the dim grey light of a television filtered out through the lower windows; the rest were dark. Riverre and Alvise would be at the windows of two of those houses, but he felt no desire to look up in their direction: he was afraid they might take it as a signal of some sort and come rushing to his aid.

He turned into the street, looking for a light-blue Panda on the right-hand side. He walked to the end of the street, seeing no car that fitted that description, turned, and came back. Nothing. He noticed that, up at the corner, there was a large rubbish bin, and he crossed to the other side, thinking again of those pictures he had seen of what little remained of Judge Falcone's vehicle. A car turned into the road, coming from the roundabout, and slowed, heading towards Brunetti. He backed between the protection of two parked cars, but it drove past and went into the parking lot. The driver got out,

locked his door, and disappeared into the tunnel to the station.

After ten minutes, Brunetti walked down the same street again, this time looking into each of the parked cars. One of them had a blanket on the floor in the back, and, conscious of how hot it was even out here in the open, Brunetti felt a surge of sympathy for whoever had been drafted in to lie under that blanket.

Half an hour passed, at the end of which Brunetti decided that Crespo wasn't going to show up. He went back to the road junction and turned left, down to where the couple in the front seat were still engaged in their exchange of intimacies. When he got to the car, Brunetti rapped with his knuckles on the hood, and Vianello pulled himself away from a red-faced Officer Maria Nardi and got out of the car.

'Nothing,' Brunetti said, looking down at his watch. 'It's almost two.'

'All right,' Vianello said, his disappointment audible. 'Let's go back.' He ducked his head into the car and said to the female officer, 'Call Riverre and Alvise and tell them to follow us back.'

'What about the man in the car?' Brunetti asked.

'Riverre and Alvise drove out with him. They'll just come out and meet at the car and drive home.'

Inside the car, Officer Nardi spoke on the radio, telling the two other officers that no one had shown up, and they were going back to Venice. She looked up at Vianello. 'All right, Sergeant. They'll be out in a few minutes.' Saying that, she got out of the car and opened the back door.

'No, stay there,' Brunetti said. 'I'll sit in the back.'

'That's all right, Commissario,' she said with a shy smile, then added, 'Besides, I'd like the chance to have a bit of distance between me and the sergeant.' She got in and closed the door.

Brunetti and Vianello exchanged a glance over the roof of the car. Vianello's smile was sheepish. They climbed in. Vianello leaned forward and turned the key. The engine sprang to life and a small buzzer sounded.

'What's that?' Brunetti asked. For Brunetti, as for most Venetians, cars were alien territory.

'Seat-belt warning,' Vianello said, pulling his down across his chest and latching it by the gear shift.

Brunetti did nothing. The buzzer continued to sound.

'Can't you turn that thing off, Vianello?'

'It'll go off by itself if you'll put your seat belt on.'

Brunetti muttered something about not liking to have machines tell him what to do, but he latched his seat belt, and then he muttered something about this being more of Vianello's ecological nonsense. Pretending not to hear, Vianello put the car into gear, and they pulled away from the kerb. At the end of the street, they waited a few minutes until the other car drew up behind them. Officer Riverre sat at the wheel, Alvise beside him, and when Brunetti turned to signal to them, he could see a third form in the back, head leaning against the seat.

The streets were virtually empty at this hour, and they were quickly back on to the road that led to the Ponte della Libertà.

'What do you think happened?' Vianello asked.

'I thought it had been set up to threaten me in some way, but maybe I was wrong and Crespo really wanted to see me.'

'So what will you do now?'

'I'll go and see him tomorrow and see what kept him from coming tonight.'

They pulled on to the bridge and saw the lights of the city ahead of them. Flat black water stretched out on either side, speckled by lights on the left from the distant islands of Murano and Burano. Vianello drove faster, eager to get to the garage and then home. All of them felt tired, let down. The second car, following close behind them, suddenly pulled out into the centre lane, and Riverre sped past them, Alvise leaning out the window and waving happily to them.

Seeing them, Officer Nardi leaned forward and put her hand on Vianello's shoulder and started to speak. 'Sergeant,' she began and then stopped abruptly as her eyes were pulled up to the rear-view mirror, in which a pair of blinding lights had suddenly appeared. Her fingers tightened on his shoulder and she had time only to shout out, 'Be careful,' before the car behind them swerved to the left, pulled abreast and then ahead of them, and then quite deliberately crashed into their left front fender. The force of the impact hurled them to the right, slamming them into the guard rail at the side of the bridge.

Vianello pulled the wheel to the left, but he reacted too slowly, and the rear of the car swung out to the left, carrying them into the middle of the road. Another car

coming from behind them at an insane velocity cut to their right and slipped into the space now opened up between them and the guard rail, and then their rear slammed into the guard rail on the left, and they were spun in another half circle, coming to rest in the middle of the road, facing back towards Mestre.

Dazed, not aware of whether he was in pain or not, Brunetti stared through the shattered windshield and saw only the radiant refraction of the headlights that approached them. One set swished past them on the right and then another. He turned to the left and saw Vianello slumped forward against his seat belt. Brunetti reached down and released his own, shifted around in his seat, and grabbed Vianello's shoulder. 'Lorenzo, are you all right?'

The sergeant's eyes opened and he turned to face Brunetti. 'I think so.' Brunetti leaned down and unsnapped the other seat belt; Vianello remained upright.

'Come on,' Brunetti said, reaching for the door on his side. 'Get out of the car or one of those maniacs will slam into us.' He pointed through what was left of the windshield at the lights that kept approaching from the direction of Mestre.

'Let me call Riverre,' Vianello said, leaning forward towards the radio.

'No. Cars have passed. They'll report it to the Carabinieri in Piazzale Roma.' As if in proof of his words, he heard the first whine of a siren from the other end of the bridge and saw the flashing blue lights as the Carabinieri sped down the wrong side of the bridge to reach them.

212

Brunetti got out and leaned down to open the back door. Officer Junior Grade Maria Nardi lay on the back seat of the car, her neck bent at a strange and unnatural angle.

Chapter Twenty

The aftermath of the incident was both predictable and depressing. Neither of them had noticed what kind of car hit them, not even the colour or general size, though it must have been a large one to have thrust them to the side with such force. No other cars had been close enough to them to see what happened, or, if they had been, no one reported it to the police. It was clear that the car, after hitting them, had merely continued into Piazzale Roma, turned, and sped back across to the mainland even before the Carabinieri had been alerted.

Officer Nardi was pronounced dead at the scene, her body taken to the *ospedale civile* for an autopsy that would merely confirm what was clearly visible from the angle at which her head rested.

'She was only twenty-three,' Vianello said, avoiding Brunetti's glance. 'They'd been married six months. Her husband's away on some sort of computer training course. That's all she kept talking about in the car, how she couldn't wait until Franco got home, how much she missed him. We sat like that for an hour, face to face, and all she did was talk about her Franco. She was just a kid.'

Brunetti could find nothing to say.

'If I had made her wear her seat belt, she'd still be alive.'

'Lorenzo, stop it,' Brunetti said, voice rough, but not with anger. They were back in the Questura by then, sitting in Vianello's office while they waited for their reports of the incident to be typed out so that they could sign them and go home. 'We can go on all night like that. I shouldn't have gone to meet Crespo. I should have seen that it was too easy, should have been suspicious when nothing happened in Mestre. Next we'll be saying we should have come back in an armoured car.'

Vianello sat beside his desk, looking past Brunetti. There was a large bump on the left side of his forehead, and the skin around it was turning blue. 'But we did what we did, or we didn't do what we didn't do, and still she's dead,' Vianello said in a flat voice.

Brunetti leaned forward and touched the other man's arm. 'Lorenzo, we didn't kill her. The men or the man in that car did. There's nothing we can do except try to find them.'

'That's not going to help Maria, is it?' Vianello asked bitterly.

'Nothing on God's earth can ever help Maria Nardi again, Lorenzo. We both know that. But I want the men in that car, and I want whoever sent them.'

Vianello nodded, but he had nothing to say to this. 'What about her husband?' Vianello asked.

'What about him?'

'Will you call him?' There was something other than curiosity in Vianello's voice. 'I can't.'

'Where is he?' Brunetti asked.

'At the Hotel Impero in Milano.'

Brunetti nodded. 'I'll call him in the morning. There's no sense in calling him now, to add time to his suffering.'

A uniformed officer came into the office carrying the originals of their statements and two Xerox copies of each. Both men sat patiently and read through the typescripts and then each signed the original and both copies and handed them back to the officer. When he was gone, Brunetti got to his feet and said, 'I think it's time to go home, Lorenzo. It's after four. Did you call Nadia?'

Vianello nodded. He had called her from the Questura an hour before. 'It was the only job Maria could get. Her father was a policeman, so someone pulled strings for her, and she got the job. Do you know what she really wanted to do, Commissario?'

'I don't want to talk about this, Lorenzo.'

'Do you know what she really wanted to do?'

'Lorenzo,' Brunetti said in a low voice, warning him.

'She wanted to be an elementary schoolteacher, but she knew there were no jobs, so she joined the police.'

All this time, they had been walking slowly down the steps and now walked across the lobby towards the double doors. The uniformed officer on guard, seeing Brunetti, saluted. The two men stepped outside, and from across the canal, from the trees in Campo San Lorenzo, came the almost deafening chorus of birds as they courted the dawn. It was no longer the full dark of night, but the light was so far only a suggestion, one that turned the world of thick impenetrability into one of infinite possibility.

They stood on the edge of the canal, looking over towards the trees, their eyes drawn by what their ears perceived. Both had their hands in their pockets and both felt the sudden chill that lay in the air before dawn.

'This shouldn't happen,' Vianello said. Then, turning off to the right and his way home, he said, '*Arrivederci*, Commissario,' and walked away.

Brunetti turned the other way and started back towards Rialto and the streets that would take him home. They'd killed her as though she were a fly; they had stretched out their hands to crush him and, instead, had snapped off her life. Just like that. One minute, she was a young woman, leaning forward to say something to a friend, hand placed lightly, confidently, affection-ately on his arm, mouth poised to speak. What had she wanted to say? Was it a joke? Did she want to tell Vianello she had been kidding back there, when she got into the car? Or had it been something about Franco, some final word of longing? No one would ever know. The fleeting thought had died with her.

He would call Franco, but not yet. Let the young man sleep now, before great pain. Brunetti knew that he couldn't, not now, tell the young man of Maria's last hour in the car with Vianello; he couldn't bear to say it. Later, Brunetti would tell him, for it was then that the young man would be able to hear it, only then, after great pain.

When he got to Rialto, he looked off to the left and saw that a vaporetto was approaching the stop, and it was that coincidence that decided him. He hurried to the stop and got on to the boat, took it to the station, and

caught the morning's first train across the causeway. Gallo, he knew, would not be at the Questura, so he took a taxi from the Mestre station, giving the driver Crespo's address.

The daylight had come when he wasn't paying attention, and with it had come the heat, perhaps worse here in this city of pavement and cement, roads and high-rise buildings. Brunetti almost welcomed the mounting discomfort of the temperature and humidity; it distracted him from what he had seen that night and from what he was beginning to fear he would see at Crespo's apartment.

As it had been the last time, the elevator was air-conditioned, already necessary even at this hour. He pushed the button and rose quickly and silently to the seventh floor. He rang Crespo's doorbell, but this time there was no response from beyond it. He rang again and then again, holding his finger on the bell for long seconds. No footsteps, no voices, no sound of life.

He took out his wallet and removed from it a small sliver of metal. Vianello had once spent an entire afternoon teaching him how to do this, and, even though he hadn't been an especially good pupil, it took him less than ten seconds to open Crespo's door. He stepped across the threshold, saying, 'Signor Crespo? Your door is open. Are you in here?' Caution never hurt.

No one was in the living-room. The kitchen glistened, fastidiously clean. He found Crespo in the bedroom, on the bed, dressed in yellow silk pyjamas. A piece of telephone wire was knotted around his neck, his face a horrible, stuffed parody of its former beauty.

Brunetti didn't bother to look around or examine the room; he went to the apartment next door and knocked on the door until a sleepy, angry man opened it, shouting at him. By the time the laboratory crew arrived from the Mestre Questura, Brunetti had also had time to call Maria Nardi's husband in Milano and tell him what had happened. Unlike the man at the door, Franco Nardi didn't shout; Brunetti had no idea if this was better or worse.

Back at the Questura in Mestre, Brunetti told a just-arrived Gallo what had happened and turned the examination of Crespo's apartment and body over to him, explaining that he had to go back to Venice that morning. He did not tell Gallo that he was returning in order to attend Mascari's funeral; already the atmosphere swirled with too much death.

Even though he came back to the city from a place of violent death, came back in order to be present at the consequences of another, he could not stop his heart from contracting at the sight of the bell towers and pastel façades that swept into view as the police car crossed the causeway. Beauty changed nothing, he knew, and perhaps the comfort it offered was no more than illusion, but still he welcomed that illusion.

The funeral was a miserable thing: empty words were spoken by people who were clearly too shocked by the circumstances of Mascari's death to pretend to mean what they said. The widow sat through it all rigid and dry-eyed and left the church immediately behind the coffin, silent and solitary.

*

The newspapers, as was only to be expected, went wild at the scent of Crespo's death. The first story appeared in the evening edition of *La Notte*, a paper much given to red headlines and the use of the present tense. Francesco Crespo was described as 'a transvestite courtesan'. His biography was given, and much attention was paid to the fact that he had worked as a dancer in a gay *discoteca* in Vicenza, even though his tenure there had lasted less than a week. The writer of this article drew the inevitable link to the murder of Leonardo Mascari, less than a week ago, and suggested that the similarity in victim indicated a person who was exacting a deadly vengeance against transvestites. The writer did not seem to believe it necessary to explain why this might be.

The morning papers picked up this idea. The *Gazzettino* made reference to the more than ten prostitutes who had been killed just in the province of Pordenone in recent years and attempted to draw a line between those crimes and the murders of the two transvestites. *Il Manifesto* gave the crime two full columns on page four, the writer using the opportunity to refer to Crespo as 'yet another of the parasites who cling to the rotting body of Italian bourgeois society'.

In its magisterial discussion of the crime, *Il Corriere della Sera* veered quickly from the murder of a relatively insignificant prostitute to that of a well-known Venetian banker. The article made reference to 'local sources' who reported that Mascari's 'double life' had been an item of common knowledge in certain quarters. His death, therefore, was simply the inevitable result of the

'spiral of vice' into which his weakness had transformed his life.

Interested by this revelation of 'sources', Brunetti put a call through to the Rome office of that newspaper and asked to speak to the writer of the article. That person, when contacted and learning that Brunetti was a commissario of police wanting to know to whom he had spoken when writing the article, said that he was not at liberty to reveal the source of his information, that the trust that must exist between a journalist and those who both speak to and read him must be both implicit and absolute. Further, to reveal his source would go against the highest principles of his profession. It took Brunetti at least three full minutes to realize that the man was serious, that he actually believed what he was saying.

'How long have you worked for the newspaper?' Brunetti interrupted.

Surprised to be cut off in the full flood of his exposition of his principles, goals, and ideals, the reporter paused a moment and then answered, 'Four months. Why?'

'Can you transfer this call back to the switchboard, or do I have to dial again?' Brunetti asked.

'I can transfer you. But why?'

'I'd like to speak to your editor.'

The man's voice grew uncertain, then suspicious, at this, the first real sign of the duplicity and underhanded dealings of the powers of the state. 'Commissario, I want to warn you that any attempt to suppress or call into question the facts I have revealed in my story will quickly be revealed to my readers. I'm not sure if you realize

221

that a new age has dawned in this country, that the people's need to know can no longer be—' Brunetti pushed down the button on his receiver and, when he got a new dial tone, redialled the central number of the newspaper. Not even the Questura should have to pay to listen to that sort of nonsense, and certainly not at long-distance rates.

When he was finally connected with the editor of the news section of the paper, he turned out to be Giulio Lotto, a man with whom Brunetti had dealt in the past when both of them had been suffering exile in Naples.

'Giulio, it's Guido Brunetti.'

'*Ciao*, Guido. I heard you were back in Venice.'

'Yes. That's why I'm calling. One of your writers' – Brunetti looked down at the byline and read out the name – 'Lino Cavaliere, has an article this morning about the transvestite who was murdered in Mestre.'

'No. My deputy read it last night. What about it?'

'He talks about "local sources" who say the other one, Mascari, who was murdered last week, was known by people here to have been leading a "double life".' Brunetti paused for a moment and then repeated the words: ' "double life". Nice phrase, Giulio, "double life".'

'Oh, Christ, did he put that in?'

'It's all right here, Giulio: "local sources. Double life".'

'I'll have his balls,' Lotto shouted into the phone and then repeated the same thing to himself.

'Does that mean there are no "local sources"?'

'No, he had some sort of anonymous phone call from

222

a man who said he had been a customer of Mascari's. Client, whatever you call them.'

'What did he say?'

'That he had known Mascari for years, had warned him about some of the things he did, some of the customers he had. He said it was a well-known secret up there.'

'Giulio, the man was almost fifty.'

'I'll kill him. Believe me, Guido, I didn't know anything about this. I told him not to use it. I'll kill the little shit.'

'How could he be that stupid?' Brunetti asked, though well he knew the reasons for human stupidity to be legion.

'He's a cretin, hopeless,' Lotto said, voice heavy, as though he had daily reminder of that fact.

'Then what's he doing working for you? You still do have the reputation of being the best newspaper in the country.' Brunetti's phrasing of this was masterful; his personal scepticism was evident, but it didn't flaunt itself.

'He's married to the daughter of that man who owns that furniture store, the one who puts in the double page ad every week. We had no choice. He used to be on the sports page, but then one day he mentioned how surprised he was to learn that American football was different from soccer. So *I* got him.' Lotto paused and both men reflected for a moment. Brunetti found himself strangely comforted to know that he was not the only man to be burdened with the likes of Riverre and Alvise. Lotto apparently found no comfort and said only, 'I'm trying to get him transferred to the political desk.'

'Perfect choice, Giulio. Good luck,' Brunetti said, thanked him for the information, and hung up.

Though he had suspected something very much like this, it still surprised him by its obvious clumsiness. Only by some stroke of extraordinary good fortune could the 'local source' have found a reporter gullible enough to repeat the rumour about Mascari without bothering to check if there was any basis in fact. And only someone who was very rash – or very frightened – would have tried to plant the story, as if it could keep the elaborate fiction of Mascari's prostitution from unravelling.

The police investigation of Crespo's murder, so far, had been as unrewarding as the press coverage. No one in the building had known of Crespo's profession; some thought he was a waiter in a bar, while others believed him to be a night porter at a hotel in Venice. No one had seen anything strange during the days before his murder, and no one could remember anything strange ever happening in the building. Yes, Signor Crespo had a lot of visitors, but he was extroverted and friendly, so it made sense that people came to visit him, didn't it?

The physical examination had been clearer: death had been caused by strangulation, his murderer taking him from behind, probably by surprise. No sign of recent sexual activity, nothing under his nails, and enough fingerprints in the apartment to keep them busy for days.

He had called Bolzano twice, but once the hotel's phone was busy, and the second time Paola had not been in her room. He picked up the phone to call her again but was interrupted by a knock on his door. He called,

'*Avanti*,' and Signorina Elettra came in, carrying a file, which she placed on his desk.

'Dottore, I think there's someone downstairs who wants to see you.' She saw his surprise at her bothering to tell him, indeed, at her even knowing this, and hastened to explain. 'I was bringing some papers down to Anita, and I heard him talking to the guard.'

'What did he look like?'

She smiled. 'A young man. Very well dressed.' This, coming from Signorina Elettra, who was today wearing a suit of mauve silk that appeared to have been made by especially talented worms, was high praise indeed. 'And very handsome,' she added, with a smile that suggested regret that the young man wanted to speak to Brunetti and not to her.

'Perhaps you could go down and bring him up,' Brunetti said, as much to hasten the possibility of meeting this marvel as to provide Signorina Elettra with an excuse to talk to him.

Her smile changed back into the one she appeared to use for lesser mortals, and she left his office. She was back in a matter of minutes, knocked, and came in, saying, 'Commissario, this gentleman would like to speak to you.'

A young man followed her into the office, and Signorina Elettra stepped aside to allow him to approach Brunetti's desk. Brunetti stood and extended his hand across the desk. The young man shook it; his grip was firm, his hand thick and muscular.

'Please make yourself comfortable, Signore,' Brunetti

said then turned to Signorina Elettra. 'Thank you, Signorina.'

She gave Brunetti a vague smile, then looked at the young man in much the same way Parsifal must have looked at the Grail as it disappeared from him. 'Yes, yes,' she said. 'If you need anything, sir, just call.' She gave the visitor one last look and left the office, closing the door softly behind her.

Brunetti sat and glanced across the desk at the young man. His short dark hair curled down over his forehead and just covered the tops of his ears. His nose was thin and fine, his brown eyes broad-spaced and almost black in contrast to his pale skin. He wore a dark grey suit and a carefully knotted blue tie. He returned Brunetti's gaze for a moment and then smiled, showing perfect teeth. 'You don't recognize me, Dottore?'

'No, I'm afraid I don't,' Brunetti said.

'We met last week, Commissario. But the circumstances were different.'

Suddenly Brunetti remembered the bright red wig, the high-heeled shoes. 'Signor Canale. No, I didn't recognize you. Please forgive me.'

Canale smiled again. 'Actually, it makes me very happy that you didn't recognize me. It means my professional self really is a different person.'

Brunetti wasn't sure just what this was supposed to mean, so he chose not to respond. Instead, he asked, 'What is it I can do for you, Signor Canale?'

'Do you remember, when you showed me that picture, I said that the man looked familiar to me?'

226

Brunetti nodded. Didn't this young man read the newspapers? Mascari had been identified days ago.

'When I read the story in the papers and saw the photo of him, what he really looked like, I remembered where I had seen him. The drawing you showed me really wasn't very good.'

'No, it wasn't,' Brunetti admitted, choosing not to explain the extent of the damage that had made that drawing so inaccurate a reconstruction of Mascari's face. 'Where was it that you saw him?'

'He approached me about two weeks ago.' When he saw Brunetti's surprise at this, Canale clarified the remark. 'No, it wasn't what you're thinking, Commissario. He wasn't interested in my work. That is, he wasn't interested in my business. But he was interested in me.'

'What do you mean?'

'Well, I was on the street. I'd just got out of a car – from a client, you know – I hadn't got back to the girls, I mean the boys, yet, and he came up to me and asked me if my name was Roberto Canale, and I lived at thirty-five, Viale Canova.

'At first, I thought he was police. He had that look.' Brunetti thought it better not to ask, but Canale explained, anyway. 'You know, ties and suits and very eager that no one misunderstand what he was doing. He asked me, and I told him that I was. I still thought he was police. In fact, he never told me he wasn't, let me go on thinking that he was.'

'What else did he want to know, Signor Canale?'

'He asked me about the apartment.'

'The apartment?'

'Yes, he wanted to know who paid the rent. I told him I did, and then he asked me how I paid it. I told him I deposited the rent in an account in the owner's name at the bank, but then he told me not to lie, that he knew what was going on, so I had to tell him.'

'What do you mean, "knew what was going on"?'

'How I pay the rent.'

'And how is that?'

'I meet a man in a bar and I give him the money.'

'How much?'

'A million and a half. In cash.'

'Who is he, this man?'

'That's exactly what he asked me. I told him he was just a man that I met every month, met at a bar. He calls me during the last week of the month and tells me where to meet him, and I do, and I give him a million and a half, and that's that.'

'No receipt?' Brunetti asked.

Canale laughed outright at this. 'Of course not. It's all cash.' And, consequently, they both knew it went unreported as income. And untaxed. It was a common enough dodge: enormous numbers of tenants probably did something similar to this.

'But I do pay another rent,' Canale added.

'Yes?' Brunetti asked.

'One hundred and ten thousand lire.'

'And where do you pay it?'

'I deposit it in a bank account, but the receipt I get doesn't have a name on it, so I don't know whose account it is.'

'What bank?' Brunetti asked, though he thought he knew.

'Banca di Verona. It's in—'

Brunetti cut him short. 'I know where it is.' Then he asked, 'How big is your apartment?'

'Four rooms.'

'A million and a half seems a lot to pay.'

'Yes, it is, but it includes other things,' Canale said, then shifted about in his chair.

'Such as?'

'Well, I won't be bothered.'

'Bothered while you work?' Brunetti asked.

'Yes. And it's hard for us to find a place to live. Once people know who we are and what we do, they want us out of the building. I was told that this wouldn't happen while I lived there. And it hasn't. Everyone in the building thinks I work on the railways: that's why I work nights.'

'Why do they think this?'

'I don't know. They just sort of all knew it when I moved in.'

'How long have you lived there?'

'Two years.'

'And you've always paid your rent like this?'

'Yes, since the beginning.'

'How did you find this apartment?'

'One of the girls on the street told me.'

Brunetti permitted himself a small smile. 'Someone you'd call a girl or someone I'd call a girl, Signor Canale?'

'Someone I'd call a girl.'

'What's his name?' Brunetti asked.

'No use my telling you. He died a year ago. Overdose.'

'Do your other friends – colleagues – have similar arrangements?'

'A few of us, but we're the lucky ones.'

Brunetti considered this fact and its possible consequences for a minute. 'Where do you change, Signor Canale?'

'Change?'

'Into your . . .' Brunetti began and then paused, wondering what to call them. 'Into your working clothes? If people think you work on the railways, that is.'

'Oh, in a car, or behind the bushes. After a while, you get to be very fast at it; doesn't take a minute.'

'Did you tell all of this to Signor Mascari?' Brunetti asked.

'Well, some of it. He wanted to know about the rent. And he wanted to know the addresses of some of the others.'

'Did you give them to him?'

'Yes, I did. I told you, I thought he was police, so I told him.'

'Did he ask you anything else?'

'No, only about the addresses.' Canale paused for a moment and then added, 'Yes, he asked one more thing, but I think it was just sort of, you know, to show that he was interested in me. As a person, that is.'

'What did he ask?'

'He asked if my parents were alive.'

'And what did you tell him?'

'I told him the truth. They're both dead. They died years ago.'

'Where?'

'In Sardinia. That's where I'm from.'

'Did he ask you anything else?'

'No, nothing.'

'What sort of reaction did he have to what you told him?'

'I don't understand what you mean,' Canale said.

'Did he seem surprised by anything you said? Upset? Were these the answers he was expecting to get?'

Canale thought for a moment and then answered, 'At first, he seemed a little surprised, but then he kept asking me questions, as if he didn't even have to think about them. As if he had a whole list of them ready.'

'Did he say anything to you?'

'No, he thanked me for the information I gave him. That was strange, you know, because I thought he was a cop, and usually cops aren't very . . .' He paused, hunting for the proper expression. 'They don't treat us very well.'

'When did you remember who he was?'

'I told you: when I saw his picture in the paper. A banker. He was a banker. Do you think that's why he was so interested in the rents?'

'I suppose it could be, Signor Canale. It's certainly a possibility we will check.'

'Good. I hope you can find the man who did it. He didn't deserve to die. He was a very nice man. He treated me well, decently. The way you did.'

'Thank you, Signor Canale. I wish only that my colleagues would do the same.'

'That would be nice, wouldn't it?' Canale said with a winsome smile.

'Signor Canale, could you give me a list of the same names and addresses you gave him? And, if you know it, when your friends moved into their apartments.'

'Certainly,' the young man said, and Brunetti passed a piece of paper and a pen across the desk to him. He bent over the paper and began to write and, as he did, Brunetti watched his large hand, holding the pen as though it were a foreign object. The list was short, and he was quickly finished with it. When he was done, Canale set the pen down on the desk and got to his feet.

Brunetti got up and came round his desk. He walked with Canale to the door, where he asked, 'What about Crespo? Do you know anything about him?'

'No, he's not someone I worked with.'

'Do you have any idea of what might have happened to him?'

'Well, I'd have to be a fool not to think it's related to the other man's murder, wouldn't I?'

This was so self-evident that Brunetti didn't even nod.

'In fact, if I had to guess, I'd say he was killed because he talked to you.' Seeing Brunetti's look, he explained, 'No, not to you, Commissario, but to the police. I'd guess he knew something about the other killing and had to be eliminated.'

'And yet you came down here to talk to me?'

'Well, Signor Mascari spoke to me like I was just an ordinary person. And you did, too, didn't you, Commissario? Spoke to me like I was a man, just like other

232

men?' When Brunetti nodded, Canale said, 'Well, then, I had to tell you, didn't I?'

The two men shook hands again, and Canale walked down the corridor. Brunetti watched as his dark head disappeared down the steps. Signorina Elettra was right, a very handsome man.

Chapter Twenty-One

Brunetti went back into his office and dialled Signorina Elettra's number. 'Would you come up to my office, please, Signorina?' he asked. 'And could you bring anything you've discovered about those men I asked you to look into this week?'

She said she would be delighted to come up; he had every confidence that this was true. Brunetti was, however, prepared for her disappointment when she knocked, came in, and looked around, only to find the young man gone.

'My visitor had to leave,' Brunetti said in answer to her unspoken question.

Signorina Elettra recovered herself immediately. 'Ah, did he?' she asked, voice level with lack of interest, and handed two separate files to Brunetti. 'The first is Avvocato Santomauro.' He took it from her hand, but even before he could open it, she said, 'There's nothing whatsoever worthy of comment. Law degree from Ca' Foscari: a Venetian born and bred. He's worked here all his life, is a member of all the professional organizations, married in the church of San Zaccaria. You'll find tax

returns, passport applications, even a permit to put a new roof on his home.'

Brunetti glanced through the file and found exactly what she described, nothing more. He turned his attention to the second, which was considerably thicker.

'That's the Lega della Moralità,' she said, making Brunetti wonder if everyone who spoke those words did so with the same heavy sarcasm or if this was perhaps no more than an indication of the kind of people he spent his time with. 'The file is more interesting, but I'll let you take a look through it and see what I mean,' she said. 'Will there be anything else, sir?'

'No, thank you, Signorina,' he said and opened the file.

She left and he spread the file flat on his desk and began to read through it. The Lega della Moralità had been incorporated as a charitable institution nine years ago, its charter proclaiming it an organization seeking to 'improve the material condition of the less fortunate so that the lessening of their worldly cares would aid them more easily to turn their thoughts and desires toward the spiritual.' These cares were to be lessened in the form of subsidized houses and apartments which were owned by various churches in Mestre, Marghera, and Venice and which had passed into the administration of the Lega. The Lega would, in its turn, assign these apartments, at minimal rents, to parishioners of the churches of those cities who were found to meet the standards established by the joint agreement of the churches and the Lega. Among those requirements were regular attendance at Mass, proof of baptism of all

children, a letter from their parish priest attesting that they were people who maintained the 'highest moral standards', and evidence of financial need.

The charter of the Lega placed the power to select among applicants in the hands of the board of directors of the Lega, all of whom, to remove any possibility of favouritism on the part of Church authorities, were to be laymen. They were themselves, as well, to be of the highest moral character and were to have achieved some prominence in the community. Of the current board of six, two were listed as 'honorary members'. Of the remaining four, one lived in Rome and another in Paris, while the third lived on the monastery island of San Francesco del Deserto. The only active member of the board living in Venice, therefore, was Avvocato Giancarlo Santomauro.

The original charter provided for the transfer of fifty-two apartments to the administration of the Lega. At the end of three years, the system had been judged to be so successful, this on the basis of letters and statements from tenants and from parish officials and priests who had interviewed them, that six other parishes were led to join, passing another forty-three apartments to the care of the Lega. Much the same thing happened three years after that, when another sixty-seven apartments, most of them in the historic centre of Venice and the commercial heart of Mestre, were passed to the Lega.

Since the charter under which the Lega operated and which gave it control of the apartments it administered was subject to renewal every three years, this process, Brunetti calculated, was due to be repeated this year.

He flipped back and read the first two reports of the evaluation committees. He checked the signatures on both: Avvocato Giancarlo Santomauro had served on both boards and had signed both reports, the second as chairman. It was shortly after that report that Avvocato Santomauro had been appointed president – an unpaid and entirely honorary position – of the Lega della Moralità.

Attached to the back of the report was a list of the addresses of the one hundred and sixty-two apartments currently administered by the Lega, as well as their total area and the number of rooms in each. He pulled the paper Canale had given him closer and read through the addresses on it. All four appeared on the other list. Brunetti liked to think of himself as a man of broad views, relatively free of prejudice, yet he wasn't sure whether he could credit five transvestite prostitutes as being people of the 'highest moral standards', even if they were living in apartments which were rented for the specific purpose of helping tenants 'turn their thoughts and desires to the spiritual'.

He turned back from the list of addresses and continued reading through the body of the report. As he had expected, all of the tenants of Lega apartments were expected to pay their rents, which were no more than nominal, to an account at the Venice office of the Banca di Verona, which bank also handled the contributions the Lega made to the 'relief of widows and orphans', donations paid out of the funds raised from the minimal rents paid on the apartments. Even Brunetti found himself surprised that they would dare a rhetorical flourish

like this – 'the relief of widows and orphans' – but then he saw that this particular form of charitable work was not undertaken until Avvocato Santomauro had assumed the leadership of the Lega. Flipping back, Brunetti saw that the five men on Canale's list had all moved into their apartments after Santomauro became president. It was almost as if, having achieved that position, Santomauro felt himself free to dare anything.

Brunetti stopped reading here and went and stood at the window of his office. The brick façade of San Lorenzo had been free of scaffolding for the last few months, but the church still remained closed. He looked at the church and told himself that he was committing an error against which he warned other police: he was assuming the guilt of a suspect, even before he had a shred of tangible evidence to connect the suspect with the crime. But just as he knew that the church would never be reopened, not in his lifetime, he knew that Santomauro was responsible for Mascari's murder and for Crespo's, and for that of Maria Nardi. He, and probably Ravanello. A hundred and sixty-two apartments. How many of them could be rented to people like Canale or to others who were willing to pay their rent in cash and ask no questions? Half? Even a third would give them more than seventy million lire a month, almost a billion lire a year. He thought of those widows and orphans, and he wondered if Santomauro could have been led so to overreach himself that they, too, were part of it, and even the minimal rents that reached the coffers of the Lega were then turned around and paid out to phantom widows and invented orphans.

He went back to his desk and paged through the report until he found the reference to the payments made to those found worthy of the charity of the Lega: yes, payments were made through the Banca di Verona. He stood with both hands braced on the desk, head bent down over the papers, and he told himself, again, that certainty was different from proof. But he was certain.

Ravanello had promised him copies of Mascari's accounts at the bank, no doubt the records of the investments he oversaw or the loans he approved. Clearly, if Ravanello was willing to supply those documents, then whatever Brunetti was looking for would not be among them. To have access to the complete files of the bank and of the Lega, Brunetti would need an order from a judge, and that could come only from a power higher than Brunetti had at his disposal.

Patta's '*Avanti*' came through the door, and Brunetti entered his superior's office. Patta looked up, saw who it was, and bent down again over the papers in front of him. Much to Brunetti's surprise, Patta seemed actually to be reading them, not using them as props to suggest his own industry.

'*Buon giorno*, Vice-Questore,' Brunetti said as he approached the desk.

Patta looked up again and waved to the chair in front of him. When Brunetti was seated, Patta asked, pushing a finger at the papers in front of him, 'Do I have you to thank for this?'

Since Brunetti had no idea of what the papers were and didn't want to lose a tactical advantage by admitting

that, he had only the Vice-Questore's tone to guide his answer. Patta's sarcasm was usually broad, but there had been no trace of it. Because Brunetti was entirely unfamiliar with Patta's gratitude, indeed, could only speculate as to its existence, much in the way a theologian would think of guardian angels, he could not be certain that this was the sentiment which underlay Patta's tone.

'Are they the papers Signorina Elettra brought you?' Brunetti ventured, playing for time.

'Yes,' Patta said, patting them, much as a man would pat the head of a favoured dog.

That was enough for Brunetti. 'Signorina Elettra did all the work, but I did suggest a few places to look,' he lied, casting his eyes down in false humility to suggest that he dare not seek praise for doing something so natural as being of use to Vice-Questore Patta.

'They're going to arrest him tonight,' Patta said with savage delight.

'Who are, sir?'

'The finance people. He lied on his application for citizenship in Monaco, so that's not valid. That means he's still an Italian citizen and hasn't paid taxes here for seven years. They'll crucify him. They'll hang him up by his heels.'

The thought of some of the tax dodges which former and current ministers of state had managed to get away with led Brunetti to doubt that Patta's dreams would be realized, but he thought this not the moment to demur. He didn't know how to ask the next question and sought to do so delicately. 'Will he be alone when he's arrested?'

'That's the problem,' Patta said, meeting his glance. 'The arrest is secret. They're going in at eight tonight. I know about it only because a friend of mine in Finance called to tell me about it.' As Brunetti watched, Patta's face clouded with preoccupation. 'If I call her and warn her, she'll tell him, and then he'll leave Milano and won't be arrested. But if I don't call her, she'll be there when they arrest him.' And then, he didn't have to say, there was no way her name could be kept from the press. And then, inevitably, Patta's. Brunetti watched Patta's face, fascinated by the emotions that played upon it as he was torn between vengeance and vanity.

As Brunetti knew it would, vanity won. 'I can't think of a way to get her out of there without warning him.'

'Perhaps, sir, but only if you think it's a good idea, you could have your lawyer call her and ask her to meet him in Milano this evening. That would get her out of, er, where she is when the police arrive.'

'Why would I want my lawyer to talk to her?'

'Perhaps he could say you were willing to discuss terms, sir? It would serve to get her somewhere else for the evening.'

'She hates my lawyer.'

'Would she be willing to talk to you, sir? If you said you were going to Milano to meet her?'

'She . . .' Patta began but pushed himself back from his desk and stood without finishing the thought. He walked over to his window and began his own silent inspection of the façade of San Lorenzo.

He stood there for a full minute, saying nothing, and Brunetti realized the peril of the moment. Should Patta

turn round and confess to some sort of emotional weakness, confess that he loved his wife and wanted her back, he would never forgive Brunetti for having been there to hear it. Worse, should he give some physical sign of weakness or need and Brunetti see it, Patta would be relentless in exacting vengeance upon the witness.

Voice level and serious, as though Patta and his personal problems were already dismissed from his mind, Brunetti said, 'Sir, the real reason I came down was to discuss this Mascari business. I think there are some things you ought to know.'

Patta's shoulders moved up and down once as he took a deep breath, and then he turned around and came back to his desk. 'What's been happening?'

Quickly, voice dispassionate and interested only in this matter, Brunetti told him about the file on the Lega and the apartments it had in its care, one of which was Crespo's, then told him about the sums which were given out each month to the deserving poor.

'A million and a half a month?' Patta said when Brunetti finished telling him about Canale's visit. 'What rent is the Lega supposed to be collecting?'

'In Canale's case, a hundred and ten thousand a month. And no one on the list pays more than two hundred thousand, sir. That is, the Lega's books say they collect no more than that for any one apartment.'

'What are the apartments like?'

'Crespo's was four rooms, in a modern building. It's the only one I've seen, but from the addresses I saw on the list, at least the addresses here in the city, and the

number of rooms, I'd say they would have to be desirable apartments, many of them.'

'Do you have any idea of how many of them are like Canale's, and the owner pays the rent in cash?'

'No, sir, I don't. At this point, I need to speak to the people who live in the apartments and find out how many of them are involved in this. I must see the bank records for the Lega. And I need the list of the names of these widows and orphans who are supposed to be getting money every month.'

'That means a court order, doesn't it?' Patta asked, his native caution seeping into his tone. To move against someone like Canale or Crespo was perfectly all right, and no one to care about how it was done. But a bank – a bank, that was a different matter entirely.

'I'm assuming, sir, that there is some tie-in here with Santomauro and that any investigation of Mascari's death will lead us to him.' Perhaps if Patta was not to have vengeance against Santomauro's wife, then he would settle for Santomauro himself.

'I suppose that's possible,' Patta said, wavering.

At the first sign of the weakness of a truthful argument, Brunetti was, as ever, willing to turn to mendacity. 'It's probable that the bank records are in order and the bank has had nothing to do with this, that it has been manipulated by Santomauro alone. Once we eliminate the possibility of irregularity at the bank, then we'll be free to move against Santomauro.'

Patta needed no more than this to tip himself over the edge. 'All right, I'll request that the instructing judge give us an order to sequester the bank records.'

'And the documents of the Lega, as well,' Brunetti risked, thought for a moment about naming Santomauro again, but resisted.

'All right,' Patta agreed, but in a voice that made it clear that Brunetti would get no more.

'Thank you, sir,' Brunetti said, getting to his feet. 'I'll start now, getting some of the men to talk to the people on the list.'

'Good, good,' Patta said, no longer much interested. He bent down over the papers on his desk again, ran a hand affectionately across their surface, then looked up as if surprised to see Brunetti standing there. 'Is there anything else, Commissario?'

'No, sir, no. That's all,' Brunetti said and went across to the door. When he let himself out, Patta was reaching for the phone.

Back in his own office, he put a call through to Bolzano and asked to speak to Signora Brunetti.

After some clicks and pauses, Paola's voice came across the line to him. '*Ciao*, Guido, *come stai*? I tried to get you at home Monday night. Why haven't you called?'

'I've been busy, Paola. Have you been reading the papers?'

'Guido, you know I'm on vacation. I've been reading The Master. *The Sacred Fount* is wonderful. *Nothing* happens, absolutely nothing.'

'Paola, I don't want to talk about Henry James.'

She had heard the words before, but never with that tone. 'What's wrong, Guido?'

Immediately, he regretted not having made more of

an effort to call her sooner. 'There's been some trouble here,' he said, trying to make little of it.

Instantly alert, she asked, 'What sort of trouble?'

'An accident.'

Voice softer, she said, 'Tell me about it, Guido.'

'I was coming back from Mestre, and someone tried to run us off the bridge.'

'Us?'

'I was with Vianello,' he said, then added, 'and Maria Nardi.'

'The girl from Canareggio? The new one?'

'Yes.'

'What happened?'

How was it that no one had called her? Why hadn't he? 'Our car was hit and we crashed into the guard rail. She wasn't wearing a seat belt, and she was tossed against the door. It broke her neck.'

'Ah, the poor girl,' Paola whispered. 'Are you all right, Guido?'

'I was shaken up, and so was Vianello, but we're all right.' He tried for a lighter tone, 'No broken bones.'

'I'm not talking about broken bones,' she said, voice still very soft, but quick, either with impatience or concern. 'I'm asking if you're all right.'

'Yes, I think I am. But Vianello blames himself. He was driving.'

'Yes, Vianello would blame himself. Try to talk to him, Guido. Keep him busy.' She paused and then asked, 'Do you want me to come back?'

'No, Paola, you barely got there. I just wanted you to know I was all right. In case you read it in the papers. Or

in case anyone asked you about it.' He heard himself talking, heard himself trying to blame her for not having called, for not having read the papers.

'Do you want me to tell the children?'

'I guess you better, in case they hear about it or read something. But play it down, if you can.'

'I will, I will, Guido. When's the funeral?'

For a moment, he didn't know which one she meant: Mascari's, Crespo's, or Maria Nardi's? No, it could only be Maria's. 'I think it's Friday morning.'

'Will you all go?'

'As many of us as can. She'd only been on the force a short time, but she had a lot of friends.'

'Who was it?' she asked, no need to explain the question.

'I don't know. The car was gone before we realized what happened. But I'd just been in Mestre to meet someone, one of the transvestites, so whoever it was knew where I was. It would have been easy to follow us. There's only the one road back.'

'And the transvestite?' she asked. 'Have you spoken to him?'

'Too late. He's been killed.'

'Same person?' she asked in that telegraphic style they'd had two decades to develop.

'Yes. Has to be.'

'And the first one? The one in the field?'

'It's all the same thing.'

He heard her say something to someone else, then her voice came back, and she said, 'Guido, Chiara's here and wants to say hello.'

246

'*Ciao*, Papà, how have you been? Do you miss me?'

'I've been fine, angel, and I miss you terribly. I miss you all.'

'But do you miss me most?'

'I miss you all the same.'

'That's impossible. You can't miss Raffi because he's never home anyway. And Mamma just sits and reads that book all day, so who'd miss her? That means you've got to miss me most, doesn't it?'

'I guess that's right, angel.'

'See, I knew it. You just had to think about it a little bit, didn't you?'

'Yes. I'm glad you reminded me.'

He heard noises on Chiara's end of the phone, then she said, 'Papà, I've got to give you back to Mamma. You tell her, will you, to come for a walk with me? She just sits here on the terrace all day and reads. What sort of vacation is that?' With that complaint, she was gone, replaced by Paola.

'Guido, if you'd like me to come back, I can.'

He heard Chiara's howl of protest at the suggestion and answered, 'No, Paola, it's not necessary. Really. I'll try to get up there this weekend.'

She had heard similar promises many times before, so she didn't ask him to swear to it. 'Can you tell me more about it, Guido?'

'No, Paola, I'll tell you when I see you.'

'Here?'

'I hope so. If not, then I'll call you. Look, I'll call you either way, whether I'm coming or not. All right?'

'All right, Guido. For God's sake, please be careful.'

'I will, Paola. I will. You be careful, too?'

'Careful? Careful of what, up here in the middle of paradise?'

'Careful you don't finish your book, the way you did in Cortina that time.' Both laughed at the memory. She had taken *The Golden Bowl* with her but finished it in the first week, leaving her with nothing to read and, consequently, nothing to do for the second week except walk in the mountains, swim, loaf in the sun, and chat with her husband. She had loathed every minute of it.

'Oh, that's all right. I'm already eager to finish it so that I can begin it all over again immediately.' For a moment, Brunetti pondered the possibility that his failure to be promoted to vice-questore might be accountable to the fact that it was common knowledge he was married to a madwoman. No, probably not.

With mutual abjurations towards caution, they took their leave of one another.

Chapter Twenty-Two

He called down to Signorina Elettra, but she was not at her desk, and her phone rang unanswered. He dialled Vianello's extension and asked him to come up to his office. After a few minutes, the sergeant came in, looking much as he had two mornings ago, when he walked away from Brunetti in front of the Questura.

'*Buon di*', Dottore,' he said as he took his usual place in the chair facing Brunetti's desk.

'Good morning, Vianello.' To avoid a return to their discussion of the other morning, Brunetti asked, 'How many men have we got free today?'

Vianello gave this a moment's thought, then answered, 'Four, if we count Riverre and Alvise.'

Nor did Brunetti want to discuss them, so he said, passing Vianello the first list from the file on the Lega, 'This is a list of names of people who rent apartments from the Lega della Moralità. I'd like you to select the addresses here in Venice and divide it up among the four of them.'

Vianello, glancing down the names and addresses on the list, asked, 'What for, sir?'

'I want to find out who they pay their rent to, and

how.' Vianello gave him a glance replete with curiosity, and Brunetti explained what Canale had told him about paying the rent in cash and about his friends who did the same. 'I'd like to know how many of the people on this list pay their rent in the same way and how much they pay. More importantly, I want to know if any of them know the person or persons to whom they actually give the money.'

'So that's it?' Vianello asked, understanding at once. He paged through the list. 'How many are there, sir? Far more than a hundred, I'd say.'

'One hundred and sixty-two.'

Vianello whistled. 'And you say this Canale's paying a million and a half a month?'

'Yes.'

Brunetti watched Vianello repeat the same calculation he had made when he first saw the list. 'Even if it's only a third of them, it would be well over half a billion a year, wouldn't it?' Vianello asked, shaking his head, and again Brunetti couldn't tell if his response was astonishment or admiration for the enormity of the thing.

'Do you recognize any of the names on the list?' Brunetti asked.

'One of them sounds like the man who owns the bar on the corner near my mother's house: same name, but I'm not sure if it's the right address.'

'If it is, then perhaps you could talk to him casually.'

'Not wearing my uniform, you mean?' Vianello asked with a smile that seemed more like his old self.

'Or send Nadia,' Brunetti joked, but as soon as he said it, he realized this might not be a bad idea. The

appearance of uniformed policemen to question people who were, in some degree, in illegal possession of apartments was sure to affect any answers they gave. Brunetti was certain that all of the accounts would be in order, sure that proof would exist that the rents had been paid into the proper bank account each month, and he had no doubt that proper receipts would exist. If Italy was nothing else, it was a place where documented evidence always existed, and that in abundance; what was often illusory was the reality it was meant to reflect.

Vianello saw it as quickly as he did, and said, 'I think there might be a more casual way to do this.'

'Asking neighbours, you mean?'

'Yes, sir. I think people would be reluctant to tell us if they were involved in anything like this. It could mean they'd lose their apartments, and anyone would lie to avoid that.' Vianello, he had no doubt, would lie to save his apartment. After sober reflection, Brunetti realized he would, too, as any Venetian would.

'Then I suppose it's better to ask around in the neighbourhoods. Send women officers to do it, Vianello.'

Vianello's smile was one of pure delight.

'And take this. It should be easier to check,' Brunetti said, pulling the second list from the file and handing it to him. 'These are people who are receiving monthly payments from the Lega. See if you can find out how many of them live at the addresses listed for them, and then see if you can find out if they're among what used to be called the deserving poor.'

'If I were a betting man,' Vianello, who was, said, 'I'd bet ten thousand lire that most of them don't live at the

251

addresses given here.' He paused a moment, flipped at the list with the tips of his fingers, and added, 'And I'd make another one that many of them are neither deserving nor poor.'

'No bet, Vianello.'

'I didn't think there would be. What about Santomauro?'

'According to everything Signorina Elettra could find, he's clean.'

'No one's clean,' Vianello shot back.

'Careful, then.'

'That's better.'

'There's something else. Gallo spoke to the manufacturer of the shoes that were found with Mascari, and he gave him a list of the stores in the area where the shoes were sold. I'd like you to get someone going round the stores on the list and see if they can find anyone who remembers selling them. They're size forty-one, so it's possible that whoever sold them might remember who they sold them to.'

'What about the dress?' Vianello asked.

Brunetti had received the report two days ago, and the results were just as he had feared. 'It's one of those cheap things you can buy at the open-air markets anywhere. Red, some sort of cheap synthetic material. Couldn't have cost more than forty thousand lire. The tag's been ripped out of it, but Gallo's trying to trace it back to the manufacturer.'

'Any chance of that?'

Brunetti shrugged. 'There's a much better chance

with the shoes. At least we know the manufacturer and the stores where they were sold.'

Vianello nodded. 'Anything else, sir?'

'Yes. Call the Finance Police and tell them we're going to need one of their best people, more than that if they'll let us have them, to take a look at whatever papers we get from the Banca di Verona and from the Lega.'

Surprised, Vianello asked, 'You actually got Patta to ask for a court order? To make a bank give up papers?'

'Yes,' Brunetti said, managing neither to smile nor to preen.

'This business must have upset him more than I thought. A court order.' Vianello shook his head at the marvel of it.

'And could you ask Signorina Elettra to come up here?'

'Of course,' Vianello said, getting to his feet. He held up the lists. 'I'll divide up the names and get to work.' He walked over to the door, but before he left, he asked the same question Brunetti had been asking himself all morning, 'How could they risk something like this? All it needs is one person, one leak, and the whole thing would come tumbling down.'

'I have no idea; well, none that makes sense.' To himself, he reflected that it might be no more than yet another manifestation of a kind of group madness, a frenzy of risk-taking that had abandoned all sane limits. In recent years, the country had been shaken by arrests and convictions for bribery at all levels, from industrialists and builders to cabinet ministers. Billions, tens of billions, hundreds of billions of lire had been paid out in

bribes, and so Italians had come to believe that corruption was the normal business of government. Hence the behaviour of the Lega della Moralità and the men who ran it could be seen as absolutely normal in a country run mad with venality.

Brunetti shook himself free from this speculation, looked towards the door, and saw that Vianello was gone.

He was quickly replaced by Signorina Elettra, who came through the door that Vianello had left open. 'You wanted to see me, Commissario?'

'Yes, Signorina,' he said, waving her to the seat beside his desk. 'Vianello just went downstairs with the lists you gave me. It seems a number of the people on one of them are paying far more in rent than what the Lega is declaring, so I want to know if the people on the second list are really getting the money the Vega says it's giving them.'

As he spoke, Signorina Elettra wrote quickly, head bent down over her notebook.

'I'd like to ask you, if you aren't busy with anything else – what is it you're working on down in the Archives this week?' he asked.

'What?' she asked and half rose to her feet. Her notebook fell to the floor, and she bent to pick it up. 'I beg your pardon, Commissario,' she said when she had the notebook open on her lap again. 'In the Archives? I was trying to see if there was anything there about Avvocato Santomauro or perhaps Signor Mascari.'

'And what luck have you had?'

'None, unfortunately. Neither of them has ever been in trouble with the police. Absolutely nothing.'

'No one in the building has any idea of the way things are filed down there, Signorina, but I'd like you to see what you can find about the people on those lists.'

'On both, Dottore?'

She had prepared them, so she knew that they contained more than two hundred names. 'Perhaps you could begin with the second one, the people who receive money. The list has their names and addresses, so you can check at the city hall and find out which of them are registered here as residents.' Though it was a holdover from the past, the law which required all citizens to register officially in the city where they resided and to inform the authorities of any change in address made it easy to trace the movements and background of anyone who came under official scrutiny.

'I'd like you to check the people on that list, find out if any of them have criminal records, either here or in other cities. Other countries, though I have no idea of what you'll be able to find.' Signorina Elettra nodded as she took notes, suggesting that all of this was child's play. 'Also,' he continued, 'once Vianello finds out who's paying rent under the table, then I'd like you to take those names and do the same.' She looked up a few seconds after he finished speaking. 'Do you think you could do this, Signorina? I have no idea what happened to the old files after we began to switch over to computers.'

'Most of the old files are still down there,' she said.

'They're a mess, but some things are still to be found in them.'

'Do you think you could do this?' She had been here less than two weeks, and already it seemed to Brunetti that she had been there for years.

'Certainly. I find myself with a great deal of time on my hands,' she said, leaving an opening wide enough for Brunetti to herd sheep through.

He gave in to the impulse and asked, 'What's happening?'

'They're having dinner tonight. In Milano. He's having himself driven over there this afternoon.'

'What do you think will happen?' Brunetti asked, though he knew he shouldn't.

'Once Burrasca's arrested, she'll be on the first plane. Or perhaps he'll offer to drive her back to Burrasca's after dinner – he'd enjoy that, I think, driving up with her and finding the cars from the Finance Police. She'll probably come back with him tonight if she sees them.'

'Why does he want her back?' Brunetti finally asked.

Signorina Elettra glanced up at him, puzzled by his density. 'He loves her, Commissario. Surely, you must realize that.'

Chapter Twenty-Three

The heat usually robbed Brunetti of all appetite, but that night he found himself really hungry for the first time since he had eaten with Padovani. He stopped at Rialto on the way home, surprised to find some of the fruit and vegetable stalls still open after eight. He bought a kilo of plum tomatoes so ripe the vendor warned him to carry them carefully and not put anything on top. At another stall, he bought a kilo of dark figs and got the same warning. Luckily, each warning had come with a plastic bag, so he arrived at home with a bag in each hand.

When he got inside, he opened all the windows in the apartment, changed into loose cotton pants and a T-shirt, and went into the kitchen. He chopped onions, dropped the tomatoes in boiling water, the more easily to peel them, and went out on the terrace to pick some leaves of fresh basil. Working automatically, not really paying attention to what he was doing, he prepared a simple sauce and then put water on to cook the pasta. When the salted water rose to a rolling boil, he threw half a package of *penne rigate* into the water and stirred them around.

As he did all of this, he kept thinking of the various

people who had been involved in the events of the last ten days, not trying to make any sense of the jumble of names and faces. When the pasta was done, he poured it through a colander, tossed it into a serving bowl, then poured the sauce on top of it. With a large spoon, he swirled it round, then went out on to the terrace, where he had already taken a fork, a glass and a bottle of Cabernet. He ate from the bowl. Their terrace was so high that the only people close enough to see what he was doing would have to be in the bell tower of the church of San Polo. He ate all the pasta, wiping the remaining sauce up with a piece of bread, then took the bowl inside and came out with a plate of freshly washed figs.

Before he started on them, he went back inside and picked up his copy of Tacitus' *Annals of Imperial Rome*. Brunetti picked up where he had left off, with the account of the myriad horrors of the reign of Tiberius, an emperor for whom Tacitus seemed to have an especial distaste. These Romans murdered, betrayed, and did violence to honour and to one another. How like us they were, Brunetti reflected. He read on, learning nothing to change that conclusion, until the mosquitoes began to attack him, driving him inside. On the sofa, until well after midnight, he read on, not at all troubled by the knowledge that this catalogue of crimes and villainies committed almost two thousand years ago served to remove his mind from those that were being committed around him. His sleep was deep and dreamless, and he awoke refreshed, as if he believed that Tacitus' fierce,

uncompromising morality would somehow help him through the day.

When he got to the Questura the following morning, he was surprised to discover that Patta had found time, before he left for Milano the previous day, to request of the instructing judge a court order that would provide them with the records of both the Lega della Moralità and the Banca di Verona. Not only that, but the order had been delivered to both institutions that morning, where the officials in charge had promised to comply. Though both institutions insisted it would take some time to prepare the necessary documents, neither had been precise on just how long that would be.

By eleven, there was still no sign of Patta. Most of the people who worked in the Questura bought a newspaper that morning, but in none of them was there mention of Burrasca's arrest. This fact came as no surprise, neither to Brunetti nor the rest of the staff, but it did a great deal to increase the eagerness, to make no mention of the speculation, about the results of the Vice-Questore's trip to Milano the evening before. Rising above all of this, Brunetti contented himself with calling the Guardia di Finanza to ask if his request for the loan of personnel to check the financial records of both the bank and the Lega had been granted. Much to his surprise, he learned that the instructing judge, Luca Benedetti, had already called and suggested that the papers be examined by the Financial Police as soon as they were produced.

When Vianello came into his office shortly before lunch, Brunetti was sure he had come to report that

259

the papers had not arrived or, more likely, that some bureaucratic obstacle had suddenly been discovered by both the bank and the Lega, and delivery of the papers would be delayed, perhaps indefinitely.

'*Buon giorno*, Commissario,' Vianello said when he came in.

Brunetti looked up from the papers on his desk and asked, 'What is it, Sergeant?'

'I've got some people here who want to talk to you.'

'Who?' Brunetti asked, placing his pen down on the papers in front of him.

'Professore Luigi Ratti and his wife,' Vianello answered, offering no explanation save the terse, 'from Milano.'

'And who are the professor and his wife, if I might ask?'

'They're the tenants in one of the apartments in the care of the Lega, have been for a little more than two years.'

'Go on, Vianello,' Brunetti said, interested.

'The professor's apartment was on the part of the list I had, so I went to speak to him this morning. When I asked him how he had come by the apartment, he said that the decisions of the Lega were private. I asked him how he paid his rent, and he explained that he paid two hundred and twenty thousand lire into the Lega's account at the Banca di Verona every month. I asked him if I might take a look at his receipts, but he said he never kept them.'

'Really?' Brunetti asked, even more interested now. Because there was never any telling when some agency

of the government would decide that a bill had not been paid, a tax not collected, a document not issued, no one in Italy threw out any official form, least of all proof that some sort of payment had been made. Brunetti and Paola, in fact, had two complete drawers filled with utility bills that went back a decade and at least three boxes filled with various documents stuffed away in the attic. For a person to say he had thrown away a rent receipt was either an act of sovereign madness, or a lie.

'Where is the professor's apartment?'

'On the Zattere, with a view across to the Giudecca,' Vianello said, naming one of the most desirable areas in the city. Then he added, 'I'd say it's six rooms, the apartment, though I saw only the entrance hall.'

'Two hundred and twenty thousand lire?' Brunetti asked, thinking that this was what Raffi had paid for a pair of Timberlands a month ago.

'Yes, sir,' Vianello said.

'Why don't you ask the professor and his wife to come in, then, Sergeant? By the way, what is the professor a professor of?'

'I don't think of anything, sir.'

'I see,' Brunetti said and screwed the cap back on to his pen.

Vianello went over to the door and opened it, then stepped back to allow Professore and Signora Ratti to come into the office.

Professore Ratti might have been in his early fifties, but he was keeping that fact at bay to the best of his ability. He was aided in the attempt by the ministrations of a barber who cut his hair so close to the scalp that the

grey would be mistaken for blond. A Gianni Versace suit in dove-grey silk added to the youthful look, as did the burgundy silk shirt which he wore open at the throat. His shoes, which he wore without socks, were the same colour as the shirt, made of woven leather that could have come only from Bottega Veneta. Someone once must have warned him about the tendency of the skin under his chin to wattle, for he wore a knotted white silk cravat and held his chin artificially high, as if compensating for a careless optician who had put the lenses in his bifocals in the wrong places.

If the professor was fighting a holding action against his age, his wife was engaged in open combat. Her hair bore an uncanny resemblance to the colour of her husband's shirt, and her face had the tautness that came only from the vibrancy of youth or the skill of surgeons. Blade-thin, she wore a white linen suit with a jacket left open to display an emerald-green silk shirt. Seeing them, Brunetti wondered how they managed to walk around in this heat and still look fresh and cool. The coolest part of them was their eyes.

'You wanted to speak to me, Professore?' Brunetti asked, rising from his chair but making no attempt to shake hands.

'Yes, I did,' Ratti said, motioning to his wife to sit in the chair in front of Brunetti's desk and then going, unasked, to pull a second from where it stood against the wall. When they were both comfortable, he continued, 'I've come to tell you how much I dislike having the police invade the privacy of my home. Even more, I want to complain about the insinuations that have been

made.' Ratti, like so many Milanesi, elided all of the R's in his speech, a sound which Brunetti could not help associating with actresses of the more pneumatic variety.

'And what insinuations are those, Professore?' Brunetti asked, resuming his seat and signalling to Vianello to stay where he was, just inside the door.

'That there is some irregularity pertaining to my tenancy.'

Brunetti glanced across at Vianello and saw the sergeant raise his eyes towards the ceiling. Not only the Milano accent but now big words to go with it.

'What makes you believe this insinuation has been made, Professore?' Brunetti asked.

'Well, why else would your police push their way into my apartment and demand that I produce rent receipts?' As the professor spoke, his wife was busy running her eyes around the office.

' "Push", Professore?' Brunetti asked in a conversational voice. ' "Demand"?' Then, to Vianello, 'Sergeant, how did you gain access to the property to which the professor has . . .' he paused, 'tenancy?'

'The maid let me in, sir.'

'And what did you tell the maid who let you in, Sergeant?'

'That I wanted to speak to Professore Ratti.'

'I see,' Brunetti said and turned his attention back to Ratti. 'And how was the "demand" made, Professore?'

'Your sergeant asked to see my rent receipts, as if I'd keep such things around.'

'You are not in the habit of keeping receipts, Professore?'

263

Ratti waved a hand, and his wife gave Brunetti a look of studied surprise, as if to suggest what an enormous waste of time it would be to keep a record of a sum so small.

'And what would you do if the owner of the apartment were ever to claim that you had not paid the rent? What proof would you offer?' Brunetti asked.

This time, Ratti's gesture was meant to dismiss the possibility of that ever happening, while his wife's look was meant to suggest that no one would ever think of questioning her husband's word.

'Could you tell me just how you pay your rent, Professore?'

'I don't see how that is any business of the police,' Ratti said belligerently. 'I'm not used to being treated like this.'

'Like what, Professore?' Brunetti asked with real curiosity.

'Like a suspect.'

'Have you been treated like a suspect before, by other police, that would make you familiar with what it feels like?'

Ratti half rose in his seat and glanced over at his wife. 'I don't have to put up with this. A friend of mine is a city councillor.' She made a slight gesture with her hand, and he slowly sat back down.

'Could you tell me how you pay your rent, Professore Ratti?'

Ratti looked directly at Brunetti. 'I deposit the rent at the Banca di Verona.'

'At San Bartolomeo?'

'Yes.'

'And how much is that rent, Professore?'

'It's nothing,' the professor said, dismissing the sum.

'Is two hundred and twenty thousand lire the sum?'

'Yes.'

Brunetti nodded. 'And the apartment, how many square metres is it?'

Signora Ratti interrupted here, as if driven past her power to put up with such idiocy. 'We have no idea of that. It's adequate for our needs.'

Brunetti pulled the list of the apartments held in trust by the Lega towards him and flipped to the third page, then ran his finger down the list until he came to Ratti's name. 'Three hundred and twelve square metres, I think. And six rooms. Yes, I suppose that would be adequate for most needs.'

Signora Ratti was on him in a flash. 'And what is that supposed to mean?'

Brunetti turned a level glance on her. 'Just what I said, Signora, and no more. That six rooms ought to be adequate for two – there are only two of you, aren't there?'

'And the maid,' she answered.

'Three, then,' Brunetti agreed. 'Still adequate.' He turned away from her, face unchanged, and returned his attention to her husband. 'How was it that you came to be given one of the apartments of the Lega, Professore?'

'It was very simple,' Ratti began, but it seemed to Brunetti that he had begun to bluster. 'I applied for it in the normal fashion, and I was given it.'

'To whom did you apply?'

'To the Lega della Moralità, of course.'

'And how did you happen to learn that the Lega had apartments which it rented?'

'It's common knowledge here in the city, isn't it, Commissario?'

'If it is not now, then it soon will be, Professore.'

Neither of the Rattis said anything to this, but Signora Ratti glanced quickly at her husband and then back at Brunetti.

'Do you remember anyone in particular who told you about the apartments?'

Both of them answered instantly, 'No.'

Brunetti allowed himself the bleakest of smiles. 'You seem very sure of that.' He made a meaningless squiggle against their name on the list. 'And did you have an interview in order to obtain this apartment?'

'No,' Ratti said. 'We filled out the paperwork and sent it in. And then we were told that we had been selected.'

'Did you receive a letter, or perhaps a phone call?'

'It's been so long ago. I don't remember,' Ratti said. He turned to his wife for confirmation, and she shook her head.

'And you've been in this apartment for two years now?'

Ratti nodded.

'And you haven't saved any of the receipts for the rent you've paid?'

This time his wife shook her head.

'Tell me, Professore, how much time do you spend in the apartment each year?'

He thought about this for a moment. 'We come for Carnevale.'

His wife finished his sentence with a firm, 'Of course.'

Her husband continued. 'Then we come for September, and sometimes for Christmas.'

His wife broke in here and added, 'We come for the odd weekend during the rest of the year, of course.'

'Of course,' Brunetti repeated. 'And the maid?'

'We bring her with us from Milano.'

'Of course,' Brunetti nodded and added another squiggle to the paper in front of him.

'May I ask you, Professore, if you are familiar with the purposes of the Lega? With its goals?'

'I know that it aims at moral improvement,' the professor answered in a tone that declared there could never be too much of *that*.

'Ah, yes,' Brunetti said, then asked, 'But beyond that, to its purpose in renting apartments?'

This time, it was Ratti who glanced at his wife. 'I think their purpose was to attempt to give the apartments to those they considered worthy of them.'

Brunetti continued, 'Knowing this, Professore, did it at any time seem strange to you that the Lega, which is a Venetian organization, had given one of the apartments it controls to a person from Milano, a person who would, moreover, make use of the apartment only a few months of the year?' When Ratti said nothing, Brunetti urged him, 'Surely, you know how difficult it is to find an apartment in this city?'

Signora Ratti chose to answer this. 'I suppose we believed that they wanted to give an apartment like this

to people who would know how to appreciate it and care for it.'

'By that are you suggesting that you would be better able to care for a large and desirable apartment than would, for example, the family of a carpenter from Cannaregio?'

'I think that goes without saying,' she answered.

'And who, if I might ask, pays for repairs to the apartment?' Brunetti asked.

Signora Ratti smiled and answered, 'So far, there has been no need to make any repairs.'

'But surely there must be a clause in your contract – if you were given a contract – which makes clear who is responsible for repairs.'

'They are,' Ratti answered.

'The Lega?' Brunetti asked.

'Yes.'

'So then maintenance is not the responsibility of the people who rent?'

'No.'

'And you are there for – ' Brunetti began and then glanced down at the paper in front of him, as though he had the number written there, ' – for about two months a year?' When Ratti said nothing, Brunetti asked, 'Is that correct, Professore?'

His question was rewarded with a grudging, 'Yes.'

In a gesture he made consciously identical to the one used by the priest who taught catechism to his grammar-school class, Brunetti folded his hands neatly in front of him, just short of the bottom of the sheet of paper on

his desk, and said, 'I think it is time to begin making choices, Professore.'

'I don't know what you mean.'

'Then perhaps I can explain it to you. The first choice is that I have you repeat this conversation and your answers to my questions into a tape recorder or that we have a secretary come in and take it down in shorthand. Either way, I would ask you to sign a copy of that statement, ask both of you to sign it, since you are telling me the same thing.' Brunetti paused long enough for that to register. 'Or you could, and I suggest this is by far the wiser course, begin to tell me the truth.' Both feigned surprise, Signora Ratti going so far as to add outrage.

'In either case,' Brunetti added calmly, 'the least that will happen to you is that you will lose the apartment, though that might take some time to happen. But you will lose it; that is little, but it is certain.' He found it interesting that neither demanded that he explain what he was talking about.

'It is clear that many of these apartments have been rented illegally and that someone associated with the Lega has been collecting rents illegally for years.' When Professore Ratti began to object, Brunetti raised a hand for an instant, then quickly folded his fingers back together. 'Were it only a case of fraud, then perhaps you would be better advised to continue to maintain that you know nothing about all of this. But, unfortunately, it is far more than a case of fraud.' He paused here. He'd have it out of them, by God.

'What is it a case of?' Ratti asked, speaking more softly than he had since he entered Brunetti's office.

'It is a case of murder. Three murders, one of them a member of the police. I tell you this so that you will begin to realize that we are not going to let this go. One of our own has been killed, and we are going to find out who did that. And punish them.' He paused a moment to let that sink in.

'If you persist in maintaining your current story about the apartment, then you will eventually become involved in a prosecution for murder.'

'We know nothing about murder,' Signora Ratti said, voice sharp.

'You do now, Signora. Whoever is at the back of this plan to rent the apartments is also responsible for the three murders. By refusing to help us discover who is responsible for renting you your apartment and collecting your rent each month, you are also obstructing a murder investigation. The penalty for that, I need not remind you, is far more severe than for being evasive in a case involving fraud. And I add, but quite at the personal level, that I will do everything in my power to see that it is imposed upon you if you continue to refuse to help us.'

Ratti got to his feet. 'I'd like some time to speak to my wife. In private.'

'No,' Brunetti said, raising his voice for the first time.

'I have that right,' Ratti demanded.

'You have the right to speak to your lawyer, Signor Ratti, and I will gladly allow you to do that. But you and your wife will decide that other matter now, in front of me.' He was way beyond his legal rights, and he knew it; his only hope was that the Rattis did not.

They looked at one another for so long that Brunetti lost hope. But then she nodded her burgundy head and they both sat back down in their chairs.

'All right,' Ratti said, 'but I want to make it clear that we know nothing about this murder.'

'Murders,' Brunetti said and saw that Ratti was shaken by the correction.

'Three years ago,' Ratti began, 'a friend of ours in Milano told us he knew someone he thought could help us find an apartment in Venice. We had been looking for about six months, but it was very difficult to find anything, especially at that distance.' Brunetti wondered if he was going to have to listen to a series of complaints. Ratti, perhaps sensing Brunetti's impatience, continued, 'He gave us a phone number we could call, a number here in Venice. We called and explained what we wanted, and the person on the other end asked us what sort of apartment we had in mind and how much we wanted to pay.' Ratti paused, or did he stop?

'Yes?' Brunetti urged, his voice just the same as that priest's had been when the children had some question or uncertainty about the catechism.

'I told him what I had in mind, and he said he'd call me back in a few days. He did, and said he had three apartments to show us, if we could come to Venice that weekend. When we came, he showed us this apartment and two others.'

'Was he the same man who answered the phone when you called?'

'I don't know. But it was certainly the same man who called us back.'

'Do you know who the man was? Or is?'

'It's the man we pay the rent to, but I don't know his name.'

'And how do you do that?'

'He calls us in the last week of the month and tells us where to meet him. It's usually a bar, though sometimes, during the summer, it's outside.'

'Where, here in Venice or in Milano?'

His wife interrupted. 'He seems to know where we are. He calls us here if we're in Venice or Milano if we're there.'

'And then what do you do?'

Ratti answered this time. 'I meet him and I give him the money.'

'How much?'

'Two and a half million lire.'

'A month?'

'Yes, though sometimes I give him a few months in advance.'

'Do you know who this man is?' Brunetti asked.

'No, but I've seen him on the street here a few times.'

Brunetti realized there would be time to get a description later and let that pass. 'And what about the Lega? How are they involved?'

'When we told this man that we were interested in the apartment, he suggested a price, but we bargained him down to two and a half million.' Ratti said this with ill-disguised self-satisfaction.

'And the Lega?' Brunetti asked.

'He told us that we would receive application forms

from the Lega and that we were to fill them out and return them, and that we would be able to move into the apartment within two weeks of that.'

Signora Ratti broke in here. 'He also told us not to tell anyone about how we had got the apartment.'

'Has anyone asked you?'

'Some friends of ours in Milano,' she answered, 'but we told them we found it through a rental agency.'

'And the person who gave you the number – do you know how he got it?'

'He told us someone had given it to him at a party.'

'Do you remember the month and year when you made that original call?' Brunetti asked.

'Why?' Ratti asked, immediately suspicious.

'I'd like to have a clearer idea of when this began,' Brunetti lied, thinking that he could have their phone records checked for calls to Venice at that time.

Though he looked and sounded sceptical, Ratti answered. 'It was in March, two years ago. Towards the end of the month. We moved in here at the beginning of May.'

'I see,' said Brunetti. 'And since you've been living in the apartment, have you had anything to do with the Lega?'

'No, nothing,' Ratti said.

'What about receipts?' Brunetti asked.

Ratti shifted uncomfortably in his chair. 'We get one from the bank every month.'

'For how much?'

'Two hundred and twenty thousand.'

'Then why didn't you want to show it to Sergeant Vianello?'

His wife broke in again and answered for him. 'We didn't want to get involved in anything.'

'Mascari?' Brunetti suddenly asked.

Ratti's nervousness seemed to increase. 'What do you mean?'

'When the director of the bank that sent you the receipts for the rent was killed, you didn't find it strange?'

'No, why should I?' Ratti said, putting anger into his voice. 'I read about how he died. I assumed he was killed by one of his "tricks".'

'Has anyone been in touch with you recently about the apartment?'

'No, no one.'

'If you should happen to receive a call or perhaps a visit from the man you pay the rent to, I expect you to call us immediately.'

'Yes, of course, Commissario,' Ratti said, restored to his role as irreproachable citizen.

Suddenly sick of them, their posing, their designer clothes, Brunetti said, 'You can go downstairs with Sergeant Vianello. Please give him as detailed a description as you can of the man you pay the rent to.' Then, to Vianello, 'If it sounds like anyone we might know, let them take a look at some pictures.'

Vianello nodded and opened the door. The Rattis both stood, but neither made any effort to shake Brunetti's hand. The professor took his wife's arm for the short trip to the door, then stood back to allow her to pass

through it in front of him. Vianello glanced across at Brunetti, allowed himself the smallest of smiles, and followed them out of the office, closing the door after them.

Chapter Twenty-Four

His conversation with Paola that night was short. She asked if there was any news, repeated her suggestion that she come down for a few days; she thought she could leave the children alone at the hotel, but Brunetti told her it was too hot even to think of coming to the city.

He spent the rest of the evening in the company of the Emperor Nero, whom Tacitus described as being 'corrupted by every lust, natural and unnatural'. He went to sleep only after reading the description of the burning of Rome, which Tacitus seemed to attribute to Nero's having gone through a marriage ceremony with a man, during which the emperor shocked even the members of his dissolute court by 'putting on the bridal veil'. Everywhere, transvestites.

The next morning, Brunetti, ignorant of the fact that the story of Burrasca's arrest had appeared in that morning's *Corriere*, a story that made no mention of Signora Patta, attended the funeral of Maria Nardi. The Chiesa dei Gesuiti was crowded, filled with her friends and family and with most of the police of the city. Officer Scarpa from Mestre attended, explaining that Sergeant Gallo could not get away from the trial in Milan and

would be there for at least another three days. Even Vice-Questore Patta attended, looking sombre in a dark blue suit. Though he knew it was a sentimental and no doubt politically incorrect view, Brunetti could not rid himself of the idea that it was worse for a woman to die in the course of police duty than a man. When the Mass was finished, he waited on the steps of the church while the coffin was carried out by six uniformed policemen. When her husband emerged, weeping brokenly and staggering with grief, Brunetti turned his eyes to the left and looked out across the waters of the *laguna* towards Murano. He was still standing there when Vianello came up to him and touched him on the arm.

'Commissario?'

He came back. 'Yes, Vianello?'

'I've got a probable identification from those people.'

'When did that happen? Why didn't you tell me?'

'I didn't know until this morning. Yesterday afternoon, they looked at a number of pictures, but they said they weren't sure. I think they were but wanted to talk to their lawyer. In any case, they were back in this morning, at nine, and they identified Pietro Malfatti.'

Brunetti gave a silent whistle. Malfatti had been in and out of their hands for years; he had a record for violent crimes, among them rape and attempted murder, but the accusations seemed always to dissipate before Malfatti came to trial, when witnesses changed their minds or said that they had been wrong in their original identification. He had been sent away twice, once for living off the earnings of a prostitute, and once for attempting to extort protection money from the owner

of a bar. The bar had burned down during the two years Malfatti was in jail.

'Did they identify him positively?'

'Both of them were pretty sure.'

'Do we have an address for him?'

'The last address we had was an apartment in Mestre, but he hasn't lived there for more than a year.'

'Friends? Women?'

'We're checking.'

'What about relatives?'

'I hadn't thought of that. It ought to be in his file.'

'See who he's got. If it's someone close, a mother or a brother, get someone into an apartment near them and watch for him. No,' he said, remembering what little he knew of Malfatti's history, 'get two.'

'Yes, sir. Anything else?'

'The papers from the bank and from the Lega?'

'Both of them are supposed to give us their records today.'

'I want them. I don't care if you have to go in there and take them. I want all the records that have to do with the payments of money for these apartments, and I want everyone in that bank interviewed to see if Mascari said anything to them about the Lega. At any time. If you have to ask the judge to go with you to get them, then do it.'

'Yes, sir.'

'When you go to the bank, try to find out whose job it was to oversee the accounts of the Lega.'

'Ravanello?' Vianello asked.

'Probably.'

278

'We'll see what we can find out. What about Santomauro, sir?'

'I'm going to speak to him today.'

'Is that . . .' Vianello stopped himself before asking if that was wise and asked, instead, 'Is that possible, without an appointment?'

'I think Avvocato Santomauro will be very interested in talking to me, Sergeant.'

And so it was. The *avvocato*'s office was in Campo San Luca, on the second floor of a building that was within twenty metres of three different banks. How fitting that proximity was, Brunetti thought, as Santomauro's secretary showed him into the lawyer's office, only a few minutes after his arrival.

Santomauro sat at his desk, behind him a large window that looked out on the *campo*. The window, however, was tightly sealed, and the office cooled to an almost uncomfortable degree, especially in view of what could be seen below: naked shoulders, legs, backs, arms all passed across the *campo*, yet here it was cool enough for a jacket and tie.

The lawyer looked up when Brunetti was shown in but didn't bother to smile or stand. He wore a conservative grey suit, dark tie, and gleaming white shirt. His eyes were wide-spaced and blue and looked out on the world with candour. He was pale, as pale as if it were midwinter: no vacations for those who labour in the vineyards of the law.

'Have a seat, Commissario,' he said. 'What is it you want to see me about?' He reached out and moved a photo in a silver frame slightly to the right so as to

provide himself with a clear view of Brunetti and Brunetti with a clear view of the photo. In it stood a woman about Santomauro's age and two young men, both of whom resembled Santomauro.

'Any one of a number of things, Avvocato Santomauro,' Brunetti replied, sitting opposite him, 'but I'll begin with La Lega della Moralità.'

'I'm afraid you'll have to ask my secretary to give you information about that, Commissario. My involvement is almost entirely ceremonial.'

'I'm not sure I understand what you mean by that, Avvocato.'

'The Lega always needs a figurehead, someone to serve as president. But as I'm sure you've already ascertained, we members of the board have no say in the day-to-day running of the affairs of the Lega. The real work is done by the bank director who handles the accounts.'

'Then what is your precise function?'

'As I explained,' Santomauro said, giving a minimal smile, 'I serve as a figurehead. I have a certain – a certain, shall I say stature? – in the community, and so I was asked to become president, a purely titular post.'

'Who asked you?'

'The authorities at the bank which handles the accounts of the Lega.'

'If the bank director attends to the business of the Lega, then what are your duties, Avvocato?'

'I speak for the Lega in those cases when a question is put to us by the press or when the Lega's view is sought on some issue.'

'I see. And what else?'

'Twice a year, I meet with the bank official charged with the Lega's account to discuss the financial status of the Lega.'

'And what is that status? If I might ask.'

Santomauro laid both palms on the desk in front of him. 'As you know, we are a non-profit organization, so it is enough to us that we manage, as it were, to keep our head above water. In the financial sense.'

'And what does that mean? In the financial sense, that is.'

Santomauro's voice grew even calmer, his patience even more audible. 'That we manage to collect enough money to allow us to continue to bestow our charitable bequests upon those who have been selected to receive them.'

'And who, if I might ask, decides who will receive them?'

'The official at the bank, of course.'

'And the apartments which the Lega has in its care, who is it that decides to whom they will be given?'

'The same person,' Santomauro said, permitting himself a small smile, then added, 'The board routinely approves his suggestions.'

'And do you, as president, have any say in this, any decision-making power?'

'If I were to choose to use it, I suppose I might have. But, as I've already told you, Commissario, our positions are entirely honorary.'

'What does that mean, Avvocato?'

Before he answered, Santomauro placed the very tip of his finger on his desk and picked up a small speck of

dust. He moved his hand to his side and shook it, removing the speck. 'As I said, my position is merely titular. I do not feel that it would be correct, knowing so many people in the city as I do, for me to attempt to select those who might profit in any way from the charity of the Lega. Nor, I am sure and if I might take the liberty of speaking for them, would my fellow members of the board.'

'I see,' Brunetti said, making no attempt to disguise his scepticism.

'You find that hard to believe, Commissario?'

'It would be unwise of me to tell you what I find hard to believe, Avvocato,' Brunetti said and then asked, 'And Signor Crespo. Are you handling his estate?'

It had been years since Brunetti had seen a man purse his lips, but that is precisely what Santomauro did before he answered. 'I am Signor Crespo's lawyer, so of course I am handling his estate.'

'Is it a large estate?'

'That is privileged information, Commissario, as you, having taken your degree in law, should know.'

'Ah, yes, and I suppose the nature of whatever dealings you might have had with Signor Crespo is similarly privileged?'

'I see you do remember the law, Commissario,' Santomauro said and smiled.

'Could you tell me if the records of the Lega, the financial records, have been given to the police?'

'You speak of them as though you were no part of the police, Commissario.'

'The records, Signor Santomauro? Where are they?'

282

'Why, in the hands of your colleagues, Commissario. I had my secretary make copies of them this morning.'

'We want the originals.'

'Of course it's the originals I've given you, Commissario,' Santomauro said, measuring out another small smile. 'I took the liberty of making copies for myself, just in case something should get lost while they are in your care.'

'How cautious of you, Avvocato,' Brunetti said, but he didn't smile. 'But I don't want to take any more of your time. I realize how precious time is to someone who has your stature in the community. I have only one more question. Could you tell me who the bank official is who handles the accounts of the Lega. I'd like to speak to him.'

Santomauro's smile blossomed. 'I'm afraid that will be impossible, Commissario. You see, the Lega's accounts were always handled by the late Leonardo Mascari.'

Chapter Twenty-Five

He went back to his office, marvelling at the skill with which Santomauro had suggested Mascari's guilt. It all rested on such fragile premises: that the papers in the bank now looked like Mascari had been in charge of them; that people at the bank would not know or could be induced not to remember if anyone else had ever handled the accounts of the Lega; that nothing would be discovered about the murders of Mascari or Crespo.

At the Questura, he discovered that the papers of both the Banca di Verona and the Lega had been given to the police who went to collect them, and a trio of men from the Guardia di Finanza were even then going over them in search of any indication of who had overseen the accounts into which rents were paid and out of which cheques were written for the Lega's charity works.

Brunetti knew that nothing was to be gained by going down and standing over them while they worked, but he couldn't stop himself from wanting at least to walk past the room in which they had been placed. To prevent this, he went out for lunch, deliberately choosing a restaurant in the Ghetto, even though this meant a long walk there and back in the worst heat of the day. When he got back,

after three, his jacket was soaked through, and his shoes felt as though they had melted to his feet.

Vianello came into his office only minutes after he got back. Without preamble, he said, 'I've been checking the list of the people who receive cheques from the Lega.'

Brunetti recognized his mood. 'And what have you found?'

'That Malfatti's mother has remarried and taken the name of her new husband.'

'And?'

'And she's receiving cheques under that name and under her former name. What's more, her new husband also receives a cheque, as do two of his cousins, but it looks like each of them is getting them under two separate names.'

'What does that make the total for the Malfatti family?'

'The cheques are all about five hundred thousand a month, so it makes it close to three million a month.' Involuntarily, the question sprang from Vianello's mouth, 'Didn't they ever think they'd be caught?'

Brunetti thought that too obvious to answer and so, instead, he asked, 'What about the shoes?'

'No luck here. You talk to Gallo?'

'He's still in Milano, but I'm sure Scarpa would have called me if they found anything. What are those men from Finance doing?'

Vianello shrugged. 'They've been in there since the morning.'

'Do they know what they're supposed to be looking

for?' Brunetti asked, unable to keep the impatience out of his voice.

'Some sign of who handled it all, I think.'

'Would you go down there and ask them if they've found anything? If Ravanello's involved, I want to move on him as soon as possible.'

'Yes, sir,' Vianello said and left the office.

While he waited for Vianello to come back, he rolled up the sleeves of his shirt, more for something to do with his hands than from any hope that it would make him feel any cooler.

Vianello came back, and the answer was written on his face. 'I just spoke to their captain. He said that, so far, from what they can tell, it looks like Mascari was in charge.'

'What's that supposed to mean?' Brunetti snapped.

'It's what they told me,' Vianello said very slowly, voice level, and then added, after a long pause, 'sir.' Neither spoke for a moment. 'Perhaps if you were to speak to them yourself, you'd get a clearer idea of what it means.'

Brunetti looked away and rolled down his sleeves. 'Let's go downstairs together, Vianello.' It was as close as he could come to an apology, but Vianello seemed to accept it. Given the heat in the office, it was probably all he was going to get.

Downstairs, Brunetti went into the office where three men in the grey uniforms of the Guardia di Finanza were working. The men sat at a long desk covered with files and papers. Two small pocket calculators and a laptop computer stood on the desk, one man in front of each. In

concession to the heat, they had removed their woollen jackets, but they still wore their ties.

The man at the computer looked up when Brunetti came in, peered over his glasses for a moment, then looked back down and tapped some more information into the keyboard. He looked at the screen, glanced down at one of the papers beside the keyboard, punched some more keys, then looked at the screen again. He picked up the sheet of paper from the pile to the right of the computer, placed it face down on the left, and started to read more numbers from the next sheet of paper.

'Which of you is in charge?' Brunetti asked.

A small red-headed man looked up from one of the calculators and said, 'I am. Are you Commissario Brunetti?'

'Yes, I am,' Brunetti answered, coming to stand beside him and extending his hand.

'I'm Captain de Luca.' Then less formally, taking Brunetti's hand, he added, 'Beniamino.' He waved his hand over the papers. 'You wanted to know who was in charge of all of this at the bank?'

'Yes.'

'It looks, right now, like it was all handled by Mascari. His key codes have been tapped into all of the transactions, and what look like his initials appear on many of the documents we've got here.'

'Could that have been faked?'

'What do you mean, Commissario?'

'Could someone else have changed these documents to make it look like Mascari had handled them?'

De Luca thought about this for a long time, then

287

answered, 'I suppose so. If whoever did it had a day or two to work on the files, I suppose he could have done it.' He considered this for a while, as if working out an algebraic formula in his head. 'Yes, anyone could have done it, if he knew the key codes.'

'In a bank, how private are those access codes?'

'I would imagine they aren't private at all. People are always checking one another's accounts, and they need to know the codes in order to get into them. I would say it could be very easy.'

'What about the initials on the receipts?'

'Easier to forge than a signature,' de Luca said.

'Is there any way to prove that someone else did it?'

Again, de Luca considered the question for a long time before he answered. 'With the computer entries, not at all. Maybe the initials could be shown to be false, but most people just scribble them on things like this; often it's difficult to tell them apart or, for that fact, to recognize your own.'

'Could a case be made that the records had been changed?'

De Luca's look was as clear as his answer. 'Commissario, you might want to make that case, but you wouldn't want to make it in a courtroom.'

'So Mascari was in charge?'

De Luca hesitated this time. 'No, I wouldn't say that. It looks like it, but it is entirely possible that the records were changed to make it look like he was.'

'What about the rest of it, the process of selection for apartments?'

'Oh, it's clear that people were chosen to get apart-

ments for reasons other than need and, in the case of those who received money, that poverty didn't have much to do with a lot of the grants.'

'How do you know that?'

'In the first case, the letters of application are all here, divided into two groups: those who did get apartments and those who were turned down.' De Luca paused for a moment. 'No, I'm overstating the case. A number of the apartments, a large number of them, went to people who seemed to have real need, but the letters of application for almost a quarter of the applications come from people who aren't even Venetian.'

'The ones who were accepted?' Brunetti asked.

'Yes. And your boys haven't even finished checking on the complete list of tenants.'

Brunetti glanced towards Vianello, who explained, 'They've gone through about half of the list, and it looks like a lot of them are rented to young people who live alone. And who work nights.'

Brunetti nodded. 'Vianello, when you have a complete report on everyone on both lists, let me have it.'

'It's going to take at least another two days, sir,' Vianello said.

'There's no longer any need to hurry, I'm afraid.' Brunetti thanked de Luca for his help and went back up to his office.

It was perfect, he reflected, about as perfect as anyone could hope. Ravanello had spent his weekend all to good purpose, and the records now showed that Mascari had been in charge of the accounts of the Lega. What better way to explain those countless millions that had been

pilfered from the Lega than to lay them at the feet of Mascari and his transvestites? Who knew what he had got up to when he travelled for the bank, what orgies he had not engaged in, what fortunes he had not squandered, this man who was too frugal to make a long-distance call to his wife? Malfatti, Brunetti was sure, was far from Venice and would not soon reappear, and he had no doubt that Malfatti would be recognized as the man who collected the rents and who had arranged that a percentage of the charity cheques be given back to him as a condition of their being granted in the first place. And Ravanello? He would reveal himself as the intimate friend who, out of mistaken loyalty, had not betrayed Mascari's sinful secret, never imagining what fiscal enormities his friend had engaged in to pay for his unnatural lusts. Santomauro? No doubt there would be a first wave of ridicule as he was revealed to have been such a gullible tool of his banker friend, Mascari, but, sooner or later, popular opinion was bound to see him as the selfless citizen whose instinct to trust had been betrayed by the duplicity to which Mascari was driven by his unnatural lust. Perfect, absolutely perfect and not the slightest fissure into which Brunetti could introduce the truth.

Chapter Twenty-Six

That night, the high moral purpose of Tacitus provided Brunetti no consolation, nor did the violent destinies of Messalina and Agrippina serve as vindication of justice. He read the grim account of their much-merited deaths but could not rid himself of the realization that the evil spawned by these malevolent women endured long beyond their passing. Finally, well after two, he forced himself to stop reading and spent what remained of the night in troubled sleep, assailed by the memory of Mascari, of that just man, dispatched before his time, his death even more sordid than those of Messalina and Agrippina. Here, as well, evil would long endure his passing.

The morning was suffocating, as though a curse had been laid upon the city, condemning it to stagnant air and numbing heat, while the breezes abandoned it to its fate and went elsewhere to play. As he passed through the Rialto market on his way to work, Brunetti noticed how many of the produce vendors were closed, their usual spots in the ordered ranks of stalls gaping open like missing teeth in a drunkard's smile. No sense trying

to sell vegetables during Ferragosto: residents fled the city, and tourists wanted only *panini* and *acqua minerale*.

He arrived early at the Questura, reluctant to walk through the city after nine, when the heat grew worse and the streets even more crowded with tourists. He turned his thoughts from them. Not today.

Nothing satisfied him, not the thought that the illegal dealings of the Lega would now be stopped, and not the hope that de Luca and his men might still find some thread of evidence that would lead them to Santomauro and Ravanello. Nor did he have any hope of tracing either the dress or the shoes that Mascari had been wearing: too much time had already passed.

In the midst of this grim reverie, Vianello burst into his office without knocking and shouted, 'We've found Malfatti!'

'Where?' Brunetti asked, getting up and moving towards him, suddenly filled with energy.

'At his girlfriend's, Luciana Vespa, over at San Barnaba.'

'How?'

'Her cousin called us. He's on the list, been getting a cheque from the Lega for the last year.'

'Did you make a deal?' Brunetti asked, not at all disturbed by the illegality of this.

'No, he didn't even dare ask. He told us he wanted to help.' Vianello's snort told how much faith he put in this.

'What did he tell you?' Brunetti asked.

'Malfatti's been there for three days.'

'Is she in the file?'

Vianello shook his head. 'Just the wife. We've had

someone in the apartment next to hers for two days, but there's been no sign of him there.' While they spoke, they walked down the stairs to the office where the uniformed branch worked.

'Did you call a launch?' Brunetti asked.

'It's outside. How many men do you want to take?'

Brunetti had never been directly involved with any of Malfatti's many arrests, but he had read the reports. 'Three. Armed. And with vests.'

Ten minutes later, he and Vianello and the three officers, these last ballooned out and already sweating from the thick bullet-proof vests they wore over their uniforms, climbed aboard the blue and white police launch that stood, motor running, in front of the Questura. The three officers filed down into the cabin, leaving Brunetti and Vianello on deck to try to catch what little breeze was created by their motion. The pilot took them out into the *bacino* of San Marco, then turned right and headed up towards the entrance to the Grand Canal. Glory swept past on both sides as Brunetti and Vianello stood, heads together, talking against the force of the wind and the roar of the motor. They decided that Brunetti would go to the apartment and try to make contact with Malfatti. Since they knew nothing about the woman, they had no idea what her involvement with Malfatti might be, and so her safety had to be their chief concern.

At that thought, Brunetti began to regret having brought the officers along. If passers-by saw four police-men, three of them heavily armed, standing near an

apartment, a crowd was sure to form, and that would draw the attention of anyone in the building.

The launch pulled up at the Ca' Rezzonico vaporetto stop, and the five men filed off, much to the surprise and curiosity of the people waiting for the boat. Single file, they walked down the narrow *calle* that led to Campo San Barnaba and then out into the open square. Though the sun had not yet reached its zenith, heat radiated up from the paving stones and seared at them from below.

The building they sought was at the far right corner of the *campo*, its door just in front of one of the two enormous boats which sold fruit and vegetables from the embankment of the canal which ran alongside the *campo*. To the right of the door was a restaurant, not yet open for the day, and beyond it a bookstore. 'All of you,' Brunetti said, conscious of the stares and comments the police and their machine-guns were causing among the people around them, 'get into the bookstore. Vianello, you wait outside.'

Awkwardly, seeming too big for it, the men trooped through the door of the store. The owner stuck her head out, saw Vianello and Brunetti, and ducked back into the shop without saying anything.

The name 'Vespa' was written on a piece of paper taped to the right of one of the bells. Brunetti ignored it and rang the one above. After a moment, a woman's voice came across the intercom. '*Si?*'

'*Posta*, Signora. I have a registered letter for you. You have to sign for it.'

When the door clicked open, Brunetti turned back to Vianello, 'I'll see what I can find out about him. Stay

down here, and keep them off the street.' The sight of the three old women who now surrounded him and Vianello, shopping trolleys parked beside them, made him regret even more bringing the other officers with him.

He opened the door and went into the entrance, where he was greeted by the heavy, thudding sound of rock music spilling down towards him from one of the upper floors. If the bells on the outside corresponded to the location of the apartments, Signorina Vespa lived one floor above, and the woman who let him in on the floor above her. Brunetti walked quickly up the stairs, passed the door to the Vespa apartment, from which the music blasted.

At the top of the next flight of steps, a young woman with a baby balanced on her hip stood at the door of an apartment. When she saw him, she stepped back and reached for the door. 'One moment, Signora,' Brunetti said, stopping where he was on the steps so as not to frighten her. 'I'm from the police.'

The woman's glance, beyond him and down the steps, to the source of the music that thundered up the stairs behind him, suggested to Brunetti that she might not be surprised by his arrival. 'It's about him, isn't it?' she asked, pointing with her chin towards the source of the heavy bass that continued to flow up the stairs.

'Signorina Vespa's friend?' he asked.

'*Si*. Him,' she said, spitting out the syllables with such force that Brunetti wondered what else Malfatti had done in the time he had been in the building.

'How long has he been here?' Brunetti asked.

'I don't know,' she said, taking another step back into her apartment. 'The music's been on all day, ever since early morning. I can't go down and complain.'

'Why not?'

She pulled her baby closer to her, as if to remind the man in front of her that she was a mother. 'The last time I did, he said terrible things to me.'

'What about Signorina Vespa, can't you ask her?'

Her shrug dismissed the usefulness of Signorina Vespa.

'Isn't she there with him?'

'I don't know who's with him, and I don't care. I just want that music to stop so my baby can get to sleep.' On that cue, the baby, which had been heavily asleep in her arms, opened his eyes, drooled, and went immediately back to sleep.

The music gave Brunetti the idea, that and the fact that the woman had already complained to Malfatti about it.

'Signora, go inside,' he said. 'I'm going to slam your door and then go down and talk to him. I want you to stay inside. Stay in the back of your apartment and don't come out until one of my men comes up and tells you that you can.'

She nodded and stepped back from the door. Brunetti bent forward, reached into the apartment, and grabbed the door by its handle. He pulled it towards him violently, crashing it shut with a sound that rang out in the stairway like a shot.

He turned and slammed his way down the steps, pounding his heels as hard as he could, creating a torrent

of noise that momentarily obscured the music. '*Basta con quella musica!*' he screamed in a wild voice, a man driven beyond the limits of patience. 'Enough of that music!' he screamed again. When he got to the landing below, he pounded on the door from behind which the music came, screaming as loud as he could, 'Turn that goddamned music down. My baby's trying to sleep. Turn it down or I'll call the police.' At the end of each sentence, he banged, then kicked, at the door.

He must have been at it for a full minute before the volume of the music suddenly grew lower, though it was still fully audible through the door. He forced his voice up into a higher register, shouting now as though he had finally lost all control of himself, 'Turn the goddamned music off. Turn it off or I'll come in there and turn it off for you.'

He heard quick footsteps approaching and braced himself. The door was pulled back suddenly, and a stocky man filled the doorway, a short metal rod gripped in his hand. Brunetti had only an instant, but in that instant he recognized Malfatti from his police photos.

Holding the rod down at his side, Malfatti took one step forward, bringing himself half-way through the door. 'Who the hell do you—' he began but stopped when Brunetti lunged forward and grabbed him, one hand on his right forearm and the other on the cloth of his shirt. Brunetti swiveled, turned on his hip, and swung out with all his strength. Caught completely off guard, Malfatti was pulled forward and off balance. For an instant, he balked at the top of the stairs, trying vainly to shift his weight and pull himself backwards, but then he

lost his balance and toppled forward down the steps. As he fell, he dropped the iron bar and wrapped both arms around his head, turning himself into an acrobatic ball that tumbled down the steps.

Brunetti scrambled down the stairs after him, screaming Vianello's name as loud as he could. Half-way down the steps, Brunetti stepped on the iron bar and slipped to his side, crashing against the wall of the stairway. When he looked up, he saw Vianello pushing open the heavy door at the bottom of the steps. But by that time, Malfatti had scrambled to his feet and was standing just behind the door. Before Brunetti could shout a warning, Malfatti kicked the door, slamming it into Vianello's face, knocking the gun from his hand and him out into the narrow *calle*. Malfatti pulled the door open and disappeared into the sunlight beyond.

Brunetti got to his feet and ran down the steps, drawing his pistol, but by the time he got to the street, Malfatti had disappeared, and Vianello lay against the low wall of the canal, blood streaming from his nose on to his white uniform shirt. Just as Brunetti bent over him, the three other officers piled out of the bookstore, machine-guns pointed in front of them but no one to point them at.

Chapter Twenty-Seven

Vianello's nose was not broken, but he was badly shaken. With Brunetti's help, he got to his feet, weaved unsteadily for a moment, wiping at his nose with his hand.

People crowded around them, old women demanding to know what was happening, the fruit vendors already explaining to their newest customers what they had seen. Brunetti turned away from Vianello and almost tripped over a metal grocery cart filled to the top with vegetables. He kicked it angrily aside and turned to the two men who worked on the nearest boat. They had a clear view of the door to the building and must have seen everything.

'Which way did he go?'

Both pointed down toward the *campo*, but then one pointed to the right, in the direction of the Accademia bridge, while the other pointed to the left and towards Rialto.

Brunetti signalled to one of the officers, who helped him lead Vianello towards the boat. Angrily, the sergeant pushed their hands away, insisting he could walk by himself. From the deck of the boat, Brunetti

radioed the Questura with a description of Malfatti, asking that copies of his photo be distributed to all the police in the city and that his description be radioed to everyone on patrol.

When the officers were aboard, the pilot backed the boat towards the Grand Canal, then swung it round and headed towards the Questura. Vianello went down into the cabin and sat with his head tilted back to stop the bleeding. Brunetti followed him. 'Do you want to go to the hospital?'

'It's only a bloody nose,' Vianello said. 'It'll stop in a minute.' He wiped at it with his handkerchief. 'What happened?'

'I banged on his door, complaining about his music, and he opened it. I pulled him out and threw him down the stairs.' Vianello looked surprised. 'It was all I could think of,' Brunetti explained. 'But I didn't think he'd recover so quickly.'

'What now?' Vianello asked. 'What do you think he'll do?'

'Try to get in touch with Ravanello and Santomauro, I'd say.'

'Do you want to warn them?'

'No,' Brunetti answered immediately. 'But I want to know where they are, and I want to see what they do. I want them watched.' The launch swung into the canal that led to the Questura, and Brunetti climbed back on deck. When they pulled up to the small dock, he jumped ashore and waited while Vianello followed him. As they passed through the front door, the officers on guard stared at the sergeant's bloody shirt but said nothing.

When the other officers came off the boat, the guards crowded round and asked for an explanation.

At the second landing, Vianello went off towards the bathroom at the end of the corridor, and Brunetti went up to his own office. He called the Banca di Verona and, using a false name, asked to speak to Signor Ravanello. When the man he spoke to asked him what this was in regard to, Brunetti explained that it was about the estimate the banker had asked for on a new computer. He was told that Signor Ravanello was not in that morning but could be reached at home. Asked, the man supplied the banker's home number, and Brunetti dialled it immediately, only to find it busy.

He found the number of Santomauro's office, dialled it, and, giving the same false name, asked if he could speak to Avvocato Santomauro. The lawyer, his secretary explained, was busy with another client and could not be disturbed. Brunetti said he would call back and hung up.

He dialled Ravanello's number again, but still it was busy. He pulled the phone book from his bottom drawer and looked up Ravanello's name, curious to find the address. From the listing, he guessed that it would have to be in the vicinity of Campo San Stefano, not far from Santomauro's office. He considered how Malfatti would get there: the obvious answer was the *traghetto*, the public gondola that plied the waters back and forth between Ca' Rezzonico and Campo San Samuele on the opposite side of the Grand Canal. From there, it was only minutes to Campo San Stefano.

He dialled the number again, but still it was busy. He

called the operator and asked her to check the line and, after waiting less than a minute, was told that the line was open though not in contact with any other number, which meant the phone was either out of order or had been left off the hook. Even before he hung up, Brunetti was mapping out the fastest way to get there: the launch was best. He went down the stairs and into Vianello's office. The sergeant, wearing a clean shirt, looked up when Brunetti came in.

'Ravanello's phone is off the hook.'

Vianello was out of his chair and on the way to the door before Brunetti said anything else.

Together, they went downstairs and out into the blanketing heat. The pilot was hosing down the deck of the launch but, seeing the two men come running out the front door, he tossed the hose to the sidewalk and jumped to the wheel.

'Campo San Stefano,' Brunetti called to him. 'Use the siren.'

Klaxon shouting out its double-noted call, the boat pulled away from the dock and once again out into the *bacino*. Boats and vaporetti slowed to allow it to speed past them; only the elegant black gondolas paid it no heed: by law, all boats had to defer to the slow passage of the gondola.

Neither of them spoke. Brunetti went down into the cabin and consulted a city guide to see where the address was located. He was right: the apartment was directly opposite the entrance to the church that gave the *campo* its name.

As the boat neared the Accademia bridge, Brunetti

went back on deck and told the pilot to cut the siren. He had no idea what they would find at San Stefano, but he would like their arrival there to go unannounced. The pilot switched the siren off and pulled the boat into the Rio del Orso and over to the landing stage on the left side. Brunetti and Vianello climbed up on to the embankment and walked quickly through the open *campo*. Lethargic couples sat at tables in front of a café, hunched over pastel drinks; everyone walking in the *campo* looked to be carrying the heat like a palpable yoke across their shoulders.

They quickly found the door, between a restaurant and a shop that sold Venetian paper. Ravanello's bell was on the top right of the two rows of names. Brunetti rang the one below it then, when there was no answer, the one under that. When a voice answered, asking who it was, he declared, '*Polizia*,' and the door snapped open immediately.

He and Vianello went into the building, and, from above them, a high, querulous voice called out, 'How did you get here so fast?'

Brunetti started up the stairs, Vianello close behind him. On the first floor, a grey-haired woman, little taller than the banister over which she leaned, called down again, 'How did you get here so fast?'

Ignoring her question, Brunetti asked, 'What's wrong, Signora?'

She moved back from the banister and pointed above her. 'Up there. I heard shouting from Signor Ravanello's, and then I saw someone run down the steps. I was afraid to go up.'

Brunetti and Vianello swept past her, taking the stairs two at a time now, both of them with their pistols in their hands. At the top, light spilled out of the apartment on to the broad landing in front of the open door. Brunetti crouched low and moved to the other side of the door, but he moved too quickly to be able to see anything inside. He looked back at Vianello, who nodded. Together they burst into the apartment, both bent low. As soon as they were through the door, they moved to either side of the room, making of themselves two separate targets.

But Ravanello was not going to shoot at them: one glance at him was enough to show that. His body lay across a low chair that had fallen to its side in the fight that must have taken place in this room. He lay on his side, facing the door, staring with unseeing eyes, eternally removed from any curiosity about these men who had burst suddenly and without invitation into his home.

Not for an instant did Brunetti suspect that Ravanello might still be alive: the marmoreal weight of his body rendered that impossible. There was very little blood: that was the first thing Brunetti noticed. Ravanello appeared to have been stabbed twice, for there were two bold red patches on his jacket, and some blood had spilled to the floor beneath his arm, but hardly enough to suggest that its passing had taken his life with it.

'*Oh Dio*,' he heard the old woman gasp behind him, turned and found her at the door, one fist clenched in front of her mouth, staring across at Ravanello. Brunetti moved two steps to his right and into her line of vision.

She looked up at him with chilled eyes. Could it be she was angry with him for having blocked her sight of the body?

'What did he look like, Signora?' he asked.

She shifted her eyes to his left, but couldn't see around him.

'What did he look like, Signora?'

Behind him, he heard Vianello moving around, going off into another room of the apartment, then he heard the phone being dialled and Vianello's voice, soft and calm, reporting to the Questura what had happened, asking for the necessary people.

Brunetti walked directly towards the woman and, as he had hoped, she retreated before him out into the corridor. 'Could you tell me exactly what you saw, Signora?'

'A man, not very tall, running down the steps. He had a white shirt. Short sleeves.'

'Would you know him if you saw him again, Signora?'

'Yes.'

So would Brunetti.

Behind them, Vianello appeared from the apartment, leaving the door open. 'They'll be here soon.'

'Stay here,' Brunetti said, moving towards the stairs.

'Santomauro?' Vianello asked.

Brunetti waved his hand in acknowledgement and ran down the steps. Outside, he turned left and hurried up to Campo San Angelo and, beyond it, Campo San Luca and the lawyer's office.

It was like wading through a heavy surf, pushing his way through the late-morning crowds of people who

gawked in front of shop windows, paused to talk to one another, or stood in the momentary relief of a cool breeze escaping from an air-conditioned shop. Down through the narrow confines of Calle della Mandorla he raced, using his elbows and his voice, careless of the angry stares and sarcastic remarks created by his passing.

In the open space of Campo Manin, he broke into a trot, though every step brought sweat pounding out on to his body. He cut round the bank and into Campo San Luca, crowded now with people meeting for a drink before lunch.

The downstairs door that led up to Santomauro's office was ajar; Brunetti pushed himself through it and took the steps two at a time. The door to the office was closed, the light below it gleaming out into the dim hallway. He took out his gun and pushed the door open, moving quickly to the side in a protective crouch, just as he had when entering Ravanello's office.

The secretary screamed. Like a character in a comic book, she covered her mouth with both hands and let out a loud shriek, then pushed herself backwards and toppled from her chair.

Seconds later, the door to Santomauro's office opened, and the lawyer came rushing from his office. In a glance, he took it all in: his secretary cowering behind her desk, butting her shoulder repeatedly against the top as she tried, vainly, to crawl under it, and Brunetti, rising to his feet and putting his gun away.

'It's all right, Louisa,' Santomauro said, going to his secretary and kneeling down beside her. 'It's all right, it's nothing.'

The woman was incapable of speech, beyond thought or reason. She sobbed, turned towards her employer and stretched out her hands to him. He put an arm round her shoulder and she pressed her face against his chest. She sobbed deeply and gasped for breath. Santomauro bent over her, patting her on the back and speaking softly to her. Gradually, the woman calmed and after a moment pushed herself back from him. '*Scusi*, Avvocato,' was the first thing she said, her formality restoring full calm to the room.

Silent now, Santomauro helped her to her feet and towards a door at the back of the office. When he closed it behind her, Santomauro turned to face Brunetti. 'Well?' he said, voice calm but no less lethal for that.

'Ravanello's been killed,' Brunetti said. 'And I thought you'd be next. So I came here to try to stop it.'

If Santomauro was surprised at the news, he gave no sign of it. 'Why?' he asked. When Brunetti didn't answer, he repeated the question, 'Why would I be next?'

Brunetti didn't answer him.

'I asked you a question, Commissario. Why would I be next? Why, in fact, would I be in any danger at all?' In the face of Brunetti's continuing silence, Santomauro continued. 'Do you think I'm somehow involved in all of this? Is that why you're here, playing cowboy and Indians and terrifying my secretary?'

'I had reason to believe he would come here,' Brunetti finally explained.

'Who?' the lawyer demanded.

'I'm not at liberty to tell you that.'

Santomauro bent down and picked up the secretary's

chair. He righted it and pushed it into place behind her desk. When he looked back at Brunetti, he said, 'Get out. Get out of this office. I am going to make a formal complaint to the Minister of the Interior. And I am going to send a copy of it to your superior. I will not be treated as a criminal, and I will not have my secretary terrified by your Gestapo techniques.'

Brunetti had seen enough anger in his life and in his career to know that this was the real thing. Saying nothing, he left the office and went down into Campo San Luca. People pushed past him, rushing home for lunch.

Chapter Twenty-Eight

Brunetti's decision to return to the Questura was an exercise of the power of the will over that of the flesh. He was closer to home than to the Questura, and he wanted only to go there, shower, and think about things other than the inescapable consequences of what had just happened. Unsummoned, he had burst violently into the office of one of the most powerful men in the city, terrorizing his secretary and making it clear, by his explanation of his behaviour, that he assumed Santomauro's guilty involvement with Malfatti and the manipulation of the accounts of the Lega. All of the good will he had, however spuriously, accumulated with Patta during the last weeks would be as of nothing in the face of a protest from a man of Santomauro's stature.

And now, with Ravanello dead, all hope of a case against Santomauro had vanished, for the only person who might implicate Santomauro was Malfatti; his guilt in Ravanello's death would render worthless any accusation he might make against Santomauro. It would come, Brunetti realized, to a choice between Malfatti's and Santomauro's stories; he needed neither wit nor prescience to know which was stronger.

When Brunetti got there, he found the Questura in tumult. Three uniformed officers huddled together in the lobby, and the people on the long line at the Ufficio Stranieri crowded together in a babble of different languages. 'They brought him in, sir,' one of the guards said when he saw Brunetti.

'Who?' he asked, not daring to hope.

'Malfatti.'

'How?'

'The men waiting at his mother's. He showed up at the door about half an hour ago, and they got him even before she could let him in.'

'Was there any trouble?'

'One of the men who was there said that he tried to run when he saw them, but as soon as he realized there were four of them, he just gave up and went along quietly.'

'Four?'

'Yes, sir. Vianello called and told us to send more men. They were just arriving when Malfatti showed up. They didn't even have time to get inside, just got there and found him at the door.'

'Where is he?'

'Vianello had him put in a cell.'

'I'll go see him.'

When Brunetti went into the cell, Malfatti recognized him immediately as the man who had thrown him down the steps, but he greeted Brunetti with no particular hostility.

Brunetti pulled a chair away from the wall and sat facing Malfatti, who was lying on the cot, back propped

310

up against the wall. He was a short, stocky man with thick brown hair, features so regular as to make him almost immediately forgettable. He looked like an accountant, not a killer.

'Well?' Brunetti began.

'Well what?' Malfatti's voice was completely matter of fact.

'Well, do you want to do this the easy way or the hard way?' Brunetti asked imperturbably, just the way the cops on television did.

'What's the hard way?'

'That you say you know nothing about any of this.'

'About any of what?' Malfatti asked.

Brunetti pressed his lips together and glanced up at the window for a moment, then back at Malfatti.

'What's the easy way?' Malfatti asked after a long time.

'That you tell me what happened.' Before Malfatti said a word, Brunetti explained, 'Not about the rents. That's not important now, and it will all come out. But about the murders. All of them. All four.'

Malfatti shifted minimally on the mattress, and Brunetti had the impression that he was going to question that number, but then Malfatti thought better of it.

'He's a respected man,' Brunetti continued, not bothering to explain whom he meant. 'It's going to come down to his word against yours, unless you've got something to link him to you and to the murders.' He paused here, but Malfatti said nothing. 'You've got a long criminal record,' Brunetti continued. 'Attempted murder and now murder.' Before Malfatti could say a word, Brunetti

continued in an entirely conversational voice, 'There's not going to be any trouble proving that you killed Ravanello.' In answer to Malfatti's surprised glance, he explained, 'The old woman saw you.' Malfatti looked away.

'And judges hate people who kill police, especially policewomen. So I don't see it any other way but a conviction. The judges are bound to ask me what I think,' he said, pausing to be sure he had Malfatti's complete attention. 'When they do, I'll suggest Porto Azzurro.'

All criminals knew the name of the prison, the worst in Italy and one from which no one had ever escaped; even a man as hardened as Malfatti could not disguise his shock. Brunetti waited a moment, but when Malfatti said nothing, he added, 'They say no one knows which are bigger, the cats or the rats.' Again, he paused.

'And if I do talk to you?' Malfatti finally asked.

'Then I'll suggest to the judges that they take that into consideration.'

'That's all?'

'That's all.' Brunetti hated people who killed police, too.

Malfatti took only a moment to decide. '*Va bene*,' he said, 'but I want it in the record that I volunteered this. I want it put down that, as soon as you arrested me, I was willing to give you everything.'

Brunetti got to his feet. 'I'll get a secretary,' he said and went to the door of the cell. He signalled to a young man who sat at a desk at the end of the hall, who came into the room with a tape recorder and a pad.

When they were ready, Brunetti said, 'Please give your name, place of birth, and present residence.'

'Malfatti, Pietro. Twenty-eight September, 1962. Castello 2316.'

It went on like this for an hour, Malfatti's voice never displaying any greater involvement than it did when answering that original question, though the story that emerged was one of mounting horror.

The original idea could have been Ravanello's or Santomauro's: Malfatti had never cared enough to ask. They had got his name from the men on Via Cappuccina and had contacted him to ask if he would be willing to make the collections for them every month in return for a percentage of the profit. He had never been in doubt as to whether he would accept their offer, only about the percentage he would get. They had settled at twelve, though it had taken Malfatti almost an hour of hard bargaining to get them to go that high.

It was his hopes of increasing his own take that had led Malfatti to suggest that some of the legitimate earnings of the Lega be paid out in cheques to people whose names he would supply. Brunetti cut off Malfatti's grotesque pride in this scheme by asking, 'When did Mascari find out about this?'

'Three weeks ago. He went to Ravanello and told him something was wrong with the accounts. He had no idea that Ravanello knew about it, thought that it was Santomauro. Fool,' Malfatti spat in contempt. 'If he had wanted, he could have got a third out of them, an easy third.' He looked back and forth between Brunetti and the secretary, asking them to share his disgust.

'And then?' Brunetti asked, keeping his own disgust to himself.

'Santomauro and Ravanello came to my place about a week before it happened. They wanted me to get rid of him, but I knew what they were like, so I told them I wouldn't do it unless they helped. I'm no fool.' Again, he looked at the other men for approval. 'You know what it's like with people like that. You do a job for them, you're never free of them. The only way to be safe is to make them get their hands dirty, too.'

'Is that what you told them?' Brunetti asked.

'In a way. I told them I'd do it but that they'd have to help me set it up.'

'How did they do that?'

'They had Crespo call Mascari and say he'd heard he was looking for information about the apartments the Lega rented and that he lived in one of them. Mascari had the list, so he could check. When Mascari told him he was leaving for Sicily that evening – we knew that – Crespo told him he had other information to give him, that he could stop on the way to the airport.'

'And?'

'He agreed.'

'Was Crespo there?'

'Oh, no,' Malfatti said with a snort of contempt. 'He was a delicate little bastard. Didn't want to have anything to do with it. So he took off – probably went and hit the pavements early. And we waited for Mascari. He showed up at about seven.'

'What happened?'

'I let him in. He thought I was Crespo, didn't have

any reason not to. I told him to sit down and offered him a drink, but he said he had a plane to catch and was in a hurry. I asked him again if he wanted a drink, and when he said no, I said I wanted one and walked behind him to the table where the drinks were. That's when I did it.'

'What did you do?'

'I hit him.'

'With what?'

'An iron bar. The same one I had today. It's very good.'

'How many times did you hit him?'

'Only once. I didn't want to get blood on Crespo's furniture. And I didn't want to kill him. I wanted them to do that.'

'And did they?'

'I don't know. That is, I don't know which one of them did it. They were in the bedroom. I called them and we carried him into the bathroom. He was still alive then; I heard him groan.'

'Why the bathroom?'

Malfatti's glance showed that he was thinking he'd overestimated Brunetti's intelligence. 'The blood.' There was a long pause, and when Brunetti didn't say anything, Malfatti continued, 'We laid him down on the floor, and then I went back and got the iron bar. Santomauro had been saying that we needed to destroy his face – we'd planned it all, put it together like a puzzle, and he had to be unrecognizable so there would be enough time to change the records in the bank. Anyway, he kept saying that we had to destroy his face, so I gave him the bar and told him to do it himself. Then I went

back into the living-room and had a cigarette. When I came back, it was done.'

'He was dead?'

Malfatti shrugged.

'Ravanello and Santomauro killed him?'

'I'd already done my share.'

'Then what?'

'We stripped him and shaved his legs. Jesus, what a job that was.'

'Yes, I imagine so,' Brunetti permitted himself. 'And then what?'

'We put the make-up on him.' Malfatti paused a moment in thought. 'No, that's wrong. They did that before they hit his face. One of them said it would be easier. Then we put his clothes back on him and carried him out, like he was drunk. But we didn't have to bother; no one saw us. Ravanello and I took him down to Santomauro's car and drove him out to the field. I knew about what goes on out there, and I thought it would be a good place to dump him.'

'What about the clothes? Where did you change them?'

'When we got there, out in Marghera. We pulled him out of the back seat and stripped him. Then we put those clothes on him, that red dress and everything, and I carried him over to a place at the other side of the field and left him there. I stuffed him under a bush so it would take longer for him to be found.' Malfatti paused for a moment, summoning memory. 'Ravanello stuffed the shoes into my pockets. I dropped one beside him. They were Ravanello's idea, the shoes, I think.'

'What did you do with his clothes?'

'I stopped on the way back to Crespo's place and put them in a garbage can. It was all right; there was no blood on them. We were very careful. We wrapped his head in a plastic bag.'

The young officer coughed but turned his head away so the sound wouldn't register on the tape.

'And afterwards?' Brunetti asked.

'We went back to the apartment. Santomauro had cleaned it up. That was the last I heard of them until the night you came out to Mestre.'

'Whose idea was that?'

'Not mine. Ravanello called me and explained things to me. I think they hoped the investigation would stop if we could get rid of you.' Malfatti sighed. 'I tried to tell them things don't work that way, that it wouldn't make any difference, killing you, but they didn't want to listen. They insisted that I help them.'

'So you agreed?'

Malfatti nodded.

'You have to give an answer, Signor Malfatti, or the tape doesn't register it,' Brunetti explained coolly.

'Yes, I agreed.'

'What made you change your mind and agree to do it?'

'They paid enough.'

Because the young officer was there, Brunetti didn't ask how much his life was worth. It would come out in time.

'Did you drive the car that tried to push us off the road?'

'Yes.' Malfatti paused for a long time and then added, 'You know, I don't think I would have done it if I'd known there was a woman in the car with you. It's bad luck to kill a woman. She was my first.' It hit him then and he looked up. 'See, it is bad luck, isn't it?'

'Probably more for the woman than for you, Signor Malfatti,' Brunetti answered, but before Malfatti could react, Brunetti asked, 'What about Crespo? Did you kill him?'

'No, I didn't have anything to do with that. I was in the car with Ravanello. We left Santomauro with Crespo. When we got back there, it was finished.'

'What did Santomauro tell you?'

'Nothing. Not about that. He just told us it had happened, and then he told me to stay out of sight, if possible to get out of Venice. I was going to, but now I guess I won't get the chance to.'

'And Ravanello?'

'I went there this morning, after you came to my place.' Malfatti stopped here, and Brunetti wondered what lie he was preparing.

'What happened?' Brunetti prodded him.

'I told him that the police were after me. I said I needed money to get out of the city and go somewhere. But he panicked. He started shouting that I had ruined everything. That's when he pulled the knife.'

Brunetti had seen the knife. A switchblade seemed a strange thing for a banker to carry on his person, but he said nothing.

'He came at me with it. He was completely wild. We

fought over it, and I think he fell on it.' He did, Brunetti remarked to himself. Twice. In the chest.

'And then?'

'Then I went to my mother's. That's where your men found me.' Malfatti stopped speaking, and the only sound in the room was the soft humming of the tape recorder.

'What happened to the money?' Brunetti asked.

'What?' Malfatti said, surprised by this sudden change of pace.

'The money. That was made from all the rents.'

'I spent mine, spent it every month. But it was nothing compared to what they got.'

'How much was it you got?'

'Between nine and ten million.'

'Do you know what they did with theirs?'

Malfatti paused for a moment, as though he had never speculated about this. 'I'd guess Santomauro spent a large part of his on boys. Ravanello, I don't know. He looked like one of those people who invested money.' Malfatti's tone turned this into an obscenity.

'Have you anything else to say about this or your involvement with these men?'

'Only that the idea to kill Mascari was theirs, not mine. I went along with it, but it was their idea. I didn't have much to lose if anyone found out about the rents, so I didn't see any reason to kill him.' It was clear that, had he believed he had anything to lose, he would have had no hesitation to kill Mascari, but Brunetti said nothing.

'That's all,' Malfatti said.

Brunetti rose and signalled to the young officer to come with him. 'I'll have this typed up and you can sign it.'

'Take your time,' Malfatti said and laughed. 'I'm not going anywhere.'

Chapter Twenty-Nine

An hour later, Brunetti took three copies of the typed statement down to Malfatti, who signed them without bothering to read it. 'Don't you want to know what you're signing?' Brunetti asked him.

'It doesn't matter,' Malfatti replied, still not bothering to raise himself from the cot. He waved the pen Brunetti had given him at the paper. 'Besides, there's no reason to think anyone's going to believe that.'

Since the same thing had occurred to Brunetti, he didn't argue the point.

'What happens now?' Malfatti asked.

'There'll be a hearing within the next few days, and the magistrate will decide if you should be offered the chance of bail.'

'Will he ask your opinion?'

'Probably.'

'And?'

'I'll argue against it.'

Malfatti moved his hand along the barrel of the pen and then reversed his hold on it and offered it to Brunetti.

'Will someone tell my mother?' Malfatti asked.

'I'll see that someone calls her.'

Malfatti shrugged his acknowledgement, moved himself lower on the pillow, and closed his eyes.

Brunetti left the cell and went up two flights of stairs to Signorina Elettra's alcove. Today she was dressed in a shade of red seldom seen beyond the confines of the Vatican, but Brunetti found it strident and out of tune with his mood. She smiled, and his mood lightened a bit.

'Is he in?' Brunetti asked.

'He got here about an hour ago, but he's on the phone and he told me not to interrupt him, not for anything.'

Brunetti preferred it this way, didn't want to be with Patta when he read Malfatti's confession. He placed a copy of the confession on her desk and said, 'Would you give him this as soon as he's finished with the call?'

'Malfatti?' she asked, looking at it with open curiosity.

'Yes.'

'Where will you be?'

When she asked that, Brunetti suddenly realized that he was completely displaced, had no idea what time it was. He glanced at his watch, saw that it was five, but the hour meant nothing to him. He didn't feel hungry, only thirsty and miserably tired. He began to consider how Patta was likely to respond; that increased his thirst.

'I'll go and get something to drink and then I'll be in my office.'

He turned and left; he didn't care if she read the confession or not, found that he didn't care about anything except his thirst and the heat and the faint grainy texture of his skin, where salt had been evaporating all

day. He raised the back of his hand to his mouth and licked it, almost glad to taste the bitterness.

An hour later, he went into Patta's office in response to his summons, and at the desk Brunetti found the old Patta: he looked like he had shed five years and gained five kilos overnight.

'Have a seat, Brunetti,' Patta said. Patta picked up the confession and tapped the six pages on his desk, aligning them neatly.

'I've just read this,' Patta said. He glanced across at Brunetti and laid the papers flat on his desk. 'I believe him.'

Brunetti concentrated on demonstrating no emotion. Patta's wife was somehow involved with the Lega. Santomauro was a figure of some political importance in a city where Patta hoped to rise to power. Brunetti realized that justice and the law were not going to play any part in whatever conversation he was about to have with Patta. He said nothing.

'But I doubt that anyone else will,' Patta added, beginning to lead Brunetti towards illumination. When it became clear that Brunetti was going to say nothing, Patta continued, 'I've had a number of phone calls this afternoon.'

It was too cheap a shot to ask if one of them had been from Santomauro, and so Brunetti did not ask.

'Not only did Avvocato Santomauro call me, but I also had long conversations with two members of the city council, both of whom are friends and political associates of the Avvocato.' Patta pushed himself back in his chair and crossed his legs. Brunetti could see the

tip of one gleaming shoe and a narrow expanse of thin blue sock. He looked up at Patta's face. 'As I said, no one is going to believe this man.'

'Even if he is telling the truth?' Brunetti finally asked.

'Especially if he's telling the truth. No one in this city is going to believe that Santomauro is capable of what this man accuses him of doing.'

'You seem to have no trouble believing it, Vice-Questore.'

'I am hardly to be considered an objective witness when it comes to Signor Santomauro,' Patta said, dropping in front of Brunetti, as casually as he had placed the papers on his desk, the first bit of self-knowledge he had ever demonstrated.

'What did Santomauro tell you?' Brunetti asked, though he had already worked out what that would have to be.

'I'm sure you've realized what he would say,' Patta said, again surprising Brunetti. 'That this is merely an attempt on Malfatti's part to divide the blame and minimize his responsibility in all of this. That a close examination of the records at the bank will surely show that it was all Ravanello's doing. That there is no evidence whatsoever that he, Santomauro, was involved in any of this, not the double rents and not the death of Mascari.'

'Did he say anything about the other deaths?'

'Crespo?'

'Yes, and Maria Nardi.'

'No, not a word. And there's nothing that links him to Ravanello's bank.'

'We have a woman who saw Malfatti running down the stairs at Ravanello's.'

'I see,' Patta said, uncrossed his legs and leaned forward. He placed his right hand on Malfatti's confession. 'It's worthless,' he finally said, just as Brunetti knew he would.

'He can try to use it at his trial, but I doubt that the judges would believe him. He'd be better off presenting himself as Ravanello's ignorant tool.' Yes, that was probably true. The judge didn't exist who could see Malfatti as the person behind this. And the judge who would see Santomauro as having any part in this couldn't even be imagined.

'Does that mean you're going to do nothing about that?' Brunetti asked, nodding his chin at the papers that lay on Patta's desk.

'Not unless you can think of something to do,' Patta said, and Brunetti listened in vain for sarcasm in his voice.

'No, I can't,' Brunetti said.

'We can't touch him,' Patta said. 'I know the man. He's too cautious ever to have been seen by any of the people involved in this.'

'Not even the boys in Via Cappuccina?'

Patta's mouth tightened in distaste. 'His involvement with those creatures is entirely circumstantial. No judge would listen to evidence presented about that. However distasteful his behaviour is, it's his private business.'

Brunetti began considering possibilities: if enough of the prostitutes, those who rented apartments from the Lega, could be found to testify that Santomauro had

325

used their services; if he could find the man who was in Crespo's apartment when he went to see him; if evidence could be found that Santomauro had interviewed any of the people who were paying the double rent.

Patta cut all this short. 'There's no proof, Brunetti. Everything rests on the word of a confessed murderer.' Patta tapped the papers. 'He talks about these murders as though he were going out to get a pack of cigarettes. No one is going to believe him when he accuses Santomauro, no one.'

Brunetti suddenly felt himself swept by exhaustion. His eyes watered, and he had to fight to keep them open. He brought one hand to his right eye and made as if to remove a speck of dust, closed them for a few seconds, and then rubbed them both with one hand. When he opened them again, he saw that Patta was looking at him strangely. 'I think you ought to go home, Brunetti. There's nothing more to be done about this.'

Brunetti pushed himself to his feet, nodded to Patta, and left the office. From there, he went directly home, bypassing his own office. Inside the apartment, he pulled the phone jack from the wall, took a long hot shower, ate a kilo of peaches, and went to bed.

Chapter Thirty

Brunetti slept twelve hours, a deep and dreamless sleep that left him refreshed and alert when he woke. The sheets were sodden, though he had not been aware of sweating through the night. In the kitchen, as he filled the coffee pot, he noticed that three of the peaches he had left in the bowl the night before were covered with soft green fuzz. He tossed them into the garbage under the sink, washed his hands, and put the coffee on to the stove.

Whenever he found his mind turning to Santomauro or to Malfatti's confession, he pulled away and thought, instead, of the approaching weekend, vowing to go up to the mountains to join Paola. He wondered why she hadn't called last night, and with that thought struck a resonant chord of self-pity: he sweltered in this fetid heat while she romped in the hills like that moron in *The Sound of Music*. But then he remembered disconnecting the phone and was jabbed by shame. He missed her. He missed them all. He'd go up Saturday. Friday night, if there was a late train.

Spirits buoyed by this resolve, he went to the Questura, where he read his way through the newspaper

accounts of Malfatti's arrest, all of which mentioned Vice-Questore Giuseppe Patta as their chief source of information. The Vice-Questore was variously quoted as having 'overseen the arrest' and having 'obtained Malfatti's confession'. The papers placed the blame for the Banca di Verona scandal at the feet of its most recent director, Ravanello, and left no doubt in the readers' minds that he had been responsible for the murder of his predecessor before becoming himself the victim of his vicious accomplice, Malfatti. Santomauro was named only in the *Corriere della Sera*, which quoted him as expressing shock and sorrow at the abuse which had been made of the lofty goals and high principles of the organization he felt himself so honoured to serve.

Brunetti called Paola and, even though he knew the answer would be no, asked if she had read the papers. When she asked what was in them, he told her only that the case was finished and that he would tell her about it when he got there Friday night. As he knew she would, she asked him to tell her more, but he said it could wait. When she allowed the subject to drop, he felt a flash of anger at her lack of perseverance; hadn't this case almost cost him his life?

Brunetti spent the rest of the morning preparing a five-page statement in which he set forth his belief that Malfatti was telling the truth in his confession, and he went on to present his own exhaustively detailed and closely reasoned account of everything that had happened from the time Mascari's body was found until the time Malfatti was arrested. After lunch, he read it through twice and was forced to see how all of it rested

on no more than his own suspicions: there was not a shred of physical evidence linking Santomauro to any of the crimes, nor was it likely that anyone else would believe that a man like Santomauro, who looked down upon the world from the empyrean moral heights of the Lega, could be involved in anything as base as greed or lust or violence. But still he typed it out on the Olivetti standard typewriter that stood on a small table in a corner of his room. Looking at the finished pages, the whited-out corrections, he wondered if he should put in a requisition slip for a computer for his office. He found himself caught up in this, planning where it could go, wondering if he could get his own printer or if everything he typed would have to be printed out down in the secretaries' office, a thought he didn't like.

He was still considering this when Vianello tapped at his door and came in, followed by a short, deeply tanned man in a wrinkled cotton suit. 'Commissario,' the sergeant began in the formal tones he adopted when addressing Brunetti in front of civilians. 'I'd like to present Luciano Gravi.'

Brunetti approached Gravi and extended his hand. 'I'm pleased to meet you, Signor Gravi. In what way may I be of help to you?' He led the man over to his desk and pointed to a chair in front of it. Gravi looked around the office and then took the chair. Vianello sat in the chair beside him, paused a moment to see if Gravi would speak and, when he did not, began to explain.

'Commissario, Signor Gravi is the owner of a shoe store in Chioggia.'

Brunetti looked at the man with renewed interest. A shoe store.

Vianello turned to Gravi and waved a hand, inviting him to speak. 'I just got back from vacation,' Gravi began, speaking to Vianello but then, when Vianello turned to face Brunetti, turning his attention towards him. 'I was down in Puglia for two weeks. There's no sense in keeping the store open during Ferragosto. No one wants to shop for shoes, anyway. It's too hot. So we close up every year for three weeks, and my wife and I go on vacation.'

'And you just got back?'

'Well, I got back two days ago, but I didn't go to the store until yesterday. That's when I found the postcard.'

'Postcard, Signor Gravi?' Brunetti asked.

'From the girl who works in my shop. She's on vacation in Norway, with her fiancé. He works for you, I think, Giorgio Miotti.' Brunetti nodded; he knew Miotti. 'Well, they're in Norway, as I said, and she wrote to tell me that the police were curious about a pair of red shoes.' He turned back to Vianello. 'I have no idea what they must have been talking about for them to think of that, but she wrote on the bottom of the card that Giorgio said you were looking for someone who might have bought a pair of women's shoes, red satin, in a large size.'

Brunetti found that he was holding his breath and forced himself to relax and breathe it out. 'And did you sell those shoes, Signor Gravi?'

'Yes, I sold a pair of them, about a month ago. To a man.' He paused here, waiting for the policemen to

remark on how strange it was that a man would buy those shoes.

'A man?' Brunetti asked obligingly.

'Yes, he said he wanted them for Carnevale. But Carnevale isn't until next year. I thought it strange at the time, but I wanted to sell the shoes because the satin was torn away from the heel on one of them. The left one, I think. Anyway, they were on sale, and he bought them. Fifty-nine thousand lire, reduced from a hundred twenty. Really a bargain.'

'I'm sure it was, Signor Gravi,' Brunetti agreed. 'Do you think you'd recognize the shoes if you saw them again?'

'I think so. I wrote the sale price on the sole of one of them. It might be there.'

Turning to Vianello, Brunetti said, 'Sergeant, could you go and get those shoes back from the lab for me? I'd like Signor Gravi to take a look at them.'

Vianello nodded and left the room. While he was gone, Gravi talked about his vacation, describing how clean the water in the Adriatic was, so long as you went far enough south. Brunetti listened, smiling when he thought it required, keeping himself from asking Gravi to describe the man who bought the shoes until Gravi had identified them.

A few minutes later, Vianello was back, carrying the shoes in their clear plastic evidence bag. He handed the bag to Gravi, who made no attempt to open it. He moved the shoes around inside the bag, turning first one and then the other upside-down and peering at the sole. He held them closer, smiled, and held the bag out to

Brunetti. 'See, there it is. The sale price. I wrote it in pencil so whoever bought it could erase it if they wanted to. But you can still see it, right there.' He pointed to faint pencil markings on the sole.

At last Brunetti permitted himself the question. 'Could you describe the man who bought these shoes, Signor Gravi?'

Gravi paused for only a moment and then asked, voice respectful in the face of authority, 'Commissario, could you tell me why you're interested in this man?'

'We believe he can provide us with important information about an on-going investigation,' Brunetti answered, telling him nothing.

'Yes, I see,' Gravi answered. Like all Italians, he was accustomed not to understand what he was told by the authorities. 'Younger than you, I'd say, but not all that much. Dark hair. No moustache.' Perhaps it was hearing himself say it that made Gravi realize how vague his description was. 'I'd say he looked pretty much like anyone else, a man in a suit. Not very tall and not short, either.'

'Would you be willing to look at some photos, Signor Gravi?' Brunetti asked. 'Perhaps that would help you recognize the man?'

Gravi smiled broadly, relieved to find it all so much like television. 'Of course.'

Brunetti nodded to Vianello, who went downstairs and was quickly back with two folders of police photos, among which, Brunetti knew, was Malfatti's.

Gravi accepted the first folder from Vianello and laid it on top of Brunetti's desk. One by one, he leafed

through the photos, placing them face down on a separate pile after he looked at them. As Vianello and Brunetti watched, he placed Malfatti's picture face down with the others and continued until he reached the bottom of the pile. He looked up. 'He's not here, not even someone who looks vaguely like him.'

'Perhaps you could give us a clearer idea of what he looked like, Signore.'

'I told you, Commissario, a man in a suit. All these men,' he said, pointing to the pile of photos that lay before him, 'well, they all look like criminals.' Vianello stole a look at Brunetti. There had been three photos of police officers mixed in with the others, one of them of Officer Alvise. 'I told you, he wore a suit,' Gravi repeated. 'He looked like one of us. You know, someone who goes to work every day. In an office. And he spoke like an educated man, not a criminal.'

The political naïvety of that remark caused Brunetti to wonder, for a moment, if Signor Gravi was really an Italian. He nodded to Vianello, who picked up the second folder from where he had set it on the desk and handed it to Gravi.

As the two policemen watched, Gravi leafed through a smaller stack of photos. When he got to Ravanello's, he paused and looked up at Brunetti. 'That's the banker who was killed yesterday, isn't it?' he asked, pointing down at the photo.

'He's not the man who bought the shoes, Signor Gravi?' he asked.

'No, of course not,' Gravi answered. 'If it had been, I would have told you when I came in.' He looked at the

photo again, a studio portrait that had appeared in a brochure which carried photos of all of the officers of the bank. 'It's not the man, but it's the type.'

'The type, Signor Gravi?'

'You know, suit and tie and polished shoes. Clean white shirt, good haircut. A real banker.'

For an instant, Brunetti was seven years old, kneeling beside his mother in front of the main altar of Santa Maria Formosa, their parish church. His mother looked up at the altar, crossed herself, and said, voice palpitant with pleading and belief, 'Maria, Mother of God, for the love of your Son who gave His life for all of us unworthy sinners, grant me this one request, and I will never ask a special grace of you in prayer for as long as I may live.' It was a promise he was to hear repeated countless times in his youth, for, like all Venetians, Signora Brunetti always placed her trust in the influence of friends in high places. Not for the first time in his life, Brunetti regretted his own lack of faith, but still he prayed.

He returned his attention to Gravi. 'Unfortunately, I don't have a photo of the other man who might have bought these shoes from you, but if you could come with me, perhaps you could help us by taking a look at him in the place where he works.'

'You mean literally take part in the investigation?' Gravi's enthusiasm was childlike.

'Yes, if you'd be willing.'

'Certainly, Commissario. I'd be glad to help you in any way I can.'

Brunetti stood, and Gravi jumped to his feet. As they walked towards the centre of the city, Brunetti

explained to Gravi what he wanted him to do. Gravi asked no questions, content only to do as told, a good citizen helping the police in their investigation of a serious crime.

When they got to Campo San Luca, Brunetti pointed out the doorway that led up to Santomauro's office and suggested to Signor Gravi that he have a drink in Rosa Salva and allow Brunetti five minutes before he came upstairs.

Brunetti went up the now familiar stairway and knocked on the door to the office. '*Avanti*,' the secretary called out, and he went in.

When she looked up from her computer and saw who it was, she couldn't resist the impulse that brought her half-way out of her chair. 'I'm sorry, Signorina,' Brunetti said, putting both hands up in what he hoped was an innocent gesture. 'I'd like to speak to Avvocato Santomauro. It's official police business.'

She seemed not to hear him, looked at him with her mouth open in a widening O, either of surprise or fear, Brunetti had no idea which. Very slowly, she reached forward and pressed a button on her desk, keeping her finger on it and getting to her feet but staying safely behind her desk. She stood there, finger still on the button, staring at Brunetti, silent.

A few seconds later, the door was pulled open from inside, and Santomauro came into the outer office. He saw his secretary, silent and still as Lot's wife, then saw Brunetti by the door.

His rage was immediate and fulminant. 'What are you doing here? I called the Vice-Questore and told him to

keep you away from me. Get out, get out of my office.' At the sound of his voice, the secretary backed away from her desk and stood against the wall. 'Get out,' Santomauro said again, almost shouting now. 'I will not be subjected to this sort of persecution. I'll have you . . .' he began but stopped as another man came into the office behind Brunetti, a man he didn't recognize, a short man in a cheap cotton suit.

'The two of you, get back to the Questura where you came from,' Santomauro shouted.

'Do you recognize this man, Signor Gravi?' Brunetti asked.

'Yes, I do.'

Santomauro stopped at this, though he still didn't recognize the little man in the cheap suit.

'Could you tell me who he is, Signor Gravi?'

'He's the man who bought the shoes from me.'

Brunetti turned away from Gravi and looked across the office at Santomauro, who seemed now to have recognized the little man in the cheap suit. 'And what shoes were they, Signor Gravi?'

'A pair of red women's shoes. Size forty-one.'

Chapter Thirty-One

Santomauro fell apart. Brunetti had observed the phenomenon often enough to recognize what was happening. The arrival of Gravi when Santomauro believed himself to have triumphed over all risk, when the police had not responded to the accusations in Malfatti's confession, had fallen so suddenly, from the very heavens themselves, that Santomauro had neither the time nor the wit to create some sort of story to explain his purchase of the shoes.

At first, he shouted at Gravi, telling him to get out of his office, but when the little man insisted that he would know Santomauro anywhere, knew that he was the man who had bought those shoes, Santomauro collapsed sideways against his secretary's desk, arms wrapped around his chest, as if he could that way protect himself from Brunetti's silent gaze and from the puzzled faces of the other two.

'That's the man, Commissario. I'm sure of it.'

'Well, Avvocato Santomauro?' Brunetti asked and signalled with his hand for Gravi to remain silent.

'It was Ravanello,' Santomauro said, his voice high and tight and close to tears. 'It was his idea, all of it.

About the apartments and the rents. He came to me with the idea. I didn't want to do it, but he threatened me. He knew about the boys. He said he'd tell my wife and children. And then Mascari found out about the rents.'

'How?'

'I don't know. Records at the bank. Something in the computer. Ravanello told me. It was his idea to get rid of him.' None of this made any sense to two of the people in the room, but neither of them said anything, riveted by Santomauro's terror.

'I didn't want to do anything. But Ravanello said we had no choice. We had to do it.' His voice had grown softer as he spoke, and then he stopped and looked up at Brunetti.

'What did you have to do, Signor Santomauro?'

Santomauro stared at Brunetti and then shook his head, as if to clear it after a heavy blow. Then he shook it again but this time in clear negation. Brunetti knew these signs, as well. 'I am placing you under arrest, Signor Santomauro, for the murder of Leonardo Mascari.'

At the mention of that name, both Gravi and the secretary stared at Santomauro, as though seeing him for the first time. Brunetti leaned over the secretary's desk and, using her phone, called the Questura and asked that three men be sent to Campo San Luca to pick up a suspect and escort him back to the Questura for questioning.

Brunetti and Vianello questioned Santomauro for two hours, and gradually the story came out. It was likely

that Santomauro was telling the truth about the details of the scheme to profit from the Lega apartments; it was unlikely that he was telling the truth about whose idea it was. He continued to maintain that it was all Ravanello's doing, that the banker had approached him with all of the details worked out, that it was Ravanello who had introduced Malfatti to the scheme. All of the ideas, in fact, had been Ravanello's: the original plan, the need to get rid of the honourable Mascari, to run Brunetti's car into the *laguna*. All of this had come from Ravanello, the product of his consuming greed.

And Santomauro? He presented himself as a weak man, a man made prisoner to the evil designs of another because of the banker's power to ruin his reputation, his family, his life. He insisted that he had not taken part in Mascari's murder, had not known what was going to happen that fatal night in Crespo's apartment. When he was reminded of the shoes, he said at first that he had bought them to wear during Carnevale, but when he was told that they had been identified as the shoes that were found with Mascari's body, he said that he had bought them because Ravanello had told him to and that he had never known what the shoes were going to be used for.

Yes, he had taken his share of the rents from the Lega apartments, but he had not wanted the money; he had wanted only to protect his good name. Yes, he had been in Crespo's apartment the night that Mascari was killed, but it had been Malfatti who did the killing; he and Ravanello had then had no choice but to help in disposing of the body. The plan? Ravanello's. Malfatti's. As to Crespo's murder, he knew nothing about it and insisted

that the murderer must have been some dangerous client that Crespo took back to his apartment with him.

He unfailingly presented the picture of a man much like many others, led astray by his lusts, then dominated by fear. Who could fail to feel some sympathy or compassion for a man such as this?

And so it went for two hours, Santomauro maintaining his innocent complicity in these crimes, insisting that his only motivation had been concern for his family and a desire to spare them from the shame and scandal of his secret life. As Brunetti listened, he heard Santomauro become more and more convinced of the truth of what he was saying. And at that, Brunetti called off the questioning, sickened by the man and his posturing.

By the evening, Santomauro's lawyer was with him, and the next morning, bail was set and he was released, though Malfatti, a confessed killer, remained in jail. Santomauro resigned his presidency of the Lega della Moralità that same day, and the remaining members of the board of directors called for a thorough investigation of his mismanagement and misconduct. So it was at a certain level of society, Brunetti mused: sodomy became misconduct, and murder mismanagement.

That afternoon, Brunetti walked down to Via Garibaldi and rang the bell of the Mascari apartment. The widow asked who it was, and he gave his name and rank.

The apartment was unchanged. The shutters still kept out the sun, though they seemed to trap the heat inside. Signora Mascari was thinner, her attention more withdrawn.

'It's very kind of you to see me, Signora,' Brunetti

began when they were seated, facing one another. 'I've come to tell you that all suspicion has been removed from your husband. He was not involved in any wrong-doing; he was a blameless victim of a vicious crime.'

'I knew that, Commissario. I knew that from the beginning.'

'I'm sorry there had to exist even a minute's suspicion about your husband.'

'It wasn't your fault, Commissario.'

'I still regret it. But the men responsible for his death have been found.'

'Yes, I know. I read it in the papers,' she said, paused, and then added, 'I don't think it makes any difference.'

'They will be punished, Signora. I can promise you that.'

'I'm afraid that's not going to be of any help. Not to me and not to Leonardo.' When Brunetti began to object, she cut him off and said, 'Commissario, the papers can print as much as they want about what really happened, but all people are ever going to remember about Leonardo is the story that appeared when his body was first discovered, that he was found wearing a dress and was believed to be a transvestite. And a whore.'

'But it will become clear that was not true, Signora.'

'Once mud has been thrown, Commissario, it cannot ever be fully washed off. People like to think badly of other people; the worse it is, the happier it makes them. Years from now, when people hear Leonardo's name, they will remember the dress, and they will think what-ever dirty thoughts they want to think.'

Brunetti knew she was right. 'I'm sorry, Signora.' There was nothing else he could say.

She leaned forward and touched the back of his hand. 'No one can apologize for human nature, Commissario. But I thank you for your sympathy.' She took her hand away. 'Is there anything else?'

Knowing dismissal when he heard it, Brunetti said there was not and took his leave of her there, leaving her in the darkened house.

That night, a tremendous thunderstorm swept across the city, tearing off roof tiles, hurling pots of geraniums to the ground, uprooting trees in the public gardens. It rained down wildly for three solid hours, filling storm gutters and sweeping bags of garbage into the canals. When the rain stopped, a sudden chill swept behind it, creeping into bedrooms and forcing sleepers to huddle together for warmth. Brunetti, alone, was forced to get up at about four and pull a blanket from the closet. He slept until almost nine, decided then that he would not go to the Questura until after lunch, and forced himself to go back to sleep. He got up well after ten, made himself coffee, and took a long shower, glad of the hot water for the first time in months. He was standing on the terrace, dressed, hair still damp, with a second coffee in his hand when he heard a sound from the apartment behind him. He turned, cup to his lips, and saw Paola. And then Chiara, and then Raffaele.

'*Ciao*, Papà,' Chiara cried with wild glee, hurling herself towards him.

'What happened?' he asked, holding her close but seeing only her mother.

Chiara pulled herself back and grinned up at him. 'Look at my face, Papà.'

He did, and had never seen a lovelier. He noticed that she had been out in the sun.

'Oh, Papà, don't you see?'

'Don't I see what, darling?'

'I've got measles and they threw us out.'

Though the chill of early autumn remained in the city, that night Brunetti needed no blanket.

All Pan Books are available at your local bookshop or newsagent, or can be ordered direct from the publisher. Indicate the number of copies required and fill in the form below.

Send to: Macmillan General Books C.S.
                Book Service By Post
                PO Box 29, Douglas I-O-M
                IM99 1BQ

or phone: 01624 675137, quoting title, author and credit card number.

or fax: 01624 670923, quoting title, author, and credit card number.

or Internet: http://www.bookpost.co.uk

Please enclose a remittance* to the value of the cover price plus 75 pence per book for post and packing. Overseas customers please allow £1.00 per copy for post and packing.

*Payment may be made in sterling by UK personal cheque, Eurocheque, postal order, sterling draft or international money order, made payable to Book Service By Post.

Alternatively by Access/Visa/MasterCard

Card No.   ☐☐☐☐☐☐☐☐☐☐☐☐☐☐☐☐☐☐☐

Expiry Date   ☐☐☐☐☐☐☐☐☐☐☐☐☐☐☐☐☐

Signature   _____

Applicable only in the UK and BFPO addresses.

While every effort is made to keep prices low, it is sometimes necessary to increase prices at short notice. Pan Books reserve the right to show on covers and charge new retail prices which may differ from those advertised in the text or elsewhere.

NAME AND ADDRESS IN BLOCK CAPITAL LETTERS PLEASE

Name _____

Address _____

_____

_____

_____

                                                        8/95

Please allow 28 days for delivery.
Please tick box if you do not wish to receive any additional information. ☐